Darkness at Dawn

Darkness at Dawn

Early Suspense Classics by
CORNELL WOOLRICH

Edited by Francis M. Nevins, Jr., & Martin H. Greenberg

Introduction by Francis M. Nevins, Jr.

Peter Bedrick Books

New York

This edition first published in 1988 by
Peter Bedrick Books
125 East 23rd Street
New York NY 10010

Library of Congress Cataloging-in-Publication Data

Woolrich, Cornell, 1903–1968.
  Darkness at dawn.

  Reprint. originally published: Carbondale:
Southern Illinois University Press, © 1985.
  1. Detective and mystery stories, American.
I. Nevins, Francis M. II. Title.
PS3515.06455A6 1988   813'.52   88-951
ISBN 0-87226-204-9 (pbk.)

Manufactured in the United States of America

Contents

Introduction ix
Francis M. Nevins, Jr.

Death Sits in the
Dentist's Chair 1

Walls That Hear You 19

Preview of Death 44

Murder in Wax 63

The Body Upstairs 82

Kiss of the Cobra 102

Red Liberty 126

Dark Melody of
Madness 149

The Corpse and the Kid 190

Dead on Her Feet 215

The Death of Me 235

The Showboat Murders 260

Hot Water 277

Introduction

FRANCIS M. NEVINS, JR.

Noir. Any French dictionary will tell you that the word's primary meaning is black, dark, or gloomy. But since the mid-1940s and when used with the nouns *roman* (novel) or *film*, the adjective has developed a specialized meaning, referring to the kind of bleak, disillusioned study in the poetry of terror that flourished in American mystery fiction during the 1930s and 1940s and in American crime movies during the 1940s and 1950s. The hallmarks of the *noir* style are fear, guilt and loneliness, breakdown and despair, sexual obsession and social corruption, a sense that the world is controlled by malignant forces preying on us, a rejection of happy endings and a preference for resolutions heavy with doom, but always redeemed by a breathtakingly vivid poetry of word (if the work was a novel or story) or image (if it was a movie).

During the 1940s many American books of this sort were published in French translation in a long-running series called the *Série Noire*, and at the end of World War II, when French film enthusiasts were exposed for the first time to Hollywood's cinematic analogue of those books, they coined *film noir* as a phrase to describe the genre. What Americans of those years tended to dismiss as commercial entertainments the French saw as profound explorations of the heart of darkness, largely because *noir* was so intimately related to the themes of French existentialist writers like Sartre and Camus and because the bleak world of *noir* spoke to the despair which so many in Europe were experiencing after the nightmare years of war and occupation and genocide. By the early 1960s cinephiles in the United States had virtually made an American phrase out of *film noir* and had acclaimed this type of movie as one of the most fascinating genres to emerge from Hollywood. *Noir* directors—not only the giants like Alfred Hitchcock (in certain moods) and Fritz Lang but relative unknowns like Edgar G. Ulmer, Jacques Tourneur, Robert Siodmak, Joseph H. Lewis, and Anthony Mann—were hailed as visual poets whose cinematic style made the bleakness of their films not only palatable but fantastically exciting.

Several first-rate books on this movie genre have recently been published in the United States, and one can attend courses on *film noir* at any number of colleges. But there has not yet developed a corresponding interest in the doom-haunted novels and tales of suspense in which *film noir* had its roots. Although Dashiell Hammett and Raymond Chandler, the poets of big-city corruption, and James M. Cain, the chronicler of sexual obsession, have received the fame they deserve, the names of countless other *noir* writers are known primarily to specialists.

Names like Cornell Woolrich.

Woolrich was born on December 4, 1903, to parents whose marriage collapsed in his youth. Much of his childhood was spent in Mexico with his father, a civil engineer. At age eight, the experience of seeing a traveling French company perform Puccini's *Madame Butterfly* in Mexico City gave Woolrich a sudden sharp insight into color and drama and his first taste of tragedy. Three years later he understood fully that someday, like Cio-Cio-San, he too would have to die, and from then on he was haunted by a sense of doom that never left him.

During adolescence he lived with his mother and maternal relatives in New York City, and in 1921 he entered Columbia College. It was there that he began writing fiction, and he quit school in his junior year to pursue his dream of becoming another F. Scott Fitzgerald. His first novel, *Cover Charge* (1926), chronicled the lives and loves of the Jazz Age's gilded youth in the manner of his and his whole generation's literary idol. This book was followed by the prize-winning *Children of the Ritz* (1927), whose success propelled Woolrich to Hollywood as a screenwriter, a job at which he failed, and into a brief marriage, at which, being homosexual, he failed even worse. Before long he fled back to New York and his mother. For the next quarter century he lived with her in residential hotels, going out only when it was absolutely essential, trapped in a bizarre love-hate relationship which dominated his external world just as the inner world of his later fiction reflects in its tortured patterns the strangler grip in which his mother and his own inability to love a woman held him.

From 1934 until his death in 1968, this tormented recluse all but created what we know as *noir*, writing dozens of haunting tales of suspense, despair, and lost love, set in a universe controlled by diabolical powers. During the '30s his work appeared only in pulp magazines like *Black Mask* and *Detective Fiction Weekly*. Then, beginning with *The Bride Wore Black* (1940), he launched his so-called Black Series of suspense novels—which appeared in France as part of the *Série Noire* and led the French to acclaim him as a master of bleak poetic vision. Much of his reputation still rests on those novels and on the other suspense classics originally published under his pseudonyms William Irish and George Hopley. Throughout the '40s and '50s Woolrich's publishers issued numerous hardcover and paperback collections of his short stories. Many of his novels and tales were adapted into movies, including such fine *films noirs* as Tourneur's *The Leopard Man* (1943), Siodmak's *Phantom Lady* (1944), Roy William Neill's *Black Angel* (1946), Maxwell Shane's *Fear in the Night* (1947), and, most famous of all, Hitchcock's *Rear Window* (1954). Even more of Woolrich's work was turned into radio and later into television drama. But despite overwhelming financial and critical success his life remained a wretched mess, and when his mother died in 1957 he cracked. From then until his own death eleven years later he lived alone, his last few months spent in a wheelchair after the amputation of a gangrenous leg, wracked by diabetes and alcoholism and homosexual self-contempt. But the best of his final "tales of love and despair" are still gifted with the magic touch that chills the heart, and in a title for a story he never wrote he captured the essence of his *noir* world in six words.

First you dream, then you die.

Woolrich wrote all sorts of stories, including quasi-police procedurals, rapid-action whizbangs, and tales of the occult, and all three varieties are represented in this collection. But he's best known as the master of pure suspense, the writer who could evoke with almost-more-than-human power the desperation of those who walk the city's darkened streets and the terror that lurks at noonday in the most commonplace settings. In his hands even such clichéd storylines as the race to save the innocent person from the electric chair and the amnesiac hunting his lost self resonate with anguish. Woolrich's world is a feverish place where the prevailing emotions are loneliness and fear and the prevailing action—as in his classics "Three O'Clock" (1938) and "Guillotine" (1939)—the race against time and death. His most characteristic detective stories end with the realization that no rational account of events is possible, and his suspense stories tend to close with terror not dissipated but omnipresent, like God.

The typical Woolrich settings are the seedy hotel, the cheap dance hall, the rundown movie house and the precinct station backroom. The dominant reality in his world is the Depression, and Woolrich has no peers when it comes to describing a frightened little guy in a tiny apartment with no money, no job, a hungry wife and children, and anxiety eating him like a cancer. If a Woolrich protagonist is in love, the beloved is likely to vanish in such a way that he not only can't find her but can't convince anyone she ever existed. Or, in another classic Woolrich situation, the protagonist comes to after a blackout—caused by amnesia, drugs, hypnosis, or whatever—and little by little becomes certain that he committed a murder or other crime while out of himself. The police are rarely sympathetic; in fact they are the earthly counterparts of the malignant powers above and their main function is to torment the helpless.

All we can do about this nightmare we live in is to create, if we are very lucky, a few islands of love and trust to sustain us and help us forget. But love dies while the lovers go on living, and Woolrich excels at making us watch while relationships corrode. He knew the horrors that both love and lovelessness can breed, yet he created very few irredeemably evil characters; for with whoever loves or needs love, Woolrich identifies, all of that person's dark side notwithstanding.

Purely as technical exercises, many of Woolrich's novels and stories are awful. They don't make the slightest bit of sense. And that of course is the point: neither does life. Nevertheless some of his tales, usually thanks to outlandish coincidence, manage to end quite happily. But since he never used a series character, the reader can never know in advance whether a particular Woolrich story will be light or dark, *allègre* or *noir*—which is one of many reasons why his stories are so hauntingly suspenseful.

Including the thirteen collected here.

Woolrich's dream of being the next Scott Fitzgerald was killed by the Depression, and during 1933 he wasn't able to sell a single word. Then in the spring of 1934 a second chance opened up for him, and he began writing a new kind of story for a market he hadn't considered before, the pulp mystery magazines. His success in this genre was as rapid as his early success in the mainstream. His first three crime stories appeared later that year in *Detective Fiction Weekly* and *Dime Detective*, and ten more were published in 1935 in those magazines plus *Dime Mystery* and *Argosy*. In these thirteen tales, collected here, he introduced a huge number of the themes and elements and devices that we think of as peculiarly his own.

His earliest published suspense story, "Death Sits in the Dentist's Chair" (*Detective Fiction Weekly*, August 4, 1934), features not only some revealing glimpses of New York City in the pit of the Depression but also a typically bizarre murder method and a taste of countless races-against-the-clock in future stories when the protagonist frantically tries to get the poison removed from his body before it kills him. "Walls That Hear You" (*Detective Fiction Weekly*, August 18, 1934) opens with the demonic invading the narrator's life as he finds his younger brother with all ten fingers cut off and his tongue severed at the roots. "Preview of Death" (*Dime Detective*, November 15, 1934) harks back to Woolrich's brief screenwriting stint in Hollywood, utilizes a grisly means of death which actually killed an actress years before,* and introduces the first of Woolrich's dozens of cop protago-

---

*In 1923, while shooting the Civil War film *The Warrens of Virginia*, actress Martha Mansfield was burned to death when someone threw a lit match on the ground and her flammable hoopskirt was ignited, turning her into a living torch. One of the scenes in Woolrich's precrime novel *Times Square* (1929) is also based on this incident.

nists. "Murder in Wax" (*Dime Detective*, March 1, 1935), which he later cannibalized for part of his classic 1943 novel *The Black Angel*, is the first Woolrich story to be narrated in first person by a woman. "The Body Upstairs" (*Dime Detective*, April 1, 1935) is a more-or-less straightforward detective tale, except for its subtext of innocent parties being casually tortured by the police: the cops stick lighted cigarettes into the husband's armpits till he's about to confess, at which point the homicide dick in charge chews the husband out as a weak sister! "Kiss of the Cobra" (*Dime Detective*, May 1, 1935) is another story of the invasion of everyday by demonic forces, and even though the situation is wilder than one usually encounters in Woolrich—the narrator's widower father brings home as his new bride a Hindu snake priestess complete with snake—the duel of poisoned cigarettes at the climax could have been written by no one else. "Red Liberty" (*Dime Detective*, July 1, 1935) combines the detective tale with woiking-class cop protagonist and a meticulously portrayed setting inside the Statue of Liberty, the first of many New York landmarks Woolrich used in his crime fiction. "Dark Melody of Madness" (*Dime Mystery*, July 1935), better known under its reprint title "Papa Benjamin," presents the first of Woolrich's fate-doomed existential fugitives, a jazz composer–bandleader who's cursed by a New Orleans voodoo cult. "The Corpse and the Kid" (*Dime Detective*, September 1935), also known as "Boy with Body," is the earliest Woolrich story of pure nail-biting suspense: a young man finds that his father has killed his slut stepmother and desperately tries to cover up by wrapping the woman's body in a rug and carrying it across part of New Jersey to the rendezvous where her lover is waiting. In "Dead on Her Feet" (*Dime Detective*, December 1935) Woolrich borrows the dance-marathon motif that his pulp confrere Horace McCoy had used earlier that year in his classic *noir* novel *They Shoot Horses, Don't They?*, but Woolrich's version features one of the most sadistic and psychotic of all his cop characters and one of the most chilling climaxes in any crime story. In "The Death of Me" (*Detective Fiction Weekly*, December 7, 1935) he borrows from another *noir* masterpiece, James M. Cain's *The Postman Always Rings Twice* (1934), for the climax of a powerful story about a man who tries to bury his past self and start life over again. "The Showboat Murders"

(*DetectiveFiction Weekly*, December 14, 1935) is the first of Woolrich's nonstop fast-action whizbangs, with another woiking-stiff cop hero, a setting clearly suggested by Oscar Hammerstein and Jerome Kern's blockbuster musical comedy of 1927, and, as usual in Woolrich tales of this sort, a concern with precise details of physical movement even during frenzied pursuit. And "Hot Water" (*Argosy*, December 28, 1935) is another whizbang, this one based on Woolrich's memories of Hollywood and its stars' below-the-border playgrounds in the transition time between the silent and talking eras.

By the end of that year he was a professional mystery writer and from then till the end of his life he wrote little else. His 1935 earnings totaled $2487.00, a sum on which in those days a man and his mother could live. More important, by the end of the year Woolrich had set in place an untold number of the building blocks of his *noir* universe. *Darkness at Dawn* shows us what a superb writer and craftsman of suspense he was even at the start of his new career.

After his death in 1968, a fragment was found among his papers in which he tried to explain his life's work. "I was only trying to cheat death," he wrote. "I was only trying to surmount for a little while the darkness that all my life I surely knew was going to come rolling in on me some day and obliterate me." In the end, of course, like Cio-Cio-San and all of us, he had to die. But as long as there are readers to be haunted by the fruit of his life, by the way he took his wretched psychological environment and his sense of entrapment and loneliness and turned them into poetry of the shadows, the world Woolrich imagined lives.

Darkness at Dawn

Death Sits in the Dentist's Chair

There was another patient ahead of me in the waiting room. He was sitting there quietly, humbly, with all the terrible resignation of the very poor. He wasn't all jittery and alert like I was, but just sat there ready to take anything that came, head bowed a little as though he had found life just a succession of hard knocks. His gaze met mine and I suppose he could tell how uncomfortable I was by the look on my face, but instead of grinning about it or cracking wise he put himself out to encourage me, cheer me up. When I thought of this afterward it did something to me.

"He not hurt you," he murmured across to me confidentially. "Odder dantist say he very good, you no feel notting at all when he drill."

I showed my gratitude by offering him a cigarette. Misery loves company.

With that, Steve Standish came in from the back, buttoning his white jacket. The moment he saw me professional etiquette was thrown to the winds. "Well, well, Rodge, so it's finally come to this, has it? I knew I'd get you sooner or later!" And so on and so on.

I gave a weak grin and tried to act nonchalant. Finally he said in oh, the most casual manner, "Come on in, Rodge, and let's have a look at you."

I suddenly discovered myself to be far more considerate of others than I had hitherto suspected. "This—er, man was here ahead of me, Steve." Anything to gain five minutes' time.

He glanced at his other patient, carelessly but by no means unkindly or disdainfully. "Yes, but you've got to get down to your office—he probably has the day off. You in a hurry?" he asked.

"Thass all right, I no mine, I got no work," the man answered affably.

"No, Steve, I insist," I said.

"Okay, if that's the way you feel about it," he answered genially. "Be right with you." And he ushered the other patient inside ahead of him. I saw him wink at the man as he did so, but at the moment I didn't much care what he thought of my courage. No man is a hero to his dentist.

And not long afterwards I was to wonder if that little attack of "cold feet" hadn't been the luckiest thing that ever happened to me.

Steve closed his office door after him, but the partition between the two rooms had evidently been put in long after everything else in the place. It was paper-thin and only reached three-quarters of the way up; every sound that came from the other side was perfectly audible to me where I sat, fidgeting and straining my ears for indications of anguish. But first of all there was a little matter of routine to be gone through. "I guess I'll have to take your name and pedigree myself," Steve's voice boomed out jovially. "It's my assistant's day off."

"Amato Saltone, plizz."

"And where do you live, Amato?" Steve had a way with these people. Not patronizing, just forthright and friendly.

"Two twanny Thirr Avenue. If you plizz, mista."

There was a slight pause. I pictured Steve jotting down the information on a card and filing it away. Then he got down to business. "Now what seems to be the trouble?"

The man had evidently adjusted himself in the chair, meanwhile. Presumably he simply held his mouth open and let Steve find out for himself, because it was again Steve who spoke: "This one?" I visualized him plying his mirror now and maybe playing around with one of those sharp little things that look like crocheting needles. All at once his voice had become impatient, indignant even. "What do you call that thing you've got in there? I never saw a filling like it in my life. Looks like the Boulder Dam! Who put it in for you—some bricklayer?"

"Docata Jones, Feefatty-nine Stree," the man said.

"Never heard of him. He send you here to me?" Steve asked sharply. "You'd think he'd have decency enough to clean up his own messes! I suppose there wasn't enough in it for him. Well, that headstone you've got in there is going to come out first of all, and you just pay me whatever you can afford as we go along. I'd be ashamed to let a man walk out of my office with a botched-up job like that in his mouth!" He sounded bitter about it.

The next thing that came to my ears was the faint whirring of the electric drill, sounding not much louder than if there had been a fly buzzing around the room over my head.

I heard Steve speak just once more, and what he said was the immemorial question of the dentist, "Hurting you much?" The man groaned in answer, but it was a most peculiar groan. Even at the instant of hearing it it struck me that there was something different about it. It sounded so hollow and faraway, as though it had come from the very depths of his being, and broke off so suddenly at the end.

He didn't make another sound after that. But whatever it was it had taken more than a mere twinge of pain to make him groan like that. Or was it just my own overwrought nerves that made me imagine it?

An instant later I knew I had been right. Steve's voice told me that something out of the ordinary had happened just then. "Here, hold your head up so I can get at you," he said. At first jokingly, and then— "Here! Here! What's the matter with you?" Alarm crept in. "Wake up, will you? Wake up!" Alarm turned into panic. "Rodge!" he called out to me.

But I was on my feet already and half across the waiting room, my own trivial fears a thing of the past. He threw the door open before I got to it and looked out at me. His face was white. "This fellow— something's happened to him, he's turning cold here in the chair and I can't bring him to!"

I brushed past him and bent over the figure huddled in the chair. Horrible to relate, his mouth was still wide open in the position Steve had had it just now. I touched his forehead; it was already cooler by far than the palm of my hand and clammy to the touch. I tried to rouse him by shaking him, no good, then felt for his heart. There was no heart any more. Steve was on the other side of him, holding his dental mirror before the open mouth. We both watched it fascinatedly; it stayed clear as crystal.

"He's gone," I muttered. "What do you make of it?"

"I'm going to try oxygen," Steve babbled. "It may have been his heart—" He was hauling down a big, clumsy looking cylinder from a shelf with jerky, spasmodic movements that showed how badly shaken he was. "You'd better send in a call for an ambulance."

The phone was outside in the waiting room; that didn't take any time at all. When I came back there was a mask over his face and a tube leading from his mouth to the cylinder. Steve was just standing there helplessly. Every few seconds he'd touch a little wheel-shaped valve on the cylinder, but the indicator showed that it was already as wide open as it could go. "Keep your hand on his heart," he said to me hoarsely.

It was no use. By the time the ambulance doctor and a policeman got there (with a deafening crashing of the rigged-up doorbell apparatus) Steve had taken the tube out of his mouth and turned off the flow of oxygen from the cylinder.

"Gave him nearly the whole tank," I remember his saying to me.

The ambulance doctor took one look at him as he came in and then told us what we already knew. "All up, eh?" he said. He then stretched him out on the floor, of all places, with the help of the cop, and began to examine him. I cleared out of the room at this point and sat down to wait outside—fully imagining I was being big-hearted and staying on of my own free will to brace Steve up instead of going somewhere more cheerful. It would all be over in another five or ten minutes, I thought unsuspectingly, and then maybe Steve and I better go and have a drink together some place and both of us take the rest of the day off.

The patrolman came out to me and asked if I'd been in there when it happened. I told him no, I'd been out here waiting my turn. I was about to add for no particular reason that I was a very good friend of Steve's and not just a stray patient, when things began to happen rapidly.

So far everything had been just pure routine on their part. But now the ambulance doctor finished his examination and came out, kit in hand, Steve trailing after him. What he had to say was to the police-man though and not to Steve at all. "It wasn't his heart," he said. "Better phone Headquarters and tell the coroner to come up here. He might want to bring a couple of boys with him."

"What's up?" Steve tried to sound casual but he wasn't very good at it. The cop was already at the phone.

"Not natural causes at all," the doctor said grimly. He wouldn't say anything more than that. The shrug he gave plainly meant, "It's not my job." I thought he looked at Steve a little peculiarly as he turned to go. The hideous bell had another spasm of its jangling and the door closed after him.

II

The cop became noticeably less friendly after that; he remained standing to one side of the door and had a watchful air about him. Once when Steve made a move to go back into the other room for something his upper lip lifted after the manner of a mastiff with a bone and he growled warningly, "Take it easy, fellow." Nice boy he was—as long as you were on his side of the fence.

They didn't take long to get there, the coroner and "a couple of the boys." They looked more like high-powered real estate agents to me, but this was the first time I'd even been in the same room with a detective.

"What's about it?" began one of them, lingering with us while the coroner and his pal went on inside and got busy.

Steve told him the little there was to tell; the man had climbed into his chair, Steve had started to drill, and the man had gone out like a light. No, he'd never treated him before, never even laid eyes on him until five minutes before he'd died.

That was all there was to this first session, a harmless little chat, you might call it. The cop went back to his beat, a stretcher arrived, and poor Amato Saltone departed, his troubles at an end. Steve's, though, were just beginning—and possibly mine with them. The second detective came out with the coroner, and the atmosphere, which hadn't been any too cordial, all at once became definitely hostile.

"Cyanide of potassium," snapped the coroner. "Just enough to kill—not a grain more, not a grain less. I pumped his stomach, but the traces were all over the roof of his mouth and the lining of his throat anyway. I'll hold him on the ice in case they want a more thorough going-over later." And he too departed. That bell was driving me slowly insane.

The second detective held the inner door open and said, "Come inside, Dr. Standish." It wasn't said as politely as it reads in print.

I've already mentioned that every word spoken could be heard through or over the partition. But I was only allowed to hear the opening broadside—and that was ominous enough, Lord knows. "Where do you keep your cyanide, Dr. Standish?"

The detective who had remained with me, as soon as he realized what the acoustics of the place were, immediately suggested with heavy emphasis: "Let's just step out in the hall."

After we'd been standing out there smoking awhile Steve's office phone rang. My guardian took it upon himself to answer it, making sure that I came with him, so I had a chance to overhear the wind-up of Steve's quizzing. The call itself was simply from a patient, and the detective took pains to inform her that Dr. Standish had cancelled all appointments for the rest of that day.

I didn't like the way that sounded; nor did I like the turn the questioning had taken.

"So a man that's going to commit suicide goes to all the trouble of having a cavity filled in his mouth just before he does it, does he?" Steve's interlocutor was saying as we came in. "What for—to make himself beautiful for St. Peter?"

Steve was plenty indignant by now. "You've got a nerve trying to tack anything on me! He may have eaten something deadly outside without knowing it and then only got the effects after he was in my chair."

"Not cyanide, pal, it works instantly. And it isn't given away for nothing either. A fellow of that type would have jumped off a subway platform, it's cheaper. Where would he have the money or drag to buy cyanide? He probably couldn't even pronounce the name. Now why don't you make it easy for yourself and admit that you had an accident?"

Steve's voice broke. "Because I had nothing to do with it, accidentally or otherwise!"

"So you're willing to have us think you did it purposely, eh? Keenan!" he called out.

We both went in there, Keenan just a step in back of me to guide me.

"There's no trace of where he kept it hidden, but it's all over his drill thick as jam," Keenan's teammate reported. He detached the apparatus from the tripod it swung on, carefully wrapped it in tissue paper, and put it in his pocket. He turned to Steve.

"I'm going to book you," he said. "Come on, you're coming down to Headquarters with me."

Steve swayed a little, then got a grip on himself. "Am I under arrest?" he faltered.

"Well," remarked the detective sarcastically, "this is no invitation to a Park Avenue ball."

"What about this fellow?" Keenan indicated me. "Bring him along too?"

"He might be able to contribute a little something," was the reply.

So down to Headquarters we went and I lost sight of Steve as soon as we got there. They kept me waiting around for awhile and then questioned me. But I could tell that I wasn't being held as an accessory. I suppose my puffed-out cheek was more in my favor than everything else put together. Although why a man suffering from toothache would be less likely to be an accessory to murder than anyone else I fail to see. They didn't even look to see if it was phony; for all they knew I could have had a wad of cotton stuffed in there.

I told them everything there was to tell (they asked me, you bet!)—not even omitting to mention the cigarette I had given the man when we were both sitting in the waiting room. It was only after I'd said this that I realized how bad it sounded for me if they cared to look at it in that way. The cyanide could just as easily have been concealed in that cigarette. Luckily they'd already picked up and examined the butt (he hadn't had time to smoke more than half of it) and found it to be okay. Who says the innocent don't run as great a risk as the guilty?

I told them all I could about Steve and, as soon as I was cleared and told I could go home, I embarked on a lengthy plea in his defense, assuring them they were making the biggest mistake of their lives. "What motive could he possibly have?" I declaimed. "Check up on him, you'll find he has a home in Forest Hills, a car, a walloping practice, goes to all the first nights at the theatre! What did that jobless Third Avenue slob have that *he* needed? Why I heard him with my own ears tell the guy not to be in a hurry about paying up! Where's your motive? They came from two different worlds!"

All I got was the remark, Why didn't I join the squad and get paid for my trouble, and the suggestion, Why didn't I go home now?

One of them, Keenan, who turned out to be a rather likable sort after all, took me aside (but toward the door) and explained very patiently as to a ten-year-old child: "There's only three possibilities in this case, see? Suicide, accidental poisoning, and poisoning on purpose. Now your own friend himself is the one that has blocked up the first two, not us. We were willing to give him every chance, in the beginning. But no, he insists the guy didn't once lift his hands from under that linen apron to give the stuff to himself—take it out of his pocket and pop it in his mouth, for instance. Standish claims he never even once turned his back on him while he was in the chair, and that the fellow's hands stayed folded in his lap *under* the bib the whole time. Says he noticed that because everyone else always grabs the arms of the chair and hangs on. So that's out.

"And secondly he swears he has never kept any such stuff around the place as cyanide, in any shape or form, so it couldn't have gotten on the drill by accident. So *that's* out too. What have you got left? Poisoning on purpose—which has a one-word name: murder. That's all today—and be sure you don't leave town until after the trial, you'll be needed on the witness stand."

But I turned and followed him back inside and started all over again. Finally when I saw that it was no use, I tried to go bail for Steve, but they told me I couldn't spring him until after he'd been indicted.

I spent the rest of the night with a wet handkerchief pasted against my cheek, doing heavy thinking. Every word Steve and the victim had spoken behind the partition passed before me in review. "Where do you live, Amato? Two-twanny Thirr Avenue, mista." I'd start in from there.

I took an interpreter down there with me, a fellow on my own office staff who knew a little of everything from Eskimo to Greek. I wasn't taking any chances. Amato himself had been no Lowell Thomas, I could imagine what his family's English would be like!

There seemed to be dozens of them; they lived in a cold-water flat on the third floor rear. The head of the clan was Amato's rather stout wife. I concentrated on her; when a fellow has a toothache he'll usually tell his wife all about it quicker than his aunts or nieces or nephews.

"Ask her where this Dr. Jones lived that sent him to Standish."

She didn't know, Amato hadn't even told her what the man's name was. Hadn't they a bill from the man to show me? (I wanted to prove that Amato had been there.) No, no bill, but that didn't matter because Amato couldn't read anyway, and even if he had been able to, there was no money to pay it with.

If he couldn't read, I persisted, how had he known where to find a dentist?

She shrugged. Maybe he was going by and saw the dentist at work through a window.

I went through the entire family, from first to last, and got no-where. Amato had done plenty of howling and calling on the saints in the depths of the night, and even kept some of the younger children quiet at times by letting them look at his bad tooth, but as for telling them where, when, or by whom it had been treated, it never occurred to him.

So I was not only no further but I had even lost a good deal of confidence. "Docata Jones" began to look pretty much like a myth. Steve hadn't known him, either. But the man had said Fifty-ninth Street. With all due respect for the dead, I didn't think Amato had brains enough to make up even that little out of his head. I'd have to try that angle next, and unaided, since Amato's family had turned out to be a flop.

I tackled the phone book first, hoping for a short cut. Plenty of Joneses, D.D.S., but no one on 59th. Nor even one on 57th, 58th, or 60th, in case Amato was stupid enough not even to know which street he'd been on. The good old-fashioned way was all that was left. At that, there have been dentists before now who couldn't afford a telephone.

III

I swallowed a malted milk, tied a double knot in my shoelaces, and started out on foot, westward from the Queensboro Bridge. I went into every lobby, every hallway, every basement; I scanned every sign in every window, every card in every mail box. I consulted every superintendent in every walk-up, every starter in every elevator building, every landlady in every rooming house.

I followed the street west until it became fashionable Central Park South (I hadn't much hope there), then further still as it turned into darkest San Juan Hill, gave a lot of attention to the Vanderbilt Clinic at 10th Avenue, and finally came smack up against the speedway bordering the Hudson, with my feet burning me like blazes. No results. No Jones. It took me all of the first day and most of the second. At 2 P.M. Thursday I was back again at the Bridge (I'd taxied back, don't worry).

I got out and stood on the corner smoking a cigarette. I'd used the wrong method, that was all. I'd been rational about it, Amato had been instinctive. What had his wife said? He was going by and most likely saw some dentist working behind a window and that decided him. I'd been looking for a dentist, he hadn't—until he happened on one. I'd have to put myself in his place to get the right set-up.

I walked back two blocks to 3rd Avenue and started out afresh from that point on. He had lived on 3rd Avenue, so he had probably walked all the way up it looking for work until he got to 59th, and then turned either east or west. West there was a department store on one side, a five-and-ten and a furniture store on the other; they wouldn't interest him. East there were a whole line of mangy little shops and stalls; I turned east. I trudged along; I was Amato now, worrying about where my next half dollar was coming from, not thinking about my tooth at all—at least not just at that moment.

A shadow fell before me on the sidewalk. I looked up. A huge, swaying, papier-mâché gold tooth was hanging out over the doorway. It was the size of a football at least. Even Amato would have known what it was there for. Maybe he'd gotten a bad twinge just then. The only trouble was—I'd seen it myself yesterday, it was almost the first thing that had caught my eye when I started out. I'd investigated, you may be sure. And the card on the window said "Dr. Carter" as big as life. That was out—or was it? Amato couldn't read; "Carter" wouldn't mean any more to him than "Jones." But then where had he gotten "Jones" from? Familiar as it is, it would have been as foreign to him as his own name was to me.

No use going any further, though. If that gold tooth hadn't made up Amato's mind for him, nothing else the whole length of the street could have. I was on the point of going in anyway, just for a quick once over, but a hurried glance at my own appearance decided me not to. Serge business suit, good hat, dusty but well-heeled shoes. Whatever had happened to Amato, if he *had* gone in there, wasn't likely to happen to anyone dressed like I was. If I was going to put myself in his place, I ought at least to try to look like him. And there were a few other things, too, still out of focus.

I jumped in a cab and chased down to Headquarters. I didn't think they'd let me see Steve, but somehow I managed to wangle it out of them. I suppose Keenan had a hand in it. And then too, Steve hadn't cracked yet, that may have had something to do with it.

"What enemies have you?" I shot out. There wasn't much time.

"None," he said. "I never harmed anyone in my life."

"Think hard," I begged. "You've got to help me. Maybe way back, maybe some little thing."

"Nope," he insisted cynically, "my life's been a bed of roses until day before yesterday." He had a purple eye at the moment and a forty-eight-hour beard.

I turned cynical myself. "Let's skip it then and look at it the other way around. Who are your best friends—outside of myself?"

He ran over a list of names as long as a timetable. He left out one, though. "And Dave Carter?" I supplied. "Know him?"

He nodded cheerfully. "Sure, but how did you know? We used to be pretty chummy. I haven't seen him in years, though; we drifted apart. We started out together, both working in the same office I have now. Then he moved out on me, thought he could do better by himself, I guess."

"And did he?"

"He hit the skids. All the patients kept on coming to me, for some reason, and he just sat there in his spic-and-span office twiddling his thumbs. Inside of six months the overhead was too much for him and here's the payoff: he ended up by having to move into a place ten times worse than the one he'd shared with me. What with one thing and another I lent him quite a bit of money which I never got back."

"And did he turn sour on you?"

"Not at all, that's the funny part of it. Last time I saw him he slapped me on the back and said, 'More power to you, Stevie, you're a better man than I am!'"

"In your hat!" I thought skeptically. "When was the last time you saw him?" I asked.

"Years back. As a matter of fact, I clean forgot him until you—"

I stood up to go without waiting for him to finish. "Excuse the rush, but I've got things to do."

"Dig me up a good lawyer, will you?" he called after me. "Price is no object. I'm getting sick of hitting these dicks in the fist with my eyes!"

"You don't need a lawyer," I shouted back. "All you need is a little dash of suspicion in your nature. Like me."

I got Keenan to take me in and introduce me to the chief while I was down there—after about an hour or so of pleading. The chief was regular, but a tough nut to crack. Still he must have been in good humor that day. If he reads this, no offense meant, but the cigars he smokes are fierce. I had a proposition to make to him, and two requests. One of them he gave in to almost at once—loving newspapermen the way he did. The other he said he'd think over. As for the proposition itself, he said it wasn't so hot, but to go ahead and try it if I felt like it, only not to blame anyone but myself if I got into trouble.

From Headquarters I went straight to a pawnshop on 3rd Avenue. It was long after dark, but they stay open until nine. I bought a suit of clothes for three dollars. The first one the man showed me I handed back to him. "That's the best I can give you—" he started in.

"I don't want the best, I want the worst," I said, much to his surprise. I got it all right.

From there I went to a second one and purchased what had once been an overcoat before the World War. Price, two fifty. The coat and suit were both ragged, patched and faded, but at least the pawnbrokers had kept them brushed off; I fixed that with the help of a barrel of ashes I passed a few doors away. I also traded hats with a panhandler who crossed my path, getting possession of a peculiar shapeless mound he had been wearing on his head. I was doing more than laying down my life for my friend; I was risking dandruff and Lord knows what else for his sake.

I trundled all this stuff home and managed to hide it from my wife in the broom closet. In the morning, though, when she saw me arrayed in it from head to foot she let out a yell and all but sank to the floor. "Now never mind the hysterics," I reproved. "Papa knows just what he's doing!"

"If this has anything to do with Steve, you're a day late," she told me when she was through giggling. "They've dismissed the case against him." She held out the morning paper to me.

I didn't bother looking at it; in the first place it was one of the two requests I'd made at Headquarters the night before; in the second place it wasn't true anyway.

Keenan was waiting for me on the southwest corner of 59th and 2nd as per agreement. Anyone watching us would have thought our behavior peculiar, to say the least. I went up to him and opened my mouth as though I was Joe E. Brown making faces at him. "It's that tooth up there, that molar on the right side. Take a good look at it." He did. This was for purposes of evidence. "Got the picture?" He nodded. "I'm going in now, where that gold tooth is, half-way down the block. Back in half an hour. Wait here for me and keep your fingers crossed."

This statement wasn't quite accurate, though. I was sure I was going in where the gold tooth was, but I wasn't sure I was coming back in half an hour—I wasn't sure I was coming back at all, any time.

I left him abruptly and went into the office of Dr. Dave Carter. I was cold and scared. The accent bothered me too. I decided a brogue would be the safest. No foreign langı ages for me. Carter was a short, dumpy little man, as good-natured and harmless looking as you'd want. Only his eyes gave him away. Slits they were, little malevolent pig eyes. The eyes had it; they told me I wasn't wasting my time. The office was a filthy, rundown place. Instead of a partition, the dental chair was right in the room, with a screen around it. There was an odor of stale gas around.

My feet kept begging me to get up and run out of there while I still had the chance. I couldn't, though; Keenan was waiting on the corner. I wanted to keep his respect.

Carter was standing over me; he didn't believe in the daily bath, either. "Well, young fellow?" he said sleekly. I pointed sorrowfully at my cheek, which had been more or less inflated for the past three days. The pain had gone out of it long ago, however. Pain and swelling rarely go together, contrary to general belief.

"So I see," he said, but made no move to do anything about it. "What brings you here to me?" he asked craftily.

"Sure 'tis the ellygant gold tooth ye have out, boss," I answered shakily. Did that sound Irish enough? I wondered. Evidently it did.

"Irishman, eh?" he told me not very cleverly. "What's your name?"

"McConnaughy." I'd purposely picked a tongue-twister, to get the point across I was trying to make.

He bit. "How do you spell it?"

"Sure, I don't know now," I smiled wanly. "I nivver in me life learned to spell." That was the point I was trying to make.

"Can't read or write, eh?" He seemed pleased rather than disappointed. "Didn't you ever go to school when you were a kid?"

"I minded the pigs and such," I croaked forlornly.

He suddenly whipped out a newspaper he'd been holding behind his back and shoved it under my nose. "What d'you think of that?" It was upside down. He was trying to catch me off my guard, hoping I'd give myself away and turn it right side up without thinking. I kept my hands off it. "What do it say?" I queried helplessly.

He tossed it aside. "I guess you can't read, at that," he gloated. But the presence of the newspaper meant that he already knew Steve was back in circulation; the item had been in all of them that morning.

He motioned me to the chair. I climbed into it. I was too curious to see what would happen next to be really frightened. Otherwise how could I have sat in it at all? He took a cursory glance into my mouth. Almost an absent-minded glance, as though his thoughts were really elsewhere. "Can you pay me?" he said next, still very absent-minded and not looking at me at all.

"I'll do my best, sorr. I have no job."

"Tell you what I'll do for you," he said suddenly, his eyes dilating. "I'll give you temporary relief, and then I'll send you to someone who'll finish the job for you. He won't charge you anything, either. You just tell him Dr. Smith sent you."

My heart started to go like a triphammer. So I was on the right track after all, was I? He'd picked a different name this time to cover up his traces, that was all. And as for the gold tooth outside the door betraying him, he was counting on something stopping me before I got around to mentioning that. I knew what that something was, too.

He got to work. He pulled open a drawer and I saw a number of fragile clay caps or crowns, hollow inside and thin as tissue paper. They were about the size and shape of thimbles. I could hardly breathe any more. Steve's voice came back to me, indignantly questioning Amato: "Looks like the Boulder Dam, some bricklayer put it in for you?"

He took one of these out and closed the drawer. Then he opened another drawer and took something else out. But this time I couldn't see what it was, because he carefully stood over it with his back to me. He glanced over his shoulder at me to see if I was watching him. I beat him to it and lowered my eyes to my lap. He closed the second drawer. But I knew which one it was; the lower right in a cabinet of six.

He came over to me. "Open," he commanded. My eyes rolled around in their sockets. I still had time to rear up out of the chair, push him back, and snatch the evidence out of his hand. But I wasn't sure yet whether it *was* evidence or not.

Those caps may have been perfectly legitimate, for all I knew; I was no dentist. So I sat quiet, paralyzed with fear, unable to move.

And the whole thing was over with almost before it had begun. He sprayed a little something on the tooth, waxed it with hot grease, and stuck the cap on over it. No drilling, no dredging, no cleansing whatsoever. "That's all," he said with an evil grin. "But remember, it's only temporary. By tomorrow at the latest you go to this other dentist and he'll finish the job for you."

I saw the point at once. He hadn't cleaned the tooth in the least; in an hour or two it would start aching worse than ever under the fake cap and I'd *have* to go to the other dentist. The same thing must have happened to Amato. I was in for it now! "Don't chew on that side," he warned me, "until you see him." He didn't want it to happen to me at home or at some coffee counter, but in Steve's office, in Steve's chair!

Then he gave me the name and place I was to go to. "Standish, 28th and Lexington, second floor." Over and over again. "Will you remember that?" That was all I needed, I had the evidence against him now. But I didn't make a hostile move toward him, instead I stumbled out into the street and swayed toward the corner where Keenan was waiting for me. Let the cops go after him. I had myself to worry about now. I was carrying Death around in my mouth. Any minute, the slightest little jolt—

Keenan had been joined by a second detective. They both came toward me and held me up by the elbows. I managed to get my mouth open, and Keenan looked in. "Get the difference?" I gasped.

"It begins to look like you were right," he muttered.

He phoned the chief at Headquarters and then got me into a taxi with him. The second man was left there to keep an eye on Carter and tail him if he left his office.

"What're you holding your mouth open like that for?" he asked me in the cab.

"A sudden jolt of the taxi might knock my teeth together," I articulated. I had seen how thin those caps were.

We raced down Lexington and got out at Steve's office. Steve had been rushed up there from the detention pen in a police car along with the chief himself and two more detectives. He had to have facilities if he was going to save me from what had happened to Amato.

"He's got the evidence," Keenan informed them as he guided me past the jangling bell. I pointed to my mouth. "In there," I gasped, and my knees buckled up under me.

Steve got me into the chair. Sweat broke out on his face after he'd taken one look at Carter's work, but he tried to reassure me. "All right, all right now, boy," he said soothingly, "You know I won't go back on you, don't you?"

He looked around at them. The chief had his usual rank cigar in his mouth, which had gone out in the excitement. One of the others held a pipe between his clenched teeth.

"Where's your tobacco pouch?" ordered Steve hoarsely. "Let me have it, I'll get you a new one."

The lining was thin rubber. He tore that out, scattered tobacco all over the floor. Then he held it up toward the light and stretched it to see if there were any holes or cracks. Then, with a tiny pair of curved scissors, he cut a small wedge-shaped hole in it. "Now hold your mouth open," he said to me, "and whatever you do, don't move!" He lined the inside of my mouth with the rubber, carefully working the tooth Carter had just treated through the hole he had cut, so that it was *inside* the pouch. The ends of the rubber sack he left protruding through my lips. I felt a little as though I were choking. "Can you breathe?" he said. I batted my eyes to show him he could go ahead.

He thrust wedges into my cheeks, so that I couldn't close my jaws whether I wanted to or not. Then he came out with a tiny mallet and a little chisel, about the size of a nail. "I may be able to get it out whole," he explained to the chief. "It's been in less than half an hour. Drilling is too risky."

His face, as he bent over me, was white as plaster. I shut my eyes and thought, "Well, here I go—or here I stay!" I felt a number of dull blows on my jawbone. Then suddenly something seemed to crumble and a puff of ice-cold air went way up inside my head. I lay there rigid and—nothing happened.

"Got it!" Steve breathed hotly into my face. He started to work the rubber lining carefully out past my lips and I felt a little sick. When it was clear he passed it over to the detectives without even a look at its contents, and kept his attention focussed on me. "Now, watch yourself, don't move yet!" he commanded nervously. He took a spray and rinsed out the inside of my mouth with water, every corner and crevice of it, about eighteen times. "Don't swallow," he kept warning me. "Keep from swallowing!" Keenan, his chief, and the others had their heads together over the spread-out contents of the little rubber sack, meanwhile.

Steve turned off the water and took the pads away from my gums finally. He sat down with a groan; I sat up with a shudder. "I wouldn't want to live the past five minutes over again for all the rice in China!" he admitted, mopping his brow. "Maybe I would!" I shivered.

"Packed with cyanide crystals," the chief said, "enough to kill a horse! Go up there and make the pinch. Two counts, murder and attempted murder." Two men started for the door.

"Top drawer left for the caps, bottom drawer right for the cy," I called after them weakly and rather needlessly. They'd find it, all right.

But I was very weary all at once and very much disinterested. I stumbled out of the chair and slouched toward the door, muttering something about going home and resting up. Steve pulled himself together and motioned me back again.

"Don't forget the nerve is still exposed in that tooth of yours. I'll plug it for you right, this time." I sat down again, too limp to resist. He attached a new drill to the pulley and started it whirring. As he brought it toward me I couldn't help edging away from it. "Can you beat it?" He turned to Keenan, who had stayed behind to watch, and shook his head in hopeless amazement. "Takes his life in his hands for a friend, but when it comes to a little everyday drilling he can't face it!"

(1934)

Walls That Hear You

When the policeman came to the door and asked if Eddie Mason lived there I knew right away something had happened to him. They always break it to you that way.

"Yeah. I'm his brother."

"Better come down and see him," he said. I got my hat and went with him.

Eddie was in the emergency ward of the Mount Eden Hospital, he told me. He'd been found lying on his back on a lonely stretch of road out toward White Plains, slowly bleeding away.

"What is it, hit and run?" I cried, grabbing him by the sleeve.

He didn't want to tell me at first. Then, just before we got there he said, "Well, you may as well know now as later, I guess." Eddie's tongue had been torn out by the roots and all ten of his fingers had been cut off at the base, leaving just the stumps of both hands.

I went all weak at the pit of my stomach when I heard it. And then when I got the full implication of the thing, it was even worse. That poor kid. Just turned twenty. Yesterday with his life all before him. And now he'd never be able to speak another word as long as he lived, never be able to feed himself or dress himself or earn a decent living after this.

"He'd have been better off dead!" I groaned. "What did it?" I kept saying. "What was it?"

"I don't know," said the cop sadly. "I'm just a sidewalk-flattener with the pleasant job of breaking these things to people."

19

Eddie hadn't come to yet, so just standing there looking at him didn't do much good. It broke my heart, though. One of the doctors gave me a good stiff drink of whiskey and tried to be encouraging.

"He'll pull through," he said. "No doubt about it. We've made a preliminary examination, and I don't even think we'll have to resort to blood transfusion. What saved him more than anything else were the makeshift bandages that were found on him. If it hadn't been for them he'd have been a goner long before he was picked up."

This went over my head at the time. I didn't understand. I thought he meant their own bandages, the hospital's.

A couple of detectives had already been assigned to the case from the moment the cop who had found him had phoned in his report. Why wouldn't they be? No car has ever yet been designed so that it can rip the tongue out of a man's mouth without leaving a scratch on the rest of his face. Or deposit him neatly on the side of the road, with his feet close together and his hat resting on his stomach as if he were dozing. There wasn't a bruise on him except the mutilations. They were waiting in the other room to talk to me when I came out of the ward, looking like a ghost.

"You his brother?"

"Yes, damn it!" I burst out. "And all I want is to get my hands on whoever did this to him!"

"Funny," said a dick dryly, "but so do we."

I didn't like him much after that. Sarcasm is out of place when a man has just been brought face to face with personal tragedy.

First they told me what they already knew about Eddie, then they had me fill in the rest for them. There wasn't very much of either. I mean that had any bearing on this.

"He runs the elevator at the Hotel Lyons, works the late shift alone, from midnight to six in the morning," I explained.

"We checked down there already. He never showed up at all last night; they had to use the night watchman as a substitute on the car. What time did he leave your house to go to work last night?"

"Same time as always. Quarter to twelve."

"That don't give him much time, does it?" remarked my pet aversion irrelevantly.

My nerves were raw and I felt like snapping, "That's no reason why he should be half torn to pieces," but instead I said, "He only has two express stops to go, the hotel's on Seventy-second."

"How do you know he rode?"

"I can give you a lead on that," I offered. "The station agent down there knows him—by sight, anyway. Kelsey's his name. Ask him if he saw him come up last night at the usual time or not." He went out to find a phone. "He don't know his name," I called after him warningly, "so just say the young fellow from the Hotel Lyons he let pass through one time when he'd lost all his change through a hole in his pocket."

"Not bad," remarked his mate admiringly while we were waiting. "You've got a good head, Mason. What do you do?"

"Master electrician. I've got my own store on upper Amsterdam."

The other one came back and said, "I had to wake him up at home, but he knew who I meant right away. Yeah, your brother came through the turnstile about five of twelve. Says he flipped his hand up and said, 'Hello, you bird in a gilded cage.'"

"Well," I said, and my voice broke, "then it's a cinch he still had—his voice and his—fingers when he got out of the train. And it's another cinch it didn't happen to him between the station and the hotel. It's right on the corner, that hotel is, and it's one of the busiest corners on Broadway. Looks like the management gave you a bum steer and he did go to work after all."

"No, that was on the up-and-up. They were even sore about it at first, until we told them he was in the hospital."

"What were those sandwiches doing in his pocket?" the other one asked. "Looks like he stopped off somewhere first to buy food. They were still on him when he was found, one in each pocket."

"No, my wife fixed them for him to take with him and eat on the job," I said. "She did that every night." I looked the other way so they wouldn't see my eyes get cloudy. "I saw him shove them in his coat before he left the house. Now they'll be feeding him through a tube, most likely."

"Any way you look at it," said the first one, "it narrows down to about five minutes in time and twenty or thirty yards in distance. He was seen leaving the station. He never got to the hotel. With lights all around as bright as day. Why, he didn't even have to go all the way across the street—the station's on an island in the middle!"

"What's the good of all that?" said the one I didn't like. "We won't get anywhere until we find out from him himself. He knows better than anyone else what happened after he came out of the station. He's the only one can tell us; we'll just have to sit tight until he's able to—"

"Tell!" I exclaimed bitterly. "How is he going to tell anybody anything after this, with no voice left and without being able to hold a pencil to paper!"

"There are ways," he said. He flagged a nurse who had just stepped out of the ward. "When are you people going to let us at young Mason?"

"Right now, if you want to finish the job," she snapped back at him. "He's out of his head from shock and loss of blood. But go right in if you want to make it a murder case; maybe you'd rather handle one of those. However, if you'll hold your horses and give us a chance to pull him through, maybe you can see him by tomorrow or the day after."

I saw the other one, Kane, grin behind his hand. She certainly had character, that person, whoever she was. He turned back to me again after that. "I don't want to make you feel bad, Mason, but we've had cases like this before. And the answer is always pretty much the same. Your brother probably got in with the wrong crowd and knew a little more than he should've. Who'd he run around with, any idea?"

"No one, good, bad or indifferent. If it's gangs you're thinking of you can drop that angle right now. He wasn't that kind; he didn't have the time. Know what that kid was doing? Working nights at the hotel, sleeping mornings, helping me out in the shop afternoons, and going to night school three times a week in the bargain! The couple of evenings he had left over he usually took his girl to the movies. He was no slouch, he wanted to get somewhere. And now look at him!" I turned away. "If they'd only broken his leg, or knocked out his teeth, or anything—anything but what they did do! I'm going home and drink myself to sleep, I can't stand thinking about it any more."

Kane gave me a slap on the back in silent sympathy. Pain-in-the-face said, "We'll want you on hand tomorrow when we try to question him; you might be some help."

II

I was with him long before they were, from the minute they'd let me in until they told us we all had to go. About all the poor kid could talk with were his eyes, and he worked them overtime. They seemed to burn out at me sometimes, and I figured I understood what he meant.

"We'll straighten it out, Eddie," I promised him grimly. "We'll get even on them—whoever they are. We'll see that they get what's coming to them!"

He nodded his head like wild and his eyes got wet, and the nurse gave me a dirty look for working him up.

Kane and his partner were only allowed fifteen minutes with him that first day, which was a hell of a long time at that, considering that the amputations had taken place less than forty-eight hours before. The questioning fell completely flat, just as I had expected it to. He was as completely shut off from all of us as though there was a wall built around him. The only kind of questions he could answer were those that took "yes" or "no" for an answer—by shaking his head up and down or from side to side—and that limited them to about one out of every ten that they wanted to put to him. I saw red when I saw how helpless he was. It was later that same afternoon that I dug up that permit I'd had ever since two years before when my shop was held up, and went out and bought a revolver with it. I didn't know what I was going to do with it, but I knew what I wanted to do with it—given the right person!

But to go back: "Did you see who did it to you?"

No, he shook.

"Well, have you any idea who it could be?"

No again.

"Been in any trouble with anyone?"

No.

"Well, where did it happen to you?"

He couldn't answer that, naturally, so they had to shape it up for him. But it wouldn't go over, no matter how they put it. He kept shrugging his shoulders, as if to say he didn't know himself. His face got all white with the effort he was making to express himself and when the nurse had examined him and found out that bleeding had set in again inside his mouth, she lost her temper and told us to get out and please question somebody else if we had to ask questions. Eddie was in a faint on the pillows when she closed the door after us. That was when I went out and bought the gun, swearing under my breath.

Kane and Frozen-face showed up the next day with a couple of those charts that opticians use for testing the eyes, with capital letters all scrambled up, big at the top and getting smaller all the way down. Instead of questioning him directly any more, they had him spell out what he wanted to say letter by letter, Deadpan pointing them out on the chart and Kane jotting them down on a piece of paper—providing Eddie nodded yes—until he had complete words and sentences made up out of them. But it was as slow and tedious as teaching a cross-eyed mental defective the alphabet. The first two or three letters sometimes gave a clue to what word he had in mind: for instance, *H, O* meant that "hotel" was coming and they could save time and skip the *T, E, L* part. But others weren't as easy as all that to figure out, and then every once in awhile they would get one all wrong and have to go back and start it over.

Well, when they were all through—and it took three or four full half-hour sessions—they were practically back where they had started from. Eddie, it turned out, was as much in the dark as the rest of us were. He had been unconscious the whole time, from a minute after leaving the subway station that night until he came to in the hospital bed where he was now, the next morning.

This was his story. Just as he got past Kelsey's ticket window in the subway station the green lights flashed on and he had to stand there waiting before he could get across to the other side of the half-roadway. He wasn't a heavy smoker, but as he was standing there waiting for the traffic to let up he absent-mindedly lit a cigarette. Then, when he got over and was ready to go in the hotel, he noticed what he'd done. The management was very strict about that; they didn't allow the employees to smoke, not even in the locker-room, on pain of dismissal. Being an economical kid he hated to throw it away right after he'd begun it. The big sidewalk clock that stood out in front of the hotel said seven to twelve—the clock must have been a couple of minutes slow—so he decided to take a turn around the block and finish the cigarette before he went in.

And another thing, he admitted—there was a laugh and a tear in this if you've ever been twenty—he didn't want to "spoil" the fellow he was relieving for the night by getting in too much ahead of time. So up the side-street he turned, killing time while he finished his cigarette.

It was dark and gloomy, after the glare of Broadway, and there wasn't anyone on it at that hour. But from one end to the other of it there was a long, unbroken line of cars parked up against the sidewalk. They seemed to be empty; in any case he didn't pay any attention to them. Halfway up the block he stopped for a moment to throw the cigarette away, and as he did so something soft was thrown up against his face from behind. It was like a hand holding a big, square folded handkerchief.

There hadn't been a sound behind him, not even a single footfall. It was done so easily, gently almost, that for a moment he wasn't even frightened but thought that it must be something like a rag or piece of goods that had fallen out of some window up above and blown up against his face. Then when he tried to raise his hand and brush it away, he felt something holding it. And he started to feel lazy and tired all over.

Then he felt himself being drawn backwards, like a swimmer caught in a current, but when he tried to pull away and fight off whatever it was that was happening to him, it was too late. Instead of being able to get any air in his lungs, all he kept breathing was something sweet and sickly, like suffocating flowers, and after that he didn't know any more. When he woke up he was in agony in the hospital.

Kane got a little vial of chloroform from the nurse and wet the stopper and held it near Eddie's face.

"Was that it? Was that what it smelt like?"

He got wild right away and tried to back his head away and nodded *yes* like a house afire and made growling sounds deep in his throat that went through me like a knife.

III

The three of us went outside to talk it over.

"Mistaken identity," decided Kane. "Whoever was waiting in that car expected somebody else to go by and thought they had him when they jumped on the kid. That's all I can make of it. Either they never found out their mistake until it was too late, or else they did but went ahead and did it anyway, afraid he'd give way on them. It's not fool-proof, but it's the best I can do."

"It's as full of holes as a Swiss cheese," his partner told him disgustedly. "It's like I told you before. The kid knows and he's not telling. He talked too much, got a little present for it from somebody, and now he's learned his lesson and isn't making the same mistake twice." He took the penciled sheets from Kane and shuffled through them. "It don't hang together. Chloroform my eye! Husky twenty-year-olds don't stand still waiting to go bye-bye like that. It don't get them that quick; their wind's too good. He was politely invited to step into that car by someone he knew and he didn't dare refuse. What they did after proves it. Why the tongue and the fingers? For talking. You can't get around that."

I had stood all of that I could.

"Listen," I flamed, "are you on a job to get whoever did it, or are you on a job to stand up for 'em and knock my brother?"

"Watch yourself," he said. "I don't like that."

Kane came between us and gave me the wink with one eye. I suppose he gave his partner the wink with the other eye at the same time; peacemakers usually do.

Poison-mouth would have the last word, though. "If your brother would open up and give us a tip or two instead of holding out, we'd probably have the guy we want by this time."

"And what if he'd been a stiff and couldn't tip you off?" I squelched him. "Does that mean the guy would beat the rap altogether?"

It was probably this little set-to more than anything else that first put the idea in my mind of working on my own hook on Eddie's behalf. Kane's partner had him down for a gangster more or less. I knew that he wasn't. I wanted to get even for him, more than I ever wanted anything before in my life.

Let them tackle it in their own way! I'd do a little work on the side. I didn't have any idea of what I was going to do—then or for some time afterwards. All I knew was whoever did that to Eddie wasn't going to get away with it—not if it took me the rest of my life to catch up with them.

They had left the charts behind while they were out rounding up small-time racketeers and poolroom-lizards that had never heard of Eddie, and I worked over them with him daily. We got so that we could handle them much faster than in the beginning.

And then one day, out of all the dozens, the hundreds of questions I kept throwing at him, the right one popped out. The minute I asked it, even before he gave me the answer, I knew I had hit something. I wondered why I hadn't asked it long ago.

He had worked at another hotel called the San Pablo before going to the Lyons. But this had been quite awhile before.

"None of the guests from there ever turned up later at the Lyons while you were there, did they?" I asked.

Yes, one did, he spelled back. His name was Dr. Avalon. He'd left the San Pablo before Eddie himself did, and then when Eddie got the job at the Lyons he found he'd moved there ahead of him, that was all.

Maybe this was just a coincidence, but all the same I kept digging at it.

"Did he recognize you?"

He nodded.

"What did he say when he first saw you?"

He'd smiled jovially at Eddie and said, "Young fellow, are you following me around?" Then he'd given him a five-dollar tip.

"Pretty big tip, wasn't it?"

Yes, but then at the San Pablo, Eddie recalled, he had once given him a ten-dollar one. This was getting interesting.

"Whew!" I said. " What for?"

Eddie smiled a little.

Something about a woman, as I might know.

"Better tell me about it," I urged.

One night about one o'clock, his message ran, a young woman who
acted kind of nervous had got on the car and asked Eddie which floor
Dr. Avalon was on. So he took her to the door and showed her. But it
was a long hallway and before he could get back to the cage again,
Avalon had let her in and he heard him say in a loud voice: "You
shouldn't have come here! I don't see anybody here! You should have
seen me in my office tomorrow."

And she had answered, "But I had to see you!"

Well, Eddie had thought it was the usual thing, some kind of a love
affair going on. But about half an hour later he was called back to the
floor and when he got up there he found Avalon standing waiting for
him, all excited, his face running with sweat, and he shoved a piece of
paper with something written on it at him and told him to run out and
find an all-night drugstore and bring back some medicine as quickly
as he could.

"Hurry! Hurry!" he said. "Every minute counts!"

Eddie did, and when he got back with it he knocked on the door, but
not very loudly because he didn't want to wake up people in the other
rooms. The doctor must have been too excited to pay any attention
because he didn't come to the door right away, so Eddie tried the
knob, found that it had been left open, and walked in. He saw the
doctor's visitor stretched out on a table with a very white light
shining down on her and a sheet or something over her. Then the
doctor came rushing over at him and for a minute he thought he was
going to kill him, he looked so terrible.

"Get out of here, you!" he yelled at him. "What do you mean by
coming in here?" and practically threw him out of the door.

About an hour later the young lady and the doctor showed up
together and rode down in Eddie's car as cool and collected as if
nothing had happened. The doctor showed her to a taxi at the door,
and it was when he came in and rode upstairs again that he gave
Eddie the ten dollars, saying he was sorry he had lost his head like
that, but she had had a very bad heart attack and it was lucky he had
pulled her through.

"Did he ask you not to say anything?"

Eddie nodded, and again smiled a little sheepishly. But I knew he didn't get the point at all. He thought it was just some love affair that the doctor wanted kept quiet. I knew better. The man was a shady doctor and ran the risk of imprisonment day and night.

"Then what happened?"

Eddie hadn't opened his mouth at all to anyone, but not long after some men had come around and stopped at the desk and asked questions about the doctor, men wearing iron hats and chewing cigars in the corner of their mouths, and when they learned he wasn't in they said they'd come back next day. But before they did the doctor had left, bag and baggage. Eddie said he never saw anyone leave in such a hurry. It was at five thirty in the morning and Eddie was still on duty.

"Did he say anything to you?"

No, he had just looked at him kind of funny, and Eddie hadn't known what to make of it.

I did, though. I was beginning to see things clearer and clearer every moment. I was beginning to have a little trouble with my breathing, it kept coming faster all the time.

"Time's up," said the nurse from the doorway.

"Not yet it isn't," I told her. "I'm not going to have to do any questioning after today, so back out while I take a couple minutes more to wind it all up." I turned to Eddie. "And when you ran into him again at the Lyons he said 'Young fellow, are you following me around?', did he? And smiled at you, did he? And gave you a finif tip for no reason at all, did he?"

Eddie nodded three times.

I clenched my teeth tight. I had everything I needed, knew all I wanted to, and yet—I couldn't have made the slimmest charge stick and I knew it; I didn't have any evidence. A ten-dollar tip, a hasty departure, an everyday wisecrack like "Are you following me around?"—you can't bring charges against anyone on the strength of those alone.

"What's he like?" I asked.

Short and dumpy, came the answer. He wore a black beard, not the bushy kind, but curly and trimmed close to his face.

"Did he always have it?"

Not at the San Pablo, no. He'd only had a mustache there, but he'd grown the beard after he moved to the Lyons.

Just in case, I thought, the cigar-chewing gentlemen with the iron hats showed up again. That wasn't very clever. Something told me that this Dr. Avalon was not quite right in his head—which made the whole thing all the more gruesome. Frozen-face's gangsters were angels of light and sweetness compared to a maniac like this.

"Did he ever act a little strangely, I mean different from other people, as far as you could notice?"

No, except that he seemed absent-minded and used to smile a lot about nothing at all.

I only asked Eddie one more question. "What was his room number at the Lyons?"

He didn't know for sure, but he had always taken him up to the eighth floor.

I got up to go.

"I won't be in to see you tomorrow," I told him casually. "I'm going to drop by the hotel and collect the half week's wages they still owe you." But there was a far bigger debt than that I was going to collect for him. "In case I don't get around for the next few days, I'll have the wife stay with you to keep you company. Not a tumble to her or to those two flatfeet, either, the next time they come around on one of their semi-annual visits."

I think he knew. He just looked at me and narrowed his eyes down, and we shook hands hard.

"Don't worry, Eddie, everything's under control—now."

IV

When I got back to my own house I put the revolver in an empty suitcase and carried it out with me. From there I stopped off at the shop and put in several lengths of copper wire and an awl and a screwdriver and some metal disks and a little black soundbox with some batteries inside it, something on the order of a telephone baseboard. I also put in several other little tools and gadgets you'd have to be a master electrician to know anything about. I told my assistant to keep things running, that I was going out to wire a concert hall, and I rode down to the Hotel Lyons and checked in. I signed the register "T. Mallory, Buffalo," and told them I was very particular about where I slept. The seventh floor wasn't quite high enough, and the ninth floor was just a little too high. How about something on the eighth? So they gave me 802. I didn't even know if he was still in the hotel at all, but it was taking too much of a chance to ask; he might have gotten wind of it. So I paid for three days in advance and said: "Don't be surprised if I ask you to change me in a day or two. I'm a very hard customer to please." Which was perfectly all right with them, they told me.

When I got up to the room I just put the valise down without unpacking it and killed a little time, and then I went downstairs with a newspaper in my pocket and grabbed a chair in the lobby that faced the entrance and sat there from then on. From six until eleven I sat there like that with the paper spread out in front of my face. I never turned a page of it because that would have covered over the two little eye-holes I'd made in it with the point of a pencil. At eleven-thirty they started to put the lights out around me and I couldn't stay there any longer without attracting attention. So I got up and went up to my room. He'd never shown up. For all I knew he'd beat it right after—what he did to Eddie; maybe he wasn't even living in the building any more. I had to find out and find out quick, otherwise I was just wasting my time. But how, without asking openly? And I couldn't do that, it would give me away.

In the morning I thought of a way, and it worked. I remembered a song of years back that strangely enough had the same name as the man I was tracking down—Avalon. When the chambermaid came in to clean up the room I got busy and started singing it for all I was worth. I didn't know the words and I didn't know the music, so I faked it, but I put in plenty of Avalon. She was a friendly old soul and stood there grinning at me.

"Like it?" I said.

"What's it supposed to be?" she asked.

"It's called Avalon," I said. "Isn't that a funny name for a song?"

"It is," she admitted. "We got a doctor in this hotel by the same name."

I laughed as though I didn't believe her.

"What room is he in?" I asked skeptically.

"815," she said. "He's a permanent, that's how I know his name."

I went down to the desk and said: "I didn't sleep a wink last night; you've got to give me something else."

The clerk unfolded a floor-plan and we began to consult it together. 815, I saw at a glance, was a suite of two-rooms-and-a-bath, at the end of the hallway. It sealed it up like the cross-bar of a T. All the others were singles, lying on each side of the hallway; only two of them, therefore, adjoined it.

I pointed to one. "That's a nice layout. 814. How about that?"

They had someone in there.

"Or this?" I put my finger on 813.

No good either.

"What's it worth to you to put me in one of those two rooms?" I said abruptly. "I'll double the rate if you switch me in and move the other tenant elsewhere."

He gave me a funny look, as if to say, "What're you up to?" but I didn't care.

"I'm a crank," I said. "At home I sleep on three mattresses." I handed him a cigar wrapped in a five-spot and half an hour later I was in 814 and had the door locked.

I spent the next half hour after that sounding out the wall, the one between me and him, with my knuckles and my eardrum. I had to go easy, because I didn't know whether he was in the room or not at the time and I didn't want to arouse his suspicions.

Just when I was wondering whether I should take a chance or not and go ahead, I got a break. The telephone on the other side of the wall, his telephone, started to ring. All that came through to where I was was a faint, faraway tinkle. It kept on for awhile and then it quit of its own accord. But it told me two things that I wanted to know very badly. It told me he wasn't there to answer it, and it gave me a very good idea of just how thick the wall was. It was too thick to hear anything through, it needed fixing. I opened my suitcase, got out my tools, and got busy drilling and boring. I kept my ears open the whole time because I knew I'd have to quit the minute I heard him open his door and come in. But he never did. He must have been out for the day.

I finished a little before four in the afternoon. Finished on my side of the wall, anyway. I had the tiny hole bored all the way through, the wiring strung through and the soundbox screwed in behind a radiator where it wasn't noticeable. I swept up all the little specks of plaster in my handkerchief and dropped them out the window. You couldn't notice anything unless you looked very closely. But I had to get in on the other side, his side of the wall, and hook up the little disk, the "mike," before it would work. Without that it was dead, no good at all.

The set-up, I had better explain, was not a dictaphone. It didn't record anything, all it did was amplify the sounds it picked up in his room and bring them through into mine, the way a loudspeaker would. In other words, it was no good as evidence without a witness. But to hell with witnesses and all legal red tape! I was out to pay him back for Eddie and I figured he'd be too clever for me if it came to an open arraignment in a criminal court. I didn't have anything on him that a smart enough lawyer couldn't have blown away like a bunch of soap-bubbles, and yet I could have sworn on a stack of Bibles that he was the guy I was looking for.

The next step was to get in there. I examined the outside of my window, which faced the same way as his, but that was no good. Neither of them had a fire-escape or even a ledge to cross over by. It was also pretty late in the afternoon by now and he might be coming in any minute. Much as I hated to waste another night, I figured I would have to put it off until the morning. Of course, I was taking a chance on his noticing any small grains of mortar or plaster that might have fallen to the floor on his side. But that couldn't be helped. It wasn't very likely anyway, I consoled myself. It was one of those thousand-to-one shots that life is full of.

I didn't undress at all that night or go to bed. I kept pacing back and forth on the carpet, stopping every few minutes to listen at the door and at the wall. There wasn't a sound the whole night through. Nobody came and nobody went. 815 might have been vacant for all the signs of life it gave.

In the morning the same chambermaid as before came to make the room up. I mussed up the bed just before she came in so it looked as if it had been slept in. When she was through she went into 815 and left the door ajar after her. House-regulations, I suppose. It was a two-room suite, remember.

I gave her about five minutes to get through with one of the rooms—either one, it didn't matter—and then I stole out of my room, closed the door after me, and edged up to the door of 815 until I could look in. If anyone coming along the corridor had seen me I was going to pretend she had forgotten to leave towels in my room and I was looking for her. She was in the living room. It was even easier than I had expected, because she was running a baby vacuum-cleaner across the floor and the buzz it made drowned out my footsteps.

I waited until she had her back to me and then I gave a quick jump in through the door and past her line of vision. The bed in the bedroom was made up, so I knew she was through in there and wouldn't come back again. I ducked down behind a big stuffed chair and waited. I had the copper disk, the rubber mat it went on, and the tools I needed in the side pocket of my coat.

I began to get cramped squatting down on my heels, but after awhile she got through and went out. I waited another minute or two after that, and then I got up, slipped into the living room and got to work. One good thing, there wasn't much noise to this part of the job, I had done all the drilling and pecking from my side. If he came in and caught me at it I was going to pretend I was the hotel elecrician and had been ordered to put in a new outlet or something. The trouble was I wasn't dressed for the part, and being a permanent in the hotel he might know the real electrician by sight. It occurred to me, now that it was too late, that I should have had the revolver with me instead of leaving it behind in my own room like a fool.

But I was through in no time at all. All I had to do was get hold of the ends of the wire, draw them the rest of the way through the hole, hook them onto the disk, and screw the disk onto the baseboard of the wall. It was no bigger than a coffee saucer, still it was coppery and bright. But I fixed that by shifting a chair over in front of it. In five minutes I was through. It was still dead, but all it needed now was to be grounded on one of the light fixtures in my own room. I let myself out, went back there, and did it. Now I was all set.

V

I went out and got some food, and then when I was through eating I did a funny thing. I went into a butcher shop to buy some more. But I knew what I was doing.

"I want a lamb's tongue," I told him. "Look in your icebox and bring me out the smallest one you've got."

When he did it was still too big.

"Cut it down," I said. "Just the tip and not much more."

He looked at me as though I was crazy, but he went ahead and did it. Then he took a nice clean piece of waxpaper and started wrapping it up.

"No, not that," I told him. "Find a piece with a lot of blood on it, all smeary, and wrap it in that. Then put a clean piece around the outside of it."

I took it back with me in my pocket, and when I got up to my room I wrote "Dr. Avalon" in pencil on the outside of it. Then I put it down outside his door, as if a delivery boy had left it there, and went back into my room and waited.

Now I was going to know for sure. If he had nothing on his conscience and came home and found that there, he wouldn't think anything of it—he'd think it was either a practical joke or that somebody else's order had been left at his door by mistake. But if he had a guilty conscience this was going to catch him off his guard and make him give himself away; he wouldn't be able to help it. It wouldn't have been human not to—even if it was only for a minute or two. And if there was anyone else in on it with him—and I had a hunch there was—the first thing he'd think of would be to turn to them for help and advice in his panic and terror. So I waited, stretched out on my bed, with the revolver in my pocket and my head close to the wall apparatus.

He came in around six. I heard his door open and then close again, and I jumped off the bed and took a peek through my own door. The package was gone, he'd taken it in with him. I went back and listened in. I could hear the paper crackling while he unwrapped it as clearly as if it had been in my own room. Then there was a gasp—the sound a man suffering from asthma makes trying to get his breath back. Then, *plop!* He had dropped it in his fright. The wiring was working without a hitch; I wasn't missing a thing.

After that I heard the clink of a glass. He was pouring himself a drink. It clinked again right after that, and then I heard him give sort of a moan. That was a dead giveaway; a man doesn't take two drinks to keep his courage up just because the butcher has left the wrong order at his door. He'd done that to my brother all right, he and nobody else. More rage and hate went through me than I ever thought I had in me. I could feel my lower jaw quivering as if I was a big dog getting ready to take a bite out of somebody. I had to hang on to the sides of the bed to stay where I was a little longer.

Then I heard his voice for the first time. The wiring played it up louder than it really was, like a projection machine. It sounded all hollow and choked. He was asking for a number at the phone. Regency, four-two-eight-one. I whipped a pencil out and scrawled it on my wall.

"Hello," he said huskily. "This is Avalon. Can you hear me? I don't want to talk very loud." His voice dropped to a mumble, but the wiring didn't let me down, it came in at ordinary conversational pitch and I could still follow it. "Somebody's on to us, and we better take a powder out while we still have the chance. I thought I'd let you know, that's all." Then he said, "No, no, no, not that at all. If that's all it was I could get around that with one hand tied behind my back. It's that other thing. You know, the night three of us went for an airing—and two of us came back. Don't ask me how I know! I can't tell you over this phone, there's someone at the switchboard downstairs. You hang up," he said, "and stand by. I'll call you right back. I'll use the direct wire from the cigar store downstairs, just to be on the safe side."

He hung up and I heard him come out and go down the hallway past my door. He sounded in a hurry.

I didn't waste any time. I grabbed my own phone and got Headquarters. "Put Kane on quick, or that other guy working with him. Never mind, you'll do, whoever you are! It's on the Mason case and it's only good for five minutes, it's got to be worked fast. Trace Regency four-two-eight-one and get whoever you find at the other end; he's on the line right now getting a call. Get him first and then look up the cases afterwards if you have to. It opened May fifteenth. Never mind who I am or where I am; I'm too busy, got no time to tell you now." I hung up, opened the door, and went out into the hall.

I was going to wait for him outside his own door and corner him when he came back, but when I looked I saw that he'd forgotten to close it in his hurry. It stood open on a crack. So I pushed it open and went in, hoping I might find something in the way of evidence to lay my hands on before he had a chance to do away with it. I closed the door after me, so that he wouldn't notice anything from the other end of the hall and be able to turn back in time.

The place was just about as I remembered it from the last time I'd been in it. That was only the afternoon before, but it already seemed like a year ago. The liquor he'd braced himself with was standing in a decanter on the table. The bloody parcel from the butcher was lying on the carpet where he'd dropped it. There was a doctor's kit on the seat of a chair, with a lot of gleaming, sharp-edged little instruments in it. I figured he'd used one of these on Eddie, and all my rage came back. I heard him fitting his key into the outside door, and I jumped back into the bathroom and got behind the shower curtain. I wanted to see what he'd do first, before I nabbed him.

What gave me time enough to get out of sight was that he was so excited it took him nearly a whole minute to get his key fitted into the keyhole straight enough to get the door open. The bathroom door had a mirror on the outside of it, and I saw his face in that as he went by. It was evil, repulsive; you could tell by his face that his reason was slowly crumbling. He had his mouth open as if he was panting for air. The black beard, short as it was, made him look a little bit like an ape standing on its hind legs. He kept going back and forth, carrying clothes out of the closet. He was getting ready to make another get-away, like that time at the San Pablo. But this time it wasn't going to work.

I waited until I heard the latches on his suitcases click shut, and then I stepped softly over the rim of the tub and edged my way to the bathroom door. I got the gun out, flicked open the safety clip and held it in my hand. Then I lounged around the angle of the doorway into the living room, like a lazy corner loafer. He didn't see me at first. The valises were standing in the middle of the room ready to move out, and he had gone over to the window and was standing looking anxiously out with his back to me. Waiting for his accomplice to stop by with a car and get him, I suppose.

I was halfway across the room now.

"You've got a visitor, Dr. Avalon," I said grimly. "Turn around and say hello to Eddie Mason's brother."

I was right in back of him by that time. He twisted around as suddenly as when you crack a whip, and when he saw me his eyes got big. I was holding the gun pressed close up against my side, muzzle trained on him. He saw that too. His face turned gray and he made a strangling sound in his throat, too frightened even to yell. He took a deep breath and I could tell that he was trying to get a grip on himself and pull himself together. Finally he managed to get his voice back to work again. "Who are you? Who's Eddie Mason? I never—"

Without taking my eyes off him I gave the bloody package on the floor a shove forward with my foot. "Now do you know why I'm here?"

He cringed and gibbered at me, more like an ape than ever. "I didn't know what I was doing! I—I didn't mean to go that far, something got the better of me. I just meant to frighten him."

"Why I don't let fly and put these six in you is more than I can understand," I growled. "That's what I came here for, and the quicker it's over the better!"

"I didn't kill him, though!" he protested. "I didn't take his life away! You can't do this to me—"

"Then you admit you did it, don't you? That's no news to me—but we're not going to keep it a secret between you and me and Regency four-two-eight-one. Get a piece of paper and write down what I tell you to—and then after you've signed it, we'll see. I'm giving you more of a break than you deserve; you ought to be stepped on like a toad and squashed!"

"Yes, yes, anything—I'll do anything you say," he murmured. He was drooling with relief. He gestured vaguely to the back of me. "There's a pen and paper—on that desk right behind you, just hand them to me—"

I should have remembered that there wasn't any; I'd come by there only a moment ago. I should have remembered there was a streak of insanity in him, and that always makes for greater cleverness when they're cornered than a normal person shows. But he caught me off my guard, and I half-turned to reach behind me.

Instantly there was a blinding flash of light and something broke all over my head and shoulders. The decanter, I suppose, that had been standing on the table alongside of us. But he must have had it ready in his hand for several moments past without my realizing it, to be able to bring it down so quickly. And at the same time he gripped me by the wrist so suddenly with his other hand, and wrenched it around so violently, that there wasn't even time to flex the trigger finger, and the gun went spinning loosely out of my hand as though I had been twirling it around on one finger.

The last thing I was conscious of was a dull thud somewhere across the room as it landed harmlessly on the carpet. I went out like a light, with whiskey, or maybe it was blood, streaming down into my ears and eyes.

VI

When my head cleared and I came to, I was no longer flat on the floor, but upright in a chair. Each ankle was tied to a leg of it by long strips torn from a shirt or piece of underwear. I was sitting on my own hands and they were fastened to the seat of it in some ingenious way—I think by another long strip running around the whole chair and passing under my body.

The position was a torture to my bent wrists, especially the one he had sprained. What I mistook at first for a fuzzy taste in my mouth turned out to be a gag loosely stuffed into it. I could see the gun out of the corner of my eye, still lying where it had fallen. I was thankful for a minute that he hadn't picked it up and turned it on me. Then, as I concentrated my full attention on him, something told me I was wrong about that—it might have been better for me if he had.

He had his back to me and I didn't know what he was doing at first. Or rather, my mind didn't know yet, but my instincts seemed to, beforehand. The way animals know things. The short hairs on the back of my neck stood up, and my heart was icy. My breath was coming like a bellows. He had a bright white light on, some kind of an adjustable doctor's lamp, like the time Eddie had caught sight of him working over that woman. That didn't frighten me. He kept making little clinking sounds, as if he was picking up and putting down metal instruments one by one. That didn't frighten me much either, although I began to have an inkling of what was up.

He wouldn't dare, I told myself. He wouldn't be crazy enough to! I wasn't Eddie, shanghaied off in the middle of the night without even a look at who had done it. We were in a hotel with hundreds of people all around us. We were in rooms he had been known to occupy for months past. Anything that happened here would point right at him. If he left me here his number was up, and on the other hand there was no way of getting me out of the place without being seen.

But when he turned around and looked at me, I knew he would dare. He'd dare anything. Not because he didn't know any better, but simply because he'd lost all caution. What the lamp and the metal instruments hadn't been able to do, one look at his sleepy eyes did.

Then I knew fear. I was in the presence of full-fledged insanity. Maybe it had always been there and he'd kept it covered up. Maybe the fright I'd given him before had brought it out in him at last. But there it was, staring me in the face and horrible to look at. Vacant eyes and an absent-minded smile that never changed. So peaceful, so gentle, like a kind-hearted old family doctor pottering around.

I sat there helpless, like a spectator at a show. And what a show! What frightened me more than anything else was to watch the deliberate, cold-blooded professional way he was saturating a number of pads with disinfectant. I would have given anything now if he had only used the gun on me. It would have been better than what was coming. I heard and whipped myself around and fell over sideways with the chair, giving myself another knock on the head. But I was too frightened to pass out any more. He came over and lifted me up and stood me straight again, chair and all, gently, almost soothingly, as if I was a kid with the colic.

"Don't be impatient," he said softly. "It will be over soon. I'm almost ready for you now."

If it's going to be like what happened to Eddie, I prayed desperately, let his hand slip and make it the throat instead!

He brought out a newspaper and spread it on the floor all around me.

"That will catch any drops that fall," he purred. "I used one with your brother too. It's the best absorbent there is."

The sweat was running down my face in streams by this time. The whole thing was like a bad dream. He had a number of sharp little scalpels laid out in a row on the table and they gleamed under the light. He selected one, breathed lovingly on it, and then turned around and came back to me, smiling dreamily.

"I suppose it's wrong of me not to use chloroform," he said, "but that's what you get for coming to me after office hours!" And then he suddenly broke out into an insane hysterical laugh that just about finished me. "Now, my friend," he said, "here's how we do it." He reached down and daintily plucked at the gag until he had drawn it all out of my mouth.

I had been waiting for that, it was the only chance I had. I let out the loudest yell that that hotel room or any other had ever heard. Tied up as I was, it actually lifted me an inch or two above the chair, I put such volume into it. What it would have sounded like in my own room, had anyone been there to hear it, I can only imagine.

He gripped me cruelly by the lower jaw and pulled it down until I thought it would fracture, so that I couldn't yell any more. Then with his other elbow he pressed my forehead and the upper part of my face back flat. I couldn't close my mouth and my head was held in a vise. One whole arm was still free from the elbow down, remember, even if it didn't have much room to swing in. And that was the one that held the scalpel. I saw the shiny thing flash before my face as he turned it to get a better leverage. I was pretty far gone, but not far enough. I knew I was going to feel everything that was going to happen.

"What's going on in here?" a voice asked somewhere in back of me. Not a very excited voice either. He let go of me and straightened up.

"How dare you come in here without knocking while I am treating one of my patients?" I heard him say. My luck was that I hadn't passed out a minute ago, as frightened as I was. His voice carried so much conviction and dignity he might have gotten away with it, whether I was tied or not. I couldn't yell any more, I couldn't even talk, but I showed whoever it was in the only way I could. I tipped myself over and hit the floor once more, and threshed around there trying to free myself.

I stayed conscious but everything around me was a blur for several minutes. When it came back in focus again I was standing up and my bonds had been loosened. They were all standing around me, the manager, the hotel detective, the porter, and everyone else.

"Did you get that guy?" was the first thing I asked. They shook their heads. Someone motioned and I turned around and looked.

The window was wide open, and the curtains were hanging on the outside of the sill instead of on the inside, as though something heavy had dragged them across it. Down below on the street you could hear some woman screaming, and people were running up from all directions.

"Better so," I said as I turned back to them. "It's a good thing you came when you did," I told the hotel dick. "How did it happen?"

He looked embarrassed.

"Well, you see," he stammered, "we happened to be in your room at the time—er—investigating that hook-up of yours, which had been reported to us by the maid, and we heard something going on in here through the wall. But until you gave that loud yell we thought he was just treating a patient. Even then we weren't sure, until I opened the door with a passkey and took a look."

"Well," I said, "outside of a sprained wrist, a stiff jaw and a bump on the head I feel a lot better than I would've if you hadn't showed up."

There was a commotion at the door and Kane's partner came hustling in, by himself. "We got that guy at Regency 428, and he broke like a toothpick! He's a hophead the doctor's been supplying and he drove the car that night—"

As I was leaving I stuck my tongue out at him, to everyone's surprise. "Just wanted to show you I've still got it," I said. I never liked that guy.

I stopped in at the hospital to see Eddie. He saw the plaster on my scalp and the gauze around my wrist and we just looked at each other quietly.

"It's all right, kid," I said after awhile. "Everything's all right—now."

It will be, too. They have artificial fingers these days that are as good as the real ones. And a man can become a good electrician without—having to talk very much.

(1934)

Preview of Death

It was what somebody or other has called life's darkest moment. My forehead was dripping perspiration and I stared miserably down at the floor. "But, Chief," I said when he got all through thundering at me, "all I had was a couple of beers and besides I wasn't on duty at the time. And how was I to know that that wasn't the right way out of the place? I only found out it was a plate-glass window when I came through on the other side of it. And my gun didn't go off, you can look for yourself. It was some car out in the street that back-fired just then and made everybody clear out in such a hurry. You're not going to break me for that, are you?"

"No," he said, "but I'm going to give you a nice quiet assignment that'll keep you out of trouble for awhile. You're going to look after Martha Meadows from now on, she's been getting threatening letters and her studio just called and asked us to furnish her with protection. That's you until further orders."

"I resign," I said when I heard that.

He switched his cigar from the left-hand corner to the right-hand corner without putting a finger to it, leaned half-way across his desk at me, and went into another electrical storm. A lot of fist-pounding on the mahogany went with it. You couldn't hear yourself think, he was making that much noise. "Resign? You can't resign! Over my dead body you'll resign! What d'ya think this squad is, a game of in-again out-again Finnigan?"

"But—but Chief," I pleaded, "bodyguard to a—a movie actress! All the rest of the boys will laugh at me, I'll never be able to live it down! And what'll the wife say? Dock me, break me—anything but that!"

He rattled some papers around and held them up in front of his face. Maybe to keep from weakening, I don't know. "*Ahem*—now not another word out of you, Galbraith. Off you go. Get right out there and don't let her out of your sight until further notice. Remember, your job isn't to trace these threats or track down whoever sent 'em, it's just to keep your eye on Martha Meadows and see that nothing happens to her. You're responsible for her safety."

"O.K., Chief," I sighed, "but I really should be wearing a dog collar."

No doubt about it, I was the unhappiest, most miserable detective that ever started out on an assignment as I walked out of headquarters that day and got in a taxi. The sooner I got busy on the job, I figured, the sooner the chief might relent and take me off it. The taxi, and everything else from now on, was at Miss Meadows' own personal expense, but that didn't make me like her any the better. Without actually wishing her any harm, I was far from being a fan of hers at the moment.

The studio, on Marathon Street, looked more like a library than anything else from the outside. The gateman picked up a phone, said: "From headquarters, to see Miss Meadows," and everything opened up high, wide and handsome. I passed from hand to hand like a volley-ball getting to her; and all of them, from the gateman right on up, seemed glad that I had been sent over to look after her. You could tell she was well liked.

She was in her bungalow dressing-room resting between scenes and having her lunch when they brought me in. Her lunch was a malted milk and a slice of sponge cake—not enough to keep a canary alive. She had a thick make-up on, but even at that she still looked like somebody's twelve-year-old sister. You sort of wanted to protect her and be her big brother the minute you set eyes on her, even if you hadn't been sent there for just that purpose—the way I had. "I'm Jimmy Galbraith from headquarters, Miss Meadows," I said.

She gave me a friendly smile. "You don't look a bit like a detective," she answered, "you look like a college boy."

Just to put her in her place I said: "And you don't look a bit like a screen star, you look like a little girl in grade school, rigged up for the school play."

Just then a colored woman, her maid I guess, looked in and started to say, "Honey lamb, is you nearly—" Then when she saw me she changed to: "Look here, man, don't you bring that cig-ret in here, you want to burn that child up?" I didn't know what she meant for a minute, I wasn't anywhere near Meadows.

"Hush up, Nellie," Martha Meadows ordered with a smile. "She means this," Meadows explained, and pointed to her dress. "It has celluloid underneath, to stiffen it. If a spark gets on it—" She was dressed as a Civil War belle, with a wide hoopskirt the size of a balloon. I pinched the cigarette out between my fingers in a hurry.

"Just cause it ain't happen', don't mean it can't happen," snapped the ferocious Nellie, and went about her business muttering darkly to herself. The dressing-room telephone rang and Meadows said: "Alright, I'm ready whenever you are." She turned to me. "I have to go back on the set now. We're shooting the big scene this afternoon."

"Sorry," I said, "but I'll have to go with you, those are my orders."

"It's agreeable to me," she said, "but the director mayn't like outsiders watching him. He's very temperamental, you know."

I wasn't even sure what the word meant, so I looked wise and said: "He'll get over it."

She started up and the three of us left the bungalow. I let the maid and her go in front and followed close behind them. They walked along a number of lanes between low one-story studio buildings and finally came to a big barn of a place that had sliding doors like a garage and a neat little sign up: *Set VIII, Meadows, Civil War Picture.* People were hanging around outside, some in costume and some not. They made way for her respectfully and she passed through them and went in. She bowed slightly to one or two and they nearly fell over themselves bowing back.

Inside, the place had a cement floor criss-crossed over with a lot of little steel rails like baby train tracks. They were for moving heavy camera trucks back and forth, and cables and ropes and wires and pulleys galore were dangling from the rafters. Canvas back-drops were stacked, like cards, up against the walls. But it wasn't out here they were going to shoot the scene at all. There was a sound-proof door with a red light over it leading in to the "stage" itself, where the action was to take place.

Before we got to it, though, a bald-headed man in a pullover sweater came up to Meadows. He was about five feet tall and with a beak like an eagle's. A girl carrying a thick notebook, like a stenographer's dictation pad, was following him around wherever he went. I had him spotted for the director as soon as I looked at him.

"Who is this man?" he asked—meaning me. Then, when she told him, he raised both hands to his head and would have torn out some hair, only, as I said before, he was bald. "No," he said, "I cannot work! There are too many people hanging around the stage already! First it was your colored maid. Now a detective! Who will it be next?"

A big argument started in then and there about whether I was to go in or stay out, with Meadows taking my part and the script-girl trying to calm the director down. "Now, Stormy," she kept saying, "please don't excite yourself, this isn't good for you, remember how sensitive you are!" Finally I cut the whole thing short by saying I'd phone the chief and leave it up to him, as he was the one who had given me the assignment. But there was no telephone in the place and I had to go outside and call up headquarters fromthe studio cafeteria next door.

The chief went off like a firecracker. "What's the matter with them anyway? First they ask me for a bodyguard for her, then they start shooing him away. You go in there, Gal, and if they try to keep you out, quit the case cold and report back here to me. I'll wash my hands of all responsibility for her safety!" Which was music to my ears, as I hadn't liked the job from the start.

Sure enough, when I got back, the sound-proof door was already closed, the red light was on above it to warn that "shooting" was going on, and they had all gone in without waiting. There was a guard stationed outside the door to keep people from opening it by accident.

"She left word for you to wait out here," he told me. "Stormann bullied her into going in without you."

"Oh, he did, did he?" I burned. "The little shrimp! Who does he think he is? He may be the whole limburger around here but he isn't even a bad smell to us down at headquarters!" The chief had told me what to do, but Stormann's opposition somehow got my goat so beautifully that instead of quitting I hung around, just for the pleasure of telling him a thing or two when he came out. To crash in now would have ruined the scene, cost the company thousands of dollars, and maybe gotten Meadows in bad with her bosses; so I didn't have the heart to do it.

"They'll be through about four," the guard told me. It was now a little before two.

Whether I would have stuck it out for two whole hours, outside that door, just to bawl Stormann out—I don't know. I never will know. At 2:10 or thereabouts the door suddenly opened from the inside without any warning and through it came the horrible unearthly screams of the dying. Nothing could scream like that and live very long.

"Something's happened!" he blurted. "That's not in the scene! I know, because they were rehearsing it all morning—"

It was Meadows' maid. Only she was almost white now. Her voice was gone from fright. "Oh, somebody—quick, somebody!" she panted. "I've been hammering on this door—" But she wasn't the victim. The screaming went right on behind her.

I rushed in, the guard with me. The sight that met us was ghastly. Martha Meadows, with the cameras still playing on her, was burning to death there before everyone's eyes. She was a living torch, a funnel of fire from head to foot, and screaming her life away. She was running blindly here and there, like some kind of a horrible human pin wheel, and they were all trying to overtake her and catch her to throw something over her and put the flames out. But she was already out of her head, mad with agony, and kept eluding them, ducking and doubling back and forth with hellish agility. What kept her going like that, with her life going up in blazing yellow-white gushes, I don't understand. I'll see that scene for years to come.

But I didn't stand there watching. I flung myself at her bodily, head first right into the flames in a football tackle. With stinging hands I grasped something soft and quivering behind that glow that had once been cool, human flesh. The pillar of fire toppled over and lay horizontal along the ground, with the flames foreshortened now and just licking upward all around it like bright scallops. With that, a blanket or something was thrown over her, and partly over me, too. As it fell with a puff of horrid black smoke spurting out all around the edges, the last scream stopped and she was still.

I held my breath, so as not to inhale any of the damned stuff. I could feel rescuing hands beating all around the two of us through the blanket. After a minute I picked myself up. My hands were smarting, my shirt cuffs were scorched brown in places and peeling back, and sparks had eaten into the front of my suit. Otherwise I was alright. But what lay under the blanket didn't move. Five minutes ago one of the most beautiful girls in America, and now something it was better not to look at if you had a weak stomach.

As if in gruesome jest, the winking eyes of the cameras were still turned upon her and, in the deathly silence that had now fallen, you could hear the whirring noise that meant they were still grinding away. No one had thought of signalling them to stop.

The guard who had been outside the door, though, had had the presence of mind to send in a call for help even before the flames had been beaten out. The studio had a first-aid station of its own a door or two away, and two men arrived with a stretcher and carried her out with them, still under the blanket. Nellie went with them, bellowing like a wounded steer and calling: "Oh, Lawd, oh Lawd, don't do this to my lamb! Change yo' mind, change yo' mind!"

Stormann was shaking like a leaf and incoherent with shock, and had to be fed whiskey by one of the electricians. The girl with the notebook, the script-girl, was the only one there who seemed to have kept her head about her. I went up to her, dabbing some oil they'd given me onto the red patches on the back of my hands and wrists, and asked: "How'd it happen?"

It turned out she wasn't as bright as I thought she'd be. "It happened right here," she said. "I was following very closely, the way I'm supposed to—that's my job." I looked to find out where "here" was, but instead of pointing any place on the set, she was pointing at her book.

"See—where it says 'Oh won't he ever come?' That's her line. She's supposed to be waiting by the window for her lover. Well, she spoke it alright, and then the next thing I knew, there was a funny flickering light on the pages of my book. When I looked up, I saw that it was coming from her. She had flames all over her. Well, just from force of habit, I quickly looked back at the book to find out whether or not this was part—"

I gave her up as a complete nut. Or at least a very efficient script-girl but a washout otherwise. I tackled Stormann next. He was on his third or fourth bracer by now and wringing his hands and moaning something about: "My picture, my beautiful picture—"

"Pull yourself together," I snapped. "Isn't there anyone around here who has a heart? She's thinking about her book, you're thinking about your picture. Well, I'm thinking about that poor miserable girl. Maybe you can tell me how it happened. You're the director and you're supposed to have been watching what went on!"

Probably no one had ever spoken to him that way in years. His mouth dropped open. I grabbed him by the shoulder, took his snifter away from him, and gave him a shake. "Let me have it, brother, before I go sour on you. I'm asking you for your testimony—as a witness. You can consider this a preliminary inquest."

I hadn't forgotten that it was his doing I'd been kept out of here earlier, either. Seeing that he wasn't up against one of his usual yes-men, he changed his mind and gave until it hurt. "No one was near her at the time, I can't understand what could have caused it. I was right here on the side-lines where I always sit, she was over there by that win—"

"Yeah, I know all that. Here's what I'm asking you. Did you or did you not see what did it?" Not liking him, I got nasty with him and tapped him ten times on the chest with the point of my finger, once for each word, so it would sink in. The idea of anyone doing that to him was so new to him he didn't dare let out a peep. "No," he said, like a little kid in school.

"You didn't. Well, was anyone smoking a cigarette in here?"

"Absolutely not!" he said. "No director allows it, except when the scene calls for it. The lenses would pick up the haze—"

"Did she touch any wires, maybe?"

"There aren't any around, you can see for yourself. This whole thing's supposed to be the inside of an old mansion."

"What about this thing?" I picked up a lighted oil lamp that was standing on the fake window sill, but when I looked, I saw that it had an electric pocket-torch hidden in it. I put it down again. "Who was playing the scene with her? She wasn't alone in it, was she?"

"Ruth Tobias. That girl crying over there." I let him go back to his pain-killer and went over to tackle her. She was having grade-A hysterics across the back of a chair, but, as I might have known, on her own account, not poor Meadows'.

"Two whole years—" she gurgled, "two whole years to make a come back. I've waited—and now, look! They won't hire me again. I'm getting older—"

"Alright sis, turn off the faucets," I said. "Uncle wants to ask you something. What happened to her?"

She had on one of the same wide dresses as the kid had, but she was gotten up to look older—black gloves and a lorgnette with her hair in a cranky knot. At that, she wasn't out of her twenties yet, but looked as though she'd been used as a filling-station for a bootlegger while she was out of work the last few years.

"I played her older sister," she sniffled, "although they really had a nerve to cast me in an older part like that. I had to take anything I could get. I was in that rocker there on the set, facing her way. I'm supposed not to approve of the fellow she's intending to run off with, but all I do to show it is to keep rocking back and forth. She had her back to me, over at the window— I tell you I was looking right at her and all of a sudden, *ffft,* she was on fire from head to foot! As quickly as that, and for no earthly reason that I could make out! All I had time to do was jump back out of the way myself—"

"You would," I thought, but without saying so.

She gave me a sort of a come-on smile and said: "You're not a bad-looking guy at all for a detective."

"That's what my wife and eighteen kids tell me," I squelched her.

"Hmf," she said, and went over to chisel a drink from Stormann. Just then they sent word in that, impossible as it sounded, Meadows was still breathing. She was going fast, though—just a matter of minutes now. They'd given her morphine to kill the pain.

"Is she conscious or out?" I asked.

"Semi-conscious."

"Quick then, let me have a look at her before she goes!"

It was a slim chance, but maybe she, herself, knew what or who had done it. Maybe she, alone, of all of them, had seen what caused it and hadn't been able to prevent it in time to save herself.

On my way out, I collared the guard, who was back at the door again keeping out the crowd of extras and employees who had heard the news.

"Consider yourself a deputy," I said to him in an undertone. "See that they all stay where they are until I get back. Whatever you do, see that nothing's touched on that set—not even a match stick. Keep everything just the way it is—"

It was a monstrous thing they showed me in that bed, dark as the room was. Without eyes, without ears, without nose, without any human attribute. An oversized pumpkin-head, a Hallowe'en goblin, made of yards and yards of interlaced gauze bandaging. It stood out whitely in the greenish dimness cast by the lowered shades. A crevice between the bandages served as a mouth. Atop the sheets were two bandaged paws. She was conscious, but partly delirious from the heat of the burns and "high" from the morphine that kept her from feeling the pain in her last moments. The faithful Nellie was there beside her, silent now and with her forehead pressed to the wall.

I bent close to the muffled figure, put my face almost up against the shapeless mound that was Martha Meadows, to try to catch the garbled muttering which came through the bandages. I couldn't make it out. "Martha Meadows," I begged, "Martha Meadows, what caused the accident?"

The muttering stopped, broke off short. I couldn't tell whether she'd heard me or not. I repeated the question. Then suddenly I saw her head move slowly from side to side, slowly and slightly. "No—accident," she mumbled. Then she repeated it a second time, but so low I couldn't catch it any more. A minute later her head had lolled loosely over to the side again and stayed that way. She'd gone.

I went outside and stood there, lost in thought. I hadn't found out what I'd come to find out—what did it—but I'd found out something else, much more important. "No—accident" meant it had been done purposely. What else could it mean? Or was I building myself a case out of thin air? Delirium, morphine—and a shaking of the head in her death-throes that I'd mistaken for "no"? I tried to convince myself I was just looking for trouble. But it wouldn't work. I had an answer for every argument. She'd known what I was asking her just now. She hadn't been out of her mind.

Death will strike during unconsciousness or sleep, maybe, but never during delirium. The mind will always clear just before it breaks up, even if only an instant before. And hadn't she gotten threatening letters and asked for protection? Anyway, I told myself, as long as there *was* a doubt in my mind, it was up to me to track it down until there *wasn't* any doubt left—either one way or the other. That was my job. I was going to sift this thing down to the bottom.

Nellie came out. She wasn't bellowing now any more like she had been on the set. "They musta been casting her in heaven today, but they sure picked a mis'able way to notify her," she said with a sort of suppressed savagery. "I'm gonna buy me a bottle a' gin and drink it down straight. If it don't kill me the fust time, I'll keep it up till it do. She'll need a maid on the set up there fust thing and I ain't gonna leave her flat!" She shuffled off, shaking her head.

I was hard-hearted enough to go after her and stop her. "That's all right about heaven, auntie, but you don't happen to know of anyone down below here who had a grudge against her, do you?"

She shook her head some more. "Stop yo' mouth. She was everybody's honey. Didn't she even go to the trouble of axing 'em and coazing 'em to give that Miss Tobias a job in her picher on account of she felt sorry for her cause she was a back-number and nobody wanted her no-how?"

"What about those threats she got, where are they?"

"She turned 'em over to her supe'visor. They weren't nothing, everybody in the business gets 'em. It means you a big-shot, that's all."

"You were there when it happened. What'd *you* see?"

"Weren't nothing to see. 'Pears like it musta been some of this here sponchaneous combusting."

That gave me an idea, but I hung it up to dry for a while. I rang headquarters and spilled what had happened to the chief. "Something new—an invisible accident. Right under everybody's nose and yet nobody saw it. Guess I better stay on it for a while, don't you?"

"You park your can on it till it breaks. I'll let the studio hot-shots know."

When I got back to the set they were all there yet—all but Stormann and Tobias! "I thought I told you—" I snarled in the guard's ear.

"They'll be right back," he whined, "they told me so. Stormy only stepped next door to get some more liquor. The electrician that was supplying him ran out of it. And she went to take off her costume. She got jittery because Stormy was nervous and started smoking around her. After what happened to— Besides, they weren't under arrest. Nobody here is, and you don't know Stormy. If I'd a' tried to stop him, it woulda been good-bye to my job—"

They were back in no time at all. Tobias was back first and I made a mental note of that. Since when does it take a man longer to dig up some liquor than it does a woman to change clothes from head to foot—besides, scraping off a stage make-up in the bargain? That was another little chip stacked against Stormann. I had three of them so far. He hadn't wanted Meadows to bring me on the set with her. He bullied her into going in alone while my back was turned. And lastly he'd found an excuse for leaving the set, taking him longer to get back than it had a conceited frail, like Tobias, to do herself over from head to toe.

The ace turned up when I checked up on the electrician who'd been supplying him.

"Why, no," he admitted, "I got another bottle left. I told him so, only he got a sudden notion his own was better quality and went out after it."

What a dead give-away that was!

He had the staggers when he showed up, but he had enough decency left to straighten up when he saw me and breathe: "How is she?"

I made the announcement I'd been saving until he got there—to see how he'd take it.

"I'm sorry to say—she's quit."

I kept my eyes on him. It was hard to tell. Plop! went the bottle he'd brought in with him and he started folding up like a jack knife. They picked him up and carried him out. It might've been the drink—but if he hadn't wanted to be questioned, for instance, it was the swellest out he could've thought up.

Maybe I should and maybe I shouldn't have, but I'm frank to admit I stuck a pin in him before they got him to the door—just to see. He never even twitched.

I turned a chair around backwards, sat down on it, and faced the rest of them. "I'm in charge of this case now," I said, "by order of police headquarters and with the consent of the studio executives. All I'm going to do, right now, is repeat the question I've already asked Mr. Stormann, Miss Tobias, Nellie, and the script-girl. Did any of you see what caused it?" This meant the electricians, stage-hands, and the two cameramen. They all shook their heads.

I got up and banged the chair down so hard one leg of it busted off. "She wasn't six feet away from some of you!" I bawled them out. "She was in the full glare of the brightest lights ever devised! All eyes were on her watching every move and she was the center of attraction at the time! She burned to death, and yet no one saw how it started! Twenty-five pairs of human eyes and they might as well have all been closed! Well, there's one pair left—and they won't let him down."

I suppose they thought I meant my own. Not by a damn sight. "Now clear out of here, all of you, and don't touch anything as you go!" I pointed to the chief electrician. "You stay and check up on those lights for defects—one of 'em might have got overheated and dropped a spark on her. And don't try to hold out anything to save your own skin. Criminal carelessness is a lot less serious than obstructing an agent of justice!" I passed my handkerchief to the guard. "You comb the floor around where she was standing. Pick up every cigarette butt and every cinder you find!"

The rest of them filed out one by one, giving me names and addresses as they went. I wasn't worried about getting them back again if I wanted them. They all reacted differently. Some were frightened, some just curious, some cracking wise. The script-girl's nose was still buried in her book. She hardly looked up at all. Tobias glided by me with a little extra hip-action and purred over her shoulder: "Lots of luck, Handsome. And if you find out you were mistaken about those eighteen kids of yours, look a lady up sometime."

"Thirtieth of next February," I told her.

The chief cameraman came out of his booth with a round, flat, tin box—packed under his arm.

"Where you going with that?" I asked him.

"Drop it in the ashcan on my way out," he said. "It's what we took today, no good now any more."

"Ashcan—hell," I snapped. "Those machines of yours are the other pair of eyes I told you about! How soon can you develop that stuff?"

"Right away," he told me, looking surprised. "But we can't use this roll—it's got her whole death-scene on it and it'll turn your hair white just to look at it."

"You do it yourself," I warned him, "don't call anybody in to help you. And don't touch it, leave it just the way it is. Can I trust you?"

"Meet me in half an hour in projection room A," he said. "She was a swell kid."

The electrician came down from way up high somewhere and reported the lights all jake. No crossed wires, not a screw out of place anywhere.

"You dig up a typewriter and get that all down on paper, sign it, have a notary witness it, and shoot it in to me at headquarters—Galbraith's the name. It better be on the level, the pay-off is withholding information from the authorities." Which didn't mean anything, but it was good enough to throw a scare into him. I never saw anyone take it on the lam so quick in my life.

The guard passed me my handkerchief back with a cigarette butt, a wire frame, and a lot of little pieces of glass in it.

"The butt's Stormann's," he pointed out. "He was smoking it after it was all over. I saw him throw it down and step on it before he went after that liquor. I remember because Tobias yapped 'Don't come near me with that thing! You want it to happen to me, too?'"

I wondered if that remark meant anything. Did he *want* it to happen to her, too? Get the point? I knew what the pieces of glass and the frame were right away—a busted lorgnette like I had seen Tobias fiddling with.

"Meadows had it around her neck I guess," he suggested, "and it fell and smashed when she started to run around crazy."

I felt like telling him he didn't know his ears from his elbow, but I kept quiet about it. These pieces of glass were clear, that burning celluloid would have smoked them up plenty if they had been anywhere near Martha Meadows. But there was an easy enough way of settling that.

"Get the wardrobe-woman in here and tell her to bring a complete list of every article she furnished Meadows and Tobias for this picture."

She was a society-looking dame, with white hair, and had had her face lifted. She had typewritten sheets with her.

"Did you supply Meadows with a lorgnette?"

"Why no," she said. "Young girls didn't wear them even in those days."

"But Tobias wore one. Is this it?" I showed her the pieces.

"It must be," she returned. "She turned in her costume a little while ago and explained that she'd broken her lorgnette while that awful thing was happening to poor Martha. You see I have everything else crossed off but that. We usually charge players for anything that isn't returned to us, but in this case of course nothing like that will happen."

That explained something that had bothered me for a minute or two. Because I'd distinctly seen the lorgnette on Tobias *after* the accident, when she was making those first passes at me. She must have broken it later—while I was outside in the infirmary with Meadows. But a chiseler like her who would cadge a drink from Stormann would try to make them believe it had happened during all the excitement—to get out of paying for it.

"You keep those two lists just the way they are now, I may want to see them again." I folded up the handkerchief with the pieces of broken glass and put it away in my pocket.

A kid came in and said: "The rushes are ready for you in projection room A," and took me over there.

It had rows of seats just like a miniature theatre and a screen on one wall. I closed the door and locked the cameraman and myself in.

"It's ghastly," he said, "better hang on tight."

"Run it through at normal speed first," I said. "I'll see if I can stand it."

I sat down in the front row with the screen almost on top of me. There wasn't much to it at regular speed—about five minutes worth of picture—what they call a "sequence." It was pretty grisly at that. It opened on Tobias sitting there in the rocker, broadside to the camera. Meadows came in almost at once.

"I'm going away with him tonight," she said.

Tobias opened her lorgnette and gave her the once-over through it. Meadows went over to the window, and the camera followed her part of the way. That left Tobias over at the left-hand side of the screen and partly out of the picture, with just one shoulder, arm, and the side of her head showing. She started to rock back and forth and tap her lorgnette against the back of her hand. I had my eyes glued to Meadows though. She turned around to look at her "sister."

"Oh, won't he ever come?" she said.

Her face sort of tightened up—changed from repose to tenseness. A look of horror started to form on it, but it never got any further. Right then and there the thing happened.

The best way I can describe it is, a sort of bright, luminous flower seemed to open up half way down her dress, spreading, peeling back. But the petals of it were flame. An instant later it was all over her, and the first screams of a voice that was gone now came smashing out at my eardrums. And in between each one, the hellish sound-track had even picked up and recorded the sizzling that her hair made.

"Cut!"

I turned around and yelled back at him: "For Pete's sake, cut, before I throw up!" and I mopped my drenched forehead. "I did— twice—while I was processing it," he confessed, looking out of the booth at me.

It hadn't told me a thing so far, but then I hadn't expected it to—the first throw out of the bag.

"Go back and start it over," I shivered, "but, whatever you do, leave out that finale! Take it up where she turns at the window. Slow-motion this time. Can you hold it when I tell you to?"

He adjusted his apparatus. "Say when," he called.

The figures on the screen hardly moved at all this time, eight times slowed down. They drifted lazily—sort of floated. I knew the place to look for on Meadows' dress now, and I kept my eyes focussed on it and let everything else ride. A moment later something had shown up there.

"Hold it!" I yelled, and the scene froze into a "still."

Now it was just a magic-lantern slide, no motion at all. I left my seat and stood close up against the screen, keeping to one side so my own shadow wouldn't blur out that place on her dress. No flame was coming from it yet. It was just a bright, luminous spot, about the size and shape of a dime.

"Back up one!" I instructed. "One" meant a single revolution of the camera. The scene hardly shifted at all, but the pin-point of light was smaller—like a pea now. You couldn't have seen it from the seat I'd been in at first.

Two heads are better than one. I called him out and showed it to him. "What do you make of this? It's not a defect in the film, is it?"

"No, it's a blob of light coming to a head at that place on her dress. Like a highlight, you might say. A gleam." Which is what I'd had it figured for, too.

"Go three forward," I said, "and then hold it."

He came out again to look. It was back to the size of a dime again, and only a turn or two before the flames were due to show up.

"There's heat in it!" I said. "See that!"

The white spot had developed a dark core, a pin-head of black or brown.

"That's the material of the dress getting ready to burn. See that thread coming out of the dot? Smoke—and all there'll ever be of it, too. Celluloid doesn't give much warning."

So far so good. But what I wanted to know was where that gleam or ray was coming from. I had the effect now, but I wanted the cause. The trouble was you couldn't follow the beam through the air—to gauge its direction. Like any beam of light, it left no trail—only showed up suddenly on her dress. The set-up, so far, seemed to fit Nellie's theory of spontaneous combustion perfectly. Maybe one of the powerful Klieg lights, high overhead and out of the picture, had developed some flaw in its glass shield, warping one of its rays. But the electrician had gone over them afterward and given them all a clean bill of health.

"Start it up again," I said wearily. "Slow motion," and went back and sat down. I was farther away now and had a better perspective of the thing as a whole; maybe that's what did it.

As the scene on the screen thawed and slowly dissolved into fluid motion once more, it gave the impression for a moment of everything on it moving at once. Therefore it was only natural that the one thing that *didn't* move should catch my eye and hold it. Tobias' lorgnette, and the wrist and hand that held it. The three objects stayed rigid, down in the lower left-hand corner of the screen, after everything else was on the go once more. The chair she was in had started to rock slowly back and forth, and her body with it, but the forearm, wrist, hand and lorgnette stayed poised, motionless. There was something unnatural about it that caught the eye at once. I remembered she had opened the scene by tapping her lorgnette *as well as* rocking.

Now, with the fire due to break out any second, she was only rocking. The lorgnette was stiff as a ramrod in her grasp. Not that she was holding it out at full length before her or anything like that, she was holding it close in, unobtrusively, but straight up and down—a little out to one side of her own body. Maybe the director's orders had been for her to stop fiddling with it at a certain point. Then again maybe not. All I wanted to find out was at what point she had stopped tapping and playing with it. I had been concentrating on Meadows until now and had missed that.

"Whoa, back up!" I called out to him. "All the way back and then start over—slow."

I let Meadows go this time and kept my eye on Tobias and her lorgnette. The minute I saw it stop—"Hold it!" I yelled and ran over to the screen and examined Meadows' dress. Nothing yet. But in three more revolutions of the camera that deadly white spot had already showed up on the celluloid-lined hoopskirt. Effect had followed cause too quickly to be disregarded.

"Lights!" I roared. "I've got it!"

He turned a switch, the room blazed all around me, and I took that handkerchief out of my pocket and examined the pieces of glass it held. Some were thicker than others—the lens had therefore been convex, not flat. I held one up and looked at my cuff through it. The weave stood out. A magnifying glass. I held it about a foot away from the back of my hand, where I'd already been burned once this after-noon, and even with the far weaker lights of the projection-room working through it, in about thirty seconds something bit me and I jumped.

He'd come out and was watching what I was doing. "Pack that film up again in the box the way you had it," I said. "I'll be back for it in a minute. I'm taking it down to headquarters with me!"

"What'd you find out?" he asked.

"Look it up in tomorrow morning's papers!"

I called Tobias' dressing-room. "How's the lay of the land?" I greeted her.

She knew me right away. "I know, it's Handsome."

"I was wrong about those eighteen kids," I told her. "I counted 'em over—only nine."

She sure was a hard-boiled customer. "Nine to go," she said cheer-fully. "When will I see you?"

"I'll pick you up in about twenty minutes."

"Where we going?" she cooed when she got in the car.

"You'll find out."

Then when we got there, she said: "Why, this looks like police headquarters to me."

"Not only does, but is," I told her. "Won't take a minute, I just want to see a man about a dog."

"Wouldn't you rather have me wait outside for you?"

I chucked her under the chin. "I'm getting so fond of you I want you with me wherever I go. Can't stand being without you even for five minutes."

She closed her eyes and looked pleased and followed me in like a lamb. Then when the bracelets snapped on her wrists she exploded: "Why you dirty doublecrossing—I thought you said you wanted to see a man about a dog."

"I do," I said, "and you're the dog."

"What're the charges?" the chief asked.

"Setting fire to Martha Meadows with a magnifying glass and causing her to burn to death. Here's the glass she used; picked up on the set. Here's the original harmless glass that was in the frame before she knocked it out; picked up in the trashbasket in her dressing room. The film, there in the box, shows her in the act of doing it. She's been eaten away with jealousy ever since she faded out and Meadows stepped into her shoes."

I never knew a woman knew so many bad words as she did; and she used them all. After she'd been booked and the matron was leading her away she called back: "You'll never make this stick. You think you've got me, but you'll find out!"

"She's right, Gal," commented the chief, after she'd gone. "The studio people'll put the crusher on the case before it ever comes up for trial. Not because they approve of what she's done—but on account of the effect it would have on the public."

"She may beat the murder rap," I said, "but she can't get around these." I took a bundle of letters and a square of blotting-paper out of my pocket and passed them to him. "Wrote them in her very dressing room at the studio and then mailed them to Meadows on the outside, even after Meadows had gotten her a job. The blotting-paper tells the story if you hold it up to a mirror. She didn't get rid of it quickly enough."

"Good work, Gal," the chief said; and then, just like him, he takes all the pleasure out of it. "Now that you're in for promotion, suppose you step around to that grill and pay the guy for that plate-glass window you busted."

(1934)

Murder in Wax

He always called me Angel Face. Always claimed I didn't have a thing inside my head, but that the outside was a honey. When he began to let up on the ribbing, I should have known something was wrong. But I figured maybe it was because we had been married four years—and didn't tumble right away.

One morning no different from any other, the pay-off comes. Everything is peaches and cream and I'm trying to make up my mind between my green and my blue with the whosis around the neck when the doorbell rings. The guy looked like a taxi-driver. It turned out he was.

"I've come to collect that dollar'n a half your husband owes me, lady. He knows where my stand is, he shoulda squared it long ago." And then to cinch the argument he flashes Jackie's cigarette case at me, the one I gave him the Christmas before. "I'm sick of carrying this around for security, it ain't worth a dime at the hock shop. The only reason I trusted him in the first place was on account of the dame he was with that night is a very good customer of mine. My stand is right outside her door—"

Plop went my heart! "Be right back," I said, and dialed Jackie's office on the phone. "Why, he quit last Saturday," they told me. This was Wednesday. I took a look in the closet where his valise was. It was locked but when I lifted it by the handle it weighed a ton. It had everything in it all ready, all set to move out. So she'd put the Indian sign on him, had she? I went back to the door again hooking my blue up and down the back.

"You're getting your dollar fifty," I said, "and you've also got a fare all the way up to where that lady lives. Step on it."

East Fifty-fourth Street, a couple of doors down from that big beer garden on the corner of Third. "Sure I know her name," he said, "it's Boinice. I hear 'em all call her that whenever she's with anybody in my cab." The other half of it was on the mailbox—Pascal.

No one saw me go in, and the elevator was automatic. She was having breakfast—bromo-seltzer and a cigarette—and if he called me Angel Face, I wonder what he called her. Helen of Troy would have been homely. She had one of those faces that only happen once in a hundred years.

"Who're you?" she snapped.

"Jackie Reardon's wife," I said, "and I've come here to ask you to give me a break."

It was no use though. I found it out that night when I tried to tell him. The coffee I got in my face wasn't hot enough to scald me, luckily, and I didn't even mind hitting the floor over in the corner of the dining nook. It was when he snatched up his valise and went for the door that it hurt. I beat it inside, fixed up the purple mark on my jaw with powder, jammed on a hat, and caught up with him at the subway station. "Jackie, listen to me! You've got to listen to me!"

"All right, I forgot," he said, and tried to pass a couple of sawbucks to me. I let them fall and the wind carried them down the tracks.

All I could say was, "Not tonight, Jackie! No, no, not tonight! Don't go near her, you'll get in trouble. Wait over until tomorrow, then go if you have to. But not tonight, Jackie, stay away—" His train came roaring in and drowned out every sound. I saw his lips say, "So long, kid," and then him and his valise and his train all went away and left me there calling out, "Don't go there, Jackie, you'll get in trouble!" on the empty platform.

I went back and bawled from then until midnight. I killed the gin he'd left behind him, from midnight until dawn; and slept from daylight until it was almost evening again.

By that time the papers were on the streets with the big scare-heads—PLAYGIRL FOUND SLAIN. My hunch must have still been with me from the night before. I signaled from the window and hauled in a batch of them. Sure enough, Bernice Pascal, 225 East Fifty-fourth street, had been found shot to death in her apartment at about nine the night before. They'd caught up with Jackie less than half an hour later at Grand Central, trying to powder out on the Montreal train—alone. With *two* tickets on him and the key to her apartment. His valise was back at her place, where he'd left it in care of the doorman while he went upstairs.

I sank to my knees, held my head in my hand and went wading down the column with swimming eyes. What a set-up! He'd shown up at 8:30 the first time, asked the doorman to mind his valise, and gone ahead up without being announced—she'd given him the key, hadn't she? The doorman had never seen him come down again. The next time the doorman had seen him the body had already been discovered and Jackie was being brought in from the outside, by the homicide men who had picked him up. Quickest pinch in years, raved the papers and the bureau.

A time-table, left in her place with the 9:40 Montreal train underlined, had tipped them off. There was one every night, but they didn't wait for the next night to make sure. Her things had been all packed, too, you see.

"Oh, you fool, you fool!" I groaned and banged my head against the windowsill a couple of times.

Two days later they finally let me at him.

"You didn't do it," I said. "I'll get you a good lawyer."

"You stay out of this," he said. "I don't want you dragged into it. I've done you enough dirt without that."

"I'm your wife, Jackie. You don't have to tell me, I know you didn't do it."

"She was dead when I let myself in," he said, "and the radio was playing *Nobody's Sweetheart Now*. I remember that. That's all I remember. I lost my head I guess. I beat it down the emergency staircase and slipped out while the doorman was out front getting a cab for someone. I got into one myself around the corner and drove around and around in a daze. Then I made for the train—"

"You'll get your lawyer, Jackie," I promised him.

My brother-in-law in Trenton turned me down flat. I had the diamond engagement-ring Jackie had given me five years before, though. And my wedding-ring was platinum. That went, too. I got Westman for him. You spell his name with dollar marks.

"I like the case," he said. "I don't like the looks of it much, but that's why I like it. Hold on tight."

I liked the looks of it even less than he did—after all, Jackie was my husband, not his—but I held on tight.

The trial opened in the middle of a freak heat wave that had got its dates mixed. At 90 in the shade, with a perspiring jury ready to convict the Angel Gabriel if they could only get out of there and into a shower bath and a cranky judge who hated his own mother, he didn't have a chance.

It was a mess all the way through. The State's proposition was that she'd agreed to beat it to Montreal with him; then when she changed her mind at the last minute for some unknown reason, he'd killed her in a fit of jealous rage. The gun was her own, but it had been found at the bottom of the elevator shaft—and she'd died instantly with a hole between her eyes. Soundproof walls, no shot heard. The doorman had seen him go up at 8:30; he was the last person he'd seen go up there; he'd known him by sight for months. And about everybody else in New York seemed to chip in their say-so after that—the State had them stepping up and stepping down all day long.

"Do something," I kept saying to Westman, "do something!"

Westman drew nothing but blanks. The night doorman, who'd come on duty at six, was obviously greased—or so he said. Then when he went out after the day doorman, who might have been able to mention any callers she'd had earlier in the day, that gentleman had chucked his job two days after the murder and gone home to Ireland or somewhere without leaving any forwarding address. He dug up a former colored maid of hers who would have been a walking card-index of the men in Pascal's life, and just as he had her nicely subpoenaed and all, she got mysteriously knocked down by a speeding car at 135th and Lenox and had a fine funeral. All wet, all wet.

I sat through it day after day, in the last row behind a pair of smoked glasses. The jury came in on the 21st with their shirts sticking to their backs and stubble on their jaws and found him guilty.

I keeled over and a court attendant carried me outside, but no one noticed because people had been passing out from the heat the whole time the trial lasted.

It was nice and cool when he came up for sentence, but it was too late to do any good by that time. Jackie got the chair.

"So my husband goes up in sparks for something he never did!" I said to Westman.

"Ten million people think he did, one little lady thinks he didn't. You can't buck the State of New York."

"No, but I can give it a run for its money. What do you need for a stay of execution?"

"New evidence—something I haven't got."

"No? Watch me. How long have we got?"

"Week of November Eighth. Six weeks to us, a lifetime to him."

At the door I turned back. "The five centuries, I suppose, was to pay for the current they're going to use on him."

He threw up his hands. "You can have the retainer back. I feel worse about it than you do."

I took it because I needed it. I'd been living in a seven-dollar-a-week furnished room and eating corn flakes, since I'd retained him. Now here was the job—to separate the one right person from the 6,999,999 wrong ones—or whatever the population of New York was at the last census—and hang the killing of Bernice Pascal on him so that it would stick and give my Jackie an out.

Six weeks to do it in. Forty-two days. A thousand hours. And here was the equipment: five hundred dollars, a face like an angel and a heart like a rock. The odds? A thousand to one against me was putting it mild. Who could stand up and cheer about anything so one-sided?

I just sat there holding my head in my hands and wondering what my next move was. Not a suspicion, not a hunch, not a ghost of an idea. It was going to be tough going all right. I couldn't figure it out and the minutes were already ticking away, minutes that ticked once and never came back again.

They let me say goodbye to Jackie next day before they took him upstate. He was cuff-linked, so we didn't have much privacy. We didn't say much.

"Look at me. What do you see?"

"You've got a funny kind of light in your eyes," he said.

"It's going to bring you back alive," I said, "so never mind the goodbyes."

When I got back to the room there was a cop there. "Oh-oh," I thought, "now what?"

"I been looking all over for you," he said. "Mr. Westman finally tipped me off where I could find you. Your husband asked us to turn his things over to you."

He passed me Jackie's packed valise, the one he'd taken up to her house that night.

"Thanks for rubbing it in," I said, and shut him out.

I never knew what punishment shirts and socks and handkerchiefs could hand out until I opened it and started going through it. His gray suit was in it, too. I held the coat up against my face and sort of made love to it. The cops had been through the pockets a million times of course but they'd put everything back. A couple of cards from liquor concerns, a crumpled pack of cigarettes, his silver pencil clamped onto the breast pocket.

Being a Sing Sing widow already, I spread them all out in front of me in a sort of funeral arrangement. It was when I started smoothing out the coat and folding it over that I felt something down at the bottom—in one of the seams. He'd had a hole in the lining of his side pocket and it had slipped through, out of reach. But when I'd worked it back up into the light again, I saw the cops hadn't missed much. It was just a folder of matches.

I put it down. Then I picked it up again. It wasn't a commercial folder of matches. There wasn't an ad on it. It was a private folder, a personal folder. Fancy. Black cover with two gilt initials on it—*T.V.* You can pick them up at the five-and-ten at a dime a throw; or at any department store for two bits. Just the same, it belonged to one single person and not to any hotel or grillroom or business enterprise of any kind. *T.V.* It hadn't been Bernice's because those weren't her initials.

Where had he gotten hold of it then? I knew who most of his friends were, she'd been the only dark horse in his life, and none of their names matched the two letters. Just to check up, I went out and called up the firm he'd worked for.

"T.V. there?" I asked off-handedly.

"No one by those intials works here," the office girl said.

It was when I went back to the room again that the brain-wave hit me. I suddenly had it. He *had* picked them up at Bernice's apartment after all, he must have—without their being hers. Somebody else had called on her, absentmindedly left his matches lying around the place, and then Jackie had showed up. He was lit up and, without noticing, put them in his pocket and walked off with them.

Even granting that—and it was by no means foolproof—it didn't mean much of anything. It didn't mean that "T.V." had anything to do with her death. But if I could only get hold of *one* person who had known her intimately, I'd be that much ahead, I could find out who some of the rest of her friends were.

"T.V." was elected. Just then I looked over in the corner and saw a cockroach slinking back to its hole. I shivered. That—and all the other cockroaches I'd been seeing for weeks—did the trick. I got an idea.

First a folder of matches, then a cockroach. I dolled up and went around to the building she'd lived in—225. I dug up the superintendent. "Listen, I want to talk to you about 3-H," I said. "Have you rented it yet?"

"No," he said, "and God knows when we'll be able to. People are funny about things like that, it was in all the papers."

I made him take me up and I took a look around. The phone was still in, disconnected, of course. The phone books were lying on the floor in the clothes closet. Everything else was gone long ago.

"Nice roomy closet you have here," I said, fluttering the leaves of the Manhattan directory. Then I put it down and came out again. You have to have good eyes to be able to see in a dim closet. Mine are good.

"I'll make you a proposition," I said. "I'm not at all superstitious, and I haven't got much money, and I don't like the brand of cockroaches over at my place. You haven't got an earthly chance of renting this place until people forget about what happened and you know it. I'll take it for exactly one quarter of what she was paying. Think it over."

He went down, phoned the real-estate agents, came back again, and the place was mine. But only for six weeks; or, in other words, until just around the time Jackie was due to hit the ceiling—which suited me fine as that was only as long as I wanted it for anyway.

The minute the door had closed behind him and I was alone in the place, I made a bee line for that clothes closet and hauled out the Manhattan directory. I held it upside down and shook it and the card fell out, the one I'd seen the first time. It was just one of those everyday quick-reference indexes ruled off into lines for names and numbers that the phone company supplies to its subscribers.

There were two or three penciled scrawls on hers. Probably had so many numbers on tap she couldn't keep them all in her head. Anyway there it was—

Ruby Moran—Wickersham, so-and-so
Gilda Johnson—Stuyvesant, such-and-such
Tommy Vaillant—Butterfield 8-14160.

This was getting hotter all the time. Butterfield is a Gold Coast exchange, Park Avenue and the Sixties. But the cream of the crop don't sport store-bought monogrammed matches—that's tin-horn flash. Which meant that this guy, whoever he was, was in quick money of some kind and hadn't caught up with himself yet. Which meant some kind of a racket, legitimate or otherwise. Which meant that maybe she had known a little too much about him and spoken out of turn, or had been about to, and therefore was now sprouting a lot of grass up at Woodlawn. At the same time, as I said before, it didn't necessarily have to mean any of those things, but that was for me to find out.

As for the police, they'd had such an open-and-shut case against Jackie that it hadn't behooved them to go around scouting for little things like folders of matches in the seams of a suit he hadn't been wearing when they arrested him nor unlisted numbers on reference cards hidden away in the leaves of a phone book. It took a little party like me, with nothing behind her face, to do that much.

I went out, thought it over for awhile, and finally went into one of the snappy theatrical dress shops on Broadway.

"Show me something with a lot of *umph*," I said. "Something that hits your eye if you're a him and makes you see stars."

The one I finally selected was the sort of a bib that you wore at your own risk if the month had an "r" on the end of it. It made a dent in the five hundred but that was all right. I wrapped it up and took it, and everything that went with it. Then I found a crummy, third-class sort of bar near where I lived and spent a good deal of time in there building myself up with the bartender and pouring a lot of poisonous pink stuff into the cuspidor whenever he wasn't looking.

"Why no," he said when I finally popped the question, "I couldn't slip you anything like that. I could get pinched for doing that. And even if I wanted to, we don't have nothing like that."

"I only wanted it for a little practical joke," I said. "All right, forget it. I never asked for it. I haven't even been in here at all, you never saw me and I never saw you."

But I paid for the next Jack Rose with a ten-dollar bill. "There isn't any change coming," I said. When he brought the drink there was a little folded white-paper packet nestled in the hollow of his hand. I took the drink from him without letting it touch the counter.

"Try this," he said out of the corner of his mouth, and sauntered up front, polishing the bar. I put it in my bag and blew.

They'd already tuned in my phone when I got back and I christened it by calling that Tommy Vaillant number. A man's voice answered. "Tommy there?" I cooed as though I'd known him all my life.

Mr. Vaillant, said the voice, was out for the evening. The "Mr." part told me it must be his man Friday. And who was this wanted to know?

"Just a little playmate of his. Where can I reach him?"

"The Gay Nineties Club." Which made it all the easier, because if he had come to the phone himself I would have been in a spot.

It took me an hour to get ready, but if my face was good before I started you should have seen it when I got through. I figured I had plenty of time, because anyone who would go to a club that early must own an interest in it and would stick around until curfew. I nearly got pneumonia going there in that come-and-get-it dress, but it was worth it.

I rocked the rafters when I sat down and wisps of smoke came up through the cracks in the floor. The floor show was a total loss, not even the waiters watched it. I ordered a Pink Lady and sat tight. Then when I took out a cigarette there were suddenly more lighters being offered me from all directions than you could shake a stick at, the air was as full of them as fireflies.

"Put 'em all down on the table," I said, "and I'll pick my own."

A guy that went in for monogrammed matches wasn't going to neglect putting his initials on his cigarette-lighter and I wanted to pick the right one. I counted nine of them. His was a little black enamel gadget with the *T.V.* engraved on it in gold.

"Who goes with this?" I said and pushed the empty chair out. He wasn't the ratty type I'd been expecting. He looked like he could play a mean game of hockey and went in for cold baths.

"Whew!" I heard someone say under his breath as the other eight oozed away. "There would have been fireworks if she hadn't picked his!"

Oh, so that was the type he was! Well, maybe that explained what had happened to Bernice.

He sent my Pink Lady back and ordered fizz water. "What's your name?"

"Angel Face," I said.

"You're telling me?" he said.

"Shay come on," he said three hours later, "we go back my plashe—hup—for a li'l nightcap."

"No, we'll make it my place," I said. "I'd like to get out of this dress and get some clothes on."

When we got out of the cab I turned back to the driver while the doorman was helping Vaillant pick himself up after he'd tripped over the doorstep going in. "Stick around, I'm coming out again by myself in about half an hour, I'll need you."

Vaillant was just plastered enough to vaguely remember the house and too tight to get the full implication of it. "I been here before," he announced solemnly, going up in the elevator with me.

"Let's hope you'll be here some more after this, too." I let him in and he collapsed into a chair. "I'll get us our nightcap," I said, and got the two full glasses I'd left cooking in the fridge before I went out. One was and one wasn't. "Now if you'll just excuse me for a minute," I said after I'd carefully rinsed the two empty glasses out in hot water.

I changed scenery and by the time I came in again he was out like a light. I got his address and his latchkey, went downstairs, got in the cab, and told him where to take me. It was Park Avenue all right and it was a penthouse; but very small—just two rooms.

I'd found out back at the Gay Nineties that his Filipino didn't sleep there but went home at about ten each night, otherwise it would have been no soap. The elevator was private.

"Expect me?" I froze the elevator-man. "He sent me home ahead of him to punch the pillows together!"

It was three A.M. when I got there and I didn't quit until seven. I went over the place with a fine-tooth comb. Nothing doing. Not a scrap of paper, a line of writing to show he'd ever known her. He must have been burning lots more than logs in that trick fireplace of his—around the time Bernice was decorating the show window at Campbell's Funeral Parlor. There was a wall-safe, but the locked desk in the bedroom was a pushover for a hairpin and I found the combination in there in a little memo book.

The safe started in to get worthwhile. Still no dope about Bernice, but he'd hung onto the stubs of a lot of canceled checks that he shouldn't have. One in particular was made out to a Joe Callahan of Third Avenue, two days after she'd died. Two hundred and some-odd bucks—just about enough to take a man and wife to the other side—third-class.

Joe Callahan had been the name of that day doorman at 225 East 54th that Westman had tried so hard to locate, only to find he'd quit and gone home to Ireland. I slipped it under my garter just for luck. If he'd also greased the night doorman to forget that he'd been a caller at Bernice's, he'd had sense enough to do it in cash. There was no evidence of it. Ditto the driver of the car that had smacked down her maid up in Harlem.

So, all in all, the inventory was a flop.

It was broad daylight out and I was afraid the Filipino would check in any minute, so I quit. In ten minutes time I had the place looking just like it had been when I first came in, everything in order.

When Vaillant came to in the chair he'd passed out in, I was sitting there looking at him all dressed and rosy as though I'd just got up feeling swell. His latchkey was back in his pocket but it had only taken a locksmith twenty minutes to make me a duplicate to it. The check stub I'd left at a photographer's to have photostatic copies made of it.

"You're a nice one," I crooned when he opened his eyes, "folding up on me like that. Come on, get under the shower, I'll fix you some coffee."

When he'd finished his second cup he looked around. "There's something familiar about this room," he said. He got up and looked out the window and I saw his face turn white. "My God, it's the same apartment," he muttered, "let me out of here!"

"Got the jitters?" I said sweetly.

"I'm not yellow, but I've got a hangover," he said. "Don't ask me to tell you about it now, this ain't the time. I've got to get some air."

He grabbed his hat and I grabbed his sleeve. "Is that a promise?" I said. "Will you tell me later on? Tonight for instance?"

"There's nothing to tell," he said and slammed the door.

I'd been close that time! I picked up his empty cup and smashed it against the wall opposite me.

"I gotta have more than that!" barked Westman when I passed him the photostat of the check stub. "What am I, a magician? This don't prove his connection with *her*. All this shows is he paid some guy named Joe Callahan two hundred bucks. There's scads of 'em in New York. How you going to identify this 'J.C.' with the one that worked as doorman at her house? And, even if you do, that still don't prove the payor had anything to do with her death. It may point to it—but that ain't enough."

"Wait," I said, "who said this was all? I'm not through yet. Always remember the old saying, 'Every little bit, added to what you've got, makes a little bit more.' I only brought you this to put away in a safe place, put it in your office vault. There's more coming, I hope, and this will tie up nicely with the rest when we get it. Meanwhile I'll be needing more jack for what I have in mind."

"I'm a lawyer, not a banker."

"I sat through your last case," I reminded him, "you're a banker, all right. Give—it'll be a good investment from your point of view." I got it.

I went to the biggest music specialty shop in town and had a talk with the head man. "I'm trying out for the stage," I said. "I want to make some records of my own voice—at home. Can it be done? Not singing, just speaking. But it's got to come out clear as a bell, no matter where I'm standing."

They had nothing like that on the market, he told me, only some of those little tin platters that you have to stand right up close to and yell at. But when I told him that expense was no object, he suggested I let him send a couple of his experts up and condition my phonograph with a sort of pick-up and string some wiring around the room. Then with some wax "master" records—blanks—and a special sort of needle I could get the same effect as the phonograph companies did at their studios.

I told him go ahead, I'd try it out. "See, there's a famous producer coming to call on me and my whole career depends on this."

He had to order the needle and dummy records from the factory. He didn't carry things like that. "Make it two dozen, just to be on the safe side," I said. "He might ask me to do Hamlet's Soliloquy." I could tell he thought I was a nut, but he said: "I'll get you a trade discount on 'em."

"Oh, and don't forget the phonograph itself," I said on my way out. "I forgot to mention I haven't got one."

They were all through by five that afternoon. There really wasn't as much to it as I thought there'd be. It looked like just another agony box. The only difference was you couldn't play anything on it like the real ones, it recorded sounds instead of giving them out.

"Now, here's one very important thing," I said. "I want to be able to start and stop this thing without going over to it each time."

But that, it turned out, was a cinch. All they did was to attach a long taped cable with a plunger on the end of it, which had been featured commercially with certain types of phonos for years. You sat across the room from it, pushed the plunger and it started, released it and it stopped. It was plugged in of course, didn't need winding.

"Move it up closer against the daybed," I said. "As close as you can get it, that's where I want it to go."

When it was all set, we put a record on and I tried it out. I stood off across the room from it and said: "Hello, how are you? You're looking well," and a lot of other junk, anything that came into my head. Then I sat down on the daybed and did it from there.

They took the record off and played it for me on a little portable machine they'd brought with them—it couldn't be played on the original machine, of course—and with a softer needle, fibre or bamboo, so as not to spoil it. The part it had picked up from across the room was blurred a little, but the part it had picked up from the daybed came out like crystal and so natural it almost made me jump.

"We'll let it go at that," I said. "Just so long as I know where I'm at, that satisfies me. By the way, how am I going to tell when a record's used up and it's time to put a new one on?"

"It's got an automatic stop, the plunger'll come back in your hand."

After they'd gone I made a couple of minor improvements of my own. I hung an openwork lace scarf over the cabinet so you couldn't tell what it was and I paid out the cable with the plunger under the daybed, where it was out of sight. But it could be picked up easily by just dropping your hand down to the floor, no matter which end you were sitting on.

He was completely sold on me when we got back from the Gay Nineties the next night. I'd purposely left there with him earlier than the night before and kept him from drinking too much. It's easier to get anyone to talk when they're cockeyed, but it doesn't carry much weight in court.

He came in eating out of my hand but grumbling just the same. "Why couldn't we have gone to my place? I tell you I don't like it here, it gives me the heebies."

This time I mixed the nightcaps right in front of him. He took the glass I passed him and then he smiled and said: "Is this another Micky Finn?"

I nearly stopped breathing. Then I did the only thing there was to do. I took the glass back from him and drank it myself. "You say some pretty careless things," I answered coldly. "Can you back that up?"

"I suppose you did it to keep me from making a pass at you," he said. I got my breath back again. Then he said: "How you going to stop me tonight?"

I hadn't exactly thought of that. Just because my mind was strictly on business, I'd forgotten that his might be on monkey business.

"Make yourself comfortable," I said quietly, "while I get off the warpaint," and I went inside. I was halfway through when I suddenly heard him say, "Where's the radio? Let's have a little music."

My God, I thought, if he finds that thing! I ran back to the doorway and stuck my head out and it must have been pretty white. "I—I haven't got any," I said.

"What's this thing?" he said, and reached over to lift up the lace scarf covering it.

"That's an electric sewing-machine," I said quickly. "I make my own clothes. Tommy, come here a minute, I want to show you something." He came over and my lungs went back to work for me again. "Isn't this a keen little dressing room?" He misunderstood and made a reach. "Oh, no, no, put on the brakes!" I said. "Come on, let's go in and sit down and talk quietly."

We sat down side by side and I parked my drink on the floor, an inch or two away from the cable connecting with the machine. "Why do you keep saying you don't like this place?" I remarked cagily. "Why do you get so shivery each time you come here? This morning you got all white when you looked out of the window—"

"Let's talk about you," he said.

"But I want to know. You promised you'd give me the lowdown."

But it wasn't going to be as easy as all that. "God, you're a sweet number, you're tops, kid," he said soft and low, "you've got me off my base, this isn't just a one-night stand, I want to marry you." He slipped his arm around me and leaned his head against me, so I knew I had him branded. I was on the inside track with him now. My hand dipped down toward the floor in the dark and felt the corded cable lying there. "You'll marry in hell, you punk!" I thought savagely.

"You're a chaser," I stalled. I groped along the cable, gathering it up in my fingers until I got to the end and felt the plunger in my hand. "You used to know someone in this very apartment, you said the same thing to her I bet."

"That rat," he said sourly, "she was no good."

"Who was she anyway?" I waited.

"You musta read about it in the papers," he said. "That Pascal woman that got bumped."

I reared up on my elbow and pushed the plunger. I raised my voice a little, spaced each word. "Why, Tommy Vaillant," I said, and I went double on it for purposes of identification. "Tommy Vaillant, did you know her, Bernice Pascal, that girl that was found dead right here in this very building?"

"Did I know her? We were like this!" He held up two fingers to show me. The record would muff that, so I quickly put in: "As thick as all that? How'd you feel when she got it in the neck?"

"I gave three cheers."

"Why, what'd you have against her?"

"She was a mutt," he said. "Her racket was blackmail. She accidentally found out something about me that wouldn't have looked good on the books. It was good for a Federal stretch. A shooting back in Detroit, in the old Prohibition days. I warned her, if she ever opened her trap, her number was up. I had her colored maid fixed and she tipped me off Pascal was all set to blow to Montreal with this Reardon guy. I knew what that meant. The first time she ran short of cash, off would come the lid—up there where I couldn't stop her!"

"What'd you do about it?"

"I came over here to the apartment to stop her. And with a dame like her, there was only one way to do that."

"You came here intending to kill her?"

"Yeah," he said, "she had it coming to her."

I suddenly cut the motor. My hand seemed to act without my telling it to. Don't ask me how I knew what he was going to say next, I wasn't taking any chances.

"She was dead when I found her," he said. "Somebody beat me to it. She was lying on the floor, cold already. First I thought she was just drunk. Then when I saw different I tipped my hat to whoever done it and closed the door again. I got out of there in a hurry."

I turned it on again between "again" and "I." "What's that whirring noise?" he said. "Is there a mosquito in here?"

"That's the frigidaire," I said. "The motor goes on and off." Westman would know enough to erase this before he had the wax record copied in hard rubber.

"I shouldn't be telling you all this," he said. "But you're not like her." I nestled a little closer to him to give him confidence, but not enough to start the fireworks up again. "What was the first thing you did after that?" I purred.

"I threw the key to her place down the sewer. Then I got a taxi on the next corner and drove over to the club and fixed myself a good alibi. Next day I went around to where the day doorman lived and paid his way back to Ireland—just to be on the safe side. He'd seen me with her too much for my own good."

"What about the night doorman?"

"He was new on the job, didn't know me by sight, didn't know which apartment I'd come into or gone out of." So he hadn't been greased, was just dumb.

"What about the colored maid, didn't she worry you?"

"That was taken care of," he said, "she had an accident." I could tell by the tone of his voice that it must have been really an accident, that he hadn't had anything to do with it, but I fixed that. I gave a loud boisterous laugh as though he'd meant it in a different way. "You think of everything!" I said, and switched the thing off.

It was a risky thing to say, but he wasn't noticing, let me get away with it. "What's funny about it?" he droned sleepily.

The phone rang all of a sudden. It was for him. They wanted him at the club on account of a raid was coming up. He'd left word where they could reach him. Just when I wanted him out of the way, too. Who said there was no Santa Claus?

"See you tomorrow night, Angel Face."

He grabbed his hat, grabbed a kiss, and breezed.

It was getting light out, and I was all in. Some night's work. And all on one record. I let the cord that had done all the dirty work slip out of my hand. I looked at it and shook my head and thought, "That poor slob." I guess I was too tired by then, myself, to feel joyful about it. Maybe that was why I didn't.

When I opened my eyes, the record was still on the turntable. You'd think the first thing I'd do would be to take a look under the lid and make sure. But I didn't go near it for a long time, and when I finally did I didn't feel much like crowing. I stood there holding it in my hand. Such a fragile thing! All I had to do was just let it fall, just let it slip out of my fingers and—goodbye. I thought of Jackie, then I put it down and ran to the phone as if I was scared of my life. Ran isn't the word—flew. I got Westman at his office, told him I had what he needed.

"Swell, bring it down," he tried to tell me.

"I can't, you'd better come up and get it! Quick, right now! Jump in a cab, don't give me time to think it over. Hurry, will you, hurry, before I—"

He came all right. He stripped off a pillowcase and slipped the record in that. "I'll get Albany on the wire," he promised. "I'll have a stay of execution for you before the day's over!" Then he wanted to know: "What're you looking so down in the mouth about? Is this a time for—"

"Go on, Westman," I said, "don't stand here chinning, get that thing out of my sight."

After awhile I went back to the phone again and called Tommy Vaillant. "Tom," I said, "how quickly can you blow town?"

"Why, in five minutes if I have to," he said. "Why? What's up?"

"You better see that you do then. I just got a hot tip—they're going to reopen the Pascal case."

"Where do I figure?" he asked. "I'm in the clear."

"Take my advice and don't hang around arguing about it. Goodbye, Tom," I sobbed. "Can you beat an extradition rap?"

"With one hand tied behind my back. What're you crying about?" he asked.

"I—I sort cf liked you, Tom," I said, and I hung up.

This morning when I opened my eyes Jackie was sitting up on one elbow looking at me in a worried sort of way. "Oh, my head," I groaned. "Never again!"

"Angel Face," he said, "promise me you won't take any more nightcaps."

"Why?"

"You talk in your sleep, you say such funny things. You say it was you killed Bernice Pascal that time."

I gave him a starry look and smiled. Then he smiled back.

"Angel Face," he said.

He always calls me that. Always says I haven't a thing inside my head, but that the outside is a honey.

(1935)

The Body Upstairs

I got home that night about 6:15. "Have a hard day?" the wife wanted to know as I pitched my hat at the chandelier. "Supper's ready."

"With you as soon as I polish off the body," I said. I went in the bathroom, stripped and hopped into the tub.

Halfway through, I stopped and looked around me. Either I was cockeyed or there was something the matter with the soap. It was Healthglo and it was red, like it always is, but the color seemed to be running from it. Apparently it was dyeing the water a pale pinkish shade all around me. Very pretty but not my type of bath.

All of a sudden something hit my shoulder and made me look up. I let out a yip. The whole ceiling over me was sopping wet. The stain kept spreading around the edges and a single drop at a time would come to a head right in the middle of it, very slowly, and then drop off. There must be a man-sized leak in the bathroom above, I thought, and what a leak—a young cloudburst to make it come all the way through like that! But that wasn't what was peculiar about it. If it had been only a leak it would have been the plumber's business and not mine. This was a *pink* leak! It was water mixed with something else. It was even changing the color of my bathwater little by little as it dripped into it. What that something else was I hated to think but I had a rough idea.

I jumped into my pants and shirt, wet the way I was, and came tearing out of there. I nearly knocked my wife down getting to the door. "It's the Frasers," I said. "Something's happened up there!"

"Oh, that poor woman!" I heard her say in back of me.

"You keep out of the bathroom for awhile," I grunted.

I chased up the stairs without waiting for the elevator. We were on the third, and they were on the fourth. There was a guy standing outside their door just taking his hand away from the knob when I got up there. When he turned around I saw that it was Fraser himself.

"I can't seem to get in," he said. "I went off and forgot my key this morning." He gave me a strained sickly sort of smile with it. He was a pale good-looking guy, with his hat over his left ear.

I didn't answer. Instead I turned and hollered down the stair-well: "Katie!" She wouldn't have been a woman at all if she hadn't been out at the foot of the stairs listening instead of staying inside the flat where she belonged. "Call up the super from our place and tell him to bring his passkey with him."

It didn't seem to dawn on Fraser that something might be up. After all, I only knew him by sight. You'd think he'd wonder why it was up to me to worry about whether he got in or not. If he did, he didn't let on. All he said was: "You don't have to do that, my wife'll be along any minute now."

"I doubt that, buddy, I doubt that," I said, but I didn't explain what I meant. That'd come soon enough.

The elevator door banged open and the super came hustling out. I put out my hand for the key. "Give it here," I said. "I'm doing it."

Fraser for the first time showed some slight surprise. "I don't get you," he said. "What do you want in my place?"

I just said: "Save your breath, you're going to need it," and went in first. The first room, the living room, was perfectly O.K., neat as a pin, not an ashtray out of place. From there a short passageway led into the bedroom (same lay-out as our place) and in between the two was the bathroom. The bathroom door was closed tight and you couldn't notice anything for a minute until you looked down at the floor. A pool of water had formed just outside the sill, still as glass. But when I opened the door—boy! It was about a foot deep in there, and the tub was brimming over. But that wasn't it, it was what was in the tub that counted! It—or she—was in the tub, completely submerged. But she wasn't undressed for a bath; she was clothed. There was a flatiron in the tub with her. Her head had been pounded to pieces and you couldn't have recognized her any more, even if you had known her. It was a blood-bath if there ever was one! No wonder it had come through to our place.

It was Fraser's wife all right. I heard a sound in back of me like air being slowly let out of a tire. Fraser had fainted dead away in the super's arms. The super himself looked pretty green in the face, and my own stomach did a half-turn. "Take him downstairs to my place," I said.

I locked up again to keep the other tenants out and followed them down. "Katie, do something for this man, will you?" I said, dialing Spring 7-3100 on our phone.

"Murder?" she breathed.

"And how. Pour me out two fingers will you, it's the fiercest thing I've ever seen." She wasn't a detective's wife for nothing; she didn't ask any more questions after that.

"This is Galbraith, chief. Reporting from home. There's been a murder right in my own building. A Mrs. Fraser, Apartment Four-C. Head mashed with a flatiron."

"Orright, get busy," he snapped. "I'll have the medical examiner with you right away." *Click!*

"You stay away from there, I told you. Keep that door closed." This to Katie, whom I caught standing outside the bathroom staring hypnotized up at our stained ceiling. "We'll have to have that replastered tomorrow."

I had my dinner by turning the little whiskey glass she'd handed me upside down over my mouth, then I ran back upstairs and let myself in.

I took a look at the chamber of horrors through the door and sized her up. She was wearing a flowered kimona and house-slippers with pom-poms. I reached over, closed my eyes, turned the tap off and pulled up the plug to let the water out of the tub. Then I got the hell out of there.

I went around and took a look in the bedroom. They had one of these double photograph-folders set up on the dresser—one of him, one of her—and that gave me a good idea what her face had looked like while she still had one. Not pretty, but intelligent—lots of brains. They were all over the bathroom now, I thought to myself, for anyone to see. I threw open the bureau drawers and had a look-see at them. His junk was all crowded into one little top drawer, all the others were full of hers. Liked her own way, had she? Next the closet. He had one suit, she had nine dresses. A funny thing though, the air in the bedroom was clear and odorless but that in the closet smelt distinctly of stale cigarette smoke. I quickly closed the door, took a deep breath on the outside, opened it again and sniffed inside. It was fainter than the first time but still there.

"Yeah, I'm in here, don't bother me, go look in the bathroom," I hollered out to the medical examiner and all the boys, who had just then arrived. A cop was hung outside the door to keep the reporters out, and everyone got down to work. When they began to get in my way I went down to my own place to give myself a little more elbow room, taking with me an insurance policy on Mrs. Fraser's life I'd found tucked away in the bottom bureau drawer and two hairpins, one from the carpet in the bedroom, one from the mess on the bathroom floor. The policy was for ten grand and the first premium had been paid just one week before, so it was now in full swing. I phoned the salesman who'd made it out and had a talk with him.

"Naw, he didn't, she took it out herself," he told me. "She said she was doing it because he wanted her to very badly, kept after her about it day and night."

"Oh-oh," I grunted. "Got any idea who this Mrs. Drew is?"

"Some woman friend of hers. She did that because she said she'd heard too many cases of people being killed for their insurance money, so she wasn't taking any chances. Wouldn't make her husband beneficiary, just in case."

But that didn't go over at all with me. No woman that crowds all her husband's belongings into one little top bureau drawer and appropriates all the rest for herself is afraid of her husband doing anything like that to her. She has too much to say over him. Or if she really had been afraid, why take out a policy at all, why not just lie low and steer clear of trouble altogether?

I went in to ask Fraser a few questions, ready or not. He was sitting on the edge of the sofa in our living room, sticking his tongue in a glass of spirits of ammonia mixed with water and having St. Vitus's dance from the waist up. Katie and the super, one on each side of him, were trying to buck him up. "Out," I said to the two of them and jerked my thumb at the door.

"Now no rough-house in here," Katie warned me out of the corner of her mouth. "I just had this room vacuumed today."

"How much do you make?" I asked him when they'd both gone outside. He told me. "How much insurance y'carrying?"

"Twenty-five hundred."

"And your wife?"

"None," he said.

I watched him hard. He wasn't lying. His eyes went up at me when he answered instead of dropping down.

I took a turn around the room and lit a butt. "What was her maiden name?" I said.

"Taylor."

"You got any married sisters?"

"No, just a single one."

"She have any?"

"No."

I went over to him and kicked his foot out of the way. "When was the last time you saw Mrs. Drew?"

"Who?" he said.

I said it over, about an inch away from his face.

He screwed his eyes up innocently. "I don't know what you're talking about. I don't know any Mrs. Drew."

I had him figured for the nervous type. Slapping around wasn't any good. It wasn't in my line anyway. "All right, Mac, come on in the bathroom with me." I hauled him in by the shoulder. He let out a moan when he saw the ceiling. I made him sit on the edge of the tub, then I grabbed him by the scruff of the neck and held his head down. It was still coming through. It was mostly water but he couldn't see that. He squirmed and tried to jerk back when the first drop landed on the back of his head. Sweat came out all over his face like rain.

"Why'd you do it?" I said.

"I didn't, my God, I didn't," he choked. "Let me out of here—"

"You're going to sit here until you tell me why you did it and who Mrs. Drew is."

"I don't know," he moaned. "I never heard of her." Another drop landed, on his pulse this time, and I thought he'd have convulsions.

"Why'd you do it? Who's Mrs. Drew?"

He could hardly talk any more. "I didn't. I don't know her. How can I tell you if I don't know her?" He kept waiting for the third drop that was coming. All of a sudden his head flopped and he fainted away again.

It may have been cruel, but I don't think so. It saved his life for him. It convinced me he hadn't done it, and that he didn't know who Mrs. Drew was. I got him over to a big chair and went and flagged Katie.

"Maybe you can help me. What made you say 'that poor woman!' when I started up the first time? How is it you didn't say 'that poor man!'?"

She looked indignant. "Why, he abused her! You were never home enough to hear what went on up there. They used to have terrible rows. She dropped in here only this morning and told me he'd threatened her life."

"I didn't know you knew her that well."

"I didn't," she said. "As a matter of fact today was the first time she'd ever been in here."

"I don't get it," I remarked. "Why should she come to you to spill a thing like that, if she hardly knew you at all?"

"She mentioned she'd found out from one of the neighbors that I was married to a detective. Maybe she was looking for protection."

Or maybe, I said to myself, she was planting evidence against her husband. First with the insurance salesman, now with Katie. Somehow it smelled a little fishy to me. Women will gossip about other women's husbands maybe, but never their own. This one had. She hadn't just talked at random either. She'd shot off her mouth where it would do the most good; she'd created two star witnesses for the state in case anything happened.

"Wait a minute," I said. I went and got the two hairpins I'd picked up upstairs and rinsed off the one I'd found on the bathroom floor. Then I went back to Katie. "You're a woman," I said. "How was she wearing her hair?"

It took her four and a half minutes to tell me all about it, without once repeating herself. Then I showed her the two hairpins. "Which would go with that?"

"Why, the amber one of course." She nearly laughed in my face.

"Only a man would ask a thing like that! How could a blonde like her use a black hairpin like this other one? It would have stood out a mile off."

"Here's four bits," I said. "Run along to the movies, you've earned it. And I don't want you around when the boys come down to see Fraser."

I jiggled the two hairpins up and down in my hand. The black one was the one I'd found in the bedroom. Something told me that Mrs. Drew, when she showed up a few months from now to cash in on that ten grand, was going to turn out to be a dark-haired lady. But I wasn't going to wait until then to make sure. I very much wanted to meet her now.

I got my claws in the superintendent and hauled him in from the hallway, where Katie had lingered to give him instructions about kalsomining our ceiling. "Mrs. Fraser had a woman visitor sometime during the day today," I told him. "Think hard."

"I don't have to," he said. "She came right up to me and asked me which entrance to take, it must have been her first visit." The building is one of those inner garden things with four wings.

"She had dark hair, didn't she?"

Then he goes and spoils my day. "Nah, she was as blond as they come."

I recovered after awhile. Just because he'd seen one caller didn't mean there hadn't been others later on that he hadn't seen. "You didn't see her when she left, did you?" That was asking too much. But not of him, it turned out; he seemed to know everything that was going on. "I think I did at that," he said. "I ain't sure."

"Whaddye mean?" I said impatiently. "If you got a good look at her going in, how could you miss knowing her when she came out?"

"I don't know if it was her or not," he said. "I saw someone come out of there that looked like her, was dressed just like her, but when she went in she was alone and when she came out there was a guy with her. I wasn't close enough to her the second time to tell if it was the same one."

"That's because y'mind ain't trained," I snapped. "Now forget all about her coming out and just concentrate on her going in. That ought to be easy because you said she stepped right up to you. All right, got it?" He nodded dumbly. "What color was she wearing?"

"Black."

"Well, wasn't there some ornament, some gadget or other on her that would strike your eye, catch your attention?"

"I didn't notice," he said.

"Close your eyes and try it."

He did, then opened them right up. "That's right, there was," he grinned happily. "I saw it just now with my eyes shut. She had a big bow on the side of her hat." He snapped his fingers. "Yeah, it must have been her I saw coming out, the second one had it too. I spotted that same bow all the way across the court."

"See how it works?" I said. "Drop around sometime and we'll be glad to give you a job—scrubbing the floor." So she had a guy with her when she left. That explained who had done the smoking in the clothes closet up there. Clothes are too sacred to a woman, whether they're her own or not, for her to risk getting sparks on them. It would take a man not to give a damn where he lit up.

It was still all balled up to me. The best I could do was this: the lady-visitor had arrived first, openly, and been let in by Mrs. Fraser. Then when Mrs. F. wasn't looking she had slipped a male accomplice into the flat and he'd hidden in the closet and waited for a favorable opportunity to jump out and give her the works. I scratched the part out of my hair. That was lousy, it stank. First, because the woman had gone right up to the super of her own free will and let him take a good look at her when it would have been easy enough to avoid that. Second, because she was a blonde, and the hairpin I'd picked up was a black one. Third, because it was Mrs. Fraser herself and not anyone else who had gone around planting suspicion against her husband. You might almost say that she had lent a hand in her own murder.

I went up to 4-C again, giving myself a scalp treatment on the way. The cop was still outside the door. "Never mind trying to hide your cigarette behind you," I said, "you're liable to burn yourself where it won't do you any good." No more reporters, they had a deadline, and the medical examiner had gone too. She was still in there, on the living-room floor now, waiting to go out. "Oh, by the way," I mentioned, "I'm holding the husband down in my place, in case you guys want to take a look at him." They almost fell over each other in their hurry to get out and at him. "He didn't do it," I called after them, but I knew better than to expect them to listen to me.

I followed them out and right away another door down the hall opened an inch or two. It was just Mrs. Katz of 4-E trying to get a free look at the body when it was carried out. I beckoned to her and she came the rest of the way out, pounds and pounds of her. I liked Mrs. K. at sight. I bet she cooked a mean bowl of noodles. "Maybe you can tell me something I'd like to know."

She finished swallowing the marshmallow she was chewing on. "Sure, sure, maybe I'll get my name in the papers, huh? Poppa, come here."

"No, never mind Poppa. Did you see anyone go in there yesterday to call on her, in a black dress?"

"No," she said, "but somebody in a black dress was coming out. I met them down by the elevator when I was coming home from the grocer, a man and a woman together. They didn't live in the building so maybe they was visiting."

"Big bow on her hat?"

She nodded excitedly. "Sure, sure."

"That's them. Blond, wasn't she?"

"Get out! Dark—darker as I am even."

I wheeled her around on her base and pushed her back in again. I had it now! The super met her coming in and he said she was blond. Mrs. Katz passed her going out and said she was dark. Well, they were both right. She'd come in blond and she'd gone out brunette.

I ran all the way downstairs to the basement and dragged the super away from his radio. "What time do you start the fire in the incinerator?"

"Not until after midnight," he said. "Let it burn out between then and morning."

"Then all today's rubbish is still intact?"

"Sure. I never touch it until the tenants are all asleep."

"Show me where it is, I've got to get at it." We took a couple of torches, a pair of rubber gloves, and an iron poker and went down into the sub-basement. We should have taken gas masks too. He threw open the doors of the big oven-like thing and I ducked my coat and started to crawl in head-first.

"You can't go in there!" he cried aghast. "They're still using the chutes at this hour, you'll get garbage all over you."

"How the hell else am I going to get at it?" I yelled back over my shoulder. "Which of these openings is fed by the C-apartments?"

"The furthest one over."

"It would be! You go up and give orders no one in the building is to empty any more garbage until I can get out of here."

I don't ever want a job like that again. Pawing around among the remains of people's suppers is the last word in nastiness. Slippery potato peels got in my shoes and fishbones pricked my fingers. Holding my breath didn't help much. I was in there over half an hour. When I was through I came out backwards an inch at a time and took a good sneeze, but what I came out with was worth it. I had two fistfuls of human hair, blond hair cut off short at the scalp. Cut off in a hurry, because one of the hairpins that had dressed it was still tangled in it. It hadn't come from the dead woman's head; there was no blood on it. The hairpin was amber, mate to the one I'd found upstairs. I also had the crumpled lid of a cardboard box that said *Sylvia, Hairdresser* on it. It looked like a hatbox but it wasn't, hairdressers don't sell hats. I didn't really need it, I had a general idea of what was what now, but as the saying goes, every little bit added to what you've got makes a little bit more.

Upstairs I hung my duds out on the fire-escape to air and put on clean ones. Then I beat it over to headquarters to talk some more to Fraser. I found him in the back room where a couple of the boys had been holding hands with him since he'd been brought in. I got the cold shoulder all around, to put it mildly. "Well, well," said one of them, "look who's here. Nice of you to drop in. Care to sign your name in the guest-book?"

"I remember now," said the other. "Isn't Galbraith the name? Weren't you assigned to this case just tonight?"

"He wouldn't know. It didn't happen close enough to get him steamed up," said the first one. "The corpse only just about landed in his—"

I stuck my hands deep in my pockets and grabbed hold of the lining. "What's that paper you've got in your hand?" I cut in.

"Why, this is just the confession of Fraser here that he killed his wife, which he is now about to sign. Aren't you, Fraser?"

Fraser nodded like a jack-in-the-box and his eyes seemed to roll around all over his head. "Anything, anything," he gasped. They read it back to him and he almost tore it away from them, he was so anxious to sign and get it over with. I just stood by and took it all in. It didn't amount to a hell of a whole lot. In fact it stacked up to exactly nothing. "Phooey!" I said. "You've got him punch-drunk, that's all. Who the hell couldn't get anything out of that nerve-wreck?"

His hand wobbled so that he could hardly put his name to it. They had to steady him by the elbow. "Now will you lemme alone, now will you lemme alone?" he kept murmuring over and over.

"Get wise," I said as I followed them outside. "Why don't you save yourselves a lot of razzing and tear that thing up before you show it to anybody?"

"Get that!" one of them laughed.

"Green with envy," added the other.

"Look," I said patiently, "let me show you. He didn't have the key, couldn't get in to do it even if he wanted to."

"That's what he tried to hand us, too."

"I know it's the truth because I found his key myself, found it on the living-room floor right in my own flat. The super had dumped him on the sofa, see, with his feet higher than his head."

Did they laugh! They made more noise than a shooting-gallery.

"Know where it had been all the time? In the cuff of his trouser. Dropped in when he was dressing this morning and stayed there all day long. It's a natural, one of those crazy little things that do happen ever once in a while. That's why I believe him. If it had disappeared altogether, I wouldn't have. But who'd think of planting a key in his own trouser-cuff? If that ain't enough for you dimwits, I checked up on where he worked, called his employer at his home, found out what time he left the office. He'd only just gotten to his door when I came up the stairs and found him standing outside of it."

But I could have saved my breath, it was like talking to the walls. They had their suspect in the bag and were going to see that he stayed there. They shook their heads pityingly at me and went on out to break the glad news to the chief. I went in to Fraser again and sent the cop out of the room. His hair was all down over his face and he was just staring out under it without seeing anything. I couldn't help feeling sorry for him, but I didn't let him know it.

"What'd you do that for?" I said quietly.

He knew I meant signing that cheesy confession. "It's no fun when they jab cigarette butts up under your armpits."

"Can that." I gave him a hard look. "I don't want to hear about your troubles. If there's anything yellower than killing your wife, it's saying you did it when you didn't. Now try to snap out of it and act like a man even if you're not. I want to ask you something." I called the cop and told him to bring him in a cup of coffee. While he was slobbering it all over the front of his shirt and sniffing into it I said: "You told me you've got an unmarried sister. She blond?"

"Yeah," he sobbed, "like me."

"Where can I get hold of her?"

"She don't live here, she's up in Pittsfield, Mass., with my folks."

"How'd she get along with your wife?"

"Not so hot," he admitted.

I let him alone after that. "Put him back in mothballs," I told the cop.

In the chief's office the two half-baked rookies were all but doing a war-dance around their embalmed confession, while the chief read it over through his glasses. Embalmed is right, it smelled out loud.

"You showed up smart on that last case," the chief said to me sourly.

"Why, it hasn't broken yet, I'm still with it," I said quietly. "That guy in there, Fraser, didn't have anything to do with it."

"Who did?"

"A Mrs. Drew," I said. "I'll show her to you as soon as I can. G'night."

I ran up a big bill by calling Pittsfield, Mass., long-distance, but it didn't take me long to find out all I wanted to know about Fraser's sister. Which was simply that she wasn't there. The last anyone had seen of her had been the night before, waiting around the depot for a train. I wondered if even a girl from Pittsfield would be dumb enough to think she was disguising herself by changing her hair from blond to dark—still, you never can tell. Every once in awhile one of those 1880 twists crops up in a 1935 case. Apart from that, I found out there wasn't anyone named Drew in the whole of Pittsfield.

Even so, I had a pretty good set-up after just twenty-four hours' work. I had the two angles of the triangle now—the two women—Fraser's wife and sister. All I needed was a third angle, the man in the case. And that wasn't Fraser, he was just the fall guy in this.

Who the guy was, that had smoked in the clothes-closet and then stepped out to turn Mrs. Fraser's head into caviar, wasn't going to be any cinch. Starting from scratch I had this much on him: both the super and Mrs. Katz had lamped him on his way out, which wasn't much but it was better than nothing at all. In addition there was one other little thing I didn't need to be told by anybody. I was as sure as though I had been present at his christening that his name was going to turn out to be Drew, the same as the lady who was down on the insurance policy as beneficiary. But that was only a detail. He could call himself Smith for all I cared just as long as I got hold of him. As far as Fraser's sister was concerned she could keep. The point being that wherever Drew was, Mrs. Drew wouldn't be very far away. And if the Fraser girl happened to be Mrs. Drew, with or without benefit of clergy, that was her tough luck.

The first thing I did was to get hold of the super and Mrs. Katz, one at a time, and quiz them to get a rough idea of what he had looked like. It took hours and used up thousands of words, because neither of them were exactly Einsteins, but I got a couple of interesting facts out of them. The super, who had been all the way across the court from him, could only contribute that on his way out he had taken the woman who was with him by the arm to help her manage the two very low, harmless steps that led down to the sidewalk level. Mrs. Katz, who had been waiting to go in the elevator as they came out, enlarged on this trait of gallantry he seemed to possess.

"Well, one thing, he was no loafer," she said approvingly. "I had my arms full with bundles, so what does he do, he turns and holds the elevator door open for me, I should go in."

Darned polite, I said to myself, for a guy who had just committed a murder. Politeness must have been an awfully strong habit with him, a hangover from whatever line of business he was in. Mrs. Katz was certainly no spring chicken, and I've seen better lookers. Who, I asked myself, is trained to be polite to women of all ages, no matter what they look like? Who has to be, in order to earn a living? A gigolo. A headwaiter. A floorwalker in a department store. An automobile salesman. A hairdresser—

Sure. I might have known that from the beginning. Hair seemed to have a lot to do with this. This woman had gone in there blond and come out brunette. I'd found a lot of blond hair cut off in a hurry in the incinerator, without any blood on it. This unknown guy had been up there at the time, although nobody saw him go in. And he's so used to handing out the oil to his customers that even when he comes out with that butchery on his conscience, he instinctively holds the door open for one woman, elaborately helps the other down a two-inch step. What you might call a reflex action. And to cinch the whole thing, there was that crumpled lid of a cardboard box that had been thrown down the garbage chute; the one that said *Sylvia, Hairdresser* on it.

That gave me a pretty good idea of how he had employed his talents up there in the flat, apart from mangling Mrs. Fraser. But all the same it took my breath away, left me with a hollow feeling in the pit of my stomach. The guy must be a monster. Was it possible for a human being to batter one woman to death and then right on top of that, in the very next room, calmly sit down and go to work giving his accomplice a quick treatment to change the color of her hair?

He must have said: "Anyone see you come in?" She must have said: "I had to ask the superintendent where it was." He must have cursed her out for being ninety-nine kinds of a fool, then said: "Well, I took a chance on someone spotting you. I brought something that'll fix it so they won't know you as you go out."

Well, I could fix it so nobody'd know either one of them this time next year, and I wasn't wasting any more time about it either. I looked up *Sylvia's* in the directory, and luckily there were only three of them to buck. If it had been *Frances* or *Renee* I would have had half a column to wade through. Nothing doing with the first two; I got to the third a little before five in the afternoon.

It was a whale of a place. Twenty-two booths going full-blast and a lot of steam and perfume and cigarette smoke all mixed up. It gave me the creeping willies to be in there, especially after somebody's face with black mud all over it nearly scared me out of ten years' growth. I stayed close to the door and asked to see the proprietor. It turned out *Sylvia* was just a trade-name and the proprietor was a man after all. He came out rubbing his hands; maybe he was just drying them off.

"You got anybody named Drew working for you?" I said.

"No," he said, "we had an expert named de la Rue here until the day before yesterday, but he isn't with us any more."

That interested me right away. "Come again, what'd you say the name was?"

He made a mouth like that guy in the hair-tonic ads. "Gaston de la Rue," he gargled.

I flashed my identification at him and he nearly jumped out of his skin and forgot about being French. "Break down," I said, "I'm not one of your customers. Nobody on two legs ever had a name like that. Was it Drew or wasn't it?"

"*Sh*, not so loud," he said, "very bad for business. They like 'em French. This is just between us. Please keep it to yourself. Well yes, in private life I think he was called Gus Drew or something like that. But what an artist, he could have put a permanent-wave in a porcupine—"

"Let me see your appointment book for the past few weeks." He took me back in his office and showed it to me. Mrs. Fraser's name was down there three times in one month, and right next to it each time were "de la Rue's" initials. "Why'd she always get him?" I wanted to know.

He shrugged. "She always asked for him. Some of them, they like to flirt a little."

"Flirt with death," I growled to myself. "Is he due back here for anything?" I asked him.

"He's got a week's pay coming to him, but when he called up and I asked him about it he said he wasn't coming in for it. He told me to mail it to where he lives."

"And did you? When?"

"Last night at closing time."

It was just about being delivered. "Quick," I said. "Got his last address on record? Fork it over."

He gave it to me, then made a crack that nearly killed me. "Why 'last,' did he move?"

"Oh no, he'll probably wave to me from the window."

He followed me back to the front of the place again, sort of worried. "What's he done?" he said. "What do they want him for?"

"The chief would like to have his mustache curled," I answered and walked out.

I took a taxi and rode right up to the door of the address Mr. "Sylvia" had given me. I didn't expect him to be there any more and he wasn't. "Just moved out yesterday," the janitor said. "Didn't say where. Nice quiet fellow, too."

"Where's that letter you're holding for him?" I said. "Did it come yet?"

"Just now. He said he'd be back for it." His mouth opened. "How'd you know?"

"This is who I am," I said. "Now get this. I can't be hanging around the hallway. He mayn't show up for days. I'll take one of your rooms. You give him his letter when he asks for it, but watch yourself, keep a straight face on you. Then ring my bell three times, like this, see? Don't let him see you do it, but don't wait too long either—do it as soon as he turns his back on you. Now have you got that straight? God help you if you muff it."

"Golly, ain't this exciting!" he said. He showed me a sliver of a hall room at the back of the ground floor, with exactly three things in it—a bed, a light-bulb, and a window. I paid him a dollar apiece for them and after that I lived there. I tested the doorbell battery by staying where I was and having the janitor ring it for me from the vestibule. It was no cathedral chime but at least you could hear it, which was all that interested me.

They say you should be able to see the two sides to any story. Sitting here like that, waiting, with the walls pressing me in at the elbows, I saw as much of Drew's side of it as I was ever likely to. No wonder ten grand had seemed a lot of money, no wonder murder hadn't stopped him, if it meant getting out of a hole like this. Not that

I felt sorry for him, I just understood a little better than before. But there was one good angle to it. The ten grand wouldn't be his for a long time yet, not for months. Meanwhile he needed what was in that envelope the janitor had, needed the little that was coming to him from "Sylvia's," needed it bad. He'd be around for it. I couldn't lose.

Once in awhile I'd hear a step on the stairs, the old wooden stairs that seemed to go right up over my room, when somebody in the house came up or went down them. Once some woman hollered down from the top floor for her kid to come up. That was all. Silence the rest of the time. The minutes went like hours and the hours like weeks. I didn't even smoke; there wasn't room enough for two kinds of air in the place. I just sat, until I had a headache.

It came a little before eight, sooner than I'd expected. He must have needed it bad to come that quickly, or maybe he thought it was safer to get it over with right away than to wait a few days. He'd probably read in the papers by now that Fraser was taking the rap, anyway. And once he had this letter in his pocket and had walked around the corner, try to locate him again, just try.

Ding-ding-ding peeped the bell battery, and the air in the room got all churned up. I hauled the door out of the way and loped down the dim hallway. The janitor was standing just inside the street door waving his arm to me like a windmill. "He just went away," he said. "There he goes, see him?" His cheap khaki waterproof was a pushover to tail.

"Get back!" I snarled and gave him a shove. "He's liable to turn around." I waited a second to get set, then I mooched out of the house, took a squint at the sky, turned my coat-collar up and started down the street in the same direction. He did look back from the corner just before he turned, but I'd finished crossing to the opposite side and was out of his line of vision.

I gave him a lot of rope for the first two blocks, then I saw a subway entrance heading toward us and I closed up on him in a hurry. He went into it like I'd been afraid he would. It's about the best way of shaking anyone off there is, but he had to change a dime or something, and when I got down the steps myself he'd only just gone through the turnstile. There was a train already in, with its doors wide open and jammed to the roof. He took it on the run along with a lot of others and wedged himself in on the nearest platform just as the doors started to slip closed. There was just room enough left to get my fingernails in by the time I got there, but that was all the leverage I needed. They were the pneumatic kind. Back they went and I was standing on his feet and we were breathing into each other's faces. "Whew!" I thought to myself, and kept my eyes fixed on the back of a newspaper the fat man next to him was reading.

He squirmed and yanked at 110th and tugged himself free. When I got up to the street myself he was just going into an A.&P. store. I took a look in the door as I went past. He was standing at the counter waiting his turn. Evidently they hadn't even had the price of groceries until he called for that money that was coming to him. I walked all the way to the next corner, then doubled back on the other side of the street and finally parked at a bus stop and stood there waiting. But the right bus for me never seemed to come along.

He was in there over ten minutes, and then when he came out his arms were still empty anyway. Meaning he'd ordered so much that he couldn't carry it himself. So they were going to stock up for the next few weeks and lie low, were they? I just barely kept him in sight after this, only close enough to tell which building he'd hit, as I knew there would be a last look back before he ducked. He finally got where he was going, gave a couple of cagy peeks, one over each shoulder, and then it was over. He was in—in Dutch.

I sized it up from where I was, tying my shoelace on somebody's railing. It was a President McKinley-model flat on the south side of 109th, crummy as they come, without even a service entrance. That meant the groceries would have to be delivered at the front door when they came around, which was a chance for a lot more than groceries to crash in. No lights showed up in any front windows after he'd gone in, so I figured they had a flat in the rear. I eased myself into the vestibule. Half of the mailboxes had no names in them, so they were no help. I hadn't expected his to have any, but if the rest of them had I could have used a process of elimination. It was so third-class the street door didn't even have a catch on it, you just opened it and walked in.

I worked my way up the stairs floor by floor, listening carefully at the rear doors on each landing. There was a radio going behind one of them, but nobody seemed to be in any of the others. If I had them cornered they were lying mighty low. I hated to think I might have slipped up in some way. I started soft-shoeing my way down again, and just below the second floor met the groceries coming up in a big box about twice the size of the lad struggling with it. "Where they going?" I said.

"Fourth floor, rear."

I had him put them down, then I thumbed him downstairs. "I'll see that they get them." He was too exhausted to argue. I unlimbered my gun, gave the door a couple of taps, and flattened myself back to one side of it.

Not a sound, not even a footfall, for a couple of minutes. Then all of a sudden a voice spoke from the other side of the door, only a few inches away from me. "Who's out there?"

I thinned my voice to make it sound like a kid's. "A.&P., boss."

A chain clanked and fell loose. The lock, I noticed, was shiny and new, must have just been put on. I reached out with my heel and kicked a can of tomatoes to give him confidence. The door cracked and before it was an inch wide I had the gun pushing in his belt buckle. "Up," I snapped. He lifted them all right but couldn't keep them from shaking. He didn't have anything on him though, so the precautions must have been just to give them time to make a get-away, and not because he'd intended fighting it out. There was no hall and the door opened right into the living room. I cuffed him to me and started to push in.

"What's all this about?" he tried to stall, and I heard a window go up.

"Hold it!" I yelled, and covered her from across his shoulder just as she raised one leg to go over. "Come on in again, baby."

There was my black-haired lady, a little pale around the gills, eyes nearly popping out of her head. There was something funny about her which I couldn't dope out at first. I took a second look and nearly keeled over. If I had, though, they wouldn't have hung around waiting for me to revive, so I gave a long whistle instead and let it go at that. I gave her a shove with my knee to show her which direction to take. "Get started, you head the daisy-chain going downstairs."

The chief was damn near bowled over when I brought them in to him. "So your Mrs. Drew wasn't a myth after all and you finally found her," he opened.

I knocked the black wig off her head with the back of my hand. "Mrs. Drew your eye. If you're holding Fraser for killing his wife better turn him loose. This is her right here." Her blond hair, clipped off short, stood up funny all over her head.

One of the boys who had used Fraser's armpits as ashtrays spoke up. "Then what was that we saw in the bathtub—"

"That was Fraser's sister, poor kid," I said. "She left Pittsfield that day and hasn't been seen since. Fraser didn't know she was coming but this pair did—maybe they got her to come down some way—but she must have walked in unannounced and spoiled their big love scene. Drew hid in the closet until time to come out and do his stuff. Mrs. Fraser probably led up to it with a quarrel. She and the sister didn't hate each other. Anyway, they had the frame all planned to pass off her body as his wife's and let him fry for it. They dressed her in Mrs. F.'s kimona, dumped her in the tub and then proceeded to mutilate her face with the iron until even her supposed husband couldn't recognize her any more. Then the real Mrs. Fraser put on the dead girl's clothes and this black wig and beat it with her side-kick. As soon as Fraser had hit the ceiling at Sing Sing she would have married Drew, and then there would have been a Mrs. Drew all right to collect that ten-grand premium on her own life."

I shoved all the evidence I had across the desk at him and went home.

"Supper's ready," the wife said. "Should I wait until you've had your bath?"

"Just open the windows," I said. "You don't catch me in that tub again until Nineteen Forty."

(1935)

Kiss of the Cobra

Mary's old man, after six years of office-managing for a tire company in India, comes heading back with a brand-new wife. He breaks it to us in a telegram first and then makes a bee-line for the place we've taken up in the hills beyond San Bernardino. It seems he wants to show her to us.

My boss has been whiter than snow to me. I'm on leave of absence with pay, and that's how we happen to be there.

When I had dragged myself in, a few weeks before, to report for duty after a tussle with the flu, I was down to 130, stripped, and saw spots in front of my eyes. He took one look at me and started swearing. "Get out of here!" he hollered. "Go 'way back someplace and sit down for six weeks. I'll see that you get your checks. It gives me the shivers to look at you!" When I tried to thank him he reached for his inkwell, maybe just to sign some report, but I didn't wait to find out.

So we hauled two centuries out of the bank, took the kid brother with us, and wound up in this dead-end up in the San Benny mountains. It hasn't even electric lights, but it isn't so bad at that. You can't quite hear the caterpillars drop. So there we are now, the three of us, Mary and me and the kid brother, waiting for her old man to show up.

He drives up around eight in the evening, smack off the boat, in a car he's hired down in L. A. He's brought her with him. She gets out and comes up to the house on his arm, while the driver starts unloading half of Asia behind them. He comes in grinning all over and shakes hands with the three of us. "This is Veda," he says.

"Where'd she ever get that name?" I think to myself.

She's a slinky sort of person, no angles at all; and magnetic—you can't take your eyes off her. She's dressed like a Westerner, but her eyes have a slant to them. They are the eyes of an Easterner. She doesn't walk like our women do, she seems to writhe all in one piece—undulates is the word.

She's smoking a ten-inch Russian cigarette, and when I touch her hand the sensation I get is of something cold wriggling in my grasp—like an eel. I can't help it, the skin on the back of my own hand crawls a little. I try to tell myself that anyone's handshake would feel like that after a drive in the open on a raw, damp night like this. But I can tell Mary doesn't like her either. She acts a little afraid of her without knowing why, and I have never known Mary to be afraid of anything in her life before. Mary keeps blinking her eyes rapidly, but she welcomes her just the same and takes her upstairs to show her her room. A peculiar odor of musk stays behind in the room after she's gone.

I go out to the pantry and I find the kid brother helping himself to a stiff nip. "The rain is bringing things up out of the ground," he mutters.

Kids don't finish growing until they're twenty-five, so I kick him in the shins, take it away from him, and kill it myself, so as not to cheat him out of an extra half inch or so. "What's your trouble?" I snap.

"She's Eurasian," he scowls, staring down at the floor. "Something mixed like that." He's been to college and I haven't, so he has me there. "Tough on sis," he says. "Damn it, I would have preferred some little digger with a pickax and baby-blue eyes. There's something musty, something creepy about her. *Brrh!*"

Me too, but I won't give in to him. "It's the house, it's been shut up all summer." And we look at each other and we know I'm lying.

All kinds of trunks, boxes, crates come in and go up to her room, the driver is paid off and takes the car back to L. A., and the five of us are left alone now in the house.

When she comes down to supper I don't like her any better; in fact, a hell of a lot less. She's put on a shiny dress, all fish-scales, like this was still India or the boat. On her head she's put a sort of beaded cap that fits close—like a hood. A mottled green-and-black thing that gleams dully in the candlelight. Not a hair shows below it, you can't tell whether she's a woman or what the devil she is. Right in front, above her forehead, there's a sort of question-mark worked into it, in darker beads. You can't be sure what it is, but it's shaped like a question-mark.

Then, when we all sit down and I happen to notice how she's sitting, all the short hairs on the back of my neck stand up. She's sort of coiled around in her chair, like there were yards and yards of her. One arm is looped sinuously around the back of the chair, like she was hanging from it, and when I pretend to drop my napkin and look under the table, I see both her feet twined around a single chair-leg instead of being flat on the floor. But I tell myself, "What the hell, they probably sit different in India than we do," and let it go at that.

Then, when Mary slaps around the soup-plates I get another jar. We're none of us very refined and we all bend our heads low over the soup, so as not to miss any of it. But when I happen to look up and take a gander at her, her head is down lower than anyone else's with that damn flat hood on it, and I get a sudden horrible impression, for a minute, of a long black-and-green snake sipping water down by the edge of a river or pool. I shake my head to clear it and keep from jumping back, and tell myself that that nip I had in the pantry just before dinner was no good. Wait'll I get hold of that guy in San Benny for selling me stuff like that!

O.K. Supper's over and Mary tickles the dishes, and then we light a log fire in the fireplace and we sit around. At ten Mary goes up to bed; she can't stand that damn Indian perfume or whatever it is. Vin, that's the kid brother, and I stick around a little longer sipping port and listening to the old man jaw about India, and I keep watching Veda.

She's facing the fire, still in that coiled-up position. She's sort of torpid, she hasn't moved for hours, but her eyes glitter like shoe-buttons in the light of the flames. There's something so reptilian about her that I keep fighting back an impulse to grab up a long stick, a fire-iron, anything at all, and batter and whack at her sitting over there.

It scares me and I sweat down the back—God, I must be going screwy! It's my father-in-law's wife, it's a woman, and me thinking things like that! But you can't see the lines of her body at all, they're lost in a thick, double coil, the top one formed by her hip, the lower one by her calf, and then that flat, hooded head of hers rising in the middle of it and brooding into the fire with its basilisk eyes.

After a long time, she moves, but it only adds to the horrid impression that I can't seem to get rid of. I'm watching her very closely and she evidently doesn't know it. But what I see is this: she sort of arches her neck, which is long and thin anyway, so that her head comes up a little higher. She holds it for a minute, reared like that, and then she lets it sink back again between her shoulder-blades. So help me God if it isn't like a snake peering out from some tall grass to see what's what!

She repeats it again a little while later, and then a third time. Vin and the old man don't see it at all, and it's barely noticeable anyway. Just like a person easing a stiff neck by stretching it. Only she does it in a sort of rounded way, almost a spiral way. But maybe it's just a nervous habit, I try to tell myself, and what's the matter with me anyway? If this keeps up, I'm a son of a so-and-so if I don't go in and see a doctor tomorrow.

I look at the wall-clock and it's five to eleven, late for the mountains, so I give Vin the eye to clear, to give the newlyweds a break alone together by the fire. Meanwhile a big orange moon has come up late and everything is as still as death for miles around, not even a mountain owl's hoot, as if the whole set-up was just waiting for something to happen.

The kid and I get up and say good-night, and, fire or no fire, her hand isn't any warmer than before, so I let go of it in a hurry. Vin goes right up but I take a minute off to lock up the windows and the door. Then, as I'm climbing, I glance around at them. They've moved closer together and the dying fire throws their shadows on the wall behind them. The old man's head looks just like what it should, but hers is flat, spade-shaped, you almost expect to see a forked tongue come darting in and out. She's moving a little and I see what she's doing, she's rouging her lips. I give a deep sigh of relief and it takes such a load off my mind to find out she's just a regular woman after all, that I stop there for a minute and forget to go on.

Then she takes something out of the little bag she has with her and offers it to him. It's one of those long reefers she seems partial to. She also takes one herself. "Cigarette," she murmurs silkily, "before we go up?" She says it in such a soft voice it almost sounds like a hiss.

I know I have no business watching, so I soft-shoe it the rest of the way up and go about my business. Only five minutes go by, less than that even, and I hear a rustling and a swishing in the upstairs hall and that's her going to her room—by herself. You don't hear any footsteps when she walks, just a soft sound that scaly dress of hers makes when it drags along the floor.

Her door closes and goodnight to her, I say to myself; and I think I wouldn't want to be in Mary's father's shoes for all the rice in China. Then, as I come out of the bathroom with my toothbrush in my hand, I hear the old man's step starting up the stairs from the floor below and I wait there out in the hall to have a last word with him.

He comes up slow, he's breathing kind of hard, sounds like sandpaper rubbing on concrete, and then when he gets halfway to where the landing is, he hesitates. Then he comes on a step or two more, stops again, and then there's a soft *plop* like something heavy falling. Right after that the woodwork starts to creak and snap a lot, as if somebody was wrestling on it. I don't wait to listen to any more, I throw my toothbrush away and I chase to the end of the hall. When I look down, I gasp in surprise.

He's lying flat on his back on the staircase landing between the two floors, and he's threshing about and squirming horribly, as if he's in convulsions. The agonized movement of his body is what's making the woodwork creak like that. Something seems to be jerking him all over, his arms and legs will stiffen to their full length and then contract again like corkscrews. His tongue's sticking all the way out of his mouth, and saliva or foam or something is bubbling around it. His eyes are glazed over.

One jump brings me down to where he is, and I lift his head and get it off the floor. As I do so, his whole face begins to blacken in my hands. There is one last hideous upheaval, as if I was trying to hold down a wild animal, and then everything stops. There's not a twitch left in his whole body after that.

Vin's heard the racket and he comes tearing out of his room.

"Whiskey," I pant. "Don't know what it is, gotta bring him to!" But there isn't any bringing to. Before the kid can sprint down past me and then up again with it, he's stiff as a board in my arms. I'm holding a lead weight, with a color that matches.

The blackness has spread all over his body like lightning and shows up in the veins in his throat and on his wrists, as if ink had been poured into his arteries. Nothing to be done, he isn't breathing. We pour the whiskey into his open mouth, but when we tilt his head to make it go down it comes right back again.

I pass him to Vin and get out from under and go down and take a miniature Keeley cure right then and there. It isn't because he's Mary's old man or because it happened right in my arms, it's those terrific spasms and that blackness that have gotten me. I get over it in a minute and we bring him down off the landing between us and lay him out. Then I let the kid have a double bracer and the hell with his extra growth.

We look at him lying there on the divan, stiff as a ramrod, and I try to flex his arms and legs. A peculiar muscular rigidity has already set in all over, even in those few minutes. I'm no medical student but I know it can't be *rigor mortis* that soon. This is the United States, but this was an unrecognizable death, a sudden, thrashing, black, tropical death—here in the States.

"Get your hat," I say to Vin, "and thumb yourself down into town and bring back the medical expert. Damn this place anyway for not having a telephone!" I push him out the door.

Now there are only four of us left in the house, two of them women and one a dead man, and the moon's peeping in at all the windows and filling the place with black shadows. From the minute the kid's dogs have left the wooden porch, you don't hear another sound outside, not the snapping of a twig, not the rustling of a dry leaf.

I'm not scared of stiffs. That's because of the unpleasant business I'm in. I cover his face to hide the blackness and then I pull down all the shades to keep the nosey moon out.

Then, as I start up the stairs to break the news to Mary, I see a thread hanging, moving in the air above the landing where he fell. It shows up against the light shining down from the upstairs hall, and that's how I happen to notice it.

It's a cigarette burning itself out where he dropped it when he fell. It's the same one she gave him when I left them before the fire. I said those Russian ones are long, it's lasted all this while, as long as a cigar would. There's still an inch or two left of it, there's still a dab of unburned tobacco in it; and the end, the mouth part, is still intact. That's all that matters, so I pinch it out and wrap it in my handkerchief.

After I've told Mary and persuaded her it's better if she doesn't go down and look at him, I knock on the other door across the hall, *her* door. No answer. So I open it and I go in. Not there. She must have gone downstairs while I was in Mary's room just now.

The air is loaded with that sticky musk smell that follows her wherever she goes. It's even worse up here though. Downstairs, it was more like a perfume; up here it's rank, fetid. It recalls stagnant, green pools and lush, slimy, decaying vegetation.

On the dresser, she had a lot of exotic scents and lotions in bottles, the same as any other woman would, the only difference being that hers hail from India. Sandalwood, attar of roses—but one of them's just ordinary everyday liquid mucilage mixed in with the others. No label on it, but my nose tells me this—and my fingertips, when I try it. I even take a pretty good-sized chance and test it on the tip of my tongue. Just mucilage. Anyone that's ever sealed an envelope or licked a stamp knows the taste. I wonder what it's doing there among those other things, but I put it back.

In the drawer, I come across a box of those extra-long cigarettes of hers, and I help myself to two or three just to see how they'll stack up against chemical analysis. She has some other peculiar junk hanging around too, that I can't make head or tail of. I know what it is all right, but I can't figure what she's doing with it.

First off, she has a cake of that stuff they call camphor ice—in a tin box. It freezes the skin, closes up the pores, is supposed to be good for chapped hands or something. But since when do they have chapped hands in India? All right, I argue to myself, maybe she brought it with her to guard against the colder climate over here, and I put that back too.

Then there's a funny little Indian contraption of wood about the size of a cup and saucer, which looks like a baby-sized pestle and mortar. The hollow part of it is all smeared red, like she was in the habit of pounding out and mixing her own rouge instead of buying it ready-made. Well, maybe they do that in India too.

Next I come across a hell of a whole lot of flannel. At first I think it is bandage, but there is too much of it for that. So the best I can figure she makes her undies out of it.

So much for the dresser, and I haven't gotten anywhere much. She has a lot of trunks, bags, boxes, etc., ranged around the room—all the stuff that I saw the driver unload from the car when she and the old man got here. One of the biggest pieces has a cover draped over it.

When I yank this off, lo and behold, a chicken-coop! Not only that, but the peculiar rank smell I've mentioned seems to come stronger from there than anywhere else. It nearly throws me over when I try to go near it. So she keeps pets, does she? I get up close to the thing and try to peer down into it between two of the slats, and I can't see a thing, there's a very close wire mesh on the inside. There's something alive in it though, all right, because while I'm standing there with my face up against it, I hear the wire netting sing out. The wing of a chicken must have brushed against it.

I *cluck* a little at it. No answering *cluck*. I shift it around a little and shake it up a little to try to get a peep out of them—it must be more than one chicken, one chicken couldn't smell that strong—and the wire sings out plenty, *zing, zing, zing.*

I go around on the other side of it and I spot a saucer of milk standing there on the floor next to it. One of the slats on that side is hinged, so that it can be opened up just about six inches from the floor. I reach down and I put my hand on it and I'm just fixing to lift it, then I think: "The hell with her and her chickens, I'd better go down and find out what she's up to instead of wasting my time up here." So I ease out of the room and go downstairs.

She's down there with the body. I stop and watch her for a minute from the stairs. She's uncovered his face and she's groveling upon him—sort of twined about him. Her face is hidden against him as if she was trying to burrow her way into his clothes and she couldn't have got any closer if she tried. Maybe it's just the Oriental mode of displaying grief, but I have my doubts. There's something pathological in this, that creature is less than human—or thinks she is.

Something snaps in me. "Don't coil up on him like that!" I bark at her. "You're like a damn snake nesting on something it's killed!"

She untwines slowly and raises her head and turns it my way, and a ghoulish smile flickers on her face. Maybe I just imagine that, for it's dark in the room.

There's a pounding outside at the door and Vin has come back with the medical expert and a policeman. There's a motorcycle throbbing against a tree out there, and it's the friendliest sound I've heard in twenty-eight years. They've parked the ambulance as close to the house as they can get it, which is about half a mile down the dirt road which gives up at about that point.

"So what's the riot?" says the medical guy. "This kid comes tearing in on a Ford without brakes, which he stole from a Jap farmer, and knocks over one of the lamp posts outside headquarters—"

"That was the only way I could stop it," explains Vin.

"Stole ain't the word," I squelch the hick. "I'm Lawton of the L. A. homicide bureau, and since he was deputizing for me, you call that commandeering. I want an autopsy from you."

"When'd it happen?"

"Five after eleven."

He goes over and he fumbles around a little, then he straightens up and his mouth is an O. "P. M., huh?"

"Not last year and not last week, eleven tonight!" I snap.

"Never saw anything like it," he mutters. "Stiff as a board and all black like that! You're gonna get your autopsy, mister."

"And make it gilt-edged, too."

There's a rustling on the stairs and we all look upward. Veda's on her way back to her room, with that damn long dress of hers trailing after her up the steps like a wriggling tail.

"Who's the spook?" asks the examiner.

"We're coming to her. First, the autopsy," I tell him. "Don't put it off, I want it right away—as soon as you get back with him!"

The driver comes in with a rubber sheet and he and the cop carry the old man out between them.

"Turn these over for me too," I say, "and get me a chemical analysis on them," and I pass him the butts I swiped in her room and the one the old man was smoking on the stairs when he fell. "And make room for my wife on the front seat. I'm sending her in with you."

He gives me a surprised look. "You sure you want her to ride with us on a death car like that?"

"One sure thing, she's not staying another minute in this house, not while I know it. Wait, I'll bring her right down!"

I go up to get her, and I find her in the hall shivering and pop-eyed. She's standing outside Veda's door bent over at the keyhole like she was rooted to the spot. But as soon as she sees me she comes running to me and goes into a clinch and hides her head on my shoulder and starts bawling and shaking all over. "Charlie, I'm afraid to stay here! That awful woman, that awful heathen woman in there, she's possessed of the devil."

I lead her downstairs and out, and walk her down the road to where the car is, and on the way she tells me about it. "It's enough to make your hair stand on end," she whispers. "Such awful goings-on in there."

"All right," I say soothingly, "tell Charlie about it, Charlie'll know if it's bad or not."

"I heard the gentlemen come downstairs," she says, "so I got up to come down and make them a cup of coffee. As I was going past her door, I heard funny sounds from there. I'm only a woman after all, so I stopped and took a look through the keyhole. And after that I couldn't move from there. I was held there against my will, until you came along. Charlie, she was *dancing*—all by herself in such a weird way, and it kept getting worse all the time. She kept getting nearer and nearer the door, until I think she would have caught me there if you hadn't come. She seemed to *know* someone was outside her door, and she kept her eyes on it. I couldn't budge!"

I know she isn't exaggerating, because I myself noticed a sort of magnetism or mild hypnotism about this Veda from the minute she came in the house. "What kind of a dance was she doing?" I ask her.

"First, she was just standing in one place and just wriggling back and forth and curving in and out like she didn't have any spine at all. She still had on that horrible, glittery dress clinging to her like a wet glove and that ugly hood on her head and she kept making a hissing noise and sticking her tongue in and out like she was tasting something. But then, afterwards, it got even worse than that. All of a sudden she went down on the floor in a heap and began crawling around on her stomach and switching her legs from side to side, like she was a fish or mermaid got stranded outside of the water—"

"Or a snake?" I put in.

She grabs my arm. "That's it, that's it! Now I know what she reminded me of! Every once in awhile she'd lift her head off the floor and raise it up and look around, and then she'd drop it back again. Then, finally, she squirms over to a little saucer of milk standing next to a big packing case and she starts drinking from it, but just with her tongue, without using her hands at all."

"O.K., Toots, get in, you're going to town."

"Charlie, I think you'd better notify the state asylum," she whispers. "I think his death has made her lose her mind. She must really think she's a snake."

This is putting it so mild that I have a hard time not laughing right in her face. That creature lurking back there in the house doesn't only think she's a snake; for all practical purposes, she is one. I don't mean in the slang sense, either. She is sub-human, some sort of monstrosity or freak that India has bred just once in all its thousands of years of history.

Now, there are two possibilities as I see it. She is what she is, either of her own free will—maybe a member of some ghastly snake-worshiping cult—or without being able to control herself. Maybe her mother had some unspeakable experience with a snake before she was born. In either case she's more than a menace to society, she's a menace to the race itself.

As for Mary's tip about the asylum, what's the sense? She could beat an insanity rap too easily. The strangeness of her ways, the far country she comes from, would be points in her favor. It would be a cinch for her to pass off the exhibition Mary saw through the keyhole as just an Asiatic way of showing grief for the departed. And even if I could get her booked in an institution, look what I'd have on my conscience, unloading her on a bunch of poor harmless nuts clipping paper dolls! She'd depopulate the place in a week. No, I tell myself, if I can only get the goods on her for the old man's death, she goes up for first-degree murder without any fancy insanity trimmings. The rope's the only sure cure for what's the matter with her.

So far I haven't got a thing, no motive and not even any evidence, and won't have until that damned medical examiner reports to me. The law being what it is, a person's innocent until you can prove him guilty. I can't prove her guilty just because I don't like how she dresses, how she hisses when she talks, how her room smells, and how she drinks milk off the floor.

I go back to the house alone. The moon's on the late shift and now there are only three of us there—one of them a kid of twenty who's just goofy enough to fall for this exotic vamp of death.

My footsteps don't make any noise on the dirt road, and as I come up on the porch, the living-room windows are orange from the fire going inside. I look in through one of them and I see her and the kid there in the room. He's standing there motionless, as if fascinated, and she's coiled up next to him and I see one of her white arms creeping, wavering like a vine up his coat sleeve. I freeze all over with dread. Their heads start coming closer together, slowly, very slowly, and in another minute their lips will meet.

Maybe this first kiss won't hurt him any, but I'm not in the mood to take a chance; I'd rather see him kissing poison ivy. Her head starts to weave a little and her neck lengthens in that old familiar movement. It's the almost hypnotic slowness of the thing that gives me a chance to do something about it. I nearly take the front door off its hinges and before they can even turn their heads to look, I've split them wide apart with my shoulder for a wedge.

They each react differently. He flops back, and I can tell the build-up she has given him has already taken effect, because he turns sore. Maybe he's ashamed too. She sinks back into a sort of coiled watchfulness and tries to look very innocent and harmless. She wets her lips a little.

"Watch what you're doing!" he shouts wrathfully, and before I can get out of the way, *wham*, right below the ear! I go down holding onto my jaw and I feel rotten, not from the blow either. Something tells me he's a goner, unless I can reason with him. If he won't listen to me nothing can save him. "Vin, for Pete's sake, you don't know what you're up against!"

"In the East," she lisps, "a kiss means only friendship, peace." But the look she squirts at me would drop an ox.

"Your kind of kiss means death, East or West!" Maybe I shouldn't show my hand like that, but my busting in has told her enough already. She goes slinking up the stairs like a noisome reptile crawling back into its hole.

"You let up on her!" the kid blusters. "You're all wrong! Being a detective has gone to your head! She told me herself you suspect her of all kinds of God-awful stuff. She didn't have anything to gain from the old guy's cashing in!"

I pick myself up and brush myself off. "No? Not much!"

He points at the fireplace. "Know what she just did before you got here? She brings down a codicil to the old guy's will, that he signed on the boat coming over, and shows it to me—makes me read it. It cut her in on his estate instead of leaving it to me and your wife, Mary. It was done against her wishes, as a wedding present to her. Then she throws it in the fire. She don't want his money, especially when there's suspicion attached to her!"

Damn clever! I swear softly to myself. Not that I believe for a minute that she isn't interested in the old guy's money. She isn't throwing it away that easy. Probably it was only a carbon-copy and the original's put away in a safe place. But, this way, she's given herself an out; gypped me out of my motive. If I jump on her now, I can't produce any—and without one where am I?

A money motive will stack up stronger in a criminal court of justice than any other you can dig up. It's liable to make an innocent person guilty in the minds of any twelve people in a jury box, I don't care who they are. If you can't produce one you may as well turn your defendant loose unless you can show them newsreel films of the crime in the act of being committed!

Veda was a pushover for a deaf, dumb and blind defense attorney now, if I dared haul her up. As a matter of fact, now that the original will was the only one left in circulation, a much stronger motive could be pinned on Mary and the kid than on her, and there was nothing to prevent the defense boomeranging and trying to show that it was to their interest to get the old guy out of the way *before* he changed his will and dished them out of it in favor of this stranger from the East. There wouldn't be much danger of its going any further than that, but at least it would free her—and then woe betide California, Oregon, Washington, while she roamed the Pacific Coast jacking up the death rate!

"So now," the kid says bitterly, "why don't you get smart to yourself, y' would-be gumshoer, and lay off her? Strain a muscle and act chivalrous even if it ain't in you!"

I close my eyes to shut out what I see coming to him. Is he sold on her! Has she got what it takes to catch 'em young and brand 'em! He's doomed if I don't break this thing up in a hurry. It may be puppy love to him, but what has he got that she wants? She don't want anything from him but his life! She would probably have picked on me instead, only she knows I'm on to her, can tell I don't trust her. The resistance ratio would be too high. Maybe guys in their prime aren't her meat; she only works on the old and the young.

What the hell can I do? I can't drive him out of the house at the point of my gun and make him stay away from her. He'd probably throw a rock at me the minute my back was turned and come right in again the back way. "All right, Sir Galahad," I tell him sadly, "have it your way."

"Aw, go to hell!" he says, and bangs out of the house to kick around among the trees outside and blow off steam. I do too. I smash last night's empty whiskey bottle across the room, then I just sit down and wait. The old man never died a natural death, and my hands are tied. It hurts where I ought to have pleasure!

The moon chokes down out of sight, it gets light, and at six there's a lot of commotion and backfiring outside and the San Benny medical expert is back with his report. No cop with him this time, I notice, which doesn't look encouraging. I can hardly wait for him to get in the house. I almost haul him in by the collar. The kid looks up scornfully, I notice, then goes ahead scuffling pebbles with the point of his shoe out there.

"All right, what's the ticket? Hurry up!" I fire at the examiner.

"I been up all night," he says. "I been working like a machine. I wouldn't do this for my own mother." He has a baffled air about him. "I'm out of my depth," he admits.

"I ain't interested in your swimming ability, I wanna know about that stiff and those cigarettes. What'd you find?"

"Well, we'll tackle the butts first. They're out. I had the tobacco and the paper analyzed, triple-ply. No narcotic, not dipped or impregnated in any poisonous solution—absolutely nothing wrong anywhere."

"Wa-a-ait a minute, wa-a-ait a minute now!" I haul up short. "I got eyes. What was that brownish stain on the mouthpiece of the one he'd smoked? Don't try to hand me it was nicotine discoloring the paper, either, because it didn't run all the way around the tip. It was just in one place and one only!"

"That," he explains, "was a dot of dried blood. He'd torn his lip there in smoking the cigarette. Too dry. Often happens."

"O.K.," I say disappointedly, "let's get on with it. What are you putting down in your report as the direct cause?"

"Paralysis of the nerve centers." He takes a turn or two around the room. "But there was no rhyme or reason for it. It wasn't a stroke, it wasn't apoplexy, it wasn't the bubonic plague—"

Through the window just then, I see the kid look up at the upper part of the house, as though a pebble or something fell near him and attracted his attention. But I'm too interested in what we're talking about to give him much thought right then. He sort of smiles in a goofy way.

I turn back to the examiner. "Then you can't tell me anything? You're a big help!"

"I can't give you any more facts than those. And since it's my business to give you facts and not theories, I'll shut up."

"The pig's aunt you will!" I blaze. "You'll give me whatever you've got whether you can back it up or not."

"Well, this is off the record then. I'd be laughed at from here to

Frisco and back. But the only close parallel to the symptoms of that corpse, the only similarity to the condition of the blood stream and to the bodily rigidity and distortion I've ever found, was in bodies I used to see every once in awhile along the sides of the roads, years ago, when I was a young medical student out in India, Java, and the Malay States."

"Write a book about it!" I think impatiently. "And what stopped 'em?" I hurry him up. It's like pulling teeth to get anything out of this guy.

"The bite of a cobra," he says in a low voice.

The front door inches open and the kid slides back in the house and tracks up the stairs sort of noiseless and self-effacing like he didn't want to attract attention. He's been up all night, and I figure he's going to bed and don't even turn my head and look around at him. Besides, I've finally got something out of this guy, and it chimes in with what's been in the back of my mind ever since she first showed up here, and I'm too excited right then to think of anything else.

"Then what's holding you up?" I holler out excitedly. "Put it down in your report, that's all I need! If you ain't sure of the species, just say 'poisonous snakebite.' What are you waiting for? You want me to catch the thing and stuff it for you before you'll go ahead? I'll produce it for you all right!"

I remember those "chickens" of hers in that crate with the wire netting—upstairs in her room at this very minute. Chickens, me eye! And a couple of hours after I should have thought of it, I realize that chickens don't drink milk, they peck corn.

"And when I do produce it, the findings aren't going to be 'accidental death.' The charge is going to be murder in the first degree—with a cobra for a weapon."

Whereupon, he goes and throws cold water all over me. "You can produce dozens of 'em," he tells me, shaking his head. "You can empty the whole zoo into this house, and I still can't put anything like that into my report."

I nearly have pups all over the carpet. "Why? For Pete's sake, why?"

"Because, for anyone to die of snake bite, there has to be a bite—

first of all. The fangs of any snake would leave a puncture, a livid mark, a zone of discoloration. What do you suppose my assistant and I were doing all night, sitting playing rummy? I tell you we went over every inch of body surface with the highest-powered microscopes available. There wasn't a blemish. Absolutely no place anywhere into which the venom could have been injected."

I throw all the possibilities that occur to me at him one after the other. I'm not a trained doc, remember. Anyway, he squelches them as fast as they come.

"When you examined the blood stream, or what was left of it, weren't there heavier traces of this stuff in some parts than others? Couldn't you track it down from there?"

"It's very volatile. It diffuses itself all over the system, like lightning, once it's in. Does away with itself as a specific. It's not a blood poison, it's a nerve poison. You can tell it's there by the effects rather than by the cause."

"How about a hypodermic needle?"

"That would have left a swelling—and a puncture too; even if smaller than the snake's fangs, even if invisible to the naked eye."

"How about internally?"

"It doesn't kill internally. We analyzed the contents of his stomach. Nothing foreign there, nothing harmful."

I move the position of one of the chairs in the room rather suddenly—with my foot. "What a temper," he says reproachfully.

"Maybe I've stuck too close to the village green," I let him know. "Maybe I should have had L. A. in on this."

"Suit yourself. But, if you go over our heads like that, you better have a direct accusation ready—and be able to back it up. I can't support you if it comes to a showdown. This report'll have to stay the way it is—'paralysis of the nerve centers, of unknown origin'—take it or leave it."

"You take it," I say violently, and I tell him a good place to keep it while I'm at it. "You get L. A. on the wire for me when you go back," I order him as he prepares to leave in a huff, "and have 'em send a squad up here with butterfly nets and insect guns. We're gonna play cops and robbers." And when he takes his departure we don't say goodbye to each other.

I lock the front door on the inside and ditto the back door and drop both keys into my pocket. Then I latch all the shutters and fasten down all the windows with a hammer and wedges of wood. She isn't going to get away from here until I've cinched this thing one way or the other, and I've got to be having some sleep soon. I can't hold out forever.

I go upstairs, and there's not a sound around me. It's been light out for a long time now, but the upstairs hallway is still dim, and at the end of it, where the kid's room is, lamplight is shining through the crack of his door. I thought he was asleep by now, and I get a little worried for a minute, but when I tap on it and hear him say, "Come in," I heave a long breath of relief, it's sweet music to my ears.

He's in bed, all right, but he's propped up reading a book, with a cigarette in his mouth. He hasn't noticed it got light and he's forgotten to turn out the lamp. That's all right—I used to do that too, when I was his age. "Didn't mean to butt in," I say. I figure it's a good time to patch up that little set-to we had downstairs before.

He beats me to the rap. "I'm sorry about what happened before."

"Forget it." I haul up a chair and sit down alongside the bed, and we're all set to bury the hatchet and smoke the pipe of peace. "You got me wrong, that was all." I frisk myself, no results. "Let's have one of your butts."

"I'm out of them myself," he grins.

"Then where'd you get that one?" I get a little uncomfortable for a minute. I give it a quick look. It's just one of the regular-size ones though.

"One of Veda's," he admits. He keeps talking around it without taking it out of his mouth. "I been dragging on it for ages, they last a long time." So that's why it's down to ordinary size! "Now don't go getting all het up again," he says as he sees me change color. "I didn't ask her for it, she offered it to me."

I try to remind myself those butts got a clean bill of health. I try to tell myself that if nothing's happened so far, after he's smoked it all this time—

I can hardly stay still on the chair. I lean forward and watch his face anxiously. He seems perfectly normal. "Feel all right, kid?"

"Never felt better."

Then I see something that I haven't noticed until now, and I go pins and needles all over. "Wait a minute, whatcha been doing? Where'd ya get all that red all over your mouth?"

He turns all colors of the rainbow and looks guilty. "Aw, there you go again! All right, she kissed me. So what? I couldn't push her away, could I?"

My heart's pounding in my ears and I can hardly talk. It's too much like the set-up she gave the old man! She was rouging her lips, she was getting set to kiss him when I left them alone, and when I found him he had one of her butts. Still, there's no use losing my head, nothing's happened to the kid so far, and if I frighten him—

I haul out my handkerchief and try to talk slow and easy. "Here, get it off with this. Get it off easy, don't rub." My wrist is jerking like sixty as I pass it to him, though. "Just sort of smooth it off, keep your tongue away from it."

That's where the mistake happens. To do it he has to get the cigarette out of the way. He touches it, he parts his lips. It goes with the upper one! It's adhered, just like the old man's!

He flips it out, there isn't time for me to stop him, he winces and he says "Ow!"

I'm on my feet like a shot. "What'd you do?"

"Caught my lip on it," he says and tosses it down angrily. He's out of bed before he knows what's happened to him and I've flung him halfway across the room to the door. "Bathroom, quick!" I pant. "One of my razor blades—cut it wide open, split it to the gums if you have to, bleed like a pig, it's your only chance!"

He does it, he must read death on my face, for once he doesn't argue. I don't go with him, can't. I'm shaking so, I'd cut his throat. The water gives a roar into the washbasin, he lets out a yell of pain, and he's done it.

Second mistake. Opening it up like that only gives all the red stuff a chance to get in. He's young, maybe he could have fought off the smaller amount that would have penetrated through the original slit. Too late, the examiner's words come back to me: "It isn't a blood poison, it's a nerve poison. Letting the blood out won't help, it isn't rattlesnake venom." I've finished him!

He's back in the doorway, white as a sheet. Blood's pouring down his chin and the front of his pajamas look like he'd had a nosebleed. It isn't a nosebleed; he's opened the cleft of his lip to the nostrils. It's started in already though, the poison; it's in him already, and he doesn't know what it is.

"What'd you make me do that for? I feel—" He tries to get to me and totters. Then I guess he knows what it is—for just one minute he knows what it is—that's all the time he has to know it in.

I get him onto the bed—that's all I can do for him—and the rest of it happens there. He just says one thing more. "Don't let me, will you? Charlie, I dowanna die!" in a voice like a worn-out record running down under a scratchy needle. After that, he's not recognizable as anything human any more.

I can't do anything for him, so I just turn my face to the wall and shut out the rustling with my hands clapped to my ears. "Charlie, I dowanna die!" He isn't saying it any more, it's over already, but it goes on and on. For years I'll probably hear it.

After awhile I cover him over without looking and I go to my own room. I've got a job to do—a job no one but me can do. While I'm in there, there's a sort of fluttery sound for a minute outside, as though something whisked itself along the hall and down the stairs just then. That's all right, I took care of the doors and windows before I came up. "Charlie, I dowanna die!" No, no insanity plea. Not this time—that's too easy. An asylum's too good.

I get my gun out of the closet where it's been since we came here, and I break it. Two slugs in it. Two are enough. I crack it shut again and shove it on my hip. Then I take a long pole that's standing in a corner, the handle of a floor-mop or something, and I go across the hall to her room. She's pounding on the door downstairs. I can hear her shaking it, clawing at it, trying to get out of the house. She can wait.

I shift the chicken coop around so it faces my way, and *zing, zing, zing* goes the wire netting. Then I step back and prod the hinged slat open with the end of the long pole. Then I dig the pole into the bedclothes and loosen them up. There's no wire mesh over the place that the one movable slat covers. There's sort of a wicket left in it there, and out through that wicket comes the hooded head, the slow, coiling, glistening length of one of the world's deadly things, the king cobra of India! I see Veda's twin before my dilating eyes. The same scaly, gleaming covering; even the same marking like a question-mark on its hood! Endless lengths of it come out, like gigantic black-and-green toothpaste out of a squeezed tube, and I want to throw up in revulsion. Twelve feet of it—a monster. The story might have ended then, right in the room there—but the thing is torpid, sluggish from the cold climate and its long confinement.

It sees me, standing back across the room from it. Slowly it rears up, waist high, balancing on tightening coils for the thrust. Quickly the horrid hood swells, fills out with animosity. There's not a sound in the room. I'm not breathing. The pounding and the lunging at the door downstairs has stopped some time ago. And in the silence I suddenly know that she's come back into the room with me, that she's standing somewhere right behind me.

I dare not turn around and look; dare not take my eyes off the swaying, dancing funnel of death before me for an instant. But I feel a weight suddenly gone from my hip. She's got my gun!

Over my shoulder comes a whisper. "You've locked death into the house with you."

The split second seems to expand itself into an hour. She edges her way along the wall until she comes into my range of vision. But my eyes can't even flicker toward her. I know my own gun's on me. But rather that than the other death.

Suddenly, I dip on buckled knees. I heave the long pole out from the bed like a fishing rod. A scarlet blanket and sheet come with it. The sheet drops off on the way, the blanket, heavier, clings to the end. The loathsome, fetid mouth of the thing below it has already gone wide. The blanket falls in swift effacement, covers the monster in stifling folds just as its head has gone back in the last preparatory move.

A fraction of an instant later, there is a lightning lunge against the blanket. A bulge appears there which soon is gone again—where the snake's head struck after its spring. After that, everything is squirm-ing, thrashing, cataleptic movement under the folds as it tries to free itself.

There's a flash of fire from the wall and my hand burns—but if I drop that pole I'm gone. I wield the mop-handle in my bleeding, tortured hand, making it hiss through the air, flattening the blanket under it. It breaks in two under the terrific impacts, but I keep on with the short end of it until there's no life under that blanket any more. Even then I step on the mess and grind and stamp with my steel-rimmed heels until the blanket discolors in places.

Veda stands there against the wall, the smoking gun in her hand, moaning: "You have killed a god!" If she really worshipped that thing, her whole world has come to an end. The gun slips from her hand, clatters to the floor. I swoop for it and get it again. She sinks down to her knees, her back against the wall, very still, looking at me. Her breath is coming very fast, she doesn't betray her feelings in any other way.

Sometimes under the greatest tension, in moments almost of insanity, you can think the clearest. I am almost insane just then. And, in a flash, the whole set-up comes to me, now that it's too late, now that the old man and the kid are gone. That lunge at the blanket just now has told me the whole story. The thick flannel I found in her drawer!

She held that before the opening in the crate and extracted the venom that way—when the cobra struck. Then she mixed it with her rouge in the little wooden mortar. Then she waxed her lips with camphor ice, freezing the pores tight shut, forming an impervious base for the red stuff. Then she kissed them, smeared them with it, offered them a cigarette to smoke—

They're still there on the dresser, her long, thick-tipped cigarettes. I take a couple out of the box. Then I take the little bottle of mucilage, standing with all the perfumes, and I let a drop of it fall on the end of each cigarette. She did that too—I know that, now.

It dries in no time, but the moisture of the human mouth will dampen it again and cause the paper to stick to the lips. She sees me do all this, and yet she doesn't move, doesn't try to escape. Her god is dead, the fatalism of the East has her in its grip. Almost, I relent. But—"Charlie, I dowanna die!" rings in my ears.

I turn to her. You'd think nothing had happened, you'd think the kid was only asleep back there in his room, the way I talk to her. "Have a cigarette."

She shakes her head and backs away along the wall.

"Better have a cigarette," I say, and I take up the gun and bead it at her forehead. This is no act, and she can tell the difference. I won't even ask her a second time. She takes a cigarette. "What have I done?" she tries to say.

"Nothing," I answer, "nothing that I can prove, or even care to prove any more. Doll up. You have it with you."

She smiles a little, maybe fatalistically, or maybe because she still thinks she can outsmart me. She rouges her lips. She raises the cigarette. But I see the half-curves it makes. "No you don't, not that end. The way it's supposed to be smoked."

She puts the glued end in and I hold the match for her. She can't tell yet about it but the smile goes and her eyes widen with fear.

I light my own—that's glued, too. "I'm going to smoke right along with you; one of these is no different from the other. See, I have a clear conscience; have you?" I'm going to match her, step by step—I want to know just when it happens. I didn't know I could be that cruel, but—"Charlie, I dowanna die!"

She begins by taking quick little puffs, not letting it stay any time in her mouth, and each time she puts it in at a different place. She thinks she'll get around it that way. That's easy to stop. "Keep your hands down. Touch it one more time and I'll shoot."

"Siva!" she moans. I think it is their goddess of death or something. Then to me: "You are going to kill me?"

"No, you are going to kill yourself. You last through that cigarette and you are welcome to your insanity plea when they get here from L.A."

We don't talk any more after that. Slowly the cigarettes burn down. I don't take mine out, either. A dozen times her hands start upward and each time the gun stops them. Time is on my side. She begins to have trouble breathing, not from fear now, from nicotine and burnt paper. Her eyes fill with moisture. Not even an inveterate smoker can consume a ten-inch fag like that without at least a couple of clear breaths between drags.

I can't stand it myself any more and out comes my own, and there's a white-hot sting to my lower lip. She holds on, though, for dear life.

So would I, if death was going to be the penalty. I can see her desperately trying to free hers by working the tip of her tongue around the edges. No good. She begins to strangle deep down in her throat, water's pouring out of her eyes. She twists and turns and retches and tries to get a free breath. It's torture, maybe, but so were the thousand red-hot needles piercing that kid's body upstairs— awhile ago.

All at once, a deep groan seems to come all the way up from her feet. The strangling and the gasping stop and the cigarette is smoldering on the floor. A thread of blood runs down her chin—purer, cleaner than the livid red stuff all around it. I lay the gun down near her and I watch her. Let her make her own choice!

"There's only one more bullet in it," I tell her. "If you think you can stand what's coming, you can pay me back with it."

She knows too well what it's going to be like, so she has no time to waste.

She grabs for the gun and her eyes light up. "I am going, but you are coming with me!" she pants.

She levels my rod at me. Four times she pulls the trigger and four times it clicks harmlessly. The first chamber and the last must have been the loaded ones, and the ones in between were empty.

Now, she has no more time to waste on getting even. The twitching has already set in. She turns the gun on herself.

"Once more will get you out of it," I say, and I turn away.

This time, there's a shattering explosion behind me and something heavy falls like a log. I don't bother looking. I wrap my handkerchief around my throbbing hand and go downstairs to the front door to wait for the men from L.A. to show up. I don't smoke while I'm waiting, either.

(1935)

Red Liberty

Katie must have been out of humor to say a thing like that, but it sure rankled. "And that's why you're no further than you are," she went on. "Ten years from now you'll still be a second-grade detective pinching pickpockets. Movies and beer—that's all you ever think of whenever you have any time to yourself. Why don't you improve your mind? Why don't you read a book? Why don't you go to a museum once in a while and look at the beautiful statues?"

I nearly fell over. "Look at statues!" I gasped. "What for?"

I seemed to have her there for a minute. "Why—why, to see how they're made," she said finally, looking bewildered.

There didn't seem to be much sense to it, but anything to keep peace in the family. I reached for my hat and gave a deep sigh. "You win," I said. "I'll try anything once."

Riding down in the sub I got a bright idea. Instead of wasting a lot of time looking at a flock of little statues I'd look at one big one instead and get the whole thing over with. So I got out at the Battery, forked over thirty-five cents for one round-trip ticket and got on the little ferry that takes you down the bay to the Statue of Liberty. It was the biggest statue around, and if there was any truth to what Katie said, it ought to improve me enough to last for the rest of the year.

There were about ten others making the trip with me, and as soon as everyone was on board, the tub gives a peep with its whistle and starts off, graceful as a hippopotamus. First the statue was about the size of your thumb. It came gliding over the water getting bigger all the time, until it was tall as an office building. It was pea-green, just like on the postcards. Finally the ferry tied up at a long pier built on piles that stuck out from the island, and everybody got off. There was another crowd there waiting to get on and go back. It seems the trip is only made once every hour.

It was certainly an eyeful once you got close up under it. The stone base alone was six stories high, and after that there was nothing but statue the rest of the way. There was just room enough left over on the island for a little green lawn with cannonballs for markers, a couple of cement paths, and some benches. But on the other wide, away from the city, there were a group of two-story brick houses, lived in by the caretakers I suppose.

Anyway, we went in through a thick, brutal-looking metal door painted black, and down a long stone corridor, and after a couple of turns came to an elevator. A spick-and-span one too, that looked as if it had just been installed. This only went up as far as the top of the pedestal, and after that you had to walk the other seventeen stories. The staircase was a spiral one only wide enough to let one person through at a time and it made tough going, but several times a little platform opened out suddenly on the way up, with an ordinary park bench placed there to rest on. There was always the same fat man sitting heaving on it by the time I got to it, with not much room left over for anybody else. When I say fat, I mean anywheres from two hundred fifty pounds up. I'd noticed him on the boat, with his thin pretty little wife. "Brother," I said the second time I squeezed in next to him on the bench, "pardon me for butting in, but why do it? You must be a glutton for punishment."

His wife had gone on the rest of the way up without waiting for him. He just wheezed for a long time, then finally he got around to answering me. "Brother," he said with an unhappy air, "she can think up more things for me to do like this. You know the old saying, nobody loves a—"

I couldn't help liking him right off. "Buck up, Slim," I said, "they're all the same. Mine thinks I'm a lowbrow and sends me out looking at statues so I'll learn something."

"And have you?" he wanted to know.

"Yep, I've learned there's no place like home," I told him. "Well, keep your chins up," I said, and with that I left him and went on up.

At the very top you had to push through a little turnstile, and then you were finally up in the head of the statue. The crown or tiara she wears, with those big spikes sticking out, has windows running from side to side in a half-circle. I picked the nearest one and stuck my head out. You could see for miles. The boats in the harbor were the size of match-boxes. Down below on the lawn the cannonballs looked like raisins in a pudding. Well, I stood there like that until I figured I'd gotten my thirty-five cents' worth. The rest were starting to drift down again, so I turned to go too.

At the window next to me I noticed the fat man's pretty little wife standing there alone. He evidently hadn't been able to make the grade yet and get up there with her. She was amusing herself by scribbling her initials or something on the thick stone facing of the window, which was about a foot deep and wider at the outside than at the inside, the tiara being a semicircle. That was nothing. Most people do that whenever they visit any monument or point of interest. All five of the facings were chock-full of names, initials, dates, addresses, and so on, and as time and the weather slowly effaced the earlier ones there was always room for more. She was using an eyebrow pencil or something for hers though, instead of plain lead, I noticed.

By that time we were alone up there. The others were all clattering down the corrugated-iron staircase again, and the ferry was on its way back from the Battery to pick us up. Much as I would have enjoyed waiting to get an eyeful of the shape her stout spouse was going to be in when he got up there, I figured I'd had enough. I started down and left her there behind me, chin propped in her hands and staring dreamily out into space, like Juliet waiting at her balcony for a high-sign from Romeo.

You went down by a different staircase than you came up, I mean it was the same spiral but the outside track this time, and there was no partition between, just a handrail. There were lights strung all along the stairs at regular intervals, of course; otherwise the place would have been pitch-dark. Some were just house bulbs; others were small searchlights turned outward against the lining of the statue, which was painted silver. In other words, anyone that was going up while you were coming down had to pass you in full view, almost rub elbows with you. No one did. The whole boatload that had come out with me was down below by now.

When I got down even with the first resting-platform, with only a rail separating me from it, something caught the corner of my eye just as my head was due to go below the platform level. I climbed back up a step or two, dipped under the railing, and looked under the bench, where it lay. Then I saw what it was and reached in and pulled it out. It was just somebody's brown felt hat, which had rolled under the bench.

I turned it upside down and looked in it. Knox—and P.G. were the initials. But more important, it hadn't been left there yesterday or last week, but just now. The sweat on the headband hadn't dried yet, and there was plenty of it—the leather strip was glistening with it. That was enough to tell me whose it was, the fat guy's. He'd been sitting on this bench when I left him—dripping with exertion—and I remembered seeing this very lid in his hand, or one the same color and shape. He'd taken it off and sat holding it in his hand while he mopped his melting brow.

He hadn't gone on up to where I'd left his wife, for he'd neither arrived while I was still up there nor had I passed him on the way down. It was a cinch he'd given it up as a bad job and gone on down from here, without tackling the last of the seventeen "stories" or twists. Still I couldn't figure how he could come to forget his hat, leave it behind like this, fagged out or not. Then I thought, "Maybe the poor gink had a heart attack, dizzy spell or something and had to be carried down, that's how it came to be overlooked." So I took it with me and went on down to try and locate him and hand it back to him.

I rang when I got to where the elevators started from, and when the car had come up for me I asked the operator: "What happened to that fat guy, know the one I mean? Anything go wrong with him? I picked up his hat just now."

"He hasn't come down yet," he told me. "I'd know him in a minute. He must be still up there."

"He isn't up above, I just came from there myself. And he's the last guy in the world who'd walk down the six stories from here when there's a car to take him. How do you figure it?"

"Tell you where he might be," said the attendant. "Outside there on the parapet. They all go out there for a last look through the telescope before they get in the car."

"Well, wait up here for a minute until I find out. If he shows up tell him I've got his hat."

I went out and made a complete circuit of the place, then doubled back and did it in reverse. Not a soul on it. It was a sort of terrace that ran around the top of the base, protected by a waist-high stone ledge on all four sides. It was lower down than the head of Miss Liberty of course, but still plenty high.

I went back to the elevator operator. "Nothing doing. You sure you didn't take him down in your car without noticing?"

"Listen," he said. "When he got on the first time he almost flattened me against the door getting in. I woulda known it the second time. I ain't seen him since."

"Are there any lavatories or restrooms on the way up?"

"Naw," he said, "nothing like that."

"Then he musta walked down the rest of the way without waiting for you. Take me down to the bottom—"

"If he did, he's the first one ever did that yet. That's what the elevators are here for." He threw the switch. "Say," he said, and I saw his face light up as if he was almost hoping something would happen to break the monotony of his job, "maybe he—you don't suppose he—"

I knew what he was driving at. "You're trying to tell me he took a jump for himself, aren't you? G'wan, he couldn't have even raised himself up over that stone ledge out there to do it! And if he had, there'd a been a crowd around him below. Everyone on the island woulda seen him land. I looked down just now. They're all strolling around down there, addressing postcards, taking it easy waiting for the boat."

His face dropped again. "They none of 'em try that from here, they always pick bridges instead. Nothing ever happens here."

"Cheer up, Suicide Johnny," I told him, "your cage will probably fall down the shaft some day and kill everyone in it."

When he let me out I made straight for the concession pavilion down near the pier, where most of the ten who had come out with me were hanging around buying postcards and ice-cream cones, waiting for the ferry to pull in. It wasn't more than fifty yards away by this time, coasting in a big half-circle from the right to get into position, with its engine already cut off.

The fat man wasn't in the refreshment house—one look inside from the doorway told me that. I asked one or two of the others if they'd seen him since they'd come out of the statue. Nobody had, although plenty had noticed him going in—especially on the way up—just as I had.

"He must be around some place," one of them suggested indifferently. "Couldn't very well get off the island until the ferry came back for him."

"No kidding?" I remarked brittlely. "And here I am thinking he went up in a puff of smoke!"

I went around to the other side of the base, following a series of cement walks bordered with ornamental cannonballs. No rotund gentleman in sight. I inquired at the dispensary at the back of the island, and even at one or two of the brick cottages the caretakers lived in, thinking he might have stopped in there because of illness or out of curiosity. Nothing doing.

I completed my circuit of the terraced lawn that surrounds the statue and returned to the front of it again. It had dawned on me by now that I was going to a hell of a whole lot of trouble just to return a man's hat to him, but his complete disappearance was an irritant that had me going in spite of myself. It was the size of the man that burned me more than anything. I wouldn't have minded if it had been somebody less conspicuous, probably wouldn't have noticed him in the first place, but to be as big as all that and then to evaporate completely—

The ferry was in when I got back and the passengers were straggling up the long, almost horizontal gangplank. It hadn't brought anybody out with it this trip, as the statue was closed to visitors after 4:30 each day and this was its last round trip. "Turn this in at the lost-and-found for me, will you?" I said, shoving the hat at one of the soldiers on pier-duty as I went by. "I just found it up there."

"Hand it in at the other end, at the Battery," he said. "That's where they come and claim things."

I was so dead-sure of lamping the lid's owner on the ferry, this being its last trip back, that I hung onto it without arguing and went looking for him in the saloon, or whatever they call the between-decks part of a ferry. Meanwhile the landing platform had been rolled back and we'd started to nose up the bay.

"He's got to be on here," I said to myself. "He's not spending the night back there on the island. And nothing that floats came to take him off between the time we all got off the first time and just now when this thing called back for us." I knew that for a fact, because the ferry only made the run once every hour, on the half-hour, and it was the only one in service. So I went all over the schooner from bow to stern, upstairs, downstairs, inside and out. In the saloon a couple of kids were sitting one on each side of their father, swinging their legs over the edge of the long bench that ran all around it. And a guy who didn't give a hoot about the skyline outside was reading Hellinger in the *Mirror*. Nobody else.

On the port deck the other half-dozen were sitting in chairs, just like they would on a transatlantic greyhound only without rugs, and one or two were leaning over the rail trying to kid themselves they were on an ocean trip. He wasn't there either. Then when I went around to the starboard deck (only maybe it was the port and the other was starboard, don't expect too much from a guy that was never further away than Coney Island), there was his wife sitting there as big as life, all by herself and the only person on that side of the scow which faced good old Joisey. I walked by her once and took a squint at her without stopping. She never even saw me. She was staring peacefully, even dreamily, out at the bay.

Now, I had no absolute proof that she was his wife, or had made the excursion with him at all. He had mentioned his wife to me, so his wife was along with him, no doubt about that. But each time I had overtaken him on one of the benches inside the statue she had gone up just ahead of him and I had missed seeing her. Then when I got up to the top this particular woman had been up there ahead of me scrawling her initials. That much I was sure of. She had been at the next observation window to me with that same "come-and-take-me" far-away look that she had now. But it was only by putting two and two together that I had her labeled as his wife; I had no definite evidence of it. So I stopped up at the other end of the narrow little deck and turned and started back toward her.

I don't care who a guy is or what his job is, it isn't easy for him to accost a woman sitting minding her own business like that, unless he's the masher type—which I'm not. "If she gives me a smack in the puss," I said to myself, "I'm gonna throw this son-of-a—hat in the water and make up my mind I never saw any fat guy; it was just a trick of the lighting effects in the statue!"

I stopped dead in my tracks in front of her and tipped my hat and said: "Pardon me, but I've got y'husband's hat here." I held it out.

She looked me up and down and a lot of little icicles went tinkling along the deck. "I don't know what you're talking about," she said. "I haven't any husband—and I'm not interested in picking one up on a ferryboat in the bay!"

This was enough to sour a saint; it was rubbing it in a little too much. First there's a fat man and his wife. Then there's no fat man. And now it seems there's no wife either. Only a hat.

"I'm no picker-upper," I growled. "Just let's get this straight though. On the way over I distinctly noticed you with a very hefty gentleman. You were talking to each other. You were sitting side by side out on this deck-bench. And you both stood up together when it was time to get off. I remember that distinctly, on account of your shapes reminded me of the number 10. Then later I saw the guy by himself in there. And that's the last; he does a fade-out. Now all I'm trying to do is get this blasted kelly back to—"

The temperature didn't go up any. "Well, why pick on me?" she said. "Why marry me off to him, and turn me into his hatcheck girl in the bargain? Who are you, anyway, the census-taker? All right, a fat clown did sit down next to me on the way out and try to take a shine to me. So what? I never saw him before in my life, don't know his name from Adam. You saw me talking to him all right—I told him a thing or two, only I'm not the kind screams for help and makes a scene. And if he stood up at the same time I did and tried to stick close to me, I outdistanced him once we hit those stairs, don't you worry. And if you think you rate any higher than he did just 'cause your stomach goes in instead of out, think again! Next time I go on an excursion I'm bringing a bulldog along—"

"Oh, just one of these strong, silent women! Not a word to say, eh?" I told her. "Well, suppose you give me your name and address just for fun."

She hoisted herself up and took a quick step away. "I'm going to get a cop!" she burst out.

I side-stepped around and got in front of her. "You've got one," I said, and let the badge slide back into my vest pocket again. "Now are you going to tell me what I asked you?"

"You can't compel me to give you my name if I don't want to!" she said hotly. "Who do you think you're dealing with, some fly-by-night chippy? I don't care whether you're a detec—"

Which was true enough, as far as that goes. But she had me steamed up by now. "Either you identify yourself, or you can consider yourself under arrest!" I didn't have a thing on her, and I knew it. I had no way of proving that what she had told me about the fat man wasn't so. True, he had mentioned his wife to me sitting on the bench in the statue, but he hadn't tagged this particular woman or anyone else in the group as being "it." He hadn't even made it clear whether his wife had accompanied him on the excursion. For all I knew she might be sitting at home at this very moment, just as my own was.

Meanwhile, "—never so insulted in my life!" she was boiling, but she was going through the motions of coming across, with angrily shaking hands. She threw back the lid of her pocketbook and fished around inside it. "I didn't expect a third degree like this," she snapped, "so I didn't bring my pedigree with me! However, I'm Alice Colman, Van Raalte Apartments, Tarrytown. Take it or leave it!"

I felt like two cents by now, especially as I noticed her eyes growing shiny with tears. Even if the fat man had met with foul play, which there was no proof of so far, she hadn't been anywhere near him at the time it happened. She had been away up at the top looking dreamy. I was only doing this because I'd seen them together on the trip out, and she needn't have made me feel like such a lug. I covered it up by going through with what I was doing, taking out my notebook and jotting down the info. "Miss Alice Colman," I said out loud, squinting down my pencil.

"I didn't say that!" she flared. "Oh, let me alone, you dog!" And she whisked herself off down the deck as if she couldn't stand any more. I could see her shoulders shaking as she went. I let her alone after that, didn't try to follow her up.

"Well, well, well," I sighed, "I certainly have the light touch with dolls!" Her last crack, I took it, meant that she was a Mrs. and not a Miss.

If I had any doubts that the fat guy might have turned out to be on the ferry after all, hiding behind a cuspidor or something, and that I had simply missed seeing him until now, they were very soon settled once the tub had tied up at the South Ferry landing. I stationed myself on the lower end of the plank ahead of everyone, and stopped them one by one as they tried to go past. "Police headquarters. . . . Name, please. . . . Address. Got anything to back it up?" And I killed the inevitable "What's this for?" each time it came with a terse "None of your business!"

When I was through I had a line on every one who had made the outing with me—at least if anything turned up now I was no longer in the dark. All but the very guy who was missing. And he was still missing. He had definitely not made the trip back on the boat. The Colman person was the last one off, and came sailing by me head in air with the cold remark: "Be sure you follow me—low-down common bully!" I just stood there and looked after her, scratching my head. It was only after she'd gone that I realized she was the only one of the lot who hadn't backed up her name and address with documentary proof.

But meanwhile there was something else I wanted to see about.

I went around to the ticket office in the ferry building; it was closed, of course. Ours had been the last trip of the day. I hammered on the wicket, and then I went around and pounded on the door. Luckily they were still in there, counting the day's receipts or something. I recognized the guy that had sold me my own ticket. "Headquarters, it's all right, lemme in a minute." And when he had, "Now look. Do you remember selling a ticket down the bay to a fat guy, puffy cheeks like this, blue suit, brown hat, when the last boatful went out?"

"Yeah," he said, "yeah, I do."

"How many did he buy? One or two?"

"Two," he said decidedly. "I been selling 'em all day long, but I can remember that all right because he was lamebrained, couldn't count straight. He wanted to tell me four-forty change was coming to him out of a finn. I says, 'Buddy,' I says, 'in my country two times thirty-five adds up to—'"

"Never mind the trailer," I squelched. "Did she—did anyone come up to the window with him when he bought them?"

"Naw, he come up to the window alone and bought two tickets. I didn't see who was with him."

"Being sore at him, you didn't take a gander out the window after him after he moved on? Most ticket-sellers would."

"They were all on line," he explained. "I didn't have time, had to wait on the next rubberneck."

Well, if he'd bought two tickets his wife was with him—he hadn't bought them just because he was overweight himself, that was a cinch. As for his wife, runner-up to himself when it came to staying out of sight, little Alice Colman was elected for the time being. Which added up to this—I was going back to that island. She could hold for awhile. If nothing had happened to him, then it was none of my business whether she was wife, girl-friend, or total stranger to him. But if something had—I wasn't forgetting that she was the only person outside myself I'd seen him talking to.

I beat it outside to the ferry again. It was still there, but fixing to go wherever it is they go for the night when they're not in service. Or maybe it was just going to stay put. But not while I knew it.

A couple of tattooed arms tried to bar my way up the gangplank. "One side," I said, and the badge was getting a high polish just from rubbing against the serge so much, "I gotta see the captain before he slips off his suspenders!"

"He uses safety-pins," he corrected me dryly, "but go ahead—"

He came out of the saloon just then struggling into a lumber-jacket, evidently going ashore to catch up on his suds.

"Say, y'gotta take me back there," I burst out. "Here's what—" And I explained all about the hefty passenger that had gone out and hadn't come back.

He was one person the badge didn't mean a thing to; he was used to being boss of the roost. "Go 'way, man, you're out of your head!" he boomed. "This boat's asleep for tonight, I wouldn't make another run there for St. Peter himself. If he missed it and got left behind, that's his tough luck. He'll just have to wait over until nine in the morning, there are plenty of benches on the island, just like Central P—" and he took the most graceful spiral spit over the rail I had ever seen—and made it.

"But y' don't get what I mean!" I howled, shoving the brown felt in his face. "He didn't just miss it—something's happened to him. Now give your orders. You know what this means, don't you? You're obstructing—"

"I take my orders from the company," he said surlily, looking longingly in the direction of the dives along South Street. "If that piece of tin means anything why don't it get you a police launch?"

But I wasn't going to be a back-room laughing-stock for the rest of the year in case I did get there with a launch and find the fat guy had stayed behind to pick dandelions or something. I went ashore again and had it out with one of the agents in the ferry house, and he in turn had to telephone one of the higher muck-a-mucks and put it up to him, and then sign an order for me to show the captain.

Some reporters had gotten wind that something was up, in the mysterious way that only reporters can, and a couple of them were already hanging around outside when I came out. "What's the excitement?" they wanted to know, licking their chops. "What's it all about?" "Wotcha doing with two hats?" one of them cracked suspiciously.

"I always carry a spare," I said, "in case the wind blows the first one off."

They looked sort of doubtful, but before they could do anything about it I was back on the ferry and gave orders to keep them off. "Here's your instructions, admiral," I told the captain, who was drooling by this time and biting his nails at the thought of being kept overtime. "I'll buy the first ten rounds," I assured him, "if this turns out to be a wild-goose chase."

"Hrrmph!" he growled, and turned around and hollered an order.

Back we plugged.

"How long you gonna be?" he wanted to know as I loped off at the island.

"When I show up again," I promised, "I'll be back." That old fellow could swear.

The thick, chilly-looking, black metal doors that led into the base were shut by this time. I had to get another permit from an officer on the island, and two soldiers were detailed to come with me. The only one who seemed to get any kick out of the proceedings was Suicide Johnny, who was routed out to run us up in the elevator. He was all grins. At last something was happening to break his monotony. "Gee," he said, throwing the switch in the car, "maybe he committed sewercide by hanging himself up there some place!"

"Nuts," I growled, "he couldn't have hoisted himself an inch—not without a derrick. We'll go up to the top," I told my two escorts when we got out of the car. "Start in from there and work our way down." They didn't say anything, but I could read their minds: "This guy was dropped on his head when he was a kid."

We climbed all that weary way back again and finally stood there panting. "He never got up this far," I said when I had my wind back, "because I was up here ahead of him. But I want to take a gander at some of these initials and names scrawled here on the stonework of the windows."

"Aw, them!" said one of the soldiers contemptuously. "Every chump that ever comes up here since the place was built has a crack at that."

"That's just the point," I said. I had a close look, first of all, at what my chief rooter and admirer Alice Colman had written, at the window next to the one I'd been standing at originally. It didn't say Alice Colman, it didn't say any name, but I knew her work. She'd used an eyebrow pencil and the mark it left was dark and greasy, different from the thin, faint pencil marks of the rest of them. It stood out like a headline on a newspaper.

I turned to one of the bored soldiers. "What's today's date?"

"The twenty-third," he said.

That's what I'd thought it was too. But Alice Colman seemed to have gotten her dates mixed. She had it down as the twenty-fourth.

Well, that could happen to anyone. But she had the hour right, at least. She'd even put that down—4 o'clock. Some people are like that, though. She'd visited this place at four o'clock and she wanted the world to know.

On top of that, though, came a hitch. She had an address down, and it wasn't her own. It was just five numbers and a letter, all run together. *254W51*. But that wasn't her own address. She'd given me that on the ferry, and I'd checked on it while I was hanging around in the ferry house waiting for the permit to come back here. Yes, the management of the Van Raalte Apartments had told me long-distance over the phone from Tarrytown, that Mrs. Alice Colman was a tenant of theirs. So she hadn't lied to me, yet she'd lied to the world at large when she was making her mark on Lady Liberty. There was something that I didn't get about it.

"Let's go down," I told the soldiers, "I want to look at that bench he was sitting on." By this time they both hated me heartily from the guts outward, I could see, but they turned and led the way.

We never got there, though. About midway between the head and where the bench was—in other words at about where the statue's shoulder came—there was a gap with a chain across it bearing the placard *Public Not Admitted*. I had noticed this twice before, the first time I came up and then later when I had gone down to look for him. Maybe the chain had thrown me off, the undisturbed chain stretched across it. And then, too, until you stood directly before it, it looked far smaller and more inaccessible than it actually was, the way the lights slurred past it and made it seem no more than a fold on the inside of the lady's gigantic metal draperies. This time, though, I stopped and asked them what it was.

"Oh, he ain't up in there!" they assured me instantly. "Nobody's allowed in there. Can't you read what that says? That used to lead up into the arm and torch in the old days. The arm started weakening little by little, so they shut the whole thing off a long time ago. It's boarded up just a little ways past the ch— Hey!" he broke off. "Where you going? You can't do that!"

"I'm going just that little ways between the chain and where the boarding is," I told him, spanning the cable with one leg. "If the arm lasted this long, one more guy ain't going to hurt it, I don't weigh enough. Throw your lights up after me. And don't tell me what I can't do when you see me already at it!"

The thing was a spiral, just like the other staircase that led to the head. Or rather, it started out to be, but at the very first half-turn-around it took, the boarding had already showed up, sealing it from top to bottom. That half-turn, however, cut off their lights, which shone in a straight line like any lights would. A triangle of blackness was left in one corner which they couldn't eliminate, no matter how they maneuvered the torches.

"Come on a little nearer with those things!" I called impatiently. "Come past the chain!"

They wouldn't budge. "Against orders," they called back.

I came down a few steps and reached for a torch myself. "Let me have one of those things. What d'ya think I'm doing, playing hide and seek with you? How we won the last war beats me!" I jumped up again and washed out the stubborn wedge of blackness with the thin beam in my hand.

Sure he was there. And fitted in just as neatly as though the space had been measured off for him ahead of time. In a sitting position on the turn of the steps, back propped against the boarding, legs drawn up under him to help keep him propped. I touched the side of his neck. He was as cold already as the metal statue that made a tomb for him.

"Got him," I shouted laconically. "Come on up and gimme a hand, you two."

"What's he doing up there?" one of those two clucks wanted to know.

"Waiting for judgment day."

They gasped and came on up, orders or no orders.

I bent down and looked at the backs of his shoes. The leather of both heels was scraped and scarred into a fuzz from lift to ankle. The backs of his trousers were dusty all the way to the knees. "Dragged up by the shoulders," I said, "by just one guy. If there'd been two, one of them would have taken him by the feet, like you're going to do getting him down out of here."

"How could one guy, any guy, haul that baby elephant all the way up there?" one of them wanted to know.

"You'd be surprised what one guy can manage to do if he's scared enough and has to work in a hurry," I assured him. "All right, get started. I'll handle your lights. It wasn't done up here anyway, so let's get down before we all take a header into the ocean, arm and all."

It wasn't easy, even for the two of them, to get down with him. Automatically, I figured that eliminated Alice Colman or any other woman as having had any part in it—except as an accessory.

The thing that had done it was lying under him when they got him up off the ground between them—a wicked-looking iron bar wrapped in a stiffened, blood-brown piece of rag. The wound—it was a deadly fracture—was on the side of the head just over the ear. He hadn't bled much, outside of the first splash on the padded weapon itself. The little there was after that had clung to the skin, running down behind the jawbone and into the collar of his shirt, hence nothing on the ground around the bench where the attack had occurred.

I examined the ground around the latter place. The two little tracks his heels had made as he was dragged backwards toward the hiding-place were there plain as day under my flashlight's beam, without the need of any powder or hocus-pocus of any kind. My only wonder was how I'd muffed seeing them when I stooped down to pick up his hat. But of course I hadn't used my torch then.

"Take him on down the rest of the way," I said. "No use parking with him here—it's gotta be done sooner or later anyway."

They loved the job—yeah they did! They must have lost ten pounds apiece in sweat, getting him down those seventeen stories of narrow, spiral staircase. When they were down at the elevator you could hear their heaving all the way up where I was. When I got down myself— I'd waited on the murder bench until the way was clear, no use dogging their footsteps an inch at a time—Suicide Johnny, with the body tucked into his car and the two guards in a state of collapse alongside of it, was wreathed in smiles. His fondest dream had come true. Something had at last happened. "Gee!" he kept murmuring. "Gee! A moider!"

I had Fatty carried over to the barracks, and an apoplectic-looking guy of Spanish War vintage whose collar was too tight for him came out to see what it was all about.

"Sorry to bother you," I said, "but there's just been a crime committed on your jurisdiction—man murdered up in the statue."

"Who are you, sirrr?" he boomed like a twenty-one gun salute. I felt like I was going to be shot at sunrise for daring to find anything the matter around his diggings.

"Denton, New York Homicide," I told him.

"Are you sure, sirrrr?" the old rooster crowed. He meant about the murder, not who I was. He wasn't going to believe me until he saw it with his own eyes, so I took him over and showed it to him.

"Now, just where do I stand?" I said, resting my hand on the stiff's knee.

"This, sirr," he orated, "is United States Government property. This is a matter for the Federal inves—"

I'd expected that. "Oh, so I get the air!" I interrupted heatedly. "After I been up and down that blank statue eighty-six times today. O.K., you put who you want on it. I'm going right ahead with it on my own. And we'll see who comes out ahead!" I got as far as the door, then I turned around and fired at him: "I'll even give your guy a head-start, just so you can't accuse me of withholding information. This guy is tagged Colman. He lived until today at the Van Raalte Apartments, Tarrytown, with his wife, who is thin, blond, pretty, blue eyes, about twenty-eight, and very ritzy front. But you won't find her there any more, so you can tell your guy to save his carfare. She didn't do it anyway. But if you want to get hold of her, and the guy that actually did it, I'll tell you where to look for them—"

"Where, sirrr?" he boomed like a great big firecracker.

"Today is Wednesday, isn't it?" I answered detachedly. "Well, send your guy around to Centre Street, say day after tomorrow, that would be Friday. We'll be holding 'em both for you down there by that time. No trouble at all, Field Marshal." He sort of blew up internally, so I got out before he did anything about calling a firing squad.

I ducked into the statue again, for what I hoped was the last time, and decided to make Suicide Johnny useful, since he seemed to be enjoying himself so. "How would you like to help?" I said. "Come on up with me."

When we got all the way up to the head, I took out my pocket notebook and opened it at the page where all the names were, the names I'd collected from the ten (eight really, excluding the two kids with their father) who had made the trip here and back on the ferry. Excluding Colman himself and his wife (who couldn't have been an actual participant for reasons I've already given) that left six. Excluding two other women who'd been in the group, that boiled it down to four. Now the name, of course, was going to be phony—I mean the name the actual murderer had handed me—that was a pushover. But that didn't matter. All I wanted was to connect the right guy with any name, phony or otherwise, just so I could remember something about what he'd looked like. Any little thing at all.

"You take a pencil," I told Suicide, "and each time I call out a name, you cross off the corresponding one written down there in that book. That's all."

"Gee!" he said. "I'm helping a real detective!"

"My chief," I answered drily, "sometimes has grave doubts about that. Ready? Let's go." I started going over the window-ledges inch by inch. They were crawling with names and initials, but I finally located one that matched one in the notebook. Johnny promptly crossed it out. Then another. Then a triple initial that matched. "Don't cross yet," I warned him, "just put a check next to that."

Well, when we got through, we had nine of the ten names, women, kids and all. Each and every one of them had scribbled their names as mementoes on the stone work. "Now, which one's left over?" I asked Suicide.

He screwed up his face and read off: "Vincent Scanlon, 55 Amboy Street, Brooklyn, real estate."

"On circumstantial alone, that's my guy."

"Hully mackerel!" said the enraptured Johnny. "Can y'tell just by hearing his name like that?"

"His name ain't Scanlon, he don't live on Amboy Street, and he's not in real estate," I tried to explain. "But he's the only one of the bunch that didn't come up here and scrawl his John Hancock. Me and the fat guy were the last ones coming up the stairs. When I left him on the bench he was still alive. When I got up here myself even his wife was up here ahead of me, and all the others had finished their signatures and were on their way down again. Therefore, this guy who tags himself Scanlon was the murderer. Don't you understand, he never went all the way to the top. He either came up the stairs behind me and the fat guy, or else if he was ahead of us switched into the opening that leads up into the arm, let everyone else go by, and then crept down again to where the bench was—and did his dirty work the minute the coast was clear."

I took a notebook from him, held it open before me, and did my damndest to try and separate the party that had given me that name from the other ten. I tried to remember some feature about him, some detail, anything at all, and couldn't, no matter how I racked my brains. There had been too many of them at one time, all getting off the ferry at once, all stopping in front of me just for a half-minute or so. He should have been nervous, just coming away from doing a thing like that, should have been pale, tense, jumpy, anything you want to call it—should have given himself away in some way, if not right then, then now that I was thinking back over it. But he either hadn't, or—what was more likely—I was pretty much of a wash-out at my own business. I couldn't even get him by elimination, the way I had gotten his phony name. One or two of the others started to come clear—the father of the two kids, the two other women besides Alice Colman—but not him. I might just as well have written down that name out of my own head for all I could remember of the man who had given it to me.

I took another look at Alice Colman's regards to the statue and wondered why she hadn't put her name down with it, and how she had come to be mixed up on her dates the way she had. And why a different address from her own. Of course the obvious answer was that she knew g.d. well what was taking place on that stairway below at the time, and was too nervous to know what she was doing. But she hadn't acted nervous at all, she had just acted dreamy. So that probably wasn't the answer at all. And just for luck I transcribed the thing into my notebook exactly as it stood in eyebrow pencil.

4/24/35/4 and then, *254W51*. Wrong date, right hour, wrong address, no name.

"I take it all back, Johnny," I said wearily. "Kick me here—and here. The guy did come up here after all—and right on top of what he did too."

"But he didn't write nothing—you looked all over them wind—"

"He didn't come up here to write, he came to read." I pointed at it. "He came to read that. Let's go down. I guess I can keep my promise to General Lafayette down there after all."

When I got ashore I halfheartedly checked Colman at the Tarrytown Apartments once more. No, neither Mr. nor Mrs. had come back yet, they told me after paging them on the house phone. I didn't tell them so, but they might just as well have hung out a to-let sign and gotten ready to rent that apartment all over again. He wasn't coming back any more because he was spending the night at the morgue. And she wasn't coming back any more either—because she had a heavy date at 4. As for Scanlon's Amboy Street address, I didn't even bother with it. Have to use your common sense once in awhile. Instead I asked Information to give me 254 West 51st Street, which was the best I could make out of the tag end of her billet-doux.

"Capital Bus Terminal," a voice answered at the other end.

So that's where they were going to meet, was it? They'd stayed very carefully away from each other on the ferry going back, and ditto once they were ashore in New York. But they were going to blow town together. So it looked like she hadn't had her days mixed after all, she'd known what she was doing when she put tomorrow's date down. "What've you got going out at four?" I said.

"A.M. or P.M.?" said the voice. But that was just the trouble, I didn't know myself. Yet if I didn't know, how was he going to know either? I mean Scanlon. The only thing to do was tackle both meridians, one at a time. A.M. came first, so I took that. He spieled off a list a foot long but the only big-time places among them were Boston and Philly. "Make me a reservation on each," I snapped.

"Mister," the voice came back patiently, "how can you go two places at once?"

"I'm twins," I squelched and hung up. Only one more phone call, this time to where I was supposed to live but so seldom did. "I may see you tomorrow. If I came home now I'd only have to set the alarm for three o'clock."

"I thought it was your day off."

"I've got statues on the brain."

"You mean you would have if you had a—" she started to say, but I ended that.

I staggered into the bus waiting room at half past three, apparently stewed to the gills, with my hat brim turned down to meet my upturned coat collar. They just missed each other enough to let my nose through, the rest was shadow. I wasn't one of those drunks that make a show of themselves and attract a lot of attention, I just slumped onto a bench and quietly went to sleep. Nobody gave me a first look, let alone a second one.

I was on the row of benches against the wall, not out in the middle where people could sit behind me. At twenty to four by the clock I suddenly remembered exactly what this guy Scanlon had looked like on the ferry that afternoon. Red hair, little pig-eyes set close together—what difference did it make now, there he was, valise between his legs. He had a newspaper up over his face in a split second, but a split second is plenty long enough to remember a face in.

But I didn't want him alone, didn't dare touch him alone until she got there, and where the hell was she? Quarter to, the clock said—ten to—five. Or were they going to keep up the bluff and leave separately, each at a different time, and only get together at the other end? Maybe that message on the statue hadn't been a date at all, only his instructions. I saw myself in for a trip to Philly, Boston, what-have-you, and without a razor, or an assignment from the chief.

The handful of late-night travelers stirred, got up, moved outside to the bus, got in, with him very much in the middle of them. No sign of her. It was the Boston one. I strolled back and got me a ticket, round-trip. Now all that should happen would be that she should breeze up and take the Philly one—and me without anyone with me to split the assignment!

"Better hurry, stew," said the ticket seller handing me my change, "you're going to miss that bus."

"Mr. Stew to you," I said mechanically, with a desperate look all around the empty waiting room. Suddenly the door of the ladies' restroom flashed open and a slim, sprightly figure dashed by, light-weight valise in hand. She must have been hiding in there for hours, long before he got here.

"Wait a minute!" she started to screech to the driver the minute she hit the open. "Wait a minute! Let me get on!" She just made it, the door banged, and the thing started.

There was only one thing for me to do. I cut diagonally across the lot, and when the driver tried to make the turn that would take him up Fifty-first Street I was wavering in front of his headlights. Wavering but not budging. "Wash'ya hurry?" I protested. His horn racketed, then he jammed on his brakes, stuck his head out the side, and showed just how many words he knew that he hadn't learned in Sunday School.

"Open up," I said, dropping the drunk act and flashing my badge. "You don't come from such nice people. And just like that"—I climbed aboard—"you're short three passengers. Me—and this gentleman here—and, let's see, oh yeah, this little lady trying so hard to duck down behind the seat. Stand up, sister, and get a new kind of bracelet on your lily-white wrist."

Somebody or other screamed and went into a faint at the sight of the gun, but I got them both safely off and waved the awe-stricken driver on his way.

"And now," I said as the red tail lights burned down Eighth Avenue and disappeared, "are you two going to come quietly or do I have to try out a recipe for making goulash on you?"

"What was in it for you?" I asked her at Headquarters. "This Romeo of yours is no Gable for looks."

"Say lissen," she said scornfully, accepting a cigarette, "if you were hog-tied to something that weighed two hundred ninety pounds and couldn't even take off his own shoes, but made three grand a month, and banked it in your name, and someone came along that knew how to make a lady's heart go pit-a-pat, you'd a done the same thing too!"

I went home and said: "Well, I've gotta hand it to you. I looked at a statue like you told me to, and it sure didn't hurt my record any." But I didn't tell which statue or why. "What's more," I said, "we're going down to Washington and back over the week-end."

"Why Washington?" my wife wanted to know.

"Cause they've got the biggest of the lot down there, called the Washington Monument. And a lotta guys that think they're good, called Federal dicks, hang out there and need help."

(1935)

Dark Melody of Madness

At four in the morning, a scarecrow of a man staggers dazedly into the New Orleans Police Headquarters building. Behind him at the curb, a lacquered Bugatti purrs like a drowsy cat, the swellest thing that ever parked out there. He weaves his way through the anteroom, deserted at that early hour, and goes in through the open doorway beyond. The sleepy desk-sergeant looks up; an idle detective scanning yesterday's *Times-Picayune* tipped back on the two hind legs of a chair against the wall raises his head; and as the funnel of light from the cone overhead plays up their visitor like a flashlight-powder, their mouths drop open and their eyes bat a couple of times. The two front legs of the detective's chair come down with a thump. The sergeant braces himself, eager, friendly, with the heels of both hands on his desk-top and his elbows up in the air. A patrolman comes in from the back room, wiping a drink of water from his mouth. His jaw also hangs when he sees who's there. He sidles nearer the detective and says behind the back of his hand, "That's Eddie Bloch, ain't it?"

The detective doesn't even take time off to answer. It's like telling him what his own name is. The three stare at the figure under the conelight, interested, respectful, almost admiring. There's nothing professional in their scrutiny, they're not the police studying a suspect; they're nobodies getting a look at a celebrity. They take in the rumpled tuxedo, the twig of gardenia that's shed its petals, the tie hanging open in two loose ends. His topcoat was slung across his arm originally; now it trails along the dusty station-house floor behind him. He gives his hat the final, tortured push that dislodges it. It drops and rolls away behind him. The cop picks

149

it up and brushes it off—he never was a bootlicker in his life, but this guy is Eddie Bloch.

Still it's his face, more than who he is or how he's dressed, that would draw stares anywhere. It's the face of a dead man—the face of a dead man on a living body. The shadowy shape of the skull seems to peer through the transparent skin; you can make out its bone-structure as though an X-ray were playing it up. The eyes are stunned, shocked, haunted gleams, set in a vast hollow that bisects the face like a mask. No amount of drink or dissipation could do this to anyone, only long illness and the foreknowledge of death. You see faces like that looking up at you from hospital cots when all hope has been abandoned—when the grave is already waiting.

Yet strangely enough, they knew who he was just now. Instant recognition of who he had been came first—realization of the shape he's in comes after that—more slowly. Possibly it's because all three of them have been called to identify corpses in the morgue in their day. Their minds are trained along those lines. And this man's face is known to hundreds of people. Not that he has ever broken or even fractured the most trivial law, but he has spread happiness around him—set a million feet to dancing in his time.

The desk sergeant's expression changes. The patrolman mutters under his breath to the detective. "Looks like he just came out of a bad smash-up with his car." "More like a binge to me," answers the detective. They're simple men, capable, but those are the only explanations they can find for what they now see before them.

The desk sergeant speaks.

"Mr. Eddie Bloch, am I right?" He extends his hand across the desk in greeting.

The man can hardly seem to stand up. He nods, he doesn't take the hand.

"Is there anything wrong, Mr. Bloch? Is there anything we can do for you?" The detective and the patrolman come over. "Run in and get him a drink of water, Latour," the sergeant says anxiously. "Have an accident, Mr. Bloch? Been held up?"

The man steadies himself by stiff-arming himself against the edge of the sergeant's desk. The detective extends an arm behind him in case he should go backwards. He keeps fumbling, continually fumbling in his clothes. The tuxedo swims on him as his movements shift it around. He's down to about a hundred pounds, they notice. Out comes the gun, and he doesn't even seem to have strength to lift it. He pushes it and it skids a little way across the desk-top, then spins around and faces back at him.

"I've killed a man. Just now. Little while ago. 3:30." He speaks, and if the unburied dead ever spoke, this is the voice they'd use.

They're completely floored. They almost don't know how to handle the situation for a minute. They deal with killers every day, but killers have to be gone out after and dragged in. And when fame and wealth enter into it, as they do once in a great while, fancy lawyers and protective barriers spring up like wildfire to hedge them in on all sides. This man is one of the ten idols of America, or was until just lately. People like him don't kill people. They don't come in out of nowhere at four in the morning and stand before a simple desk sergeant and a simple detective, stripped to their naked souls, shorn of almost all resemblance to humanity.

There's silence in the room—for just a minute—a silence you could cut with a knife. Then he speaks again, in agony. "I tell you I've killed a man! Don't stand looking at me like that! I've k—!"

The sergeant speaks, gently, sympathetically. "What's the matter, Mr. Bloch, been working too hard?" The sergeant comes out from behind the desk. "Come on inside with us. You stay here, Latour, and take the phone."

And when they've taken him into the back room: "Get him a chair, Humphries. Here, drink some of this water, Mr. Bloch. Now what's it all about?" The sergeant has brought the gun in with him. He passes it before his nose, then cracks it open. He looks at the detective. "He's used it all right."

"Was it an accident, Mr. Bloch?" the detective prompts respectfully. The man in the chair shakes his head. He's started to shiver all over, although the New Orleans night outside is warm and mellow. "Who'd you do it to? Who was it?" the sergeant puts in.

"I don't know his name," Bloch mumbles. "I never have. They call him Papa Benjamin."

His two interrogators exchange a puzzled look. "Sounds like—" The detective doesn't finish it. Instead he turns to the seated figure and asks almost perfunctorily: "He was a white man, of course, wasn't he?"

"He was colored," is the unexpected answer.

The thing gets more crazy, more inexplicable, at every turn. How should a man like Eddie Bloch, one of the country's ace bandsmen, pulling down his two-and-a-half grand every week for playing at the Bataclan, come to kill a nameless colored man—then be pulled all to pieces by it? These two men in their time have never seen anything like it; they have put suspects through forty-eight-hour grillings and yet compared to him now, those suspects were fresh as daisies when they got through with them.

He has said it was no accident and he has said it was no hold-up. They shower him with questions, not to break him down but rather to try and pull him together. "What'd he do, talk out of turn to you? Forget himself? Get wise?" This is the Southland, remember.

The man's head goes from side to side like a pendulum.

"Did you go out of your head for a minute? Is that how it was?"

Again a nodded no.

The man's condition has suggested one angle to the detective's mind. He looks around to make sure the patrolman outside isn't listening. Then very discreetly: "Are you a needle-user, Mr. Bloch? Was he your source?"

The man looks up at them. "I've never touched a thing I shouldn't. A doctor will tell you that in a minute."

"Did he have something on you? Was it blackmail?"

Bloch fumbles some more in his clothes; again they dance around on his skeletonized frame. Suddenly he takes out a cube of money, as thick as it is wide, more money than these two men have ever seen before in their lives. "There's three thousand dollars there," he says simply, and tosses it down like he did the gun. "I took it with me tonight, tried to give it to him. He could have had twice as much, three times as much, if he'd said the word, if he'd only let up on me. He wouldn't take it. That was when I had to kill him. That was all there was left for me to do."

"What was he doing to you?" They both say it together.

"He was killing me." He holds out his arm and shoots his cuff. The wristbone is about the size of the sergeant's own thumb-joint. The expensive platinum wrist-watch that encircles it has been pulled in to the last possible notch and yet it still hangs almost like a bracelet. "See? I'm down to 102. When my shirt's off, my heart's so close to the surface you can see the skin right over it move like a pulse with each beat."

They draw back a little, almost they wish he hadn't come in here. That he had headed for some other precinct instead. From the very beginning they have sensed something here that is over their heads, that isn't to be found in any of the instruction-books. Now they come out with it. "How?" Humphries asks. "How was he killing you?"

There's a flare of torment from the man. "Don't you suppose I would have told you long ago, if I could? Don't you suppose I would have come in here weeks ago, months ago, and demanded protection, asked to be saved—if I could have told you what it was? If you would have believed me?"

"We'll believe you, Mr. Bloch," the sergeant says soothingly. "We'll believe anything. Just tell us——"

But Bloch in turn shoots a question at them, for the first time since he has come in. "Answer me! Do you believe in anything you can't see, can't hear, can't touch——?"

"Radio," the sergeant suggests not very brightly, but Humphries answers more frankly: "No."

The man slumps down again in his chair, shrugs apathetically. "If you don't, how can I expect you to believe me? I've been to the biggest doctors, biggest scientists in the world—— They wouldn't believe me. How can I expect you to? You'll simply say I'm cracked, and let it go at that. I don't want to spend the rest of my life in an asylum——" He breaks off and sobs. "And yet it's true, it's true!"

They've gotten into such a maze that Humphries decides it's about time to snap out of it. He asks the one simple question that should have been asked long ago, and the hell with all this mumbo-jumbo. "Are you sure you killed him?" The man is broken physically and he's about ready to crack mentally too. The whole thing may be an hallucination.

"I know I did. I'm sure of it," the man answers calmly. "I'm already beginning to feel a little better. I felt it the minute he was gone."

If he is, he doesn't show it. The sergeant catches Humphries' eye and meaningfully taps his forehead in a sly gesture.

"Suppose you take us there and show us," Humphries suggests. "Can you do that? Where'd it happen, at the Bataclan?"

"I told you he was colored," Bloch answers reproachfully. Bataclan is tony. "It was in the Vieux Carré. I can show you where, but I can't drive any more. It was all I could do to get down here with my car."

"I'll put Desjardins on it with you," the sergeant says, and calls through the door to the patrolman: "Ring Dij and tell him to meet Humphries at corner of Canal and Royal right away!" He turns and looks at the huddle on the chair. "Buy him a bracer on the way. It don't look like he'll last till he gets there."

The man flushes a little—it would be a blush if he had any blood left in him. "I can't touch alcohol any more. I'm on my last legs. It goes right through me like——" He hangs his head, then raises it again. "But I'll get better now, little by little, now that he's——"

The sergeant takes Humphries out of earshot. "Pushover for a padded cell. If it's on the up-and-up, and not just a pipe dream, call me right back. I'll get the commissioner on the wire."

"At this hour of the night?"

The sergeant motions toward the chair with his head. "He's Eddie Bloch, isn't he?"

Humphries takes him under the elbow, pries him up from the chair. Not roughly, but just briskly, energetically. Now that things are at last getting under way, he knows where he's at; he can handle them. He'll still be considerate, but he's business-like now; he's into his routine. "All right, come on, Mr. Bloch, let's get up there."

"Not a scratch goes down on the blotter until I'm sure what I'm doing," the sergeant calls after Humphries. "I don't want this whole town down on my neck tomorrow morning."

Humphries almost has to hold him up on the way out and into the car. "This it?" he says. "Wow!" He just touches it with his nail and they're off like velvet. "How'd you ever get this into the Vieux Carré without knocking over the houses?"

Two gleams deep in the skull jogging against the upholstery, dimmer than the dashboard lights, are the only sign that there's life beside him. "Used to park it blocks away—go on foot."

"Oh, you went there more than once?"

"Wouldn't you—to beg for your life?"

More of that screwy stuff, Humphries thinks disgustedly. Why should a man like Eddie Bloch, star of the mike and the dance-floor, go to some colored man in the slums and beg for his life?

Royal Street comes whistling along. He swerves in toward the curb, shoves the door out, sees Desjardins land on the running-board with one foot. Then he veers out into the middle again without even having stopped. Desjardins moves in on the other side of Bloch, finishes dressing by knotting his necktie and buttoning his vest. "Where'd you get the Aquitania?" he wants to know, and then, with a look beside him: "Holy Kreisler, Eddie Bloch! We had you only tonight on my Emerson——"

"Matter?" Humphries squelches. "Got a talking-jag?"

"Turn," says a hollow sound between them, and three wheels take the Bugatti around into North Rampart Street. "Have to leave it here," he says a little later, and they get out. Congo Square, the old stamping-ground of the slaves.

"Help him," Humphries tells his mate tersely, and they each brace him by an elbow.

Staggering between them with the uneven gait of a punch-drunk pug, quick and then slow by turns, he leads them down a ways, and then suddenly cuts left into an alley that isn't there at all until you're smack in front of it. It's just a crack between two houses, noisome as a sewer. They have to break into Indian file to get through at all. But Bloch can't fall down; the walls almost scrape both his shoulders at once. One's in front, one behind him. "You packed?" Humphries calls over his head to Desjardins, up front.

"Catch cold without it," the other's voice comes back out of the gloom.

A slit of orange shows up suddenly from under a windowsill and a shapely coffee-colored elbow scrapes the ribs of the three as they squirm by. "This far 'nough, honey," a liquid voice murmurs.

"Bad girl! Wash y'mouth out with soap," the unromantic Humphries warns over his shoulder without even looking around. The sliver of light vanishes as quickly as it came . . . .

The passage widens out in places into mouldering courtyards dating back to French or Spanish colonial days, and once it goes under an archway and becomes a tunnel for a short distance. Desjardins cracks his head and swears with talent and abandon.

"Y'left out——" the rearguard remarks dryly.

"Here," pants Bloch weakly, and stops suddenly at a patch of blackness in the wall. Humphries washes it with his torch and crumbling mildewed stone steps show up inside it. Then he motions Bloch in, but the man hangs back, slips a notch or two lower down against the opposite wall that supports him. "Lemme stay down here! Don't make me go up there again," he pleads. "I don't think I can make it any more. I'm afraid to go back in there."

"Oh no!" Humphries says with quiet determination. "You're showing us," and scoops him away from the wall with his arm. Again, as before, he isn't rough about it, just business-like. Dij keeps the lead, watering the place with his own torch. Humphries trains his on the band-leader's forty-dollar custom-made patent-leathers jerking frightenedly upward before him. The stone steps turn to wood ones splintered with usage. They have to step over a huddled black drunk, empty bottle cradled in his arms. "Don't light a match," Dij warns, pinching his nose. "There'll be an explosion."

"Grow up," snaps Humphries. The Cajun's a good dick, but can't he realize the man in the middle is roasting in hell-fire? "This is no time——"

"In here is where I did it. I closed the door again after me." Bloch's skull-face is all silver with his life-sweat as one of their torches flicks past it.

Humphries shoves open the sagging mahogany panel that was first hung up when a Louis was still king of France and owned this town. The light of a lamp far across a still, dim room flares up and dances crazily in the draught. They come in and look.

There's an old broken-down bed, filthy with rags. Across it there's a motionless figure, head hanging down toward the floor. Dij cups his hand under it and lifts it. It comes up limply toward him, like a small basketball. It bounces down again when he lets it go—even seems to bob slightly for a second or two after. It's an old, old colored man, up in his eighties, even beyond. There's a dark spot, darker than the weazened skin, just under one bleared eye, and another in the thin fringe of white wool that circles the back of the skull.

Humphries doesn't wait to see any more. He turns, flips out, and down, and all the way back to wherever the nearest telephone can be found, to let headquarters know that it's true after all and they can rouse the police commissioner. "Keep him there with you, Dij," his voice trails back from the inky stairwell, "and no quizzing. Pull in your horns till we get our orders!" That scarecrow with them tries to stumble after him and get out of the place, groaning: "Don't leave me here! Don't make me stay here——!"

"I wouldn't quiz you on my own, Mr. Bloch," Dij tries to reassure him, nonchalantly sitting down on the edge of the bed next to the corpse and retying his shoelace. "I'll never forget it was your playing *Love in Bloom* on the air one night in Baton Rouge two years ago gave me the courage to propose to my wife—"

But the Commissioner would, and does, in his office a couple hours later. He's anything but eager about it, too. They've tried to shunt him, Bloch, off their hands in every possible legal way open to them. No go. He sticks to them like flypaper. The old colored man *didn't* try to attack him, or rob him, or blackmail him, or kidnap him, or anything else. The gun didn't go off accidentally, and he didn't fire it on the spur of the moment either, without thinking twice, or in a flare of anger. The Commissioner almost beats his own head against the desk in his exasperation as he reiterates over and over: "But why? Why? Why?" And for the steenth time, he gets the same indigestible answer: "Because he was killing me."

"Then you admit he did lay hands on you?" The first time the poor Commissioner asked this, he said it with a spark of hope. But this is the tenth or twelfth and the spark died out long ago.

"He never once came near me. I was the one looked him up each time to plead with him. Commissioner Oliver, tonight I went down on my knees to that old man and dragged myself around the floor of that dirty room after him, on my *bended knees,* like a sick cat—begging, crawling to him, offering him three thousand, ten, any amount, finally offering him my own gun, asking him to shoot me with it, to get it over with quickly, to be kind to me, not to drag it out by inches any longer! No, not even that little bit of mercy! Then I shot—and now I'm going to get better, now I'm going to live——"

He's too weak to cry; crying takes strength. The Commissioner's hair is about ready to stand on end. "Stop it, Mr. Bloch, stop it!" he shouts, and he steps over and grabs him by the shoulder in defense of his own nerves, and can almost feel the shoulder-bone cutting his hand. He takes his hand away again in a hurry. "I'm going to have you examined by an alienist!"

The bundle of bones rears from the chair. "You can't do that! You can't take my mind from me! Send to my hotel—I've got a trunkful of reports on my condition! I've been to the biggest minds in Europe! Can you produce anyone that would dare go against the findings of Buckholtz in Vienna, Reynolds in London? They had me under observation for months at a time! I'm not even on the borderline of insanity, not even a genius or musically talented. I don't even write my own numbers, I'm mediocre, uninspired—in other words completely normal. I'm saner than you are at this minute, Mr. Oliver. My body's gone, my soul's gone, and all I've got left is my mind, but you can't take that from me!"

The Commissioner's face is beet-red. He's about ready for a stroke, but he speaks softly, persuasively. "An eighty-odd-year-old colored man who is so feeble he can't even go upstairs half the time, who has to have his food pulleyed up to him through the window in a basket, is killing—whom? A white stumble-bum his own age? No-o-o, Mr. Eddie Bloch, the premier bandsman of America, who can name his own price in any town, who's heard every night in all our homes, who has about everything a man can want—that's who!" He peers close, until their eyes are on a level. His voice is just a silky whisper. "Tell me just one thing, Mr. Bloch." Then like the explosion of a giant firecracker, "How?" He roars it out, booms it out.

There's a long-drawn intake of breath from Eddie Bloch. "By thinking thoughtwaves of death that reached me through the air." The poor Commissioner practically goes all to pieces on his own rug. "And you don't need a medical exam!" he wheezes weakly.

There's a flutter, the popping of buttons, and Eddie Bloch's coat, his vest, his shirt, undershirt, land one after another on the floor around his chair. He turns. "Look at my back! You can count every vertebra through the skin!" He turns back again. "Look at my ribs. Look at the pulsing where there's not enough skin left to cover my heart!"

Oliver shuts his eyes and turns toward the window. He's in a particularly unpleasant spot. New Orleans, out there, is stirring, and when it hears about this, he's going to be the most unpopular man in town. On the other hand, if he doesn't see the thing through now that it's gone this far he's guilty of a dereliction of duty, malfeasance in office.

Bloch, slowly dressing, knows what he's thinking. "You want to get rid of me, don't you? You're trying to think of a way of covering this thing up. You're afraid to bring me up before the Grand Jury on account of your own reputation, aren't you?" His voice rises to a scream of panic. "Well, I want protection! I don't want to go out there again—to my death! I won't accept bail! If you turn me loose now, even on my own cognizance, you may be as guilty of my death as he is. How do I know my bullet stopped the thing? How does any of us know what becomes of the mind after death? Maybe his thoughts will still reach me, still try to get me. I tell you I want to be locked up, I want people around me day and night, I want to be where I'm safe——"

"Shh, for God's sake, Mr. Bloch! They'll think I'm beating you up——" The Commissioner drops his arms to his side and heaves a gigantic sigh. "That settles it! I'll book you all right. You want that and you're going to get it! I'll book you for the murder of one Papa Benjamin, even if they laugh me out of office for it!"

For the first time since the whole thing has started, he casts a look of real anger, ill-will, at Eddie Bloch. He seizes a chair, swirls it around, and bangs it down in front of the man. He puts his foot on it and pokes his finger almost in Bloch's eye. "I'm not two-faced. I'm not going to lock you up nice and cozy and then soft-pedal the whole thing. If it's coming out at all, then all of it's coming out. Now start in!

Tell me everything I want to know, and what I want to know is—everything!"

The strains of *Goodnight Ladies* die away; the dancers leave the floor; the lights start going out, and Eddie Bloch throws down his baton and mops the back of his neck with a handkerchief. He weighs about two hundred pounds, is in the pink, and is a good-looking brute. But his face is sour right now, dissatisfied. His outfit starts to case its instruments right and left, and Judy Jarvis steps up on the platform, in her street clothes, ready to go home. She's Eddie's torch singer, and also his wife. "Coming, Eddie? Let's get out of here." She looks a little disgusted herself. "I didn't get a hand tonight, not even after my rumba number. Must be staling. If I wasn't your wife, I'd be out of a job, I guess."

Eddie pats her shoulder. "It isn't you, honey. It's us. We're beginning to stink. Notice how the attendance has been dropping the past few weeks? There were more waiters than customers tonight. I'll be hearing from the owner any minute now. He has the right to cancel my contract if the intake drops below five grand." A waiter comes up to the edge of the platform. "Mr. Graham'd like to see you in his office before you go home, Mr. Bloch."

Eddie and Judy look at each other. "This is it now, Judy. You go back to the hotel. Don't wait for me. G'night, boys." Eddie Bloch calls for his hat and knocks at the manager's office.

Graham rustles a lot of accounts together. "We took in forty-five hundred this week, Eddie. They can get the same ginger ale and sandwiches any place, but they'll go where the band has something to give 'em. I notice the few that do come in don't even get up from the table any more when you tap your baton. Now, what's wrong?"

Eddie punches his hat a couple of times. "Don't ask me. I'm getting the latest orchestrations from Broadway sent to me hot off the griddle. We sweat our bald heads off rehearsing——"

Graham swivels his cigar. "Don't forget that jazz originated here in the South, you can't show this town anything. They want something new."

"When do I scram?" Eddie asks, smiling with the southwest corner of his mouth.

"Finish the week out. See if you can do something about it by Monday. If not, I'll have to wire St. Louis to get Kruger's crew. I'm sorry, Eddie."

"That's all right," broadminded Eddie says. "You're not running a charity bazaar."

Eddie goes out into the dark danceroom. His crew has gone. The tables are stacked. A couple of old colored crones are down on hands and knees slopping water around on the parquet. Eddie steps up on the platform a minute to get some orchestrations he left on the piano. He feels something crunch under his shoe, reaches down, picks up a severed chicken's claw lying there with a strip of red rag tied around it. How the hell did it get up there? If it had been under one of the tables, he'd have thought some diner had dropped it. He flushes a little. D'ye mean to say he and the boys were so rotten tonight that somebody deliberately threw it at them while they were playing?

One of the scrubwomen looks up. The next moment, she and her mate are on their feet, edging nearer, eyes big as saucers, until they get close enough to see what it is he's holding. Then there's a double yowl of animal fright, a tin pail goes rolling across the floor, and no two stout people, white or colored, ever got out of a place in such a hurry before. The door nearly comes off its hinges, and Eddie can hear their cackling all the way down the quiet street outside until it fades away into the night. "For gosh sake!" thinks the bewildered Eddie. "They must be using the wrong brand of gin." He tosses the object out onto the floor and goes back to the piano for his music scores. A sheet or two has slipped down behind it and he squats to collect them. That way the piano hides him.

The door opens again and he sees Johnny Staats (traps and percussion) come in in quite a hurry. He thought Staats was home in bed by now. Staats is feeling himself all over like he was rehearsing the shim-sham and he's scanning the ground as he goes along. Then suddenly he pounces—and it's on the very scrap of garbage Eddie just now threw away! And as he straightens up with it, his breath comes out in such a sigh of relief that Eddie can hear it all the way across the still room. All this keeps him from hailing Staats as he was going to a minute ago and suggesting a cup of java. But—"Superstitious," thinks broadminded Eddie. "It's his good-luck charm, that's all, like some people carry a rabbit's foot. I'm a little that way myself, never walk under a ladder——"

Then again, why should those two mammies go into hysterics when they lamp the same object? And Eddie recalls now that some of the boys have always suspected Staats has colored blood, and tried to tell him so years ago when Staats first came in with them, but he wouldn't listen to them.

Staats slinks out again as noiselessly as he came in, and Eddie decides he'll catch up with him and kid him about his chicken-claw on their way home together. (They all roost in the same hotel.) So he takes his music-sheets, some of which are blank, and he leaves. Staats is way down the street—in the *wrong direction,* away from the hotel! Eddie hesitates for just a minute, and then he starts after Staats on a vague impulse, just to see where he's going—just to see what he's up to. Maybe the fright of the scrubwomen and the way Staats pounced on that chicken-claw just now have built up to this, without Eddie's really knowing it.

And how many times afterward he's going to pray to his God that he'd never turned down that other way this night—away from his hotel, his Judy, his boys—away from the sunlight and the white man's world. Such a little thing to decide to do, and afterwards no turning back—ever . . . .

He keeps Staats in sight, and they hit the Vieux Carré. That's all right. There are a lot of quaint places here a guy might like to drop in. Or maybe he has some Creole sweetie tucked away, and Eddie thinks: I'm lower than a ditch to spy like this. But then suddenly right before his eyes, halfway up the narrow lane he's turned into—there isn't any Staats any more! And no door opened and closed again either. Then when Eddie gets up to where it was, he sees the crevice between the old houses, hidden by an angle in the walls. So that's where he went! Eddie almost has a peeve on by now at all this hocus-pocus. He slips in himself and feels his way along. He stops every once in a while and can hear Staats' quiet footfall somewhere way up in front. Then he goes on again. Once or twice the passage spreads out a little and lets a little green-blue moonlight part way down the walls. Then later, there's a little flare of orange light from under a window and an elbow jogs him in the appendix. "You'd be happier here. Doan go the rest of the way," a soft voice breathes. A prophecy if he only knew it!

But hardboiled Eddie just says: "G'wan to bed, y'dirty stay-up!" out of the corner of his mouth, and the light vanishes. Next a tunnel and he bangs the top of his head and his eyes water. But at the other end of it, Staats has finally come to a halt in a patch of clear light and seems to be looking up at a window or something, so Eddie stays where he is, inside the tunnel, and folds the lapels of his black jacket up over his white shirt-front so it won't show.

Staats just stands there for a spell, with Eddie holding his breath inside the tunnel, and then finally he gives a peculiar, dismal whistle. There's nothing carefree or casual about it. It's a hollow swampland sound, not easy to get without practice. Then he just stands there waiting, until without warning, another figure joins him in the gloom. Eddie strains his eyes. A gorilla-like, Negro roustabout. Something passes from Staats' hand to his—the chicken claw possibly—then they go in, into the house Staats has been facing. Eddie can hear the soft shuffle of feet going up stairs on the inside, and the groaning, squeaking of an old decayed door—and then silence . . . . He edges forward to the mouth of the tunnel and peers up. No light shows from any window, the house appears to be untenanted, deserted.

Eddie hangs onto his coat collar with one hand and strokes his chin with the other. He doesn't know just what to do. The vague impulse that has brought him this far after Staats begins to peter out now. Staats has some funny associates—something funny is going on in this out-of-the-way place at this unearthly hour of the morning—but after all, a man's private life is his own. He wonders what made him do this, he wouldn't want anyone to know he did it. He'll turn around and go back to his hotel now and get some shut-eye; he's got to think up some novelty for his routine at the Bataclan between now and Monday or he'll be out on his ear.

Then just as one heel is off the ground to take the turn that will start him back, a vague, muffled wailing starts from somewhere inside that house. It's toned down to a mere echo. It has to go through thick doors and wide, empty rooms and down a deep, hollow stairwell before it gets to him. Oh, some sort of a revival meeting, is it? So Staats has got religion, has he? But what a place to come and get it in!

A throbbing like a far-away engine in a machine-shop underscores the wailing, and every once in a while a *boom* like distant thunder across the bayou tops the whole works. It goes: *Boom-putta-putta-boom-putta-putta-boom!* And the wailing, way up high at the moon: *Eeyah-eeyah-eeyah . . . !*

Eddie's professional instincts suddenly come alive. He tries it out, beats time to it with his arm as if he were holding a baton. His fingers snap like a whip. "My God, that's grand! That's gorgeous! Just what I need! I gotta get up there!" So a chicken-foot does it, eh?

He turns and runs back, through the tunnel, through the courtyards, all the way back where he came from, stooping here, stooping there, lighting matches recklessly and throwing them away as he goes. Out in the Vieux Carré again, the refuse hasn't been collected. He spots a can at the corner of two lanes, topples it over. The smell rises to heaven, but he wades into it ankle-deep like any levee-rat, digs into the stuff with both forearms, scattering it right and left. He's lucky, finds a verminous carcass, tears off a claw, wipes it on some newspaper. Then he starts back. Wait a minute! The red rag, red strip around it! He feels himself all over, all his pockets. Nothing that color. Have to do without it, but maybe it won't work without it. He turns and hurries back through the slit between the old houses, doesn't care how much noise he makes. The flash of light from Old Faithful, the jogging elbow. Eddie stoops, he suddenly snatches in at the red kimono sleeve, his hand comes away with a strip of it. Bad language, words that even Eddie doesn't know. A five-spot stops it on the syllable, and Eddie's already way down the passage. If only they haven't quit until he can get back there!

They haven't. It was vague, smothered when he went away; it's louder, more persistent, more frenzied now. He doesn't bother about giving the whistle, probably couldn't imitate it exactly anyhow. He dives into the black smudge that is the entrance to the house, feels greasy stone steps under him, takes one or two and then suddenly his collar is four sizes too small for him, gripped by a big ham of a hand at the back. A sharp something that might be anything from a pocket-knife blade to the business edge of a razor is creasing his throat just below the apple and drawing a preliminary drop or two of blood.

"Here it is, I've got it here!" gasps Eddie. What kind of religion is this, anyway? The sharp thing stays, but the hand lets go his collar and feels for the chicken-claw. Then the sharp thing goes away, too, but probably not very far away. "Whyfor you didn't give the signal?"

Eddie's windpipe gives him the answer. "Sick here, couldn't."

"Light up, lemme see yo' face." Eddie strikes a match and holds it. "Yo' face has never been here before."

Eddie gestures upward. "My friend—up there—he'll tell you!"

"Mr. Johnny you' friend? He ax you to come?"

Eddie thinks quickly. The chicken-claw might carry more weight than Staats. "That told me to come."

"Papa Benjamin sen' you that?"

"Certainly," says Eddie stoutly. Probably their deacon, but it's a hell of a way to—— The match stings his fingers and he whips it out. Blackness and a moment's uncertainty that might end either way. But a lot of savoir-faire—a thousand years of civilization are backing Eddie up. "You'll make me late, Papa Benjamin wouldn't like that!"

He gropes his way on up in the pitch-blackness, thinking any minute he'll feel his back slashed to ribbons. But it's better than standing still and having it happen, and to back out now would bring it on twice as quickly. However, it works, nothing happens.

"Fust thing y'know, all N'yorleans be comin' by," growls the African watchdog sulkily, and flounders down on the staircase with a sound like a tired seal. There was some other crack about "darkies lookin' lak pinks," and then a long period of scratching.

But Eddie's already up on the landing above and so close to the boom-putta-boom now it drowns out every other sound. The whole framework of the decrepit house seems to shake with it. The door's closed but the thread of orange that outlines it shows it up to him. Behind there. He leans against it, shoves a little. It gives. The squealings and the grindings it emits are lost in the torrent of noise that comes rushing out. He sees plenty, and what he sees only makes him want to see all the more. Something tells him the best thing to do is slip in quietly and close it behind him before he's noticed, rather than stay there peeking in from the outside. Little Snowdrop might always come upstairs in back of him and catch him there. So he widens it just a little more, oozes in, and kicks it shut behind him with his heel—and immediately gets as far away from it as he can. Evidently no one has seen him.

Now, it's a big shadowy room and it's choked with people. It's lit by a single oil-lamp and a hell of a whole lot of candles, which may have shone out brightly against the darkness outside but are pretty dim once you get inside with them. The long flickering shadows thrown on all the walls by those cavorting in the center are almost as much of a protection to Eddie as he crouches back amidst them as the darkness outside would be. He's been around, and a single look is enough to tell him that whatever else it is, it's no revival meeting. At first he takes it for just a gin or rent party with the lid off, but it isn't that either. There's no gin there, and there's no pairing off of couples in the dancing—rather it's a roomful of devils lifted bodily up out of hell. Plenty of them have passed out cold on the floor all around him and the others keep stepping over them as they prance back and forth, only they don't always step over but sometimes *on*—on prostrate faces and chests and outstretched arms and hands. Then there are others who have gone off into a sort of still trance, seated on the floor with their backs to the wall, some of them rocking back and forth, some just staring glassy-eyed, foam drooling from their mouths. Eddie quickly slips down among them on his haunches and gets busy. He too starts rocking back and forth and pounding the flooring beside him with his knuckles, but he's not in any trance, he's getting a swell new number for his repertoire at the Bataclan. A sheet of blank score-paper is partly hidden under his body, and he keeps dropping one hand down to it every minute jotting down musical notes with the stub of pencil in his fingers. "Key of A," he guesses. "I can decide that when I instrument it. Mi-re-do, mi-re-do. Then over again. Hope I didn't miss any of it."

Boom-putta-putta-boom! Young and old, black and tawny, fat and thin, naked and clothed, they pass from right to left, from left to right, in two concentric circles, while the candle flames dance crazily and the shadows leap up and down on the walls. The hub of it all, within the innermost circle of dancers, is an old, old man, black skin and bones, only glimpsed now and then in a space between the packed bodies that surround him. An animal-pelt is banded about his middle;

he wears a horrible juju mask over his face—a death's-head. On one side of him, a squatting woman clacks two gourds together endlessly, that's the "putta" of Eddie's rhythm; on the other, another beats a drum, that's the "boom." In one upraised hand, he holds a squalling fowl, wings beating the air; in the other, a sharp-bladed knife. Something flashes in the air, but the dancers mercifully get between Eddie and the sight of it. Next glimpse he has, the fowl isn't flapping any more. It's hanging limply down and veins of blood are trickling down the old man's shrivelled forearm.

"That part don't go into my show," Eddie thinks facetiously. The horrible old man has dropped the knife; he squeezes the life-blood from the dead bird with both hands now, still holding it in mid-air. He sprinkles the drops on those that cavort around him, flexing and unflexing his bony fingers in a nauseating travesty of the ceremony of baptism.

Drops spatter here and there about the room, on the walls. One lands near Eddie and he edges back. Revolting things go on all around him. He sees some of the crazed dancers drop to their hands and knees and bend low over these red polka-dots, licking them up from the floor with their tongues. Then they go about the room on all fours like animals, looking for others.

"Think I'll go," Eddie says to himself, tasting last night's supper all over again. "They ought to have the cops on them."

He maneuvers the score-sheet, filled now, out from under him and into his side-pocket; then he starts drawing his feet in toward him preparatory to standing up and slipping out of this hell-hole. Meanwhile a second fowl, black this time (the first was white), a squeaking suckling-pig, and a puppy-dog have gone the way of the first fowl. Nor do the carcasses go to waste when the old man has dropped them. Eddie sees things hapening on the floor, in between the stomping feet of the dancers, and he guesses enough not to look twice.

Then suddenly, already reared a half-inch above the floor on his way up, he wonders where the wailing went. And the clacking of the gourds and the boom of the drum and the shuffling of the feet. He blinks, and everything has frozen still in the room around him. Not a move, not a sound. Straight out from the old man's gnarled shoulder stretches a bony arm, the end dipped in red, pointing like an arrow at

Eddie. Eddie sinks down again that half-inch. He couldn't hold that
position very long, and something tells him he's not leaving right
away after all. "White man," says a bated breath, and they all start
moving in on him. A gesture of the old man sweeps them into
motionlessness again.

A cracked voice comes through the grinning mouth of the juju
mask, rimmed with canine teeth. "Whut you do here?"

Eddie taps his pockets mentally. He has about fifty on him. Will that
be enough to buy his way out? He has an uneasy feeling however that
none of this lot is as interested in money as they should be—at least
not right now. Before he has a chance to try it out, another voice
speaks up. "I know this man, papaloi. Let me find out."

Johnny Staats came in here tuxedoed, hair slicked back, a cog in
New Orleans' night life. Now he's barefooted, coatless, shirtless—a
tousled scarecrow. A drop of blood has caught him squarely on the
forehead and been traced, by his own finger or someone else's, into a
red line from temple to temple. A chicken-feather or two clings to his
upper lip. Eddie saw him dancing with the rest, groveling on the floor.
His scalp crawls with repugnance as the man comes over and squats
down before him. The rest of them hold back, tense, poised, ready to
pounce.

The two men talk in low, hoarse voices. "It's your only way, Eddie. I
can't save you——"

"Why, I'm in the very heart of New Orleans! They wouldn't dare!"
But sweat oozes out on Eddie's face just the same. He's no fool. Sure
the police will come and sure they'll mop this place up. But what will
they find? His own remains along with that of the fowls, the pig and
the dog.

"You'd better hurry up, Eddie. I can't hold them back much longer.
Unless you do, you'll never get out of this place alive and you may as
well know it! If I tried to stop them, I'd go too. You know what this is,
don't you? This is voodoo!"

"I knew that five minutes after I was in the room." And Eddie
thinks to himself, "You son-of-a-so-and-so! You better ask Mombo-
jombo to get you a new job starting in tomorrow night!" Then he grins

internally and, clown to the very end, says with a straight face: "Sure I'll join. What d'ye suppose I came here for anyway?"

Knowing what he knows now, Staats is the last one he'd tell about the glorious new number he's going to get out of this, the notes for which are nestled in his inside pocket right now. And he might even get more dope out of the initiation ceremonies if he pretends to go through with them. A song or dance for Judy to do with maybe a green spot focussed on her. Lastly, there's no use denying there *are* too many razors, knives, and the like, in the room to hope to get out and all the way back where he started from without a scratch.

Staats' face is grave though. "Now don't kid about this thing. If you knew what I know about it, there's a lot more to it than there seems to be. If you're sincere, honest about it, all right. If not, it might be better to get cut to pieces right now than to tamper with it."

"Never more serious in my life," says Eddie. And deep down inside he's braying like a jackass.

Staats turns to the old man. "His spirit wishes to join our spirits."

The papaloi burns some feathers and entrails at one of the candle-flames. Not a sound in the room. The majority of them squat down all at once. "It came out all right," Staats breathes. "He reads them. The spirits are willing."

"So far so good," Eddie thinks. "I've fooled the guts and feathers."

The papaloi is pointing at him now. "Let him go now and be silent," the voice behind the mask cackles. Then a second time he says it, and a third, with a long pause between.

Eddie looks hopefully at Staats. "Then I can go after all, as long as I don't tell anyone what I've seen?"

Staats shakes his head grimly. "Just part of the ritual. If you went now, you'd eat something that disagreed with you tomorrow and be dead before the day was over."

More sacrificial slaughtering, and the drum and gourds and wailing start over again, but very low and subdued now as at the beginning. A bowl of blood is prepared and Eddie is raised to his feet and led forward, Staats on one side of him, an anonymous colored man on the other. The papaloi dips his already caked hand into the bowl and traces a mark on Eddie's forehead. The chanting and wailing grow louder behind him. The dancing begins again. He's in the middle of all of them. He's an island of sanity in a sea of jungle frenzy. The bowl is being held up before his face. He tries to draw back, his sponsors grip him firmly by the arms. "Drink!" whispers Staats. "Drink—or they'll kill you where you stand!"

Even at this stage of the game, there's still a wisecrack left in Eddie, though he keeps it to himself. He takes a deep breath. "Here's where I get my vitamin A for today!"

Staats shows up at orchestra rehearsal next A.M. to find somebody else at drums and percussion. He doesn't say much when Eddie shoves a two-week check at him. Spits on the floor at his feet and growls: "Beat it, you filthy——"

Staats only murmurs: "So you're crossing them? I wouldn't want to be in your shoes for all the fame and money in this world, guy!"

"If you mean that bad dream the other night," says Eddie, "I haven't told anybody and I don't intend to. Why, I'd be laughed at. I'm only remembering what I can use of it. I'm a white man, see? The jungle is just trees to me; the Congo, just a river; the night-time, just a time for 'lectric-lights." He whips out a couple of C's. "Hand 'em these for me, will ya, and tell 'em I've paid up my dues from now until doomsday and I don't want any receipt. And if they try putting rough-on-rats in my orange juice, they'll find themselves stomping in a chain gang!"

The C's fall where Eddie spat. "You're one of us. You think you're pink? Blood tells. You wouldn't have gone there—you couldn't have stood that induction—if you were. Look at your fingernails sometime, look in a mirror at the whites of your eyes. Goodbye, dead man."

Eddie says goodbye to him, too. He knocks out three of his teeth, breaks the bridge of his nose, and rolls all over the floor on top of him. But he can't wipe out that wise, knowing smile that shows even through the gush of blood.

They pull Eddie off, pull him up, pull him together. Staats staggers away, smiling at what he knows. Eddie, heaving like a bellows, turns to his crew. "All right, boys. Altogether now!" *Boom-putta-putta-boom-putta-putta-boom!*

Graham shoots five C's on promotion and all New Orleans jams its way into the Bataclan that Saturday night. They're standing on each other's shoulders and hanging from the chandeliers to get a look. "First time in America, the original VOODOO CHANT," yowl the three-sheets on every billboard in town. And when Eddie taps his baton, the lights go down and a nasty green flood lights the platform from below and you can hear a pin drop. "Good evening, folks. This is Eddie Bloch and his Five Chips, playing to you from the Bataclan. You're about to hear for the first time on the air the Voodoo Chant, the age-old ceremonial rhythm no white man has ever been permitted to listen to before. I can assure you this is an accurate transcription, not a note has been changed." Then very soft and faraway it begins: *Boom-putta-putta-boom!*

Judy's going to dance and wail to it, she's standing there on the steps leading up to the platform, waiting to go on. She's powdered orange, dressed in feathers, and has a small artificial bird fastened to one wrist and a thin knife in her other hand. She catches his eye, he looks over at her, and he sees she wants to tell him something. Still waving his baton he edges sideways until he's within earshot. "Eddie, don't! Stop them! Call it off, will you? I'm worried about you!"

"Too late now," he answers under cover of the music. "We've started already. What're you scared of?"

She passes him a crumpled piece of paper. "I found this under your dressing room door when I came out just now. It sounds like a warning. There's somebody doesn't want you to play that number!" Still swinging with his right hand, Eddie unrolls the thing under his left thumb and reads it:

You can summon the spirits but can you dismiss them again? Think well.

He crumples it up again and tosses it away. "Staats trying to scare me because I canned him."

"It was tied to a little bunch of black feathers," she tries to tell him. "I wouldn't have paid any attention, but my maid pleaded with me not to dance this when she saw it. Then she ran out on me—"

"We're on the air," he reminds her between his teeth. "Are you with me or aren't you?" And he eases back center again. Louder and louder the beat grows, just like it did two nights ago. Judy swirls on in a green spot and begins the unearthly wail Eddie's coached her to do.

A waiter drops a tray of drinks in the silence of the room out there, and when the headwaiter goes to bawl him out he's nowhere to be found. He has quit cold and a whole row of tables has been left without their orders. "Well, I'll be—" says the captain, and scratches his head.

Eddie's facing the crew, his back to Judy, and as he vibrates to the rhythm, some pin or other that he's forgotten to take out of his shirt suddenly catches him and sticks into him. It's a little below the collar, just between the shoulder-blades. He jumps a little, but doesn't feel it any more after that . . . .

Judy squalls, tears her tonsils out, screeches words that neither he nor she know the meaning of but that he managed to set down on paper phonetically the other night. Her little body goes through all the contortions, tamed down of course, that that brownskin she-devil greased with lard and wearing only earrings performed that night. She stabs the bird with her fake knife and sprinkles imaginary blood in the air. Nothing like this has ever been seen before. And in the silence that suddenly lands when it's through, you can count twenty. That's how it's gotten under everyone's skin.

Then the noise begins. It goes over like an avalanche. But just the same, more people are ordering strong drinks all at once than has ever happened before in the place, and the matron in the women's restroom has her hands full of hysterical sob-sisters.

"Try to get away from me, just try!" Graham tells Eddie at curfew time. "I'll have a new contract, gilt-edged, ready for you in the morning. We've already got six grand worth of reservations on our hands for the coming week—one of 'em by telegram all the way from Shreveport!"

Success! Eddie and Judy taxi back to their rooms at the hotel, tired but happy. "It'll be good for years. We can use it for our signature on the air, like Whiteman does the Rhapsody."

She goes into the bedroom first, snaps on the lights, calls to him a minute later. "Come here and look at this—the cutest little souvenir!" He finds her holding a little wax doll, finger high, in her hands. "Why, it's you, Eddie, look! Small as it is, it has your features! Well isn't that the clev——"

He takes it away from her and squints at it. It's himself all right. It's rigged out in two tiny patches of black cloth for a tuxedo, and the eyes and hair and features are inked onto the wax.

"Where'd you find it?"

"It was in your bed, up against the pillow."

He's fixing to grin about it, until he happens to turn it over. In the back, just a little below the collar between the shoulder blades, a short but venomous-looking black pin is sticking.

He goes a little white for a minute. He knows who it's from now and what it's trying to tell him. But that isn't what makes him change color. He's just remembered something. He throws off his coat, yanks at his collar, turns his back to her. "Judy, look down there, will you? I felt a pin stick me while we were doing that number. Put your hand down. Feel anything?"

"No, there's nothing there," she tells him.

"Musta dropped out."

"It couldn't have," she says. "Your belt-line's so tight it almost cuts into you. There couldn't have been anything there or it'd still be there now. You must have imagined it."

"Listen, I know a pin when I feel one. Any mark on my back, any scratch between the shoulders?"

"Not a thing."

"Tired, I guess. Nervous." He goes over to the open window and pitches the little doll out into the night with all his strength. Damn coincidence, that's all it was. To think otherwise would be to give them their inning. But he wonders what makes him feel so tired just the same—Judy did all the exercising, not he—yet he's felt all in ever since that number tonight.

Out go the lights and she drops off to sleep right with them. He lies very quiet for awhile. A little later he gets up, goes into the bathroom where the lights are whitest of all, and stands there looking at himself close to the glass. "Look at your fingernails sometime; look at the whites of your eyes," Staats had said. Eddie does. There's a bluish, purplish tinge to his nails that he never noticed before. The whites of his eyes are faintly yellow.

It's warm in New Orleans that night but he shivers a little as he stands there. He doesn't sleep any more that night . . . .

In the morning his back aches as if he were sixty. But he knows that's from not closing his eyes all night, and not from any magic pins.

"Oh, my God!" Judy says, from the other side of the bed, "look what you've done to him!" She shows him the second page of the *Picayune*. "John Staats, until recently a member of Eddie Bloch's orchestra, committed suicide late yesterday afternoon in full view of dozens of people by rowing himself out into Lake Pontchartrain and jumping overboard. He was alone in the boat at the time. The body was recovered half an hour later."

"I didn't do that," says Eddie grimly. "I've got a rough idea what did, though." Late yesterday afternoon. The night was coming on, and he couldn't face what was coming to him for sponsoring Eddie, for giving them all away. Late yesterday after—that meant *he* hadn't left that warning at the dressing-room or left that death sentence on the bed. He'd been dead himself by then—not white, not black, just yellow.

Eddie waits until Judy's in her shower, then he phones the morgue. "About Johnny Staats. He worked for me until yesterday, so if nobody's claimed the body send it to a funeral parlor at my exp——"

"Somebody's already claimed the remains, Mr. Bloch. First thing this morning. Just waited until the examiner had established suicide beyond a doubt. Some colored organization, old friends of his it seems——"

Judy comes in and remarks: "You look all green in the face."

Eddie thinks: "I wouldn't care if he was my worst enemy, I can't let that happen to him! What horrors are going to take place tonight somewhere under the moon?" He wouldn't even put cannibalism beyond them. The phone's right at his fingertips, and yet he can't denounce them to the police without involving himself, admitting that he was there, took part at least once. Once that comes out, bang!

goes his reputation. He'll never be able to live it down—especially now that he's played the Voodoo chant and identified himself with it in the minds of the public.

So instead, alone in the room again, he calls the best-known private agency in New Orleans. "I want a bodyguard. Just for tonight. Have him meet me at closing-time at the Bataclan. Armed, of course."

It's Sunday and the banks are closed, but his credit's good anywhere. He raises a G in cash. He arranges with a reliable crematorium for a body to be taken charge of late tonight or early in the morning. He'll notify them just where to call for it. Yes, of course! He'll produce the proper authorization from the police. Poor Johnny Staats couldn't get away from them in life, but he's going to get away from them in death, all right. That's the least anyone could do for him.

Graham slaps a sawbuck cover on that night, more to give the waiters room to move around in than anything else, and still the place is choked to the roof. This Voodoo number is a natural, a wow.

But Eddie's back is ready to cave in, while he stands there jogging with his stick. It's all he can do to hold himself straight.

When the racket and the shuffling are over for the night, the private dick is there waiting for him. "Lee is the name."

"Okay, Lee, come with me." They go outside and get in Eddie's Bugatti. They whizz down to the Vieux, scrounge to a stop in the middle of Congo Square, which will still be Congo Square when its official name of Beauregard is forgotten. "This way," says Eddie, and his bodyguard squirms through the alley after him. "'Lo, suga' pie," says the elbow-pusher, and for once, to her own surprise as much as anyone else's, gets a tumble. "'Lo, Eglantine," Eddie's bodyguard remarks in passing, "so you moved?"

They stop in front of the house on the other side of the tunnel. "Now here's what," says Eddie. "We're going to be stopped halfway up these stairs in here by a big ourangoutang. Your job is to clean him, tap him if you want, I don't care. I'm going into a room up there, you're going to wait for me at the door. You're here to see that I get out of that room again. We may have to carry the body of a friend of mine down to the street between us. I don't know. It depends on whether it's in the house or not. Got it?"

"Got it."

"Light up. Keep your torch trained over my shoulder."

A big, lowering figure looms over them, blocking the narrow stairs, ape-like arms and legs spread-eagled in a gesture of malignant embrace, receding skull, teeth showing, flashing steel in hand. Lee jams Eddie roughly to one side and shoves up past him. "Drop that, boy!" Lee says with slurring indifference, but then he doesn't wait to see if the order's carried out or not. After all, a weapon was raised to two white men. He fires three times, from two feet away and considerably below the obstacle, hits where he aimed to. The bullets shatter both knee-caps and the elbow-joint of the arm holding the knife. "Be a cripple for life now," he remarks with quiet satisfaction. "I'll put him out of his pain." So he crashes the butt of his gun down on the skull of the writhing colossus, in a long arc like the overhand pitch of a baseball. The noise of the shots goes booming up the narrow stair-well to the roof, to mushroom out there in a vast rolling echo. "Come on, hurry up," says Eddie, "before they have a chance to do away with——"

He lopes on up past the prostrate form, Lee at his heels. "Stand here. Better reload while you're waiting. If I call your name, for Pete's sake don't count ten before you come in to me!"

There's a scurrying back and forth and an excited but subdued jabbering going on on the other side of the door. Eddie swings it wide and crashes it closed behind him, leaving Lee on the outside. They all stand rooted to the spot when they see him. The papaloi is there and about six others, not so many as on the night of Eddie's initiation. Probably the rest are waiting outside the city somewhere, in some secret spot, wherever the actual burial, or burning, or—feasting—is to take place.

Papa Benjamin has no juju mask on this time, no animal pelt. There are no gourds in the room, no drum, no transfixed figures ranged against the wall. They were about to move on elsewhere, he just got here in time. Maybe they were waiting for the dark of the moon. The ordinary kitchen chair on which the papaloi was to be carried on their shoulders stands prepared, padded with rags. A row of baskets covered with sacking is ranged in a row along the back wall.

"Where is the body of John Staats?" raps out Eddie. "You claimed it, took it away from the morgue this morning." His eyes are on those baskets, on the bleared razor he catches sight of lying on the floor near them.

"Better far," cackles the old man, "that you had followed him. The mark of doom is on yo' even now——" A growl goes up all around.

"Lee," grates Eddie, "in here!" Lee stands next to him, gun in hand. "Cover me while I take a look around."

"All of you over in that corner there," growls Lee, and kicks viciously at one who is too slow in moving. They huddle there, cower there, glaring, spitting like a band of apes. Eddie makes straight for those baskets, whips the covering off the first one. Charcoal. The next. Coffee-beans. The next. Rice. And so on.

Just small baskets that negro women balance on their heads to sell at the market-place. He looks at Papa Benjamin, takes out the wad of money he's brought with him. "Where've you got him? Where's he buried? Take us there, show us where it is."

Not a sound, just burning, shriveling hate in waves that you can almost feel. He looks at that razor-blade lying there, bleared, not bloody, just matted, dulled, with shreds and threads of something clinging to it. Kicks it away with his foot. "Not here, I guess," he mutters to Lee and moves toward the door. "What do we do now, boss?" his henchman wants to know. "Get the hell out of here, I guess, where we can breathe some air," Eddie says, and moves on out to the stairs.

Lee is the sort of man who will get what he can out of any situation, no matter what it is. Before he follows Eddie out, he goes over to one of the baskets, stuffs an orange in each coat-pocket, and then prods and pries among them to select a particularly nice one for eating on the spot. There's a thud and the orange goes rolling across the floor like a volleyball. "Mr. Bloch!" he shouts hoarsely. "I've found—him!" And he looks pretty sick.

A deep breath goes up from the corner where the negroes are. Eddie

just stands and stares, and leans back weakly for a minute against
the door-post. From out the layers of oranges in the basket, the five
fingers of a hand thrust upward, a hand that ends abruptly, cleanly at
the wrist.

"His signet," says Eddie weakly, "there on the little finger—I
know it."

"Say the word! Should I shoot?" Lee wants to know.

Eddie shakes his head. "They didn't—he committed suicide. Let's
do what—we have to—and get out of here!"

Lee turns over one basket after the other. The stuff in them spills
and sifts and rolls out upon the floor. But in each there's something
else. Bloodless, pallid as fish-flesh. That razor, those shreds clinging
to it, Eddie knows now what it was used for. They take one basket,
they line it with a verminous blanket from the bed. Then with their
bare hands they fill it with what they have found, and close the ends
of the blanket over the top of it, and carry it between them out of the
room and down the pitch-black stairs, Lee going down backwards
with his gun in one hand to cover them from the rear. Lee's swearing
like a fiend. Eddie's trying not to think what the purpose, the destina-
tion of all those baskets was. The watchdog is still out on the stairs,
with a concussion.

Back through the lane they struggle, and finally put their burden
down in the before-dawn stillness of Congo Square. Eddie goes up
against a wall and is heartily sick. Then he comes back again and
says: "The head—did you notice—?"

"No, we didn't," Lee answers. "Stay here, I'll go back for it. I'm
armed. I could stand anything now, after what I just been through."

Lee's gone about five minutes. When he comes back, he's in his
shirt, coatless. His coat's rolled up under one arm in a bulky bulge. He
bends over the basket, lifts the blanket, replaces it again, and when
he straightens up, the bulge in his folded coat is gone. Then he throws
the coat away, kicks it away on the ground. "Hidden away in a
cupboard," he mutters. "Had to shoot one of 'em through the palm of
the hand before they'd come clean. What were they up to?"

"Practice cannibalism maybe, I don't know. I'd rather not think."

"I brought your money back. It didn't seem to square you with them."

Eddie shoves it back at him. "Pay for your suit and your time."

"Aren't you going to tip off the squareheads?"

"I told you he jumped in the lake. I have a copy of the examiner's report in my pocket."

"I know, but isn't there some ordinance against dissecting a body without permission?"

"I can't afford to get mixed up with them, Lee. It would kill my career. We've got what we went there for. Now just forget everything you saw."

The hearse from the crematorium contacts them there in Congo Square. The covered basket's taken on, and what's left of Johnny Staats heads away for a better finish than was coming to him.

"G'night, boss," says Lee. "Anytime you need any other little thing——"

"No," says Eddie. "I'm getting out of New Orleans." His hand is like ice when they shake.

He does. He hands Graham back his contract, and a split week later he's playing New York's newest, in the frantic Fifties. With a white valet. The Chant, of course, is still featured. He has to; it's his chief asset, his biggest draw. It introduces him and signs him off, and in between, Judy always dances it for a high-spot. But he can't get rid of that backache that started the night he first played it. First he goes and tries having his back baked for a couple of hours a day under a violet-ray. No improvement.

Then he has himself examined by the biggest specialist in New York. "Nothing there," says the big shot. "Absolutely nothing the matter with you: liver, kidneys, blood—everything perfect. It must be all in your own mind."

"You're losing weight, Eddie," Judy says, "you look bad, darling." His bathroom scales tell him the same thing. Down five pounds a week, sometimes seven, never up an ounce. More experts. X-rays this time, blood analysis, gland treatments, everything from soup to nuts.

Nothing doing. And the dull ache, the lassitude, spreads slowly, first to one arm, then to the other.

He takes specimens of everything he eats, not just one day, but every day for weeks, and has them chemically analyzed. Nothing. And he doesn't have to be told that anyway. He knows that even in New Orleans, way back in the beginning, nothing was ever put into his food. Judy ate from the same tray, drank from the same coffee-pot he did. Nightly she dances herself into a lather, and yet she's the picture of health.

So that leaves nothing but his mind, just as they all say. "But I don't believe it!" he tells himself. "I don't believe that just sticking pins into a wax doll can hurt me—me or anyone!"

So it isn't his mind at all, but some other mind back there in New Orleans, some other mind *thinking,* wishing, ordering him dead, night and day.

"But it can't be done!" says Eddie. "There's no such thing!"

And yet it's being done; it's happening right under his own eyes. Which leaves only one answer. If going three thousand miles away on dry land didn't help, then going three thousand miles away across the ocean will do the trick. So London next, and the Kit-Kat Club. Down, down, down go the bathroom scales, a little bit each week. The pains spread downward into his thighs. His ribs start showing up here and there. He's dying on his feet. He finds it more comfortable now to walk with a stick—not to be swanky, not to be English—to rest on as he goes along. His shoulders ache each night just from waving that lightweight baton at his crew. He has a music-stand built for himself to lean on, keeps it in front of him, body out of sight of the audience while he's conducting, and droops over it. Sometimes he finishes up a number with his head lower than his shoulders, as though he had a rubber spine.

Finally he goes to Reynolds, famous the world over, the biggest alienist in England. "I want to know whether I'm sane or insane." He's under observation for weeks, months; they put him through every known test, and plenty of unknown ones, mental, physical, metabolic. They flash lights in front of his face and watch the pupils of his eyes; they contract to pinheads. They touch the back of his throat with sandpaper; he nearly chokes.

They strap him to a chair that goes around and around and does somersaults at so many revolutions per minute, then ask him to walk across the room; he staggers. Reynolds takes plenty of pounds, hands him a report thick as a telephone book, sums it up for him. "You are as normal, Mr. Bloch, as anyone I have ever handled. You're so well-balanced you haven't even got the extra little touch of imagination most actors and musicians have." So it's not his own mind, it's coming from the outside, is it?

The whole thing from beginning to end has taken eighteen months. Trying to outdistance death, with death gaining on him slowly, but surely, all the time. He's emaciated. There's only one thing left to do now, while he's still able to crawl aboard a ship—that's to get back to where the whole thing started. New York, London, Paris haven't been able to save him. His only salvation, now, lies in the hands of a decrepit colored man skulking in the Vieux Carré of New Orleans.

He drags himself there, to that same half-ruined house, without a bodyguard, not caring now whether they kill him or not, almost wishing they would and get it over with. But that would be too easy an out, it seems. The gorilla that Lee crippled that night shuffles out to him between two sticks, recognizes him, breathes undying hate into his face, but doesn't lift a finger to harm him. The spirits are doing that job better than he could ever hope to. Their mark is on this man, woe betide anyone who comes between them and their hellish satisfaction. Eddie Bloch totters up the stairs unopposed, his back as safe from a knife as if he wore steel armor. Behind him the negro sprawls upon the stairs to lubricate his long-awaited hour of satisfaction with rum—and oblivion.

He finds the old man alone there in the room. The Stone Age and the 20th Century face each other, and the Stone Age has won out. "Take it off me," says Eddie brokenly. "Give me my life back—I'll do anything, anything you say!"

"What has been done cannot be undone. Do you think the spirits of the earth and of the air, of fire and water, know the meaning of forgiveness?"

"Intercede for me then. You brought it about. Here's money, I'll give you twice as much, all I earn, all I ever hope to earn——"

"You have desecrated the obiah. Death has been on you from that night. All over the world and in the air above the earth you have mocked the spirits with the chant that summons them. Nightly your wife dances it. The only reason she has not shared your doom is because she does not know the meaning of what she does. You do. You were here among us."

Eddie goes down on his knees, scrapes along the floor after the old man, tries to tug at the garments he wears. "Kill me right now, then, and be done with it. I can't stand any more——" He bought the gun only that day, was going to do it himself at first, but found he couldn't. A minute ago he pleaded for his life, now he's pleading for death. "It's loaded, all you have to do is shoot. Look! I'll close my eyes—I'll write a note and sign it, that I did it myself——"

He tries to thrust it into the witch-doctor's hand, tries to close the bony, shriveled fingers around it, tries to point it at himself. The old man throws it down, away from him. Cackles gleefully, "Death will come, but differently—slowly, oh, so slowly!" Eddie just lies there flat on his face, sobbing dryly. The old man spits, kicks at him weakly. He pulls himself up somehow, stumbles toward the door. He isn't even strong enough to get it open at the first try. It's that little thing that brings it on. Something touches his foot, he looks, stoops for the gun, turns. Thought is quick but the old man's mind is even quicker. Almost before the thought is there, the old man knows what's coming. In a flash, scuttling like a crab, he has shifted around to the other side of the bed, to put something between them. Instantly the situation's reversed, the fear has left Eddie and is on the old man now. He's lost the aggressive. For a minute only, but that minute is all Eddie needs. His mind beams out like a diamond, like a lighthouse through a fog. The gun roars, jolting his weakened body down to his shoes. The old man falls flat across the bed, his head too far over, dangling down over the side of it like an overripe pear. The bed-frame sways gently with his weight for a minute, and then it's over . . .

Eddie stands there, still off-balance from the kick-back. So it was as easy as all that! Where's all his magic now? Strength, will-power flood back through him as if a faucet was suddenly turned on. The little smoke there was can't get out of the sealed-up room, it hangs there in thin layers. Suddenly he's shaking his fist at the dead thing on the bed. "I'm gonna live now! I'm gonna live, see?" He gets the door open, sways for a minute. Then he's feeling his way down the stairs, past the unconscious watchdog, mumbling it over and over but low, "Gonna live now, gonna live!"

The Commissioner mops his face as if he was in the steam room of a Turkish bath. He exhales like an oxygen tank. "Judas, Joseph and Mary, Mr. Bloch, what a story! Wish I hadn't asked you; I won't sleep tonight." Even after the accused has been led from the room, it takes him some time to get over it. The upper right-hand drawer of his desk helps some—just two fingers. So does opening the windows and letting in a lot of sunshine.

Finally he picks up the phone and gets down to business. "Who've you got out there that's absolutely without a nerve in his body? I mean a guy with so little feeling he could sit on a hatpin and turn it into a paper-clip. Oh yeah, that Cajun, Desjardins, I know him. He's the one goes around striking parlor-matches off the soles of stiffs. Well, send him in here."

"No, stay outside," wheezes Papa Benjamin through the partly-open door to his envoy. "I'se communin' with the obiah and yo' unclean, been drunk all last night and today. Deliver the summons. Reach yo' hand in to me, once fo' every token, yo' knows how many to take."

The crippled negro thrusts his huge paw through the aperture, and from behind the door the papaloi places a severed chicken-claw in his upturned palm. A claw bound with a red rag. The messenger disposes of it about his tattered clothing, thrusts his hand in for another. Twenty times the act is repeated, then he lets his arm hang stiffly at his side. The door starts closing slowly. "Papaloi," whines the figure on the outside of it, "why you hide yo' face from me, is the spirits angry?"

There's a flicker of suspicion in his yellow eyeballs in the dimness, however. Instantly the opening of the door widens. Papa Benjamin's familiar wrinkled face thrusts out at him, malignant eyes crackling like fuses. "Go!" shrills the old man, "'liver my summons. Is you want me to bring a spirit down on you?" The messenger totters back. The door slams.

The sun goes down and it's night-time in New Orleans. The moon rises, midnight chimes from St. Louis Cathedral, and hardly has the last note died away than a gruesome swampland whistle sounds outside the deathly-still house. A fat Negress, basket on arm, comes trudging up the stairs a moment later, opens the door, goes in to the papaloi, closes it again, traces an invisible mark on it with her forefinger and kisses it. Then she turns and her eyes widen with surprise. Papa Benjamin is in bed, covered up to the neck with filthy rags. The familiar candles are all lit, the bowl for the blood, the sacrificial knife, the magic powders, all the paraphernalia of the ritual are laid out in readiness, but they are ranged about the bed instead of at the opposite end of the room as usual. The old man's head, however, is held high above the encumbering rags, his beady eyes gaze back at her unflinchingly, the familiar semicircle of white wool rings his crown, his ceremonial mask is at his side. "I am a little tired, my daughter," he tells her. His eyes stray to the tiny wax image of Eddie Bloch under the candles, hairy with pins, and hers follow them.

"A doomed one, nearing his end, came here last night thinking I could be killed like other men. He shot a bullet from a gun at me. I blew my breath at it, it stopped in the air, turned around, and went back in the gun again. But it tired me to blow so hard, strained my voice a little."

A revengeful gleam lights up the woman's broad face. "And he'll die soon, papaloi?"

"Soon," cackles the weazened figure in the bed. The woman gnashes her teeth and hugs herself delightedly. She opens the top of her basket and allows a black hen to escape and flutter about the room.

When all twenty have assembled, men and women, old and young, the drum and the gourds begin to beat, the low wailing starts, the orgy gets under way. Slowly they dance around the three sides of the bed at first, then faster, faster, lashing themselves to a frenzy, tearing at their own and each other's clothes, drawing blood with knives and fingernails, eyes rolling in an ecstasy that colder races cannot know. The sacrifices, feathered and furred, that have been fastened to the two lower posts of the bed, squawk and flutter and fly vertically up and down in a barnyard panic. There is a small monkey among them tonight, clawing, biting, hiding his face in his hands like a frightened child. A bearded negro, nude torso glistening like patent-leather, seizes one of the frantic fowls, yanks it loose from its moorings, and holds it out toward the witch-doctor with both hands. "We'se thirsty, papaloi, we'se thirsty fo' the blood of ou' enemies."

The others take up the cry. "We'se hung'y, papaloi, fo' the bones of ou' enemies!"

Papa Benjamin nods his head in time to the rhythm.

"Sac'fice, papaloi, sac'fice!"

Papa Benjamin doesn't seem to hear them.

Then back go the rags in a gray wave and out comes the arm at last. Not the gnarled brown toothpick arm of Papa Benjamin, but a bulging arm thick as a piano-leg, cuffed in serge, white at the wrist, ending in a regulation police-revolver with the clip off. The erstwhile witch-doctor's on his feet at a bound, standing erect atop the bed, back to the wall, slowly fanning his score of human devils with the mouth of his gun, left to right, then right to left again, evenly, unhurriedly. The resonant bellow of a bull comes from his weazened slit of a mouth instead of the papaloi's cracked falsetto. "Back against that wall there, all of you! Throw down them knives and jiggers!" But they're slow to react; the swift drop from ecstasy to stupefaction can't register right away. None of them are overbright anyway or they wouldn't be here. Mouths hang open, the wailing stops, the drums and gourds fall still, but they're still packed close about this sudden changeling in their midst, with the familiar shriveled face of Papa Benjamin and the thick-set body, business-suit, of a white man—too close for comfort. Blood-lust and religious mania don't know fear of a gun. It takes a cool head for that, and the only cool head in the room is the withered cocoanut atop the broad shoulders behind that gun. So he shoots twice, and a woman at one end of the semicircle, the drumbeater, and

a man at the other end, the one still holding the sacrificial fowl, drop
in their tracks with a double moan. Those in the middle slowly draw
back step by step across the room, all eyes on the figure reared up on
the bed. An instant's carelessness, the wavering of an eye, and they'll
be on him in a body. He reaches with his free hand and rips the dead
witch-doctor's features from his face, to breathe better, see better.
They dissolve into a crumpled rag before the blacks' terrified eyes,
like a stocking-cap coming off someone's head—a mixture of paraffin
and fiber, called moulage—a death-mask taken from the corpse's own
face, reproducing even the fine lines of the skin and its natural color.
Moulage. So the 20th Century has won out after all. And behind them
is the grinning, slightly-perspiring, lantern-jawed face of Detective
Jacques Desjardins, who doesn't believe in spirits unless they're
under a neat little label. And outside the house sounds the twenty-
first whistle of the evening, but not a swampland sound this time; a
long, cold, keen blast to bring figures out of the shadows and door-
ways that have waited there patiently all night.

Then the door bursts inward and the police are in the room. The
survivors, three of them dangerously wounded, are pushed and carried downstairs to join the crippled door-guard, who has been in
custody for the past hour, and single-file, tied together with ropes,
they make their way through the long tortuous alley out into Congo
Square.

In the early hours of that same morning, just a little more than
twenty-four hours after Eddie Bloch first staggered into Police Headquarters with his strange story, the whole thing is cooked, washed
and bottled. The Commissioner sits in his office listening attentively
to Desjardins.

And spread out on his desk as strange an array of amulets, wax
images, bunches of feathers, balsam leaves, ouangas (charms of nail
parings, hair clippings, dried blood, powdered roots), green mildewed
coins dug up from coffins in graveyards, as that room has ever seen
before. All this is state's evidence now, to be carefully labelled and
docketed for the use of the prosecuting attorney when the proper time
comes. "And this," explains Desjardins, indicating a small dusty

bottle, "is methylene blue, the chemist tells me. It's the only modern thing we got out of the place, found it lying forgotten with a lot of rubbish in a corner that looked like it hadn't been disturbed for years. What it was doing there or what they wanted with it I don't——"

"Wait a minute," interrupts the commissioner eagerly. "That fits in with something poor Bloch told me last night. He noticed a bluish color under his fingernails and a yellowness to his eyeballs, but *only* after he'd been initiated that first night.

"This stuff probably has something to do with it, an injection of it must have been given him that night in some way without his knowing it. Don't you get the idea? It floored him just the way they wanted it to. He mistook the signs of it for a give-away that he had colored blood. It was the opening wedge. It broke down his disbelief, started his mental resistance to crumbling. That was all they needed, just to get a foothold in his mind. Mental suggestion did the rest, has been doing it ever since. If you ask me, they pulled the same stunt on Staats originally. I don't believe he had colored blood any more than Bloch has. And as a matter of fact the theory that it shows up in that way generations later is all the bunk anyway, they tell me."

"Well," says Dij, looking at his own grimy nails, "if you're just going to judge by appearances that way, I'm full-blooded Zulu."

His overlord just looks at him, and if he didn't have such a poker face, one might be tempted to read admiration or at least approval into the look. "Must have been a pretty tight spot for a minute with all of them around while you put on your act!"

"Nah, I didn't mind," answers Dij.

Eddie Bloch, the murder charge against him quashed two months ago, and the population of the State Penitentiary increased only this past week by the admission of twenty-three ex-voodoo worshippers for terms varying from two to ten years, steps up on the platform of the Bataclan for a return engagement. Eddie's pale and washed-out looking, but climbing slowly back up through the hundred-and-twenties again to his former weight. The ovation he gets ought to do anyone's heart good, the way they clap and stamp and stand up and cheer. And at that, his name was kept out of the recently-concluded trial. Desjardins and his mates did all the states-witnessing necessary.

The theme he comes in on now is something sweet and harmless. Then a waiter comes up and hands him a request. Eddie shakes his head. "No, not in our repertoire any more." He goes on leading. Another request comes, and another. Suddenly someone shouts it out at him, and in a second the whole place has taken up the cry. "The Voodoo Chant! Give us the Voodoo Chant!"

His face gets whiter than it is already, but he turns and tries to smile at them and shake his head. They won't quit, the music can't be heard, and he has to tap a lay-off. From all over the place, like a cheering-section at a football game, "We want the Voodoo Chant! We want——!"

Judy's at his side. "What's the matter with 'em anyway?" he asks. "Don't they know what that thing's done to me?"

"Play it, Eddie, don't be foolish," she urges. "Now's the time, break the spell once and for all, prove to yourself that it can't hurt you. If you don't do it now, you'll never get over the idea. It'll stay with you all your life. Go ahead. I'll dance it just like I am."

"Okay," he says.

He taps. It's been quite some time, but he can rely on his outfit. Slow and low like thunder far away, coming nearer. *Boom-putta-putta-boom!* Judy whirls out behind him, lets out the first preliminary screech, *Eeyaeeya!*

She hears a commotion in back of her, and stops as suddenly as she began. Eddie Bloch's fallen flat on his face and doesn't move again after that.

They all know somehow. There's an inertness, a finality about it that tells them. The dancers wait a minute, mill about, then melt away in a hush. Judy Jarvis doesn't scream, doesn't cry, just stands there staring, wondering. That last thought—did it come from inside his own mind just now—or outside? Was it two months on its way, from the other side of the grave, looking for him, looking for him, until it found him tonight when he played the Chant once more and laid his mind open to Africa? No policeman, no detective, no doctor, no scientist, will ever be able to tell her. Did it come from inside or from outside? All she says is: "Stand close to me, boys—real close to me, I'm afraid of the dark."

(1935)

The Corpse and the Kid

Larry didn't even know his father was in the house until he met him coming down the stairs. It was a little after five and he'd just come in from the beach. "Hello, Dad," he said, and held his hand out in welcome. "You didn't tell us you were coming down from New York tonight!" Then he said: "Gee, you look white! Been working too hard?"

Larry idolized his father and worried continually about the way he kept slaving to provide for and indulge his family. Not that they weren't comfortably well off now—but the doctor had told the elder Weeks that with that heart of his— It was only a matter of months now.

Mr. Weeks didn't answer, nor did he take his son's outstretched hand. Instead he sat down suddenly in the middle of the staircase and hid his face behind his own hands. "Don't go upstairs, kid!" he groaned hollowly. "Keep away from there!"

Larry did just the opposite. His own face grown white in dread premonition, he leaped past his father and ran on up. He turned down the cottage's short upper hallway and threw open the door at the end of it and looked in. It was the first room he'd come to. The right room.

She lay partly across the bed with her head hanging down above the floor and her light brown hair sweeping the carpet. One arm was twisted behind her back; the other one flailed out stiff and straight, reaching desperately for the help that had never come. She was his father's wife, Larry's stepmother. The dread he had felt on the stairs became a certainty now as he looked in. He had expected something like this sooner or later.

190

He turned her over, lifted her up, tried to rouse her by shaking her, by working her lower jaw back and forth with his hand. It was too late. Her eyes stared at him unblinkingly, her head rolled around like a rubber ball. Her neck had been broken. There were livid purple marks on her throat where fingers had pressed inward.

Larry let her drop back again like a rag doll, left the room and closed the door behind him. He stumbled down the hall to the head of the stairs. His father was still sitting there halfway down, his head bowed low over his knees. Larry slumped down beside him. After a while he put one hand on his father's shoulder, then let it slip off again. "I'm with you," he said.

His father lifted his head. "She gone?"

Larry nodded.

"I knew she must be," his father said. "I heard it crack." He shuddered and covered his ears, as though he were afraid of hearing it over again.

"She asked for it and she got it," Larry remarked bitterly.

His father looked up sharply. "You knew?"

"All the time. He used to come down week-ends and she'd meet him at the Berkeley-Carteret."

"Why didn't you tell me?"

"She was your wife," Larry said. "Wouldn't I have looked great."

On a little table down at the foot of the stairs the telephone started to ring, and they both stiffened and their pale faces grew even paler. They turned and looked at each other without a word while it went on shattering the ominous stillness of the house with its loud pealing.

"I'll get it," Larry said suddenly. "I know all the answers." He got up and went down to it, while his father gazed after him fearfully. He waited a minute to brace himself, then swiftly unhooked the receiver. "Hello," he said tensely. Then with a quick let-down of relief, "No, she hasn't come back from the beach yet." He exchanged a glance with his father, halfway up the stairs. "Why don't you pick her up there instead of calling for her here at the house? You know where to find her. She won't be back for hours yet, and you'd only have to hang around here waiting." Then he added: "No, I don't mean to be inhospitable, only I thought it would save time. 'Bye." He puffed his cheeks and blew out his breath with relief as he hung up. A couple of crystal drops oozed out on his

192 / Cornell Woolrich

forehead. "Helen's boy-friend," he said, turning to the man on the stairs. Helen was his sister. "If he does what I told him, it'll give us a couple of hours at least."

The older man spoke without lifting his head at all. "What's the use? Better phone the police and get it over with."

Larry said: "No." Then he yelled it at the top of his voice. "No, I tell you! You're my father—I can't, I won't let you! She wasn't worth your life! You know what the doctors said, you haven't much time anyway— Oh, God." He went close and jabbed his knee at Weeks to bring him to. "Pull yourself together. We've got to get her out of here. I don't care where it happened, only it didn't happen here—it happened some place else."

Twenty-one years of energy pulled forty-two years of apathy to its feet by the shoulders. "You—you were in New York. You *are* in New York right now, do you get me? You didn't come down here, just as none of us expected you to." He began to shake his father, to help the words and the idea that was behind them to sink in. "Did anyone see you on the train, at the depot just now, or coming into the house? Anyone who knows you by sight? Think hard, try to remember, will you, Dad?"

Weeks ran his hand across his forehead. "Coming in, no," he said. "The street was dead, they were all down at the beach or on the boardwalk. The depot I'm not sure about, some of the redcaps might know me by sight—"

"But they only see you one day every week. They might get mixed up after a day or two in remembering just the exact day. We gotta take a chance. And make sure they see you tomorrow when you *do* come down, that'll cover today. Talk to one of them, lose something, stumble and get helped up, anything at all. Now about the train. The conductor must know you by sight—"

Weeks' face brightened all of a sudden, as the idea began to catch on, take hold of him. The self-preservation instinct isn't easily suppressed. He grasped his son by the lapel of his coat. "Larry," he said eagerly, "I just remembered—my commutation ticket—"

Larry's face paled again. "And I," he groaned, "forgot all about that. The date'll be punched—we can't get around that—"

"No, wait a minute. Just today—something that never happened before all summer—my mind was haywire I guess on account of what I'd found out—but when I got to Penn Station I found I didn't have it with me, I'd left it at the office. I had to buy an ordinary ticket to get down here—"

"Then it's a push-over!" exclaimed Larry. "It's a Godsend. It'd be a crime not to take advantage of a break like that. Doesn't it convince you what the best thing to do is? If I were superstitious I'd call it—" He stopped short. "Wait a minute, round-trip I hope? Or will you have to step up and buy a return ticket at this end?"

"It's here," panted Weeks, fumbling in his coat. "I was burning so, I didn't even notice—" He dragged it out and they both gave a simultaneous sigh of relief. "Swell," said Larry. "That unpunched commutation ticket is going to be an A-one alibi in itself. Hang onto it whatever you do. But we'll fix it all up brown. Can you get hold of someone in the city to pass the evening with you—or better still two or three friends?"

"I can get in touch with Fred German. He always rolls up a gang of stay-outs as he goes along."

"Go to a show with 'em, bend the elbow, get a little lit, stay with them as late as you possibly can manage it. And before you leave them—not after but *before*, so they all can see and hear you—call me long-distance down here. That means your name'll go down on the company's records from that end. I'll have your cue ready for you by that time. If she's not dead yet, then the rotgut made you sentimental and you wanted to talk to your family, that's all. But if I have everything under control by that time, then I'll have bad news for you then and there. You can stage a cloudburst in front of them and continue under your own speed from that point on. But until that happens, watch your step. Keep the soft pedal on. Don't be jerky and nervous and punchy. Don't give 'em an idea you've got anything on your mind. The better you know people, the better they can tell when something's wrong with you. Now all that is your job. Mine"—he drew in his breath—"is upstairs. Got your hat?" He took out his watch. "Get back to the station, the six o'clock pulls out in ten minutes. They're starting to drift back from the beach, so go to

Charlton Street, one over, and keep your head down. Don't look at anyone. Thank God she wasn't much on getting acquainted with her neighbors—" He was leading him toward the door as he spoke.

"What're you going to do?" asked Weeks with bated voice.

"I don't know," said Larry, "but I don't want an audience for it, whatever it is. All I need is darkness, and thinking how swell you've been to me all my life—and I can do the rest, I'll pull through. Stand behind the door a minute till I take a squint." He opened the door, sauntered out on the bungalow doorstep, and looked casually up in one direction, then down in the other, as though seeking a breath of air. Then suddenly he was back in again, pushing his father irresistibly before him. "Hurry up, not a living soul in sight. It may not be this way again for the rest of the evening. They all sit on their porches after dark—"

Weeks' body suddenly stiffened, held back. "No, I can't do it, can't let you! What am I thinking of anyway, letting my own son hold the bag for me? If they nab you doing this they'll hang it on you—"

"Do you want to die at Trenton?" Larry asked him fiercely. The answer was on Weeks' face, would have been on anyone's face. "Then lemme do it my way!" They gripped hands for a second. Something like a sob sounded in Weeks' throat. Then he was over the threshold and Larry was pushing the door silently after him.

Just before it met the frame Weeks pivoted abruptly, jumped back, and rammed his foot into the opening. There was a new urgency in his voice. "Helen. I see her coming! She just turned the corner!"

"Get back in!" snapped Larry. "Can't make it now. Her eyes are too good, she'll spot you even from a distance." He closed the door on the two of them. "He with her?"

"No."

"Then they missed connections. I'll send her right out again after him." He swore viciously. "If you're not out of here in five minutes, you don't make that train—and the later you get back the riskier it gets. As it is, you have three hours you can't account for. Here—the clothes closet—be ready to light out the first chance you get. It's just a step to the door."

Weeks, pulling the door of the hall closet after him, murmured: "Don't you think the kid would—"

All Larry said was: "She was pretty chummy with Doris."

Her key was already jiggling in the front door. Larry seemed to be coming toward it as she got it open and they met face to face. She was in her bathing suit. He'd overlooked that when he'd spoken to her boy friend. He swore again, silently this time.

"Who was that came to the door just now, before I got here?" she asked.

"Me," he said curtly. "Who'd you think?"

"I know, I saw you, but I thought I saw someone else too, a minute later. It looked like two people from where I was."

"Well, it wasn't," he snapped. "Whatta ya been drinking?"

"Oh, grouchy again." She started for the stairs. "Doris back yet?"

"No," he said firmly.

"Good, then I can swipe some of her face powder while she's out." She ran lightly up the stairs. He went cold for a minute, then he passed her like a bullet passing an arrow. He was standing in front of the door with his back to it when she turned down the upstairs corridor. "What's the matter with *you*?" she asked dryly. "Feel playful?" She tried to elbow him aside.

"Lay off," he said huskily. "She raised Cain just before she went out about your helping yourself to her things, said she wants it stopped." He got the key out of the door behind his back and dropped it into his back pocket.

"I don't believe it," she said. "That isn't like her at all. I'm going to ask her to her face when she comes ba—" She rattled the doorknob unsuccessfully, gave him a surprised look.

"See, what'd I tell you?" he murmured. "She must have locked it and taken the key with her." He moved down the hall again, as if going to his own room.

"If it was already locked," she called after him, "why did you jump up here in such a hurry to keep me out?"

He had an answer for that one though, too. "I didn't want you to find out. It's hell when trouble starts between the women of a family."

"Maybe I'm crazy," she said, "but I have the funniest feeling that there's something going on around here today—everything's suddenly different from what it is other days. What was the idea freezing Gordon out when he tried to call for me?"

She had stopped before her own door, which was next to their stepmother's. He was nearer the stair-well than she was, almost directly over it. From below came the faint double click of a door as it opened then shut again. Even he could hardly hear it, she certainly couldn't. The front door—he'd made it. Larry straight-armed himself against the stair railing and let a lot of air out of his lungs. He was trembling in strange places, at the wrists and in back of his knees. It was his job now. He was scared sick of it, but he was going to do it.

Without turning his head he knew she was standing there up the hall, watching him, waiting. What the hell was she waiting for? Oh yes, she'd asked him a question, she was waiting for the answer. That was it. Absently he gave it to her. "You weren't here, I only told him where to find you." She went into her room and banged the door shut.

And with that sound something suddenly exploded in his brain. The connecting bathroom, between her room and Doris's! She could get in through there! Not only could but most certainly would, out of sheer stubbornness now, because she thought Doris was trying to keep her out. Women were that way. And when she did—there in full view upon the bed, what *he* had seen, what his own loyalty had been strong enough to condone, but what might prove too much for hers. He couldn't take the chance. His father's life was at stake, he couldn't gamble with that. It had to be a sure thing—

He dove back to that door again and whipped the key from his pocket. He got the door open as quietly as he could, but he was in too much of a hurry and it was too close to her own room to be an altogether soundless operation. Then when he was in, with the twisted body in full view, he saw what had covered him. She was in the bathroom already, but she had the water roaring into the washbasin and that kept her from hearing. But the door between was already open about a foot, must have been that way all afternoon. Just one look was all that was needed, just one look in without even opening it any more than it already was. She hadn't given that look yet. He could be sure of that because her scream would have told him, but any minute now, any fraction of a second— He could see her in the mirror. She had the straps of her bathing suit down and was rinsing her face with cold water.

There was no time to get the body out of the room altogether. He didn't dare try. That much movement, the mere lifting and carrying of it, would surely attract her attention. And the long hall outside— where could he take it? The thought of trying deftly to compose and rearrange it where it lay, into the semblance of taking a nap, came to him for a moment and was rejected too. There wasn't time enough for that, and anyway he'd already told her she was out. All this in the two or three stealthy cat-like steps that took him from the door to the side of the bed.

As he reached it he already knew what the only possible thing to do was, for the time being. Even to get it into the clothes closet was out of the question. It meant crossing the room with it, and then clothes hangers have a way of rattling and clicking.

He dropped to his knees, crouched below the level of the bed on the side away from the bathroom, pulled the corpse toward him by one wrist and one ankle, and as it dropped off the side, his own body broke its fall. It dropped heavily athwart his thighs. The way the arms and legs retained their posture betokened rigor already, but made it easier to handle if anything. From where it was, across his lap, two good shoves got it under the bed and he left it there. It was a big enough bed to conceal it completely, unless you got down on the floor where he was.

Under and beyond the bed, on a level with his eyes, he could see the threshold of the bathroom. While he looked, and before there was any chance to scurry across the room to the hall door, Helen's feet and ankles came into view. They paused there for a moment, toes pointed his way, and he quickly flattened himself out, chin on floor. She was looking in. But she couldn't see under the bed, nor beyond it to the other side where he was, without bending over. And only old maids, he thought with a dismal chuckle, look under beds the first thing when they come into a room.

He held his breath. Maybe she'd go away again, now that she'd glanced in. But she didn't. The bare ankles in house-slippers crossed the threshold into the room. They came directly over toward him, growing bigger, like in a nightmare, as they drew nearer. They stopped on the other side of the bed from him, so close that her knees must be touching it. And one slipper was an inch away from Doris's rigidly outstretched hand. Oh my God, he thought, if she looks down at the floor—or if she comes around to this side!

What did she want there by the bed, what did she see, what was she looking at? Was there blood on it? No, there couldn't be, no skin had been broken, only her neck. Had something belonging to the dead woman been left on the bed, something he'd overlooked, a ring maybe or a necklace?

The bedclothes on his side brushed his face suddenly, moved upward a little. The danger signal went all over his body like an electric shock, until he understood. Oh, that was it! In dislodging the body he'd dragged them down a little. Woman-like she was smoothing the covers out again, tugging them back in place. Her feet shifted down toward the foot a little, then back toward the head again, as she completed her task. Momentarily he expected to see one of them go in too far and come down on the dead flesh of that upturned palm. Momentarily he expected her to come around to his side. Or even see him over the top of the bed, if she leaned too far across it. He lived hours in those few seconds. But she didn't do any of those things.

The feet turned, showed him their heels, and started back across the room growing smaller again. He was too prostrated even to sigh, he just lay there with his mouth open like a fish. She didn't go out, though. The feet skipped the opening to the bathroom and stopped before Doris's dresser over to one side. Helping herself to the face powder. But now she had a mirror in front of her, damn it! And he knew what mirrors were. If, for instance, it was tilted at a slight angle, it would show her the floor behind her—better than she could see it herself. Like a periscope in reverse, it might even reveal what lay under the bed, what her own unaided eyes would never have shown her.

He heard the thud of Doris's powder-box as she put it down again. He waited for the scream that would surely come as she raised her eyes to the quicksilver before her. He lay there tense, as rigid as that other form next to him even if a little warmer. He wondered why he didn't get it over with by jumping up and showing himself, saying,

"Yes, I'm here—and look what's beside me!" But he didn't. The time to do that had been when she first came in downstairs. That time was past now. There was no going back.

And then just when he'd quit hoping, there was a little shuffling sound and her feet had carried her back over the threshold and out of the room, and he was alone with the dead.

He couldn't get up for a while—even though he knew that right now was the best time, while she was busy dressing in her own room, to get out of there. He felt weak all over. When he finally did totter upright it wasn't to the outside door that he went but to the one to the bathroom.

He carefully eased it shut and locked it on his side. Let her suspect what she wanted, she wasn't going to get back in there again until the grisly evidence was out of the way! And that would have to wait until she was out of the house. He cursed her bitterly, and her pal Gordon even more so, for unknowingly adding to his troubles like this. He even cursed the dead woman for not dissolving into thin air once she was dead. He cursed everyone but the man who was by now speeding back to New York and safety; he was loyal to him to the last breath in his body. He went out into the hall and once more locked the dead woman's door behind him, once more extracted the key.

Just as he got in the clear once more, the phone started downstairs. It wasn't New York yet, too early. The train hadn't even gotten there yet. Helen stuck her head out of her room and called: "If it's Gordon, tell him I'm ready to leave now, not to be so impatient!" But it wasn't Gordon. It was an older voice, asking for Doris. The masculine "hello" Larry gave it seemed to leave it at a loss. Larry caught right on; he did some quick thinking. She'd been ready to leave an hour ago, she'd been going to this voice, and had never gotten there because death had stopped her in her own room. Still, an hour isn't much to a pretty woman—or to the man who's smitten with her.

Larry thought savagely, "It was your party. You're going to pay for it!" He tried to make his voice sound boyish, cordial. "She's gone out," he said with a cheerful ring, "but she left a message in case anyone called up for her. Only I don't know if you're the right party—"

"Who is this speaking?" said the voice suspiciously.

"I'm Helen's boy friend." That ought to be all right. He must know by now that Doris had been pretty thick with Helen, that therefore any friends of the latter would be neutral, not hostile like himself.

The voice was still cagey though. "How is it you're there alone?"

"I'm not. Helen's here with me, but she's upstairs dressing. Can't come to the phone, so she asked me to give the message—"

"What is it? This is the right party," the voice bit in.

"Well, Mrs. Weeks was called out this afternoon. Some people dropped in from the city and she couldn't get away from them. She said if anyone called, to say she'd gone to the Pine Tree Inn for dinner. You know where that is?" Why wouldn't he? Larry himself had seen the two of them dancing there more than once, and had promptly backed out again in a hurry each time.

But the voice wasn't committing itself. "I think so—it's a little way out on the road to Lakewood, isn't it?"

"You can't miss it," said Larry pointedly. "It's got a great big sign that lights up the road."

The voice caught on. "Oh, then she's going to wai— Then she'll be there?"

"These people are only passing through, they're not staying. She'll be free at about nine thirty. You see they're not bringing her back, so she thought if you wanted to pick her up with your car out there— Otherwise she'd have to phone for a taxi and wait until it got out there."

"Yeah, I could do that," said the voice hesitantly. "Y'sure she said she'll be—free by nine thirty?" Alone, was the word he wanted to use, Larry knew.

"That's the time Helen told me to say," he reassured. "Oh, and I nearly forgot—" Like hell he had! It was more important than everything else put together, but it had to be dished out carefully so as not to awaken suspicion. "She said you don't have to drive right up to the place if you don't feel like it, you can sound your horn from that clump of pines down the road. You can wait there. She'll come out to you."

He would go for that idea, Larry felt, if only to avoid getting stuck with any possible bill she might have run up in the roadhouse. That clump of pines wasn't new to him anyway. Larry'd already seen his car berthed in it while they were inside dancing—all to get out of paying the extra fifty cents the inn charged for parking. He'd known whose it was because he'd seen them both go back to it once to smoke a cigarette out under the stars.

He heard Helen coming down the stairs, dressed at last and ready to clear out, yet he didn't dare break the connection too abruptly.

"Who you talking to?" she said in her clear, shrill voice and stopped beside him. But he'd counted on her saying something, and the mouthpiece was already buried against his shirt-front by the time she spoke. Her voice couldn't reach it.

"Sweetie of mine," he said limply. "Have a heart, don't listen—" His eyes stared tensely at her. While she stood there he couldn't uncover the thing and speak into it himself. One peep from her and the voice at the other end would ask to speak to her, and she wasn't in on the set-up. On the other hand he had to keep talking, couldn't just stand there like that. Cold feet can be awfully catching, even over a wire.

"All right, son," the voice sounded into his ear. "I'll do that. You sure you got the message straight now?"

"Looks like you've got a bad case of it," said Helen derisively. "Your eyes are staring out of your head. I wish you could see yourself—" But she moved away, started for the front door.

"Absolutely. Just like I told you," he said into the instrument.

"All right, thanks a lot," the voice came back. There was a click at the other end. He felt himself caving in at his middle.

"Give her my love," Helen was saying from the open doorway.

"There's a fresh dame here sends you her love, honey," he said into the dead phone. "But she's not as pretty as you are."

As his sister banged the front door after her, the fake grin left his face with it. He parked the phone and leaned his head weakly against the wall for a minute or two. He'd been through too much in just one hour, too much to take without leaning against something. And there was lots to come yet, he knew. Plenty.

He was alone in the house now with the body of a murdered woman. That didn't frighten him. It was getting out of there that worried him—with a double row of porches to buck in either direction, porches jammed with the rocking-chair brigade on sentinel duty. Yet out it must go, and not cut up small in any valise either. That body had a date with its own murder. It had to travel to get there, and it had to travel whole. Though at this very minute it was already as dead as it would ever be, its murder was still several hours off and a good distance away. Nine thirty, in a clump of trees near Pine Tree Inn, just as a starting-point. Details could come later. The important thing was to get it away from this house, where no murder had ever taken place, and have it meet up with its murderer, who didn't know that was what he was yet, and wasn't expecting to kill.

Let him worry about getting rid of it after that! Let him find out how much harder it is to shake off the embrace of dead arms than it is of living ones! Let him try to explain what he was doing with it in a lonely clump of trees at the side of the road, at that hour and that far from town—and see if he'd be believed! That is, if he had guts enough to do the only thing there was for him to do—raise a holler, report it then and there, brazen it out, let himself in for it. But he wouldn't, he was in too deep himself. He'd lose his head like a thousand others had before him. He'd leave it where it was and beat it like the very devil to save his own skin. Or else he'd take it with him and try to dump it somewhere, cover it somehow. Anything to shake himself free of it. And once he did that, woe betide him!

The eyes of the living were going to be on hand tonight, at just the wrong time for him—just when he was pulling out of that clump of trees, or just as he went flashing past the noon-bright glare in front of the inn on the road away from Asbury, to get rid of her in the dark open country somewhere beyond.

She would be reported missing the first thing in the morning, or even before—when his father phoned—Larry would see to that. Not many people had seen them dancing together and lapping their Martinis together and smoking cigarettes in a parked car together— but just enough of them had to do the damage. A waiter here, a gas-station attendant there, a bellboy somewhere else. Larry'd know just which ones to get.

He said to himself what he'd said when he answered the man's phone call. "It was your party; you're gonna pay for it, not Dad.

She's gonna be around your neck tonight choking you, like he choked her!"

Only a minute had gone by since Helen had banged the front door after her. Larry didn't move, he was still standing there leaning his head against the wall. She might come back, she might find out she'd forgotten something. He gave her time to get as far as the Boardwalk, two blocks over. Once she got that far she wouldn't come back any more, even if she had forgotten something. She'd be out until twelve now with Gordon. Three minutes went by—five. She'd hit the Boardwalk now.

He took his head away from the wall but he didn't move. He took out a cigarette and lit it. He had all the time in the world and he wanted that last silvery gleam of twilight out of the sky before he got going. It was a lot safer here in the house with her than out in the open under those pine trees. He smoked the cigarette down to its last inch, slowly not nervously. He'd needed that. Now he felt better, felt up to what was ahead of him. He took a tuck in his belt and moved away from the wall. Anyone who had seen him would have called him just a lazy young fellow slouching around the house on a summer evening.

He wasn't bothering with any fake alibi for himself. His father had a peach and that was all he cared about. If through some unforeseen slip-up the thing boomeranged back to their own doorstep in spite of everything, then he'd take it on—himself. He didn't give a rap, as long as it wasn't fastened on his father. His own alibi, if worst came to worst, would be simply the truth—that he'd been in the house here the whole time. And, he told himself wisely, when you don't bother tinkering with an alibi is usually when you don't need one anyway.

He pulled down all the shades on all the windows. Then he lit just one light, so he could see on the stairs. From the street it would look like no one was home and a night-light had been left burning. Then he went upstairs and got her out from under the bed.

He was surprised at how little she weighed. The first thing he did was carry her downstairs and stretch her on the floor, over to one side of the stairs. To go out she had to leave by the ground floor anyway.

Then he sat down next to her, on the lowest step of the stairs, and for a long time nothing else happened. He ws thinking. The quarter hour chimed from somewhere outside. Eight fifteen that was. He still had loads of time. But he'd better be starting soon now, the Pine Tree Inn wasn't any five minutes from here. The thing was—how to go about it.

It was right there under his eyes the whole time, while he'd been racking his brains out. A spark from his cigarette did it—he'd lit another one. It fell down next to her, and he had to put his foot on it to make it go out. That made him notice the rug she was lying on. About eight by ten it was, a lightweight bright-colored summer rug. He got up and beat it over to the phone directory and looked under *Carpet Cleaners*.

He called a number, then another, then another, then another. Finally he got a tumble from someone called Saroukian. "How late do you stay open tonight?"

They closed at six, but they'd call for the article the first thing in the morning.

"Well, look," he said, "if I bring it over myself tonight, won't there be someone there to take it in? I'll just leave it with you tonight, and you don't need to start work on it until you're ready."

They evidently lived right in back of, or right over, their cleaning shop. At first they tried to argue him out of it. Finally they told him he could bring it around and ring the bell, but they wouldn't be responsible for it.

"That's O.K.," he said. "I won't have time in the morning and it's gotta be attended to." He hung up and went over to get it ready for them.

He moved her over right into the middle of it, the long way. Then he got his fountain pen out, shoved back the plunger, and wrecked the border with it until there was no more ink in the thing. It took ink beautifully, that rug. He went and got some good strong twine, and he rolled the rug around her tight as a corset and tied it at both ends, at about where her ankles were and at about where her broken neck was. It bulged a little in the middle, so he tied it there too and evened it out. When he got through it wasn't much thicker than a length of sewer pipe. Her loosened hair was still spilling out at one end though, and there was another round opening down where her feet were. He shoved the hair all back in on top of her head where it belonged, and got two small cushions off the sofa and wedged one in at each end, rammed it down with all his might. They could stand cleaning too, just like the rug. That was the beauty of a bloodless murder, you weren't afraid to leave anything at the cleaner's. He hoisted the long pillar up onto his shoulder to try it out. It wasn't too heavy, he could make it. No heavier than carrying a light-weight canoe.

He put it down again and went upstairs to the room where it had happened, and lit up and looked around for the last time. Under the bed and on top of it and all over, to make sure nothing had been overlooked. There wasn't a speck of anything. He went to her jewel case and rummaged through it. Most of the gadgets just had initials, but there was a wrist-watch there that had her name in full on the inside of the case. He slipped that in his pocket. He also took a powder compact, and slipped a small snapshot of herself she'd had taken in an automatic machine under the lid, just for luck. He wanted to make it as easy for them as he could.

He put out the lights and went downstairs. He opened the front door wide and went back in again. "From now on," he told himself, "I don't think; I let my reflexes work for me!" He picked the long cylinder up with both arms, got it to the porch, and propped it upright against the side of the door for a minute while he closed the door after him. Then he heaved it up onto his right shoulder and kept it in place with one upraised arm, and that was all there was to it. It dipped a little at both ends, but any rolled-up rug would have. Cleopatra had gone to meet Caesar like this, he remembered. The present occupant was going to keep a blind date with her murderer—three or four hours after her own death.

Someone on the porch of the next cottage was strumming *Here Comes Cookie* on a ukulele as he stepped down to the sidewalk level with the body transverse to his own. He started up the street with it, with his head to one side to give it room on his shoulder. He came to the first street-light and its snowy glare picked him out for a minute, then handed him back to the gloom. He wasn't walking fast, just trudging along. He was doing just what he'd said he'd do: not thinking about it, letting his reflexes work for him. He wasn't nervous and he wasn't frightened, therefore he didn't look nervous and he didn't look frightened.

"This is a rug," he kept repeating. "I'm taking it to the cleaners. People taking rugs to the cleaners don't go along scared of their shadows."

A rocking chair squeaked on one of the wooden platforms and a woman's nasal voice said: "Good evening, Larry. What on earth are you doing, trying to reduce?"

He showed his teeth in the gloom. "Gotta get this rug to the cleaners."

"My stars, at this hour?" she queried.

"I'll catch it if I don't," he said. "I was filling my fountain pen just now and I got ink all over it." He had deliberately stopped for a moment, set the thing down, shifted it to his other shoulder. He gave her another flash of his teeth. "See you later," he said, and was on his way again.

She gave a comfortable motherly laugh. "Nice young fellow," he heard her say under her breath to someone beside her. "But that stepmother of his—" The sibilant whispers faded out behind him.

So Doris was already getting a bad name among the summer residents—good. "Go to it!" he thought. "You'll have more to talk about in a little while."

Every porch was tenanted. It was like running the gauntlet. But he wasn't running, just strolling past like on any other summer evening. He saw two glowing cigarette ends coming toward him along an unlighted stretch of the sidewalk. As they passed under the next light he identified one—a girl he knew, a beach acquaintance, and her escort. He'd have to stop. He would have stopped if he only had a rug with him, so he'd have to stop now. The timing wasn't quite right though. Instead of coming up to them in one of the black stretches between lights, the three of them met face to face in one of the glaring white patches right at the foot of a street lamp.

"Hello, old-timer."

"Hello, babe." He tilted his burden forward, caught it with both arms, and eased it perpendicularly to the pavement.

"Johnny, this is Larry." Then she said: "What in the world have you got there?"

"Rug," he said. "I just got ink all over it and I thought I could get it taken out before I get bawled out."

"Oh, they'll charge like the dickens for that," she said helpfully. "Lemme look, maybe I could do it for you, we've got a can of wonderful stuff over at our house." She put her hand toward the top opening and felt one of the wedged-in cushions.

He could feel his hair going up. "Nah, I don't want to undo it," he said. "I'll never get it together again if I do." He didn't, however, make the mistake of pushing her hand away, or immediately trying to tip the thing back on his shoulders again. He was too busy getting his windpipe open.

"What's that in the middle there?" she said, poking her hand at the cushion.

"Sofa pillows," he said. "They got all spotted, too." He didn't follow the direction of her eyes in time.

"How come you didn't get it all over your hands?" she said innocently.

"I was holding the pen out in front of me," he said, "and it squirted all over everything." He didn't let a twitch get past his cuff and shake the hand she was looking at, although there were plenty of them stored up waiting to go to work.

Her escort came to his aid; he didn't like it because Larry'd called her "babe." "Come on, I thought you wanted to go to the movies—"

He started to pull her away.

Larry tapped his pockets with his free hand; all he felt was Doris's wrist-watch. "One of you got a cigarette?" he asked. "I came out without mine." The escort supplied him, also the match. Larry wanted them to break away first. They'd put him through too much, he couldn't afford to seem anxious to get rid of them.

"My, your face is just dripping!" said the girl, as the orange glare swept across it.

Larry said: "You try toting this on a warm night and see how it feels."

"'Bye," she called back, and they moved off into the shadows.

He stood there and blew a long cloud of smoke to get into gear again. That was the closest yet, he thought. If I got away with that, I can get away with anything.

He got back under the thing again and trudged on, cigarette in mouth. The houses began to thin out; the paved middle of the street began to turn into the road that led out toward Pine Tree Inn, shorn of its two sidewalks. But it was still a long hike off, he wasn't even halfway there yet. He was hugging the side of the roadway now, salt marshes spiked with reeds on all sides of him as far as the eye could reach. A car or two went whizzing by. He could have gotten rid of her easy enough along here by just dropping her into the ooze. But that wasn't the answer, that wouldn't be making him pay for his party.

There was another thing to be considered though. Those occasional cars tearing past. Their headlights soaked him each time. It had been riskier back further where the houses were, maybe, but it hadn't looked so strange to be carrying a rug there. The surroundings stood for it. It was a peculiar thing to be doing this far out. The biggest risk of all might be the safest in the end; anything was better than attracting the attention of each separate driver as he sped by. A big rumbling noise came up slowly behind him, and he turned and thumbed it with his free hand. The reflexes would look out for him, he hoped, like they had so far.

The truck slowed down and came to a stop a foot or two ahead; it only had a single driver. "Get in," he said facetiously. "Going camping?" But it had been a rug back further, so it was still going to be a rug now, and not a tent or anything. Switching stories didn't pay. Only instead of going to the cleaners it would have to be coming from there now; there weren't any cottages around Pine Tree Inn.

"Nah," Larry said. "I gotta get this rug out to Pine Tree Inn, for the manager's office. Somebody got sick all over it and he had to send it in to be cleaned. Now he's raising hell, can't wait till tomorrow, wants it back right tonight."

He handed it up to the driver and the man stood it upright against the double seat. Larry followed it in and sat down beside it, holding it in place with his body. It shook all over when the truck got going and that wasn't any too good for the way it was rolled up. Nor could he jump down right in front of the inn with it, in the glare of all the lights and under the eyes of the parking attendants.

"Who do you work for?" said the driver after a while.

"Saroukian, an Armenian firm."

"What's the matter, ain't they even got their own delivery truck?"

"Nah, we used to," said Larry professionally, "but we gave it up. Business been bad."

The ground grew higher as they got back inland; the marshes gave way to isolated thickets and clumps of trees. The truck ate up the road. "Got the time?" said Larry. "I'm supposed to get it there by nine thirty."

"It's about nine now," said the driver. "Quarter to when I started." Then he looked over at Larry across the obstacle between them. "Who d'ya think you're kidding?" he said suddenly.

Larry froze. "I don't get you."

"You ain't delivering that nowhere. Whatever it is, it's hot. You swiped it. You're taking it somewhere to sell it."

"How do you figure that?" said Larry, and curled his arm around it protectively.

"I wasn't born yestidday," sneered the driver.

Larry suddenly hauled it over his way, across his own lap, and gave it a shove with his whole body that sent it hurtling out the side of the truck. It dropped by the roadside and rolled over a couple of times. He got out on the step to go after it. "Thanks for the lift," he said. "I'll be leaving you here."

"All right, bud, if that's how you feel about it," agreed the driver. "Hell, it's not my look-out, I wasn't going to take it away from you—." Without slowing up he reached out and gave Larry a shove that sent him flying sideways out into the night. His red tail-lights went twinkling merrily up the road and disappeared in the dark.

Larry had fortunately cleared the asphalt roadbed and landed in the soft turf alongside. None too soft at that, but nothing was broken, his palms and knees were just skinned a little. He picked himself up and went back to where the rug was. Before he bent for it he looked around. And then his swearing stopped. Even this hadn't gone wrong, had come out right, very much right. He was so close to the inn that the reflection of its lights could be seen above the treetops off to one side. And the clump of pines would be even nearer, a five-minute walk from where he was. All that driver had done was save him the necessity of getting out in front of it and giving himself away.

But now, as he stooped over his grisly burden, he was horrified to see that one of the cords had parted, that a pillow had fallen to the road and that the body had slid down till the forehead and eyes showed beneath the blond hair that cascaded over the roadway. Larry looked up as a pair of approaching headlights floated around a distant corner. Hurriedly he worked the body back into position, shielding it with his own form from any curious glances that might be directed at him from the oncoming car. He had managed to get the pillow stuffed back in position and was retying the burst cord as the car whizzed by without even a pause of interest. Larry heaved a sigh of relief and, shouldering the load, got going again. This time he kept away from the side of the road, going deeper and deeper among the trees. It made the going tougher, but he wasn't coming up the front way if he could help it.

The glare from the roadhouse grew stronger and kept him from losing his bearings. After a while a whisper of dance music came floating to him through the trees, and he knew he was there. He edged back a little closer toward the road again, until he could see the circular clearing in the pines just ahead of him. It was just big enough to hold a single car, but there wasn't any car in it. He sank down out of sight with what he'd carried all the way out here, and got to work undoing the cords that bound it. By the time he was through, the rug and the two pillows were tightly rolled up again and shoved out of the way, and the body of the woman who had died at five that afternoon lay beside him. He just squatted there on the ground next to it, waiting. In life, he knew, Doris had never been the kind of woman who was stood up; he wondered if she would be in death.

When it felt like half the night was gone—actually only about twenty minutes had passed—a sudden flash of blinding light exploded among the trees as a car turned into the nearby clearing from the road. He was glad he hadn't gone any nearer to it than he had. As it was he had to duck his head, chin almost touching the ground, for the farflung headlight beams to pass harmlessly above him. They missed him by only two good feet. The lights swept around in a big arc as the car half turned, then they snapped out and the engine died. He couldn't see anything for a minute, but neither could whoever was in that car. Nothing more happened after that. When his eyes readjusted themselves he knew by its outline that it was the right car. Then there was a spurt of orange as the occupant lit a cigarette, and that gave his face away. Same face Larry had seen with Doris. It was the right man, too.

Larry stayed where he was, didn't move an inch. To do so would only have made every twig and pine needle around him snap and rustle. He couldn't do anything anyway while the man stayed there at the wheel; the first move would have to come from him. True, he might get tired waiting and light out again—but Larry didn't think he would. Not after coming all the way out here to get her. No one likes to be made a fool of, not even by a pretty woman. When she didn't show up he'd probably boil over, climb out and go up to the inn himself to see what was keeping her. It became a case of seeing which one of them would get tired waiting first. Larry knew it wasn't going to be himself.

The cushions of the roadster creaked as the man shifted his hips around. Larry could see the red dot of his cigarette through the trees, and even get a whiff of the smoke now and then. He folded his lapels close over his shirt-front and held them that way so the white wouldn't gleam out and give him away. The red dot went out. The leather creaked again. The man was getting restless now. About ten minutes had passed. The creakings became more frequent.

All of a sudden there was a loud honking blast, repeated three times. Larry jumped and nearly passed out. He was giving her the horn, trying to attract her attention. Then the door of the car cracked open, slammed shut again, and he was standing on the ground, swearing audibly. Larry got the head of the corpse up off the ground and held it on his lap, waiting. About a minute more now.

Scuffling, crackling footsteps moved away from the car and out onto the road. He stood there looking down it toward the inn. Larry couldn't see him but the silence told him that. No sign of her coming toward him. Then the soft scrape of shoe-leather came from the asphalt, moving away toward the inn. He was going up to the entrance to take a look in. Larry waited long enough to let him get out of earshot. Then he reared up, caught the body under the arms, and began to struggle toward the car with it, half carrying and half dragging it. The car was a roadster and Larry had known for a long time what he was going to do. The underbrush crackled and sang out, but the music playing at the inn would cover that.

When he got up to the car Larry let the body go for a minute and climbed up and got the rumble-seat open. It was capacious, but he had a hard time getting the stiffened form into it. He put her in feet first, and she stuck out like a jack-in-the-box. Then he climbed up after her, bent her over double, and shoved her down underneath. He dug the wrist-watch with her name on it out of his pocket and tossed it in after her. Then he closed the rumble-seat and she was gone.

"You're set for your last joy-ride, Doris," he muttered. He would have locked the rumble, to delay discovery as long as possible, if he had had the key. He took the powder-compact with her snapshot under the lid and dropped it on the ground in back of the car. Let him deny that he'd been here with her! Then he moved off under the trees and was lost to sight.

A few minutes later he showed up at the door of the inn, as though he'd just come out from inside. The doorman was just returning to his post, as though someone had called him out to the roadway to question him. Larry saw a figure moving down the road toward the clump of pines he'd just come from. "What was his grief?" he asked, as though he'd overheard the whole thing.

"Got stood up," the doorman grinned. He went back inside and Larry went down to the edge of the road. The headlights suddenly flared out in the middle of the pines and an engine whined as it warmed up. A minute later the roadster came out into the open backwards, straightened itself. It stayed where it was a moment. A taxi came up to the inn and disgorged a party of six. Larry got in. "Back to town," he said, "and slow up going past that car down there."

The man in the roadster, as they came abreast of it, was tilting a whiskey bottle to his lips. Larry leaned out the window of the cab and called: "Need any help? Or are you too cheap to go in and buy yourself a chaser?"

The solitary drinker stopped long enough to give Larry a four-letter word describing what he could do with himself, then resumed.

"Step on it," Larry told the driver. "I'm expecting a phone call."

When he let himself into the house once more, something stopped him before he was even over the threshold. Something was wrong here. He hadn't left that many lights turned on, he'd only left one dim one burning, and now— He pulled himself together, closed the door, and went forward. Then as he turned into the living room he recoiled. He came face to face with his father, who'd just gotten up out of a chair.

Weeks looked very tired, all in, but not frightened any more. "I took the next train back," he said quietly. "I'd come to my senses by the time I got there. What kind of a heel do you take me for anyway? I couldn't go through with it, let you shoulder the blame that way."

Larry just hung his head. "My God, and I've been through all that," he groaned, "for nothing!" Then he looked up quickly. "You haven't phoned in yet, or anything—have you?"

"No. I was waiting for you to come back. I thought maybe you'd walk over to the station-house with me. I'm not much of a hero," he admitted. Then he straightened up. "No use arguing about it, my mind's made up. If you won't come with me, then I'll go alone."

"I'll go with you," said Larry bitterly. "Might as well—I made a mess of it anyway. I see that now! It never would have held together. The whole thing came out wrong. I left the rug I carried her in, there under the trees. A dozen people saw me with it. I showed myself at the inn. I even told the taxi driver I was expecting a phone call. That alone would have damaged your alibi. How was I supposed to know you were going to call, if it wasn't a set-up? And last of all my prints are all over her powder-compact and her wrist-watch. A big help I turned out to be!" He gave a crooked smile. "Let's go. And do me a favor, kick me every step of the way getting there, will you?"

When they got to the steps of the headquarters building, they stopped and looked at each other. Larry rested his hand on his father's shoulder for a minute. "Wait here, why don't you?" he said in a choked voice. "I'll go in and break it for you. That'll be the easiest way." He went in alone.

The sergeant on duty looked across the desk. "Well, young feller, what's your trouble?"

"The name is Weeks," said Larry, "and it's about Doris Weeks, my stepmother—"

The sergeant shook his head as though he pitied him. "Came to report her missing, is that it?" And before Larry could answer the mystifying question, "Recognize this?" He was looking at the wrist-watch he'd dropped into the rumble seat less than an hour ago.

Larry's face froze. "That's hers," he managed to say.

"Yeah," agreed the sergeant, "the name's on it. That's the only thing we had to go by." He dropped his eyes. "She's pretty badly hurt, young feller," he said unwillingly.

"She's dead!" Larry exclaimed, gripping the edge of the desk with both hands.

The sergeant seemed to mistake it for apprehension and not the statement of a known fact. "Yeah," he sighed, "she is. I didn't want to tell you too suddenly, but you may as well know. Car smash-up only half an hour ago. Guy with her must have been driving stewed or without lights. Anyway a truck hit them and they turned over. He was thrown clear but he died instantly of a broken neck. She was caught under the car, and it caught fire, and—well, there wasn't very much to go by after it was over except this wrist-watch, which fell out on the roadway in some way—"

Larry said: "My father's outside, I guess I'd better tell him what you told me—" and he went weaving crazily out the doorway.

"It sure must be tough," thought the sergeant, "to come and find out a thing like that!"

(1935)

Dead on Her Feet

"And another thing I've got against these non-stop shindigs," orated the chief to his slightly bored listeners, "is they let minors get in 'em and dance for days until they wind up in a hospital with the D.T.'s, when the whole thing's been fixed ahead of time and they haven't got a chance of copping the prize anyway. Here's a Missus Mollie McGuire been calling up every hour on the half-hour all day long, and bawling the eardrums off me because her daughter Toodles ain't been home in over a week and she wants this guy Pasternack arrested. So you go over there and tell Joe Pasternack I'll give him until tomorrow morning to fold up his contest and send his entries home. And tell him for me he can shove all his big and little silver loving-cups—"

For the first time his audience looked interested, even expectant, as they waited to hear what it was Mr. P. could do with his loving-cups, hoping for the best.

"—back in their packing-cases," concluded the chief chastely, if somewhat disappointingly. "He ain't going to need 'em any more. He has promoted his last marathon in this neck of the woods."

There was a pause while nobody stirred. "Well, what are you all standing there looking at me for?" demanded the chief testily. "You, Donnelly, you're nearest the door. Get going."

Donnelly gave him an injured look. "Me, Chief? Why, I've got a red-hot lead on that payroll thing you were so hipped about. If I don't keep after it it'll cool off on me."

"All right, then you, Stevens!"

"Why, I'm due in Yonkers right now," protested Stevens virtuously.

"Machine-gun Rosie has been seen around again and I want to have a little talk with her—"

"That leaves you, Doyle," snapped the merciless chief.

"Gee, Chief," whined Doyle plaintively, "gimme a break, can't you? My wife is expecting—" Very much under his breath he added: "—me home early tonight."

"Congratulations," scowled the chief, who had missed hearing the last part of it. He glowered at them. "I get it!" he roared. "It's below your dignity, ain't it! It's too petty-larceny for you! Anything less than the St. Valentine's Day massacre ain't worth going out after, is that it? You figure it's a detail for a bluecoat, don't you?" His open palm hit the desk-top with a sound like a firecracker going off. Purple became the dominant color of his complexion. "I'll put you all back where you started, watching pickpockets in the subway! I'll take some of the high-falutinness out of you! I'll—I'll—" The only surprising thing about it was that foam did not appear at his mouth.

It may have been that the chief's bark was worse than his bite. At any rate no great amount of apprehension was shown by the culprits before him. One of them cleared his throat inoffensively. "By the way, Chief, I understand that rookie, Smith, has been swiping bananas from Tony on the corner again, and getting the squad a bad name after you told him to pay for them."

The chief took pause and considered this point.

The others seemed to get the idea at once. "They tell me he darned near wrecked a Chinese laundry because the Chinks tried to pass him somebody else's shirts. You could hear the screeching for miles."

Doyle put the artistic finishing touch. "I overheard him say he wouldn't be seen dead wearing the kind of socks you do. He was asking me did I think you had lost an election bet or just didn't know any better."

The chief had become dangerously quiet all at once. A faint drumming sound from somewhere on the desk told what he was doing with his fingers. "Oh, he did, did he?" he remarked, very slowly and very ominously.

At this most unfortunate of all possible moments the door blew open and in breezed the maligned one in person. He looked very tired and at

the same time enthusiastic, if the combination can be imagined. Red
rimmed his eyes, blue shadowed his jaws, but he had a triumphant look
on his face, the look of a man who has done his job well and expects a
kind word. "Well, Chief," he burst out, "it's over! I got both of 'em. Just
brought 'em in. They're in the back room right now—"

An oppressive silence greeted him. Frost seemed to be in the air. He
blinked and glanced at his three pals for enlightenment.

The silence didn't last long, however. The chief cleared his throat.
"*Hrrrmph*. Zat so?" he said with deceptive mildness. "Well now, Smitty,
as long as your engine's warm and you're hitting on all six, just run over
to Joe Pasternack's marathon dance and put the skids under it. It's been
going on in that old armory on the west side—"

Smitty's face had become a picture of despair. He glanced mutely at
the clock on the wall. The clock said four—A.M., not P.M. The chief, not
being a naturally hard-hearted man, took time off to glance down at
his own socks, as if to steel himself for this bit of cruelty. It seemed to
work beautifully. "An election bet!" he muttered cryptically to himself, and came up redder than ever.

"Gee, Chief," pleaded the rookie, "I haven't even had time to shave
since yesterday morning." In the background unseen nudgings and
silent strangulation were rampant.

"You ain't taking part in it, you're putting the lid on it," the chief
reminded him morosely. "First you buy your way in just like anyone
else and size it up good and plenty, see if there's anything against it
on moral grounds. Then you dig out one Toodles McGuire from under,
and don't let her stall you she's of age either. Her old lady says she's
sixteen and she ought to know. Smack her and send her home. You
seal everything up tight and tell Pasternack and whoever else is
backing this thing with him it's all off. And don't go 'way. You stay
with him and make sure he refunds any money that's coming to
anybody and shuts up shop good and proper. If he tries to squawk
about there ain't no ordinance against marathons, just lemme know.
We can find an ordinance against anything if we go back far enough
in the books—"

Smitty shifted his hat from northeast to southwest and started
reluctantly toward the great outdoors once more. "Anything screwy

like this that comes up, I'm always It," he was heard to mutter rebelliously. "Nice job, shooing a dancing contest. I'll probably get bombarded with powder-puffs—"

The chief reached suddenly for the heavy brass inkwell on his desk, whether to sign some report or to let Smitty have it, Smitty didn't wait to find out. He ducked hurriedly out the door.

"Ah, me," sighed the chief profoundly, "what a bunch of crumbs. Why didn't I listen to me old man and join the fire department instead!"

Young Mr. Smith, muttering bad language all the way, had himself driven over to the unused armory where the peculiar enterprise was taking place. "Sixty cents," said the taxi-driver.

Smitty took out a little pocket account-book and wrote down *Taxi-fare—$1.20.* "Send me out after nothing at four in the morning, will he!" he commented. After which he felt a lot better.

There was a box-office outside the entrance but now it was dark and untenanted. Smitty pushed through the unlocked doors and found a combination porter and doorman, a gentleman of color, seated on the inside, who gave him a stub of pink pasteboard in exchange for fifty-five cents, then promptly took the stub back again and tore it in half. "Boy," he remarked affably, "you is either up pow'ful early or up awful late."

"I just is plain up," remarked Smitty, and looked around him.

It was an hour before daylight and there were a dozen people left in the armory, which was built to hold two thousand. Six of them were dancing, but you wouldn't have known it by looking at them. It had been going on nine days. There was no one watching them any more. The last of the paid admissions had gone home hours ago, even the drunks and the Park Avenue stay-outs. All the big snow-white arc lights hanging from the rafters had been put out, except one in the middle, to save expenses. Pasternack wasn't in this for his health. The one remaining light, spitting and sizzling way up overhead, and sending down violet and white rays that you could see with the naked eye, made everything look ghostly, unreal. A phonograph fitted with an amplifier was grinding away at one end of the big hall, tearing a dance-tune to pieces, giving it the beating of its life. Each time the needle got to the end of the record it was swept back to the beginning by a sort of stencil fitted over the turn-table.

Six scarecrows, three men and three girls, clung ludicrously together in pairs out in the middle of the floor. They were not dancing and they were not walking, they were tottering by now, barely moving enough to keep from standing still. Each of the men bore a number on his back. *3, 8,* and *14* the numbers were. They were the "lucky" couples who had outlasted all the others, the scores who had started with them at the bang of a gun a week and two days ago. There wasn't even a coat or vest left among the three men—or a necktie. Two of them had replaced their shoes with carpet-slippers to ease their aching feet. The third had on a pair of canvas sneakers.

One of the girls had a wet handkerchief plastered across her forehead. Another had changed into a chorus-girl's practice outfit— shorts and a blouse. The third was a slip of a thing, a mere child, her head hanging limply down over her partner's shoulder, her eyes glazed with exhaustion.

Smitty watched her for a moment. There wasn't a curve in her whole body. If there was anyone here under age, it was she. She must be Toodles McGuire, killing herself for a plated loving-cup, a line in the newspapers, a contract to dance in some cheap honky-tonk, and a thousand dollars that she wasn't going to get anyway—according to the chief. He was probably right, reflected Smitty. There wasn't a thousand dollars in the whole set-up, much less three prizes on a sliding scale. Pasternack would probably pocket whatever profits there were and blow, letting the fame-struck suckers whistle. Corner-lizards and dance-hall belles like these couldn't even scrape together enough to bring suit. Now was as good a time as any to stop the lousy racket.

Smitty sauntered over to the bleachers where four of the remaining six the armory housed just then were seated and sprawled in various attitudes. He looked them over. One was an aged crone who acted as matron to the female participants during the brief five-minute rest-periods that came every half-hour. She had come out of her retirement for the time being, a towel of dubious cleanliness slung over her arm, and was absorbed in the working-out of a crossword puzzle,

mumbling to herself all the while. She had climbed halfway up the
reviewing stand to secure privacy for her occupation.

Two or three rows below her lounged a greasy-looking counterman
from some one-arm lunchroom, guarding a tray that held a covered
tin pail of steaming coffee and a stack of wax-paper cups. One of the
rest periods was evidently approaching and he was ready to cash in
on it.

The third spectator was a girl in a dance dress, her face twisted
with pain. Judging by her unkempt appearance and the scornful
bitter look in her eyes as she watched the remaining dancers, she had
only just recently disqualified herself. She had one stockingless foot
up before her and was rubbing the swollen instep with alcohol and
cursing softly under her breath.

The fourth and last of the onlookers (the fifth being the darky at the
door) was too busy with his arithmetic even to look up when Smitty
parked before him. He was in his shirt-sleeves and wore blue elastic
armbands and a green celluloid eye-shade. A soggy-looking stogie
protruded from his mouth. A watch, a megaphone, a whistle, and a
blank-cartridge pistol lay beside him on the bench. He appeared to be
computing the day's receipts in a pocket notebook, making them up
out of his head as he went along. "Get out of my light," he remarked
ungraciously as Smitty's shadow fell athwart him.

"You Pasternack?" Smitty wanted to know, not moving an inch.

"Naw, he's in his office taking a nap."

"Well, get him out here, I've got news for him."

"He don't wanna hear it," said the pleasant party on the bench.

Smitty turned over his lapel, then let it curl back again. "Oh, the
lor," commented the auditor, and two tens left the day's receipts and
were left high and dry in Smitty's right hand. "Buy yourself a drop of
schnapps," he said without even looking up. "Stop in and ask for me
tomorrow when there's more in the kitty—"

Smitty plucked the nearest armband, stetched it out until it would
have gone around a piano, then let it snap back again. The business
manager let out a yip. Smitty's palm with the two sawbucks came up
flat against his face, clamped itself there by the chin and bridge of the
nose, and executed a rotary motion, grinding them in. "Wrong guy,"

he said and followed the financial wizard into the sanctum where Pasternack lay in repose, mouth fixed to catch flies.

"Joe," said the humbled sidekick, spitting out pieces of ten-dollar-bill, "the lor."

Pasternack got vertical as though he worked by a spring. "Where's your warrant?" he said before his eyes were even open. "Quick, get me my mouth on the phone, Moe!"

"You go out there and blow your whistle," said Smitty, "and call the bally off—or do I have to throw this place out in the street?" He turned suddenly, tripped over something unseen, and went staggering halfway across the room. The telephone went flying out of Moe's hand at one end and the sound-box came ripping off the baseboard of the wall at the other. "*Tch, tch,* excuse it please," apologized Smitty insincerely. "Just when you needed it most, too!"

He turned back to the one called Moe and sent him headlong out into the auditorium with a hearty shove at the back of the neck. "Now do like I told you," he said, "while we're waiting for the telephone repairman to get here. And when their dogs have cooled, send them all in here to me. That goes for the cannibal and the washroom dame, too." He motioned toward the desk. "Get out your little tin box, Pasternack. How much you got on hand to pay these people?"

It wasn't in a tin box but in a briefcase. "Close the door," said Pasternack in an insinuating voice. "There's plenty here, and plenty more will be coming in. How big a cut will square you? Write your own ticket."

Smitty sighed wearily. "Do I have to knock your front teeth down the back of your throat before I can convince you I'm one of these old-fashioned guys that likes to work for my money?"

Outside a gun boomed hollowly and the squawking of the phonograph stopped. Moe could be heard making an announcement through the megaphone. "You can't get away with this!" stormed Pasternack. "Where's your warrant?"

"Where's your license," countered Smitty, "if you're going to get technical? C'mon, don't waste any more time, you're keeping me up! Get the dough ready for the pay-off." He stepped to the door and called out into the auditorium: "Everybody in here. Get your things and line up." Two of the three couples separated slowly like sleepwalkers and began to trudge painfully over toward him, walking zig-zag as though their metabolism was all shot.

The third pair, Number 14, still clung together out on the floor, the man facing toward Smitty. They didn't seem to realize it was over. They seemed to be holding each other up. They were in the shape of a human tent, their feet about three feet apart on the floor, their faces and shoulders pressed closely together. The girl was that clothes-pin, that stringbean of a kid he had already figured for Toodles McGuire. So she was going to be stubborn about it, was she? He went over to the pair bellicosely. "C'mon, you heard me, break it up!"

The man gave him a frightened look over her shoulder. "Will you take her off me, please, Mac? She's passed out or something, and if I let her go she'll crack her conk on the floor." He blew out his breath. "I can't hold her up much longer!"

Smitty hooked an arm about her middle. She didn't weigh any more than a discarded topcoat. The poor devil who had been bearing her weight, more or less, for nine days and nights on end, let go and folded up into a squatting position at her feet like a shriveled Buddha. "Just lemme stay like this," he moaned, "it feels so good." The girl, meanwhile, had begun to bend slowly double over Smitty's supporting arm, closing up like a jackknife. But she did it with a jerkiness, a deliberateness, that was almost grisly, slipping stiffly down a notch at a time, until her upside-down head had met her knees. She was like a walking doll whose spring has run down.

Smitty turned and barked over one shoulder at the washroom hag. "Hey you! C'mere and gimme a hand with this girl! Can't you see she needs attention? Take her in there with you and see what you can do for her—"

The old crone edged fearfully nearer, but when Smitty tried to pass the inanimate form to her she drew hurriedly back. "I—I ain't got the stren'th to lift her," she mumbled stubbornly. "You're strong, you carry her in and set her down—"

"I can't go in there," he snarled disgustedly. "That's no place for me! What're you here for if you can't—"

The girl who had been sitting on the sidelines suddenly got up and came limping over on one stockingless foot. "Give her to me," she said. "I'll take her in for you." She gave the old woman a long hard look before which the latter quailed and dropped her eyes. "Take hold of her feet," she ordered in a low voice. The hag hurriedly stooped to obey. They sidled off with her between them, and disappeared around the side of the orchestra-stand, toward the washroom. Their burden sagged low, until it almost touched the floor.

"Hang onto her," Smitty thought he heard the younger woman say. "She won't bite you!" The washroom door banged closed on the weird little procession. Smitty turned and hoisted the deflated Number 14 to his feet. "C'mon," he said. "In you go, with the rest!"

They were all lined up against the wall in Pasternack's "office," so played-out that if the wall had suddenly been taken away they would have all toppled flat like a pack of cards. Pasternack and his shill had gone into a huddle in the opposite corner, buzzing like a hive of bees.

"Would you two like to be alone?" Smitty wanted to know, parking Number 14 with the rest of the droops.

Pasternack evidently believed in the old adage, "He who fights and runs away lives to fight, etc." The game, he seemed to think, was no longer worth the candle. He unlatched the briefcase he had been guarding under his arm, walked back to the desk with it, and prepared to ease his conscience. "Well, folks," he remarked genially, "on the advice of this gentleman here" (big pally smile for Smitty) "my partner and I are calling off the contest. While we are under no legal obligation to any of you" (business of clearing his throat and hitching up his necktie) "we have decided to do the square thing, just so there won't be any trouble, and split the prize money among all the remaining entries. Deducting the rental for the armory, the light bill, and the cost of printing tickets and handbills, that would leave—"

"No, you don't!" said Smitty. "That comes out of your first nine days profits. What's on hand now gets divvied without any deductions. Do it your way and they'd all be owing you money!" He turned to the doorman. "You been paid, sunburnt?"

"Nossuh! I'se got five dolluhs a night coming at me—"

"Forty-five for you," said Smitty.

Pasternack suddenly blew up and advanced menacingly upon his partner. "That's what I get for listening to you, know-it-all! So New York was a sucker town, was it? So there was easy pickings here, was there? Yah!"

"Boys, boys," remonstrated Smitty, elbowing them apart.

"Throw them a piece of cheese, the rats," remarked the girl in shorts. There was a scuffling sound in the doorway and Smitty turned in time to see the lamed girl and the washroom matron each trying to get in ahead of the other.

"You don't leave me in there!"

"Well, I'm not staying in there alone with her. It ain't my job! I resign!"

The one with the limp got to him first. "Listen, mister, you better go in there yourself," she panted. "We can't do anything with her. I think she's dead."

"She's cold as ice and all stiff-like," corroborated the old woman.

"Oh my God, I've killed her!" someone groaned. Number 14 sagged to his knees and went out like a light. Those on either side of him eased him down to the floor by his arms, too weak themselves to support him.

"Hold everything!" barked Smitty. He gripped the pop-eyed doorman by the shoulder. "Scram out front and get a cop. Tell him to put in a call for an ambulance, and then have him report in here to me. And if you try lighting out, you lose your forty-five bucks and get the electric chair."

"I'se pracktilly back inside again," sobbed the terrified darky as he fled.

"The rest of you stay right where you are. I'll hold you responsible, Pasternack, if anybody ducks."

"As though we could move an inch on these howling dogs," muttered the girl in shorts.

Smitty pushed the girl with one shoe ahead of him. "You come and show me," he grunted. He was what might be termed a moral coward at the moment; he was going where he'd never gone before.

"Straight ahead of you," she scowled, halting outside the door. "Do you need a road-map?"

"C'mon, I'm not going in there alone," he said, and gave her a shove through the forbidden portal.

She was stretched out on the floor where they'd left her, a bottle of rubbing alcohol that hadn't worked uncorked beside her. His face was flaming as he squatted down and examined her. She was gone all right. She was as cold as they'd said and getting more rigid by the minute. "Overtaxed her heart most likely," he growled. "That guy Pasternack ought to be hauled up for this. He's morally responsible."

The cop, less well-brought-up than Smitty, stuck his head in the door without compunction.

"Stay by the entrance," Smitty instructed him. "Nobody leaves." Then, "This was the McGuire kid, wasn't it?" he asked his feminine companion.

"Can't prove it by me," she said sulkily. "Pasternack kept calling her Rose Lamont all through the contest. Why don't-cha ask the guy that was dancing with her? Maybe they got around to swapping names after nine days. Personally," she said as she moved toward the door, "I don't know who she was and I don't give a damn!"

"You'll make a swell mother for some guy's children," commented Smitty following her out. "In there," he said to the ambulance doctor who had just arrived, "but it's the morgue now, and not first-aid. Take a look."

Number 14, when he got back to where they all were, was taking it hard and self-accusing. "I didn't mean to do it, I didn't mean to!" he kept moaning.

"Shut up, you sap, you're making it tough for yourself," someone hissed.

"Lemme see a list of your entries," Smitty told Pasternack.

The impresario fished a ledger out of the desk drawer and held it out to him. "All I got out of this enterprise was kicks in the pants! Why didn't I stick to the sticks where they don't drop dead from a little dancing? Ask me, why didn't I?"

"Fourteen," read Smitty. "Rose Lamont and Gene Monahan. That your real name, guy? Back it up." 14 jerked off the coat that someone had slipped around his shoulders and turned the inner pocket inside out. The name was inked onto the label. The address checked too. "What about her, was that her real tag?"

"McGuire was her real name," admitted Monahan, "Toodles

McGuire. She was going to change it anyway, pretty soon, if we'dda won that thousand"—he hung his head—"so it didn't matter."

"Why'd you say you did it? Why do you keep saying you didn't mean to?"

"Because I could feel there was something the matter with her in my arms. I knew she oughtta quit, and I wouldn't let her. I kept begging her to stick it out a little longer, even when she didn't answer me. I went crazy, I guess, thinking of that thousand dollars. We needed it to get married on. I kept expecting the others to drop out any minute, there were only two other couples left, and no one was watching us any more. When the rest-periods came, I carried her in my arms to the washroom door, so no one would notice she couldn't make it herself, and turned her over to the old lady in there. She couldn't do anything with her either, but I begged her not to let on, and each time the whistle blew I picked her up and started out from there with her—"

"Well, you've danced her into her grave," said Smitty bitterly. "If I was you I'd go out and stick both my feet under the first trolley-car that came along and hold them there until it went by. It might make a man of you!"

He went out and found the ambulance doctor in the act of leaving. "What was it, her heart?"

The A.D. favored him with a peculiar look, starting at the floor and ending at the top of his head. "Why wouldn't it be? Nobody's heart keeps going with a seven- or eight-inch metal pencil jammed into it."

He unfolded a handkerchief to reveal a slim coppery cylinder, tapering to needle-like sharpness at the writing end, where the case was pointed over the lead to protect it. It was aluminum—encrusted blood was what gave it its copper sheen. Smitty nearly dropped it in consternation—not because of what it had done but because he had missed seeing it.

"And another thing," went on the A.D. "You're new to this sort of thing, aren't you? Well, just a friendly tip. No offense, but you don't call an ambulance that long after they've gone, our time is too val—"

"I don't getcha," said Smitty impatiently. "She needed help; who am I supposed to ring in, potter's field, and have her buried before she's quit breathing?"

This time the look he got was withering. "She was past help hours ago." The doctor scanned his wrist. "It's five now. She's been dead since three, easily. I can't tell you when exactly, but your friend the medical examiner'll tell you whether I'm right or not. I've seen too many of 'em in my time. She's been gone two hours anyhow."

Smitty had taken a step back, as though he were afraid of the guy. "I came in here at four thirty," he stammered excitedly, "and she was dancing on that floor there—I saw her with my own eyes—fifteen, twenty minutes ago!" His face was slightly sallow.

"I don't care whether you saw her dancin' or saw her doin' double-hand-springs on her left ear, she was dead!" roared the ambulance man testily. "She was celebrating her own wake then, if you insist!" He took a look at Smitty's horrified face, quieted down, spit emphatically out of one corner of his mouth, and remarked: "Somebody was dancing with her dead body, that's all. Pleasant dreams, kid!"

Smitty started to burn slowly. "Somebody was," he agreed, gritting his teeth. "I know who Somebody is, too. His number was Fourteen until a little while ago; well, it's Thirteen from now on!"

He went in to look at her again, the doctor whose time was so valuable trailing along. "From the back, eh? That's how I missed it. She was lying on it the first time I came in and looked."

"I nearly missed it myself," the intern told him. "I thought it was a boil at first. See this little pad of gauze? It had been soaked in alcohol and laid over it. There was absolutely no external flow of blood, and the pencil didn't protrude, it was in up to the hilt. In fact I had to use forceps to get it out. You can see for yourself, the clip that fastens to the wearer's pocket, which would have stopped it halfway, is missing. Probably broken off long before."

"I can't figure it," said Smitty. "If it went in up to the hilt, what room was there left for the grip that sent it home?"

"Must have just gone in an inch or two at first and stayed there," suggested the intern. "She probably killed herself on it by keeling over backwards and hittin the floor or the wall, driving it the rest of the way in." He got to his feet. "Well, the pleasure's all yours." He flipped a careless salute and left.

"Send the old crow in that had charge in here," Smitty told the cop.

The old woman came in fumbling with her hands, as though she had the seven-day itch.

"What's your name?"

"Josephine Falvey—Mrs. Josephine Falvey." She couldn't keep her eyes off what lay on the floor.

"It don't matter after you're forty," Smitty assured her drily. "What'd you bandage that wound up for? D'you know that makes you an accessory to a crime?"

"I didn't do no such a—" she started to deny whitely.

He suddenly thrust the postage-stamp of folded gauze, rusty on one side, under her nose. She cawed and jumped back. He followed her retreat. "You didn't stick this on? C'mon, answer me!"

"Yeah, I did!" she cackled, almost jumping up and down. "I did, I did—but I didn't mean no harm. Honest, mister, I—"

"When'd you do it?"

"The last time, when you made me and the girl bring her in here. Up to then I kept rubbing her face with alcohol each time he brought her back to the door, but it didn't seem to help her any. I knew I should of gone out and reported it to Pasternack, but he—that feller you know—begged me not to. He begged me to give them a break and not get them ruled out. He said it didn't matter if she acted all limp that way, that she was just dazed. And anyway, there wasn't so much difference between her and the rest any more, they were all acting dopy like that. Then after you told me to bring her in the last time, I stuck my hand down the back of her dress and I felt something hard and round, like a carbuncle or berl, so I put a little gauze application over it. And then me and her decided, as long as the contest was over anyway, we better go out and tell you—"

"Yeah," he scoffed, "and I s'pose if I hadn't shown up she'd still be dancing around out there, until the place needed disinfecting! When was the first time you noticed anything the matter with her?"

She babbled: "About two thirty, three o'clock. They were all in here—the place was still crowded—and someone knocked on the door. He was standing out there with her in his arms and he passed her to me and whispered, 'Look after her, will you?' That's when he begged me not to tell anyone. He said he'd—" She stopped.

"Go on!" snapped Smitty.

"He said he'd cut me in on the thousand if they won it. Then when the whistle blew and they all went out again, he was standing there waiting to take her back in his arms—and off he goes with her. They all had to be helped out by that time, anyway, so nobody noticed anything wrong. After that, the same thing happened each time— until you came. But I didn't dream she was dead." She crossed herself. "If I'da thought that, you couldn't have got me to touch her for love nor money—"

"I've got my doubts," Smitty told her, "about the money part of that, anyway. Outside—and consider yourself a material witness."

If the old crone was to be believed, it had happened outside on the dance floor under the bright arc lights, and not in here. He was pretty sure it had, at that. Monahan wouldn't have dared try to force his way in here. The screaming of the other occupants would have blown the roof off. Secondly, the very fact that the floor had been more crowded at that time than later had helped cover it up. They'd probably quarreled when she tried to quit. He'd whipped out the pencil and struck her while she clung to him. She'd either fallen and killed herself on it, and he'd picked her up again immediately before anyone noticed, or else the Falvey woman had handled her carelessly in the washroom and the impaled pencil had reached her heart.

Smitty decided he wanted to know if any of the feminine entries had been seen to fall to the floor at any time during the evening. Pasternack had been in his office from ten on, first giving out publicity items and then taking a nap, so Smitty put him back on the shelf. Moe, however, came across beautifully.

"Did I see anyone fall?" he echoed shrilly. "Who didn't? Such a commotion you never saw in your life. About half-past two. Right when we were on the air, too."

"Go on, this is getting good. What'd he do, pick her right up again?"

"Pick her up! She wouldn't get up. You couldn't go near her! She just sat there swearing and screaming and throwing things. I thought we'd have to send for the police. Finally they sneaked up behind her and hauled her off on her fanny to the bleachers and disqualified her—"

"Wa-a-ait a minute," gasped Smitty. "Who you talking about?"

Moe looked surprised. "That Standish dame, who else? You saw her, the one with the bum pin. That was when she sprained it and couldn't dance any more. She wouldn't go home. She hung around saying she was framed and gypped and we couldn't get rid of her—"

"Wrong number," said Smitty disgustedly. "Back where you came from." And to the cop: "Now we'll get down to brass tacks. Let's have a crack at Monahan—"

He was thumbing his notebook with studied absorption when the fellow was shoved in the door. "Be right with you," he said offhandedly, tapping his pockets, "soon as I jot down—Lend me your pencil a minute, will you?"

"I—I had one, but I lost it," said Monahan dully.

"How come?" asked Smitty quietly.

"Fell out of my pocket, I guess. The clip was broken."

"This it?"

The fellow's eyes grew big, while it almost touched their lashes, twirling from left to right and right to left. "Yeah, but what's the matter with it, what's it got on it?"

"You asking me that?" leered Smitty. "Come on, show me how you did it!"

Monahan cowered back against the wall, looked from the body on the floor to the pencil, and back again. "Oh no," he moaned, "no. Is that what happened to her? I didn't even know—"

"Guys as innocent as you rub me the wrong way," said Smitty. He reached for him, hauled him out into the center of the room, and then sent him flying back again. His head bonged the door and the cop looked in inquiringly. "No, I didn't knock," said Smitty, "that was just his dome." He sprayed a little of the alcohol into Monahan's stunned face and hauled him forward again. "The first peep out of you was, 'I killed her.' Then you keeled over. Later on you kept saying, 'I'm to blame, I'm to blame.' Why try to back out now?"

"But I didn't mean I did anything to her," wailed Monahan. "I thought I killed her by dancing too much. She was all right when I helped her in here about two. Then when I came back for her, the old dame whispered she couldn't wake her up. She said maybe the motion of dancing would bring her to. She said, 'You want that thousand dollars, don't you? Here, hold her up, no one'll be any the wiser.' And I listened to her like a fool and faked it from then on."

Smitty sent him hurling again. "Oh, so now it's supposed to have happened in here—with your pencil, no less! Quit trying to pass the buck!"

The cop, who didn't seem to be very bright, again opened the door, and Monahan came sprawling out at his feet. "Geez, what a hard head he must have," he remarked.

"Go over and start up that phonograph over there," ordered Smitty. "We're going to have a little demonstration—of how he did it. If banging his conk against the door won't bring back his memory, maybe dancing with her will do it." He hoisted Monahan upright by the scruff of the neck. "Which pocket was the pencil in?"

The man motioned toward his breast. Smitty dropped it in point first. The cop fitted the needle into the groove and threw the switch. A blare came from the amplifier. "Pick her up and hold her," grated Smitty.

An animal-like moan was the only answer he got. The man tried to back away. The cop threw him forward again. "So you won't dance, eh?"

"I won't dance," gasped Monahan.

When they helped him up from the floor, he would dance.

"You held her like that dead, for two solid hours," Smitty reminded him. "Why mind an extra five minutes or so?"

The moving scarecrow crouched down beside the other inert scarecrow on the floor. Slowly his arms went around her. The two scarecrows rose to their feet, tottered drunkenly together, then moved out of the doorway into the open in time to the music. The cop began to perspire.

Smitty said: "Any time you're willing to admit you done it, you can quit."

"God forgive you for this!" said a tomb-like voice.

"Take out the pencil," said Smitty, "without letting go of her—like you did the first time."

"This is the first time," said that hollow voice. "The time before—it dropped out." His right hand slipped slowly away from the corpse's back, dipped into his pocket.

The others had come out of Pasternack's office, drawn by the sound of the macabre music, and stood huddled together, horror and unbelief written all over their weary faces. A corner of the bleachers hid both Smitty and the cop from them; all they could see was that grisly couple moving slowly out into the center of the big floor, alone under the funeral heliotrope arc light. Monahan's hand suddenly went up, with something gleaming in it; stabbed down again and was hidden against his partner's back. There was an unearthly howl and the girl with the turned ankle fell flat on her face amidst the onlookers.

Smitty signaled the cop; the music suddenly broke off. Monahan and his partner had come to a halt again and stood there like they had when the contest first ended, upright, tent-shaped, feet far apart, heads locked together. One pair of eyes was as glazed as the other now.

"All right, break, break!" said Smitty.

Monahan was clinging to her with a silent, terrible intensity as though he could no longer let go.

The Standish girl had sat up, but promptly covered her eyes with both hands and was shaking all over as if she had a chill.

"I want that girl in here," said Smitty. "And you, Moe. And the old lady."

He closed the door on the three of them. "Let's see that book of entries again."

Moe handed it over jumpily.

"Sylvia Standish, eh?" The girl nodded, still sucking in her breath from the fright she'd had.

"Toodles McGuire was Rose Lamont—now what's your real name?" He thumbed at the old woman. "What are you two to each other?"

The girl looked away. "She's my mother, if you gotta know," she said.

"Might as well admit it, it's easy enough to check up on," he agreed. "I had a hunch there was a tie-up like that in it somewhere. You were too ready to help her carry the body in here the first time." He turned to the cringing Moe. "I understood you to say she carried on like nobody's never-mind when she was ruled out, had to be hauled off the floor by main force and wouldn't go home. Was she just a bum loser, or what was her grievance?"

"She claimed it was done purposely," said Moe. "Me, I got my doubts. It was like this. That girl the feller killed, she had on a string of glass beads, see? So the string broke and they rolled all over the floor under everybody's feet. So this one, she slipped on 'em, fell and turned her ankle and couldn't dance no more. Then she starts hollering blue murder." He shrugged. "What should we do, call off the contest because she couldn't dance no more?"

"She did it purposely," broke in the girl hotly, "so she could hook the award herself! She knew I had a better chance than anyone else—"

"I suppose it was while you were sitting there on the floor you picked up the pencil Monahan had dropped," Smitty said casually.

"I did like hell! It fell out in the bleachers when he came over to apolo—" She stopped abruptly. "I don't know what pencil you're talking about."

"Don't worry about a little slip-up like that," Smitty told her. "You're down for it anyway—and have been ever since you folded up out there just now. You're not telling me anything I don't know already."

"Anyone woulda keeled over; I thought I was seeing her ghost—"

"That ain't what told me. It was seeing him pretend to do it that told me he never did it. It wasn't done outside at all, in spite of what your old lady tried to hand me. Know why? The pencil didn't go through her dress. There's no hole in the back of her dress. Therefore she had her dress off and was cooling off when it happened. Therefore it was done here in the restroom. For Monahan to do it outside he would have had to hitch her whole dress up almost over her head in front of everybody—and maybe that wouldn't have been noticed!

"He never came in here after her; your own mother would have been the first one to squawk for help. You did, though. She stayed a moment after the others. You came in the minute they cleared out and stuck her with it. She fell on it and killed herself. Then your old lady tried to cover you by putting a pad on the wound and giving Monahan the idea she was stupefied from fatigue. When he began to notice the coldness, if he did, he thought it was from the alcohol rubs she was getting every rest-period. I guess he isn't very bright anyway—a guy like that, that dances for his coffee-and. He didn't have any motive. He wouldn't have done it even if she wanted to quit, he'd have let her. He was too penitent later on when he thought he'd tired her to death. But you had all the motive I need—those broken beads. Getting even for what you thought she did. Have I left anything out?"

"Yeah," she said curtly, "look up my sleeve and tell me if my hat's on straight!"

On the way out to the Black Maria that had backed up to the entrance, with the two Falvey women, Pasternack, Moe, and the other four dancers marching single file ahead of him, Smitty called to the cop: "Where's Monahan? Bring him along!"

The cop came up mopping his brow. "I finally pried him loose," he said, "when they came to take her away, but I can't get him to stop laughing. He's been laughing ever since. I think he's lost his mind. Makes your blood run cold. Look at that!"

Monahan was standing there, propped against the wall, a lone figure under the arc light, his arms still extended in the half-embrace in which he had held his partner for nine days and nights, while peal after peal of macabre mirth came from him, shaking him from head to foot.

(1935)

The Death of Me

As soon as the front door closed behind her I locked it on the inside. I'd never yet known her to go out without forgetting something and coming back for it. This was one time I wasn't letting her in again. I undid my tie and snaked it off as I turned away. I went in the living-room and slung a couple of pillows on the floor, so I wouldn't have to fall, could take it lying down. I got the gun out from behind the radio console where I'd hidden it and tossed it onto the pillows. She'd wondered why there was so much static all through supper. We didn't have the price of new tubes so she must have thought it was that.

It looked more like a relic than an up-to-date model. I didn't know much about guns; all I hoped was that he hadn't gypped me. The only thing I was sure of was it was loaded, and that was what counted. All it had to do was go off once. I unhooked my shaving mirror from the bathroom wall and brought that out, to see what I was doing, so there wouldn't have to be any second tries. I opened the little flap in back of it and stood it up on the floor, facing the pillows that were slated to be my bier. The movie show wouldn't break up until eleven-thirty. That was long enough. Plenty long enough.

I went over to the desk, sat down and scrawled her a note. Nothing much, just two lines. *"Sorry, old dear, too many bills."* I unstrapped my wrist watch and put it on top of the note. Then I started emptying out the pockets of my baggy suit one by one.

It was one of those suits sold by the job-lot, hundreds of them all exactly alike, at seventeen or nineteen dollars a throw, and distributed around town on the backs of life's failures. It had been carrying around hundreds of dollars—in money owed. Every pocket had its bills, its reminders, its summonses jabbed through the crack of the door by process-servers. Five days running now, I'd gotten a different summons each day. I'd quit trying to dodge them any more. I stacked them all up neatly before me. The notice from the landlord to vacate was there too. The gas had already been turned off the day before— hence the gun. Jumping from the window might have only broken my back and paralyzed me.

On top of the whole heap went the insurance policy in its blue folder. That wasn't worth a cent either—right now. Ten minutes from now it was going to be worth ten thousand dollars. I stripped off my coat, opened the collar of my shirt and lay down on my back on the pillows.

I had to shift the mirror a little so I could see the side of my head. I picked up the gun in my right hand and flicked open the safety catch. Then I held it to my head, a little above the ear. It felt cold and hard; heavy, too. I was pushing it in more than I needed to, I guess. I took a deep breath, closed my eyes, and jerked the trigger with a spasmodic lunge that went all through me. The impact of the hammer jarred my whole head, and the click was magnified like something heard through a hollow tube or pipe—but that was all there was, a click. So he'd gypped me, or else the cartridges were no good and it had jammed.

It was loaded all right. I'd seen them in it myself when he broke it open for me. My arm flopped back and hit the carpet with a thud. I lay there sweating like a mule. What could have been easier than giving it another try? I couldn't. I might as well have tried to walk on the ceiling now.

Water doesn't reach the same boiling-point twice. A pole-vaulter doesn't stay up in the air at his highest point more than a split second. I lay there five minutes maybe, and then when I saw it wasn't going to be any use any more, I got up on my feet again.

I slurred on my coat, shoved the double-crossing gun into my pocket, crammed the slew of bills about my person again. I kicked the mirror and the pillows aside, strapped on my wrist watch. I'd felt sorry for myself before; now I had no use for myself. The farewell note

I crumpled up, and the insurance policy, worthless once more, I flung violently into the far corner of the room. I was still shaking a little from the effects of the let-down when I banged out of the place and started off.

I found a place where I could get a jiggerful of very bad alcohol scented with juniper for the fifteen cents I had on me. The inward shaking stopped about then, and I struck on from there, down a long gloomy thoroughfare lined with warehouses, that had railroad tracks running down the middle of it. It had a bad name, in regard to both traffic and bodily safety, but if anyone had tried to hold me up just then they probably would have lost whatever they had on *them* instead.

An occasional arc-light gleamed funereally at the infrequent intersections. Presently the sidewalk and the cobbles petered out, and it had narrowed into just the railroad right-of-way, between low-lying sheds and walled-in lumber yards. I found myself walking the ties, on the outside of the rails. If a train had come up behind me without warning, I would have gotten what I'd been looking for a little while ago. I stumbled over something, went down, skinned my palm on the rail. I picked myself up and looked. One had come up already it seemed, and somebody who hadn't been looking for it had gotten it instead. His body was huddled between two of the ties, on the outside of the rail, had tripped me as I walked them. The head would have been resting on the rail itself if there had been any head left. But it had been flattened out. I was glad it was pretty dark around there; you didn't have to see if you didn't want to.

I would have detoured around him and notified the first cop I came to, but as I started to move away, my raised leg wasn't very far from his stiffly outstreched one. The trouser on each matched. The same goods, the same color gray, the same cheap job-lot suit. I reached down and held the two cuffs together with one hand. You couldn't tell them apart. I grabbed him by the ankle and hauled him a little further away from the rail. Now he was headless all right.

I unbuttoned the jacket, held it open and looked at the lining. Sure enough—same label, "Eagle Brand Clothes." I turned the pocket inside out, and the same size was there, a 36. He was roughly my own

238 / Cornell Woolrich

build, as far as height and weight went. The identification tag in the
coat was blank though; had no name and address on it. I got a pencil
out and I printed *"Walter Lynch, 35 Meadowbrook"* on it, the way it
was on my own.

I was beginning to shake again, but this time with excitement. I
looked up and down the tracks, and then I emptied out every pocket
he had on him. I stowed everything away without looking at it, then
stuffed all my own bills in and around him. I slipped the key to the flat
into his vest-pocket. I exchanged initialled belts with him. I even
traded his package of cigarettes for mine—they weren't the same
brand. I'd come out without a necktie, but I wouldn't have worn that
howler of his to—well, a railroad accident. I edged it gingerly off the
rail, where it still lay in a loop, and it came away two colors, green at
the ends, the rest of it garnet. I picked up a stray scrap of newspaper,
wrapped it up, and shoved it in my pocket to throw away somewhere
else. Our shirts were both white, at least his had been until it
happened. But anyway, all this wasn't absolutely necessary, I
figured. The papers in the pockets would be enough. They'd hardly
ask anyone's wife to look very closely at a husband in the shape this
one was. Still, I wanted to do the job up brown just to be sure. I took off
my wrist watch and strapped it on him. I gave him a grim salute as I
left him. "They can't kill you, boy," I said, "you're twins!"

I left the railroad right-of-way at the next intersection, still without seeing anybody, and struck out for downtown. I was free as air,
didn't owe anybody a cent—and in a couple weeks from now there'd
be ten grand in the family. I was going back to her, of course. I wasn't
going to stay away for good. But I'd lie low first, wait till she'd
collected the insurance money, then we'd powder out of town
together, start over again some place else with a ten grand nest-egg.

It was a cruel stunt to try on her, but she'd live through it. A couple
weeks grief was better than being broke for the rest of our lives. And
if I'd let her in on it ahead of time, she wouldn't have gone through
with it. She was that kind.

I picked a one-arm restaurant and went in there. I took my meal
check with me to the back and shut myself up in the washroom. I was
about to have an experience that very few men outside of amnesia

victims have ever had. I was about to find out who I was and where I hung out.

First I ripped the identification tag out of my own suit and sent it down the drain along with the guy's stained necktie. Then I started unloading, and sorting out. Item one was a cheap, mangy-looking billfold. Cheap on the outside, not the inside. I counted them. Two grand in twenties, brand new ones, not a wrinkle on them. There was a rubber band around them. Well, I was going to be well-heeled while I lay low, anyway.

Item two was a key with a six-pointed brass star dangling from it. On the star was stamped "Hotel Columbia, 601." Item three was a bill from the same hotel, made out to George Kelly, paid up a week in advance. Items four and five were a smaller key to a valise or bag, and two train tickets. One was punched and one hadn't been used yet. One was a week old and the other had been bought that very night. He must have been on his way back with it when he was knocked down crossing the tracks. The used ticket was from Chicago here, and the one intended to be used was from here on to New York.

But "here" happened not to be in a straight line between the two, in fact it was one hell of a detour to take. All that interested me was that he'd only come to town a week ago, and had been about to haul his freight out again tomorrow or the next day. Which meant it wasn't likely he knew anyone in town very well, so if his face had changed remarkably overnight who would be the wiser—outside of the clerk at his hotel? And a low-tipped hat-brim would take care of that.

The bill was paid up in advance, the room-key was in my pocket and I didn't have to go near the desk on my way in. I wanted to go over there and take a look around Room 601 with the help of that other little key. Who could tell, there might be some more of those nice crisp twenties stowed away there? As long as the guy was dead anyway, I told myself, this wasn't robbery. It was just making the most of a good thing.

I put everything back in my pockets and went outside and ordered a cup of coffee at the counter. I needed change for the phone call I was going to make before I went over there. Kelly, strangely enough, hadn't had any small change on him; only those twenties.

I stripped one off and shoved it at the counterman. I got a dirty look. "That the smallest you got?" he growled. "Hell, you clean the till out all for a fi' cent cup of coffee!"

"If it's asking too much of you," I snarled, "I can drink my coffee any other place."

But it already had milk in it and couldn't be put back in the boiler. He almost wore the twenty out testing it for counterfeitness, stretched it to the tearing point, held it up to the light, peered at it. Finally, unable to find anything against it, he jotted down the serial number on a piece of paper and grudgingly handed me nineteen-ninety-five out of the cash register.

I left the coffee standing there and went over to call up the Columbia Hotel from the open pay telephone on the wall. 601, of course, didn't answer. Still he might be sharing it with someone, a woman for instance, even though the bill had been made out to him alone. I got the clerk on the wire.

"Well, is he alone there? Isn't there anybody rooming with him I can talk to?" There wasn't. "Has he had any callers since he's been staying there?"

"Not that I know of," said the clerk. "We've seen very little of him." A lone wolf, eh? Perfect, as far as I was concerned.

By the time I got to the Columbia I had a hat, the brim rakishly shading the bridge of my nose. I needn't have bothered. The clerk was all wrapped up in some girl dangling across his desk and didn't even look up. The aged colored man who ran the creaking elevator was half blind. It was an eerie, moth-eaten sort of place, but perfect to hole up in for a week or two.

When I got out of the cage I started off in the wrong direction down the hall. "You is this heah way, boss, not that way," the old darky reminded me.

I snapped my fingers and switched around. "Need a road map in this dump," I scowled to cover up my mistake. He peered near-sightedly at me, closed the door, and went down. 601 was around a bend of the hall, down at the very end. I knocked first, just to be on the safe side, then let myself in. I locked the door again on the inside and wedged a chair up against the knob. This was my room now; just let anyone try to get in!

He'd traveled light, the late Kelly. Nothing there but some dirty shirts over in the corner and some clean ones in the bureau drawer. Bought right here in town too, the cellophane was still on some and the sales slip lying with them. He must have arrived without a shirt to his back.

But that small key I had belonged to something, and when I went hunting it up I found the closet door locked and the key to it missing. For a minute I thought I'd overlooked it when I was frisking him down by the tracks, but I was sure I hadn't. The small key was definitely not the one to the closet door. It nearly fell through to the other side when I tried it. I could have called down for a passkey, but I didn't want anyone up here. Since the key hadn't been on him, and wasn't in the door, he must have hidden it somewhere around the room. Meaning he thought a lot of whatever was behind that door and wasn't taking any chances with it. I started to hunt for the key high and low.

It turned up in about an hour's time, after I had the big rug rolled up against the wall and the bed stripped down and the mattress gashed all over with a razor blade and the whole place looking like a tornado had hit it. The funny little blur at the bottom of the inverted light-bowl overhead gave it away when I happened to look up. He'd tossed it up there before he went out.

I nearly broke my neck getting it out of the thing, had to balance on the back of a chair and tilt the bowl with my fingertips while it swayed back and forth and specks of plaster fell on my head. It occurred to me, although it was only a guess, that the way he'd intended to go about it was smash the bowl and let it drop out just before he checked out of the hotel. I fitted the key into the closet door and took a gander.

There was only a small Gladstone bag over in the corner with a hotel towel over it. Not another thing, not even a hat or a spare collar. I hauled the bag out into the room and got busy on it with the small key I'd taken from his pocket. A gun winked up at me first of all, when I got it open. Not a crummy relic like the one I'd bought that afternoon, but a brand new, efficient-looking affair, bright as a dollar. When I saw what it was lying on I tossed it aside and dumped the bag upside down on the floor, sat down next to it with a thump.

I only had to break open and count the first neat little green brick of bills, after that I just multiplied it by the rest. Twenty-one times two, very simple. Forty-two thousand dollars, in twenties; unsoiled, crisp as autumn leaves. Counting the two thousand the peculiar Mr. Kelly had been carrying around with him for pin-money, and a few loose ones papering the bottom of the bag—he'd evidently broken open one pack himself—the sum total wasn't far from forty-five. I'd been painlessly run over and killed by a train to the tune of forty-five thousand dollars!

The ten grand insurance premium that had loomed so big a while ago dwindled to a mere bagatelle, with all this stuff lying in my lap. Something to light cigarettes with if I ran out of matches! And to think I'd nearly rung down curtains on myself for that! I could've hugged the chiseler that sold me that faulty gun.

But why go through with the scheme now? I had money. Let them keep the insurance. I would come back to life. It was all in cash too—good as gold wherever we went; better, gold wasn't legal any more.

I jammed everything back into the bag, everything but the gun. That I shoved under one of the pillows. Let them find it after I was gone; it was Kelly's anyway. I locked the bag, tossed it temporarily into the closet, and hurriedly went over his few personal belongings once more. The guy didn't have a friend in the world seemingly. There wasn't a scrap of writing, wasn't a photograph, wasn't a thing to show who or what he was. He wasn't in his own home town, the two railroad tickets told that, so who was there to step forward and report him missing? That would have to come from the other end if at all, and it would take a long time to percolate through. My title to the dough was clear in every sense but the legal one; I'd inherited it from him. I saw now the mistake I'd made, though. I shouldn't have switched identities with him. I should have left him as he was, just taken the key to the bag, picked up the money, gone home and kept on being Walter Lynch. No one knew he had the money. I wouldn't have even had to duck town. This way, I was lying dead by the tracks; and if Edith powdered out with me tonight it would look funny, and would most likely lead to an investigation.

I sat down for a minute and thought it out. Then it came to me. I could still make it look on the up-and-up, but she'd have to play ball with me. This would be the set-up: she would write a note addressed to me and leave it in the flat, saying she was sick of being broke and was quitting me cold. She'd get on the train tonight—alone—and go. That would explain her disappearance and also my "suicide" down by the tracks, a result of her running off. We'd arrange where to meet in New York. I'd follow her on a different train, taking care not to be seen getting on, and using the very ticket Kelly had bought. That way I didn't even have to run the risk of a station agent recalling my face later.

I was almost dizzy with my own brilliance; this took care of everything. My only regret was I had destroyed my own original suicide note to her. It would have been a swell finishing touch to have left it by the body. But her fake note at the flat would give the police the motive for the suicide if they were any good at putting two and two together. "And here I've been going around trying to convince employers I have brains!" I gloated.

She'd only just be getting back from the movie show about now. There'd be nothing to alarm her at first in my not being there. I'd taken the gun out with me and the farewell note too. But she'd turn on the lights, maybe give the radio a try, or ask one of the neighbors if they'd seen me. She mustn't do any of those things, she was supposed to have gone long ago. I decided to warn her ahead over the phone to lie low until I got there and explained, to wait for me in the dark.

I picked up the room phone and asked for our number. It was taking a slight chance, but it was better than letting her give herself away; she might stand by the brightly-lighted window looking up and down the street for me, in full view of anyone happening along. He put through the call for me. It rang just once at our end, where she and I lived, and then was promptly answered—much quicker than Ethel ever got to it.

A deep bass voice said: "Yeah?" I nearly fainted. "Yeah? What is it?" the voice said a second time. I pulled myself together again. "I'm calling Saxony 4230," I said impatiently. "They've given me the wrong num—Damn that skirt-chasing clerk downstairs."

The answer came back, "This is Saxony 4230. What is it?" I put out one hand and leaned groggily against the table, without letting go the receiver. "Who are you?" I managed to articulate.

"I'm a patrolman," he boomed back.

My face was getting wetter by the minute. "Wh-what's up?" I choked.

"You a friend of the Lynches? They've just had a death here." Then in the background, over and above his voice, came a woman's screams—screams of agony from some other room, carried faintly over the wire. Blurred and distorted as they were, I recognized them; they were Ethel's. A second feminine voice called out more distinctly, presumably to the cop I was talking to: "Get her some spirits of ammonia or something to quiet her!" One of the neighbors, called in in the emergency.

Pop! went my whole scheme, like a punctured balloon. My body had already been found down by the tracks. A cop had already broken the news to her. He and the ministering neighbor were witnesses to the fact that she hadn't run off and left me *before* I did it. For that matter, the whole apartment building must be hearing her screams.

The entire set-up shifted back again into its first arrangement, and left me where I'd been before. She couldn't leave town now, not for days, not until after the funeral anyway. The affair at the tracks was an accident once more, not a suicide. I daren't try to get word to her now, after making her go through this. She'd either give herself away in her relief, or uncontrollable anger at finding out might make her turn on me intentionally and expose me.

"Just a friend of theirs," I was saying, or something like that. "I'll call up tomorrow, I guess—"

"Okay," he said, and I heard the line click at the other end.

I forked the receiver as though it weighed a ton and slumped down next to it. It took me a little time to get my breathing back in shape. There was only one thing to do now—get out of town by myself without her. To stay on indefinitely was to invite being recognized by someone sooner or later, and the longer I stayed the greater the chances were of that happening. I'd blow to New York tonight. I'd use Kelly's ticket, get the Flyer that passed through at midnight.

I stealthily eased the chair away from under the doorknob, picked up the bag, unlocked the door, gave it a push. As though it was wired to set off some kind of an alarm, the phone began to ring like fury just as the door swung out. I stood there thunderstruck for a minute. They'd traced my call back! Maybe Ethel had recovered enough to ask them to find out who it was, or maybe the way I'd hung up had looked suspicious. Let it ring its head off. I wasn't going near it. I was getting out of here while the getting out was good! I hotfooted it down the hall, its shrill clamor behind me.

Just before I got to the turn in the hallway, the elevator-slide sloshed open. I stopped dead in my tracks. I could hear footsteps coming toward me along the carpet, softened to a shuffle. I hesitated for a minute, then ducked back, to wait for whoever it was to go by. I closed the door after me, stood listening by it. The bell was still ding-donging in back of me. The knock, when it came, was on my own door, and sent a quiver racing through me. I started to back away slowly across the room, bag still in my hand. The knock came again.

"What is it?" I called out.

It was the old colored man's whine. "Mista Kelly, somebody wants you on de foam pow'ful bad. We done tole 'em you must be asleep if'n you don't answer, but dey say wake you up. Dey say dey know you dere—"

I set the bag down noiselessly, looked at the window. No soap, six stories above the street and no fire-escape, regulations to the contrary. The damn phone kept bleating away there inside the room, nearly driving me crazy.

"Mista Kelly—" he whined again.

I pulled myself together; a voice on the phone wasn't going to kill me. "All right," I said curtly.

If they knew I was here, then they knew I was here. I'd bluff it out—be a friend of the late Lynch's that his wife had never heard about. I took in a chestful of air, bent down and said, "Yep?"

The second word out of the receiver, I knew that it was no check-up on the call I'd made ten minutes ago. The voice was very cagey, almost muffled.

"Getting restless, Hogan?" I lowered my own to match it. Hogan?

First I was Lynch, then I was Kelly, now I was Hogan! But it wasn't much trouble to figure out Kelly and Hogan wore the same pair of shoes; I'd never had much confidence in the names on hotel-blotters in the first place.

"Sorta," I shadow-boxed. "Kelly's the name, though."

The voice went in for irony by the shovelful. "So we noticed," he drawled. Meaning about my being restless, evidently, and not what my name was. "You got so restless you were figuring on taking a little trip, without waiting for your friends, is that it? Seems you even walked down to the depot, asking about trains, and bought yourself a ticket ahead of time. I had a phone call from somebody that saw you, about eight this evening. I s'pose you woulda just taken an overnight bag—" A pause. "—a little black bag, and hopped aboard."

So others beside Kelly knew what was in that Gladstone! Nice cheering thought.

The voice remonstrated with a feline purr: "You shouldn't be so impatient. You knew we were coming. You shoulda given us more time. We only got in late this afternoon." Another pause. "Tire trouble on the way. We woulda felt very bad to have missed you. It woulda inconvenienced us a lot. You see, you've got my razor in your bag, and some shirts and socks belonging to some of the other boys. Now, we'd like to get everything sorted out before you go ahead on any little trips because, if you just go off like that without letting us know, never can tell when you'd be coming back."

I could almost feel the threat that lurked under the slurring surface of the words flash out of the receiver into my ear like a steel blade. He was talking in code, but the code wasn't hard to decipher; wasn't meant to be. They wanted a split of what was in the black bag; maybe they were entitled to it, maybe they weren't, but they sounded like they were going to get it, whoever they were. Kelly, I gathered, had been on the point of continuing his travels without waiting for that little formality—only he'd taken the back way to and from the depot to avoid being seen, had been seen anyway, and then a freight train had come along and saved him any further trouble. But since I was now Kelly, his false move had gotten me in bad and it was up to me to do the worrying for him.

I hadn't said two words so far; hadn't had a chance to. I already had a dim suspicion in the back of my mind about where, or rather how, all that crisp new money had been obtained. But that thought could wait until later. I had no time just now to bother with it. All I knew was there wasn't going to be any split, big or little; just one look at my face was all they needed and I'd be left with only memories.

I had one trump-card though: they couldn't tag me. I could walk right by them with the whole satchelful of dough and they wouldn't know the difference. All I needed was to stall a little, to keep them from coming up here.

"You've got me wrong," I murmured into the phone. "I wouldn't think of keeping anyone's razors or shirts or socks—"

"Can't hear you," he said. "Take the handkerchief off the thing, you don't need it." He'd noticed the difference in voices and thought I was using a filter to disguise mine.

"You do the talking," I suggested. "It was your nickel."

"We don't talk so good with our mouths," he let me know. "We talk better with other things. You know where to find us. All that was arranged, but you got a poor memory, it looks like. Check out and come on over here—with everything. Then we'll all see you off on the train, after everything's straightened out."

Another of those threats flashed out. I sensed instinctively what Kelly's "seeing off" would be like if he had been fool enough to go near them at this point. He was in too bad to redeem himself. He'd never make that New York train standing on his own feet.

"How soon you want me to be over?" I stalled.

The purr left the voice at this point. "We'll give you thirty minutes." Then, while the fact that a net was closing in on me slowly sank in, he went on: "I wouldn't try to make the depot without stopping by here first. Couple of the boys are hanging around there in the car. They like to watch people get off the trains. They like to watch them get off much better than they like to watch 'em get on, funny isn't it?"

"Yeah, funny," I agreed dismally.

"You're in 601, over at that dump," he told me. "You can see the street from there. Step over to the window for a minute, I'll hold the wire—" I put down the receiver, edged up to the window, took a tuck in the dusty net curtains and peered down. It was a side-street, not the one the hotel entrance faced on. But at the corner, which commanded both the window and the entrance, a negligent figure slouched under the white sputtering arc-light, hat-brim down, idly scanning a newspaper. While I watched he raised his head, saw me with the light behind me, stared straight up at the window. Unmistakably my window and no other. I let the curtains spread out again, went back to the phone.

"Like the view?" the voice at the other end suggested. "Nice quiet street, hardly anyone on it, right?"

"Nice quiet street, hardly anyone on it," I intoned dazedly.

"Then we'll be seeing you in—twenty-five minutes now." The line clicked closed, but not quickly enough to cut off a smothered monosyllable. "Rat," it had sounded like. It wouldn't have surprised me if it was, old-fashioned and overworked as the expression was.

All of which left me pretty well holed-in. I knew the penalty now for trying to get on the New York train, or any other. I knew the penalty for simply walking away from the hotel in the wrong direction. I knew the penalty for everything in fact but one thing—for staying exactly where I was and not budging.

And what else could that be but a little surprise visit on their part, preferably in the early morning hours? This place was a pushover with just a night clerk and an old myopic colored man. I certainly couldn't afford to call in police protection beforehand any more than the real Kelly could have.

There was always the alternative of dropping the bag out the window and letting that finger-man out there pick it up and walk off with it intact, but I wasn't quite yellow enough to go for that idea. Forty-five grand was forty-five grand; why should a voice on the wire and a lizard on a street corner dish me out of it? The postman may knock twice, but not Opportunity.

The obvious thing was to get out of 601 in a hurry. I split the phone for the third time that night. "This is Kelly, six-one. I'd like my room changed. Can you gimme an inside room on the top floor?"

The broad I'd seen him with must have put him in good humor. "That shouldn't be hard," he said. "I'll send the key up."

"Here's the idea," I went on. "I want this transfer kept strictly between you and me, I don't want it on the blotter. Anyone stops by, I'm in 601 as far as you know. They don't find me there, then I'm not in the building."

"I don't see how I can do that, we've got to keep the record straight," he said for a come-on.

"I'm sending a sealed envelope down to you," I said. "You open it personally. I'll keep 601—keep paying for it—if that'll make it easier for you. I'm in a little personal trouble, wife after me. Don't want any callers. You play along with me and you won't come out the short end. Send Rastus up with the key."

"I'm your man," he said. When the old darky knocked I left the black bag in the closet, locked 601 after me and took the key with me. The lights were out and he didn't notice the dummy I'd formed out of Kelly's shirts under the bedding. Nor the bulge all those packages of twenties gave my person. The bag was full of toilet-paper to give it the right weight if snatched up in a hurry. They wouldn't be likely to show their faces a second time after filling a perfectly good mattress with lead in the middle of the night and rousing the whole hotel. Kelly's dandy little gun I took with me.

He showed me into a place on the eighth floor back with a window that looked out on a blank brick shaft, and I had him wait outside the door for a minute. I put three of the twenties into an envelope, sealed it for the clerk, and told him to take it down to him.

"Yessa, Mr. Kelly," he bobbed.

"No, Mr. Kelly's down in 601, there's no one in this room," I told him, and I gave him a twenty for himself. "You ask your boss downstairs if you don't believe me. He'll put you right. You didn't show me up here; this is so you remember that." His eyes bulged when he looked at the tip.

"Yas, sir!" he yammered.

I locked the door, but didn't bother with any mere chair this time. I sealed it up with a big top-heavy chest of drawers that weighed a ton. The room had its own bath. I stretched out on the bed fully dressed with the money still on me and the gun under my pillow and lay there in the dark waiting.

I didn't have such a long wait at that. The firecrackers went off at about three in the morning. I could hear it plainly two floors above, where I was. It sounded like the guts were being blown out of the building. The shots came so close together I couldn't count them; there must have been three or four revolvers being emptied at one time. All into Kelly's rolled-up shirts, in the dark.

The whole thing was over within five minutes, less than that. Then, minutes after, like one last firecracker on the string going off, there came a single shot, much further away this time. It sounded as though it came from the lobby—either a cop had tried to head them off, or they'd taken care of the clerk on their way out.

The keening of police-cars, whistling up from all directions at once, jerked me upright on the bed. I hadn't thought of that. They'd want to know what all the shooting was for. They'd want to ask the guy who'd been in 601 a lot of questions, especially after they saw the proxy he'd left on the bed to take his medicine for him. They'd want to know why and wherefore, and how come all that money, and the nice shiny gun, was it licensed? Lots and lots of questions, that Kelly-Hogan-Lynch was in no position to answer.

It behooved me to dodge them every bit as much as my would-be murderers. It was out for me. Now was the time for it anyway. Kelly's friends would lie low until the police had cleared away. It was now or never, while the police cars were keeping them away.

I rolled the chest of drawers aside, unlocked the door, and squinted out. The building was humming with sounds and voices. I went back for the gun, laid it flat against my stomach under my shirt, with my belt to hold it up, buttoned my coat over it and started down the hall. An old maid opened her door and gawked. "Wha—what was that down below just now?"

"Backfiring in the street," I said reassuringly, and she jumped in again.

The elevator was just rising flush with the floor. I could see the light and I had an idea who was on it. I dove down the fireproof stairs next to it, which were screened by frosted-glass doors on each floor.

When I got down to the sixth, there was a shadow parked just outside them, on the hall side. A shadow wearing a visored cap. There was no light on my side. The lower half of the doors was wood. I bent double, slithered past without blurring the upper glass half, and pussyfooted on down.

The other four landings were unguarded as yet. The staircase came out in the rear of the lobby, behind a potted plant. The lobby was jammed, people in bathrobes and kimonos milling about, reporters barging in and out the two rickety phone booths the place boasted, plainclothesmen and a cop keeping a space in front of the desk clear.

Over the desk, head hanging down on the outside, dangled the clerk, showing his baldspot like a target, with a purple-black sworl in the exact middle of it. Outside the door was another cop, visible from where I was. I took the final all-important step that carried me off the staircase into the crowd. Someone turned around and saw me. "What happened?" I asked, and kept moving.

A press photographer was trying to wedge himself into one of the narrow coffin-like booths ahead of two or three others; evidently he doubled as a reporter, newspaper budgets being what they are. He unlimbered the black apparatus that was impeding him, shoved it at me.

"Hold this for me a sec," he said, and turned to the phone and dropped his nickel in. I kept moving toward the door, strapped the camera around my own shoulder as I went and breezed out past the cop in a typical journalistic hurry.

"Hey, you!" he said, then: "Okay; take one of me, why don'tcha?"

"Bust the camera," I kidded back. I unloaded it into an ashcan the minute I got around the corner, and kept going.

I was all the way across town from the Columbia when the first streak of dawn showed. The gun and the packs of twenties were both weighing me down, and I was at the mercy of the first patrolman who didn't like my shape. But this was no time of night to check in at a second hotel. The last train in or out had been at midnight and the next was at seven. I had never realized until now how tough it was getting out of a town at odd hours—especially when you were two guys, neither one of whom could afford to be recognized. I had no car. A long-distance ride in a taxi would have been a dead giveaway; the driver would only have come back and shot his mouth off. To start off

252 / Cornell Woolrich

on foot wasn't the answer either. Every passing car whose headlights
flicked me stemming the highway would be a possible source of
information against me later.

All I needed was just about an hour—hour and a half—until I could
get that New York train. Kelly's friends might still be covering the
station, police or no police, but how were they going to pick me out in
broad daylight? I certainly wasn't wearing Kelly's face, even if I was
wearing his clothes. But the station waiting-room was too conspicuous a spot. The way to do it was hop on at the last minute when the
train was already under way.

I saw a light through plate glass, and went into another of those
all-night beaneries; sitting mum in there was a shade less risky than
roaming the streets until I was picked up. I went as far to the back as I
could, got behind a bend in the wall, and ordered everything in sight
to give myself an excuse for staying awhile. It was all I could do to
swallow the stuff, but just as I had about cleaned it up and had no
more alibi left, a kid came in selling the early morning editions. I
grabbed one and buried my nose in it.

It was a good thing I'd bought it. What I read once more changed
the crazy pattern of my plans that I was trying to follow through like
a man caught in a maze.

I was on the last page, just two or three lines buried in the middle of
a column of assorted mishaps that had taken place during the pre-
vious twenty-four hours. I'd been found dead on the tracks. I was
thirty-three, unemployed, and lived at 35 Meadowbrook. And that
was that.

But the murder at the Columbia Hotel was splashed across page
one. And Mr. George Kelly was very badly wanted by the police for
questioning, not only about who his callers had been so they could be
nailed for killing the clerk, but also about brand new twenty-dollar
bills that had been popping up all over town for the past week or
more. There might be some connection, the police seemed to feel, with
a certain bank robbery in Omaha. Kelly might be someone named
Hogan, and Hogan had been very badly wanted for a long time. Then
again Kelly might not be. The descriptions of the twenty dollar bill
spendthrift that were coming in didn't always tally, but the serial

numbers on his money all checked with the list that had been sent out by the bank.

The picture of Kelly given by a haberdashery clerk who had sold him shirts and by the station-agent who had sold him a ticket to New York didn't quite line up with that given by the elevator boy at the hotel nor a coffee pot counterman who'd sold him java he hadn't drunk—except that they all agreed he was wearing a light-gray suit.

The colored man's description, being the most recent and detailed, was given more credence than the others; he had rubbed elbows with Kelly night and day for a week. It was, naturally, my own and not the other Kelly's. He was just senile enough and frightened enough not to remember that I had looked different the first six days of the week from what I had the seventh, nutty as it seems.

And then at the tag end, this: all the trains were being watched and all the cars leaving town were being stopped on the highway and searched.

So I was staying in town and liking it; or to be more exact, staying, like it or not. A stationery store across from the lunchroom opened up at eight, and I ducked in there and bought a light tan briefcase. The storekeeper wasn't very well up on his newspaper reading, there wasn't any fuss raised about the twenty I paid for it with, any more than there had been in the eating place I'd just left. But the net was tightening around me all the time. I knew it yet I couldn't do anything about it. I'd just presented them with two more witnesses to help identify me. I sent him into the back room looking for something I didn't want, and got the money into the briefcase; it didn't take more than a minute. The gun I had to leave where it was. I patted myself flat and walked out.

There was a respectable-looking family hotel on the next block. I had to get off the streets in a hurry, so I went in there, and they sold a room to James Harper. My baggage was coming later, I explained. Yes, I was new in town. Just as I was stepping into the elevator ahead of the bellhop, someone in horn-rimmed glasses brushed by me getting off. I could feel him turning around to look after me, but he wasn't anyone that I knew, so I figured I must have jostled him going by.

I locked my new door, shoved the briefcase under the mattress, and lay down on top of it. I hadn't had any sleep since two nights before. Just as I was fading out there was a slight tap at the door. I jacked myself upright and reached for the gun. The tap came again, very genteel, very apologetic. "Who is it?" I grated.

"Mr. Harper?" said an unctuous voice.

That was my name, or supposed to be. I went up close to the door and said, "Well?"

"Can I see you for a minute?"

"What about?" I switched a chair over, pivoted up on it, and peered over the transom, which was open an inch or two. The man with glasses who'd been in the lobby a few minutes ago was standing there. I could see the whole hall. There wasn't anyone else in it. I jumped down again, pushed the chair back, hesitated for a minute, then turned the key and faced him.

"Harper's the name, all right," I said, "but I think you've got your wires crossed, haven't you? I don't know you."

"Mr. Harper, I represent the Gibraltar Life Insurance Company, here in town. Being a new arrival here, I don't know whether you've heard of us or not—" I certainly had. Ethel had ten thousand coming to her from them. He was way past the door by now. I closed it after him, and quietly locked him in the room with me. He was gushing sales talk. My eyes never left his face.

"No, no insurance," I said. "I never have and never will. Don't believe in it, and what's more I can't afford it—"

"There's where you're wrong," he said briskly. "Let me just give you an instance. There was a man in this town named Lynch—" I stiffened and hooked my thumb into the waistband of my trousers, that way it was near the opening of my shirt. He continued. "He was broke, without a job, down on his luck—but he did have insurance. He met with an accident." He spread his hands triumphantly. "His wife gets ten thousand dollars." Then very slowly, "As soon as we're convinced, of course, that he's dead." Smack, between the eyes!

"Did you sell him his policy?" I tried to remember what the salesman who'd sold me mine looked like. I was quivering inside like a vibrator.

"No," he said, "I'm just an investigator for the company, but I was present when he took his examination."

"Then, if you're an investigator," I said brittlely, "how can you sell me one?"

"I'll be frank with you," he said with a cold smile. "I'm up here mainly to protect the company's interests. There's a remarkable resemblance between you and this Lynch, Mr. Harper. In fact, downstairs just now I thought I was seeing a ghost. Now don't take offense, but we have to be careful what we're doing. I may be mistaken of course, but I have a very good memory for faces. You can establish your own identity, I suppose?"

"Sure," I said truculently, "but I'm not going to. What's all this got to do with me anyway?"

"Nothing," he admitted glibly. "Of course this widow of his is in desperate need, and it will hold up the payment to her indefinitely, that's all. In fact until I'm satisfied beyond the shadow of a doubt that there hasn't been any—slipup."

"What'll it take to do that?"

"Simply your word for it, that you are not Walter Lynch. It's just one of those coincidences, that's all."

"If that's all you want, you've got it. Take my word for it, I'm not." I tried to laugh as if the whole thing were preposterous.

"Would you put that in writing for me?" he said. "Just so my conscience will be clear, just so I can protect myself if the company says anything later. After all, it's my bread and butter—"

I pulled out a sheet of hotel stationery. "What's the catch in this?" I asked.

His eyes widened innocently. "Nothing. You don't have to put your signature in full if that's what's worrying you. Just initial it. 'I am not Walter Lynch, signed J. H.' It will avoid the necessity for a more thorough investigation by the company—"

I scrawled it out and gave it to him. He blotted it, folded it, and tore off a strip before he tucked it in his wallet.

"Don't need the second half of the sheet," he murmured. He moved toward the door. "Well, I'll trot down to the office," he said. "Sorry I can't interest you in a policy." He turned the key without seeming to notice that the door had been locked, went out into the hall.

I pounced on the strips of paper he'd let fall. There were two of them. "*I am not—*" was on one and "*J. H.*" on the other. I'd fallen for him. He had my own original signature, standing by itself now, to compare with the one on file. He suspected who I was!

I ran out after him. The elevator was just going down. I rang for it like blazes, but it wouldn't come back. I chased back to the room, got the briefcase, and trooped down the stairs. When I came out into the lobby he'd disappeared. I darted out into the street and looked both ways. No sign of him. He must have gone back to his own room for a minute. Just as I was turning to go in again, out he came. He seemed surprised to see me, then covered it by saying, "If you ever change your mind, let me know."

"I have," I said abruptly. "I think I will take out a policy after all. That your car?"

His eyes lighted up. "Good!" he said. "Step in. I'll ride you down to the office myself, turn you over to our ace salesman." I knew what he was thinking, that the salesman could back him up in his identification of me.

I got in next to him. When the first light stopped him I had the gun out against his ribs, under my left arm.

"You don't need to wait for that," I said. "Turn up the other way, we're lighting out. Argue about it and I'll give it to you right here in the car."

He shuddered a little and then gave the wheel a turn. He didn't say anything.

"Don't look so hard at the next traffic cop you pass," I warned him once. When we got out of the business district, I said: "Take one hand off the wheel and haul that signature out of your wallet." I rolled it up with one hand, chewed it to a pulp, and spit it out in little soggy pieces. He was sweating a little. I was too, but not as much.

"What's it going to be?" he quavered. "I've got a wife and kids—"

"You'll get back to 'em," I reassured him, "but you'll be a little late, that's all. You're going to clear me out of town. I'll turn you back alone."

He gave a sigh of relief. "All right," he said. "I'll do whatever you say."

"Can you drive without your glasses?" He took them off and handed them to me and I put them on. I could hardly see anything at first. I took off the light-gray coat and changed that with him too. The briefcase on my lap covered my trousers from above and the car door from the side.

"If we're stopped and asked any questions," I said, "one wrong word out of you and I'll give it to you right under their noses, state police or no state police."

He just nodded, completely buffaloed.

The suburbs petered out and we hit open country. We weren't, newspapers to the contrary, stopped. A motorcycle cop passed us coming into town; he just glanced in as he went by, didn't look back. I watched him in the mirror until he was gone. Twenty miles out we left the main highway and took a side road, with fewer cars on it. About ten minutes later his machine started to buck.

"I'm running out of gas," he said.

"See if you can make that clump of trees over there," I barked. "Get off the road and into it. Then you can start back for gas on foot and I'll light out."

He swerved off the road, bumped across grassy ground and came to a stop on the other side of the trees. He cut the engine and we both got out.

"All right," I said, "now remember what I told you, keep your mouth shut. Go ahead, never mind watching me."

I stood with one elbow on the car door and one leg on the running-board. He turned and started shuffling off through the knee-deep grass. I let him get about five yards away and then I shot him three times in the head. He fell and you couldn't see him in the grass, just a sort of hole there where it was pressed down. I looked around and there wasn't anyone in sight on the road, so I went up to him and gave him another one right up against his ear to make sure.

I got back in the car and started it. He'd lied about the gas; I saw that by looking at his tank-meter. It was running low, but there was enough left to get back on the road again and make the next filling station.

When I'd filled up, an attendant took the twenty inside with him and stayed in there longer than I liked. I sounded the horn and he came running out.

"I can't make change," he said.

"Well, keep it then!" I snapped and roared away.

I met the cops that his phone call had tipped off about ten minutes later, coming *toward* me not after me. Five of them—too many to buck. I'd thrown the gun away after leaving the gas-station, and I was sitting on the briefcase. I braked and sat there looking innocently surprised.

"Driver's license?" they said. I had the insurance fellow's in the coat I was wearing.

"Left it home," I said.

They came over and frisked me, and then one of them took it out of my pocket. "No, you didn't," he said, "but it's got the wrong guy's description on it. Get out a minute."

I had to. Two of them had guns out.

"Your coat don't match your trousers," he said dryly. "And you ought to go back to the optician and see about those glasses. Both side-pieces stick out about three inches in back of your ears." Then he picked up the briefcase and said, "Isn't it uncomfortable sitting this way?" He opened it, looked in. "Yeah," he said, "Hogan," and we started back to town, one of them riding with me with my wrist linked to his. The filling-station fellow said, "Yep, that's him," and we kept going.

"I'm Walter Lynch," I said. "The real Hogan died down by the tracks. I took the money from his room, that's all—changed places with him. Maybe I can go to jail for that, but you can't pin a murder rap on me. My wife will identify me. Take me over to 35 Meadowbrook, she'll tell you who I am!"

"Better pick a live one," he said. "She jumped out a window early this morning—went crazy with grief, I guess. Don't you read the papers?"

When we got to the clump of trees, they'd found the insurance guy already. I could see some of them standing around the body. A detective came over and said, "The great Hogan at last, eh?"

"I'm Walter Lynch," I said.

The detective said, "That saves me a good deal of trouble. That insurance guy, lying out there now, put in a call to his office just before he left his hotel—something about a guy named Lynch trying to pull a fast one on the company. When he didn't show up they notified us." He got in. "I'll ride back with you," he said.

I didn't say anything any more after that. If I let them think I was Hogan, I went up for murder. If I succeeded in proving I was Lynch, I went up for murder anyway. As the detective put it on the way to town, "Make up your mind who you wanna be—either way y'gonna sit down on a couple thousand volts."

(1935)

The Showboat Murders

"Just one night," Miss Dulcy Harris was saying dramatically. "Just one night is all I ask! One night without hearing all about who you arrested and what they were wanted for and what their past record was and what they said in the line-up! Just one night away from crime!"

She put her foot down, both literally and metaphorically. A little puff of dust rose from the ground at the impact. "Is this your night off, or isn't it? Well, you can take those tickets to 'X-Men' and just tear them up, because I'm not going to sit through any more crime pictures with you and then spend the rest of the night listening to why the detectives aren't like detectives in real life. *I've* planned our evening for us, for once! You're taking me out to that showboat in the river."

Inspector Whittaker (Whitey) Ames, her affianced, unhappily swiveled his neck around inside his starched collar. "Aw, gee, honey," he pleaded, "not a showboat. Anything but that."

"Just why so?" she queried suspiciously.

"Because I'm a total loss on anything floating. It upsets me—"

She hooted incredulously. "You mean you get seasick? But it's anchored, it isn't even moving!"

"But it probably jiggles a little with the current."

Dulcy narrowed her eyes determinedly. "Everyone but me has been there by now—" She had more to say, much more. Before she had half finished he took her heroically by the arm.

"You win," he said, "let's get the tickets. But I shoulda skipped that cocoanut pie at dinner."

Dance music came blaring up, and the excursion tug that linked the showboat to the shore fitted its apron neatly into the pier. The crowd made a dive for the floating bar it boasted, and sounds of ice rattling against metal filled the night.

"Let's go round to the other side," gulped Whitey, "away from the smell of that orange peel."

"It's just your imagination," Dulcy told him. "Don't give in. Keep saying the multiplication table over to yourself. It works wonders."

The sail down-river lasted for about three-quarters of an hour, and Ames held out manfully. The last outlying lights of St. Louis on the right had petered out before a playful searchlight beam sent a shaft of pale blue up into the sky ahead of them. The excursion tug tracked it down, and presently a low-lying hulk showed up on the river bosom, garlanded with colored lights. The tug came alongside, nudged it, retreated, and finally stuck as closely as a stamp to a letter.

A ribbed incline on castors was wheeled out, the showboat lying lower in the water, and down it poured the audience. Almost before the last stragglers had cleared it, it was hauled up again, the tug gave a toot, beat the water white, and headed back where it had come from. The crowd it had brought was left there in midstream, cut off from the shore until the end of the show on something that had been a freighter and was no longer fit to go to sea.

The whole superstructure had been planed off, leaving a flat surface not more than ten feet above water level. An awning on metal stanchions roofed it, leaving the sides open to the breeze. Under this were ranged rows of folding wooden chairs packed tightly together with an aisle running down the middle of them. The bow, which was the stage, was curtained off. There were no footlights, but the same rickety platform back at the stern that lodged the sky-writing searchlight also held a couple of spots with gelatin slides. These were trained out across the heads of the audience, giving people red or green necks if they sat up too high.

A scramble for seats began and Dulcy, who was very dexterous in crowds, shot ahead and got two on the aisle before Whitey had disentangled himself from everyone else's arms and legs.

"How you getting along with yourself?" she wanted to know when he joined her.

"I'm up in the fourteens now," he muttered tensely. "I'm going to need an adding machine pretty soon."

Jazz blared out, the curtain rolled out of the way, and a long line of little ladies without much clothing pranced out onto the stage. They began to imitate people who have eaten green apples and have a pain in the stomach. It may have been that thought more than anything else, but Whitey suddenly gave up the struggle.

"'Scuse me, be right back," he said in a strangled voice, and bolted up the aisle, hand soldered to his mouth. A bartender on duty at that end mercifully caught him by the arm and guided him down a short, steep companionway to the lower level. At the bottom of it he found a short elbow of passageway, an open porthole—and peace.

The footsteps of the dancers on the planks over his head sounded like thunder down here. Just as he was about to duck in again he saw something out of the corner of his eye. From where he was, by turning his head sidewise, he could look along the whole hull. The row of lighted portholes was like a succession of orange circles, diminishing in perspective toward the bow.

A hand was sticking out of the one next in line. It stood out white against the black hull. It was slowly moving, drooping downward as it lengthened. The forearm showed up, and told him it was a woman's. As the elbow cleared the porthole the whole limb sagged bonelessly, like a white vine growing out of the side of the ship, and dangled there against the hull.

Meanwhile a second hand showed up, obviously the mate of the first. Then between them came a head of wavy red hair, hanging downward like the arms, so that the face was hidden. The slowness of the whole thing held Whitey there pop-eyed.

"What's she fixing to do, crawl halfway out to get a breath of air?" he muttered.

But when people want a breath of air they lift their heads. Her nose was practically scraping the rusty side of the hull. From the first glimpse of her fingertips she had been slowly emerging, like a human snail from its shell; now she stopped and went into reverse, began to disappear backwards. He guessed the reason at once: the porthole wasn't wide enough to let her shoulders through. Then suddenly he saw something that made his hair stand up. She was a freak! A third hand had showed up. It trailed down the nearest arm, got a grip on it at the elbow, and began to pull it in again after it. It was a heavier hand than the woman's; darker, rougher.

He got it at once, after the first momentary optical illusion had passed. It was a man's hand, pulling her back inside again. Her head disappeared, then her upper arms. Last of all went her two hands, crossed at the wrists and inanimate as severed chicken-claws. Then the porthole was empty, just an orange circle. He decided he wanted to see what was going on in there. If she'd fainted, he knew better ways of bringing her to than ramming her in and out of the porthole like a laundry bag.

Somebody else had beaten him to the door when he rounded the corner of the passageway. A very nautical-looking lady stood there, knocking peremptorily. She wore a white yachting cap atop frizzed gray hair, a jacket with brass buttons, and tennis shoes. Her only concession to femininity was her skirt. A cigarette dangled from her lower lip.

"C'mon, Toots," she was saying in a raspy voice. "You're holding up my show. I'm gonna dock you for this. Y'shoulda been on long ago! Quit stalling and open up this door!" She saluted Whitey with a terse "Upstairs! No customers allowed down here!" Then went back to rattling the doorknob again.

"Upstairs yourself. I'm homicide squad, St. Louis," grunted Whitey, crowding her aside. "Dig me up a passkey, or I'll bust down this door."

"I'm in the red enough," rasped the nautical lady. "If you want to get in that bad, go through the chorus dressing room at the end. There's a door between that won't cost as much to repair."

Whitey ran. The dressing room, luckily, was empty. The chorines were all onstage just then. One shoulder cracked the communicating door like a match box, it was that flimsy.

The girl was seated at her dressing table. She was alone in the room; the third hand and whoever it had belonged to had vanished. She was motionless, slumped before the mirror with her head on her arms. She had on even less than the girls upstairs, and that held Whitey for a minute.

"Hey!" he shouted. "Hey, you!" Then he went over to her and noticed that the top of the dressing table was all messed up with rouge.

Only it wasn't rouge. He lifted her head and for a moment had a horrible impression that it had come off in his hands. A yawning red mouth opened, lower down than the real one. Her throat had been gashed from ear to ear. At her feet was the jagged sliver of glass that had done it, with the rag that had protected the wielder's hand still folded around the upper half of it.

That let suicide out then and there. Who cares about cutting their hand if they're going to cut their own throat anyway? The glass had come from the porthole—the casing stood inward, just an empty hoop bolted to the frame. Under it the floor was iced with fragments, and with them lay the heavy curling iron that had smashed the glass.

She had probably thrown it at her murderer in the struggle and unwittingly furnished him with a weapon. Or else broken the porthole purposely in a vain attempt to top the blare of the show and attract the attention of those above. The slow-motion pantomime he had seen, Whitey realized, must have been an unsuccessful attempt to get rid of her body. And the line of escape was fairly obvious—the same side-door he had come through, locked by the murderer on his way out. But of all the quick getaways! He must have just missed the killer by the skin of his teeth. But what counted was that the murderer was still on board, and had to stay there until the tug came back—unless he jumped for it and swam the Mississippi River.

II

Whitey threw something over the dead girl, raced out the way he had come, and continued along the passage to the upper end, careening crazily from side to side in his hurry. He whizzed up the stairs there

and found himself in the wings—or what passed as such, since the
showboat used no scenery. The chorus was still dancing—less than
ten minutes had gone by since he'd left his seat. Between them and
the backdrop, instead of in front as in a regular theater, was the band.
The stage manager materialized from between two folds in the curtain and Whitey flashed his badge.

"Who's missing out there?" he asked.

"Carrots, leading lady. She's gonna get hell for it, too."

"She has already," snapped Whitey. "Then that's the whole show,
outside of her? What do they do, dance all evening?"

"The comedian and his stooge spell them. That's them, those two
standing across from us in the other wing."

"How long have they been there?"

"From the time the curtain went up. I seen 'em myself. They always
do that. It's cooler up here."

"Save it till later!" said Whitey, and dived down the stairs again,
along the passage, and up at the other end. He made it as quickly as
he would have by jumping out on the stage and running through the
audience, which might have started a panic on the overcrowded boat.
He ran up the short vertical ladder to the crow's-nest containing the
searchlight and the bored-looking sailor who manipulated it. Just at
present, however, he was letting it shoot skyward while he followed
the performers with a colored spot.

"Never mind them," ordered Whitey breathlessly, "train that other
thing down on the water, close in as you can get it, and keep it going
from side to side, so that you'll throw the light on anyone who slips
overboard and starts swimming ashore—"

"I take orders from—" the sailor tried to say.

"From me from now on," barked Whitey, "or else I'll knock you offa
here and do it myself!" He waited just long enough to see the big
metal hood give a half-revolution and splash a big patch of water to
daylight, then slowly wheel around to the other side. Every ripple on
the surface stood out in the fierce glare.

"Will it go all the way around?" Whitey asked.

"Just halfway," sweated the sailor, "and then back again."

"That'll do it," said Whitey. "Train one of those colored ones backwards, into the arc the big one doesn't cover, and leave it that

way—that'll give us the whole circle. And keep the other one on the go. The minute you spot anything that doesn't belong out there—I don't care what it is—lemme know, if you value your tattooed hide."

"I ain't got so much as a—" the sailor tried to contradict, but Whitey was already on his way down again. When he hit the below-deck passageway again, the lady captain was still parked outside the locked door. She had quit trying the knob and was deftly rolling herself a cigarette instead. She promptly dropped it at the sight of him.

"Where'd you come from?" she gawked. "I've been waiting all this time for you to get in the side way."

"I've been in and out again," he told her. "Follow me. You don't look like the kind that throws faints, and I want to talk to you." They went through the still empty chorus dressing room and beyond. The lady captain glimpsed the prone figure under the mirror and immediately went into an employer's rage.

"You holder-outer! You letterdowner!" she bellowed. "What d'ye mean by gumming up my opening number? Who d'ye think you are, Ethel Merman?"

"Close what's left of that door and shut up," said Whitey sourly. "She's dead."

The lady captain was not, to put it mildly, the nervous type. She went over, tossed aside the towel, and spaded one hand under the girl's flabby arm. "Yep," she snapped, "cold as yesterday's headline." She came away stroking her chin like a man. "Have to get that gal from Tony's to take her place. Get her five bucks cheaper, too," she commented.

"Have a murder like this every night?" Whitey said bitingly. "No? Then why not show a little surprise?"

"Boo! I'm surprised!" she came right back at him. "What d'ye want me to do, turn handsprings? All I know is, this throws a hitch into my show. Look at that door! And look at that porthole! They put them in for nothing, you know; don't cost a cent!"

"I've come across some tough cases in my time," he let her know. "I'd offer you a cigar, only I haven't got the kind that blows up in your face. Now let's get going. Who was she?"

"Carrots Kirby, twenty-four, fifty a week for showing her vaccination mark."

"Run around with anybody?"

"Anybody," she agreed.

"Big help, aren't you?" he glared. "Any way of getting word ashore that we have a murder case aboard?"

"Nope," she said calmly. "Have to wait until the tug comes back at twelve."

"What's the idea? Why doesn't it stand by?"

"That would cost do-re-mi," she stated. "I'd have to hire it for the whole evening. This way I just charter it for the two trips, coming and going."

"You mean you haven't any small boats on this thing? You're crowded to the rails! What would you do if anything happened?"

"This isn't a sea-going boat. We're all lighted up from head to stern, if it's a collision you're thinking about. We've got fire-extinguishers, if that's what y'mean. And my bartender doubles as a bouncer, in case of a riot."

"With water all around, where does he bounce them to?" Whitey demanded.

"He don't bounce 'em *to* anywhere," she stated elegantly. "He just bounces 'em *on* the button, and they stay quiet."

"Just a sissy enterprise from start to finish. How long were you in front of that door?"

"Just got there ahead of you."

"How do I know that?" Whitey challenged.

"You don't," she agreed, "but you can check up on it with the bartender. I was watching the show from in back when I saw Carrots missed her cue. As a matter of fact, I saw you stumble by. Only came down after you did, while you were at the porthole."

Your luck is, Whitey thought grimly, that it was a man's hand I saw hauling her in. He said, "If you were standing in back watching, then who was missing from the show—outside of her?"

"Nobody," she snapped. "I only have the chorus, the two comics, her and the stage manager working for me. The stage manager was on that side, signaling me from the curtain to go page her. The two comics were on the other side, kibitzing with the girls like they always do. I could see both of 'em. Every girl was in place, not one missing."

"Who else y'got on your payroll?"

"Just Shorty behind the light up there, Butch the bartender, and an electrician down in the power room in case anything goes wrong with the lights. We generate our own power, y'know."

"How about the audience? Anyone leave their seats before I did?"

"Not a blessed soul. They never start wandering back for refills until the show's past the halfway mark, anyway."

"Well, did anyone *go* to their seats after everyone else was seated, then?" Whitey demanded.

"Nope, they all sat down at once. You saw the scramble for seats that went on yourself."

"Well, if I'm going to take your word for it," he remarked, "I'll end up by believing a swordfish took a leap in the window and did it to her. All I know is she's been turned into a tomato surprise and whoever did it is still on board."

There was a tap at the shattered door and the bartender's homely face peered through the split panel. "Shorty just picked up something with the big light—" he began. Whitey nearly flattened him going by, and was up on the platform in no time flat.

"It went down," the sailor apologized. "Only your orders was, anything that didn't belong out there, to tip you off—"

"What the hell was it?"

"Something silver, looked like a big oil or gasoline can. Musta been dropped over the side. It was so close to us I couldn't get the light square down on it, but I caught the reflection. It made me nervous," he admitted. "If anything like that spreads around us, all somebody's gotta do is toss a butt overboard, and—"

"How'd it go down, straight?"

"No, sort of sideways and slow."

"Then it was empty."

Shorty sighed. "Gee, that's good."

"Bad, you mean! Whatever was in it is still with us, probably spread around nice and lovely . . . How do I get to this power room, where this electrician is?"

"It's under the stairs that lead up to the stage," explained the sailor. "You've gotta look close or you'll miss seeing the door."

Down went Whitey again. He had the rather chilling suspicion that the murderer, failing to get rid of the body through the porthole, intended to try a little wholesale arson to cover up the traces of the crime.

And yet the murderer himself was on board, would be trapped with the rest if he did such a thing. What the murderer didn't know, since the show was still going full blast and no alarm had been raised as yet, was that the crime had already been unearthed, and that there was a detective on board. He intended taking his time, probably, and then swimming for it—with a good head-start. Whitey detoured into the audience for a moment to single out Dulcy and hustle her to the rear.

"What's the idea, making me give up a perfectly good seat?" she said.

"I want you back here where you won't get trampled on in case anything happens," Whitey said. "Now don't get nervous, but just stand here where I can find you in a hurry—"

"Well, aren't you the cheerful little ray of sunshine!"

"Tell me about the part of the show that I missed. Did you notice anyone who came on later than the others?"

"No," she said, then added, "Anyone at all?"

"Anyone at all. I don't care who!"

"None of the performers did, but the bandmaster keeps wandering off and on all the time, I've noticed. I mean he just introduces each new turn and then strolls off again and lets the other five do the playing—"

"I could kiss you!" Whitey said fervently. "None of the others mentioned that. I suppose they thought I meant only the performers. I muffed it myself when I was in the wings before, forgot about him."

"What do you mean? Who's 'he'? What's the band leader done?" Dulcy wanted to know.

"Played a sour note. Remember what I told you—don't move!"

III

The music was playing no longer. The two comedians had just come on, but the five musicians were sitting in full view. Only their leader was missing. When Whitey got down to the passageway below it was choked with chorus girls, all trying to get into their dressing room at once and do a quick change. They not only slowed him down, they resented his presence in their half-clad midst and began to squeal and claw at him.

"Get out of here! Go back where you belong!" Whitey emerged, protecting his bent head with both arms, and a dance-shoe came flying after him and glanced harmlessly off his skull. They banged their door after them resentfully and the corridor was suddenly quiet.

Just under the stairs was the power room doorway. A heavy smell of oil and machinery seeped out as he got the door open. The place was a labyrinth of greasy generators and what not, shot through with weird, futuristic shadows. It was empty—and it looked very much as if it needed someone in charge of it at the moment.

Quantities of newspapers were scattered about wholesale, all transparent with oil, soaked with it. Nobody read that many newspapers and drenched them that way. The door clapped back on its hinges behind him and the smell became almost overpowering. The two overworked bulbs overhead couldn't get into the corners and angles and light them up.

He advanced warily and an overturned copper oiler on the floor clanged loudly under his foot. A moment later he stumbled over one of the newspapers and a man's upturned shoe was revealed. Whitey crouched down and found a man in the dungarees of an engineer lying flat on his back in a narrow lane of blackness between two pieces of machinery, only his feet protruding into the light. A hefty wrench lying at his heels told most of the story.

The engineer was out cold, but still breathing. Whitey crouched down above him to haul him out into the open, careless of which way he turned his back. It was then that the wrench started to move slowly along the floor like something possessed. The corner of his eye saw it—but not quickly enough. The wrench swung up into the air just as he turned his head, then came down again. Whitey just had time to see the arm wielding it, the face behind it—then both were wiped out in a flash of white fire that seemed to come from his own head.

The fire was still there when he came to a minute or so later, but it wasn't white and it wasn't at his head any more. It was down near his legs. The way it was stinging and biting him would have brought the dead to life. And the blow hadn't been as accurate as intended, or it would have finished him; too much emotion and not enough aim had been put into it. The biting and stinging made him jackknife his legs up out of the way before he had even opened his eyes.

When he did so, bright yellow flame was fluttering from the scattered newspapers all over the room, in three or four places at once. One of the burning papers had been lying across his own legs. He was partly across the body of the engineer, who was still motionless. His splitting head was still trying to drag him back into unconsciousness again, but pain defeated it. He shoved backward with his buckled legs, and felt his back slip up the oily wall behind him until he was totteringly erect.

He still saw everything double, but the oil-soaked overalls of the man at his feet were already smoking, and the air was full of dancing sparks from the papers. Grease-rags began to smoulder ominously here and there and make it tough to breathe. The room got hot. One of the two bulbs overhead suddenly popped into nothingness. The fire was past the stamping-out stage now.

Whitey grabbed the engineer by one ankle and dragged him out of the little lane that had hidden him. The slippery floor made it easier. Half of the burning papers had taken wings now and were swirling about in the torturing air like huge fire-birds. One of Whitey's own lisle socks began to peel back in a red thread, and he rubbed it out against his other leg like a mosquito bite. He struggled through the inferno toward the door, the body of the man he was dragging after him snuffing out buttercups of flame along the floor as it passed over them. A belt on the machinery suddenly burned in two and sent up a shower of sparks like a rocket.

He had just enough strength left, in the wilting heat-waves swirling about him, to claw at the door like some idiot thing wanting out and unable to show it in any other way. The door wouldn't move—was either warped by the heat or else locked. Whitey could feel himself going, knew he'd never get up again, would be cremated in here. But his fall was his salvation. As his body slumped against the door it gave outward under his weight—and quite easily. In his torment he'd forgotten it opened that way.

Air that was air came rushing past him. He fell on his hands and knees, and behind him the room gave a roar and turned itself into a furnace as it found the draught it had been waiting for. He tugged, strained, and the body of the engineer came slipping over the threshold after him, bringing patches of fire with it like a human torch. The door, released, clapped back again.

He beat out the fire on the man he had saved with his bare hands, listened for heart-action. Too late. There wasn't any; he was dead. Whitey had been through all that for nothing. Chalk up two murders now instead of one. And there were the living to be thought of, dozens of them, up above. He knew better than to yell "Fire!"

He staggered to his feet, reeled down the passageway he had traversed so often tonight, looked in at the chorus girls' dressing room. It was empty, they were onstage once more. The clink of a glass attracted him and he looked beyond, into the room where Carrots Kirby's body was. The lady commodore sat there big as life, a bottle of gin in one hand, a glass in the other.

"Heresh lookin' atcha, sport," she announced blithely. "I'm the only mourner."

She had probably never been torn away from a bottle so suddenly in her life before. It actually bounced and cracked in two.

"Never mind lookin' at me!" he rasped. "There's a fire—keep still about it and get the extinguishers, quick!" One look at his face and she was sober. She came tottering out after him.

"Oh, Lord, and I don't even carry insurance!" she mourned.

"Rockets!" he yelled back. "Send up rockets if you've got any—attract someone on shore or some other boat!"

The clatter of a rumba held the audience spellbound as his head emerged from the companionway. Dulcy was standing there where he'd left her, looking very sulky. He flashed past and on up to the searchlight-nest. The sailor had a grievance.

"Now you come," he growled. "First you tell me to watch the water, then you don't show up! I picked up a guy out there five minutes ago—I'm following him with the light, but he's halfway across the river already."

"Yeah? Well, I was busy having my nails manicured," Whitey said. He peered out into the searchlight beam, his eyes still smarting from the fire.

"See him?" encouraged the sailor. "Mean to say you can't see him?"

A black dot bobbed up and down, the head of a swimmer desperately trying to make land. He was going diagonally with the current.

"The Missouri side," said Whitey. "He'll have all St. Louis to hide in once he steps out!" He turned and hopped down again to the deck, twisting out of his coat.

The lady captain was busy fanning herself weakly with one hand, a new gin-bottle in the other.

"The fire's under control," she panted. "A minute more and it would have sent the lighting system out of commish! After this, I stick to running a tea shop."

The bartender came up from below, face smudged, dragging an empty extinguisher after him. "Wotta evening!" he grunted. Whitey was kicking off his shoes. Dulcy appeared beside him.

"Wait a minute, you can't walk out on me like this—" she began. He clambered up on the low rail. "You just finish seeing your show, honey. I gotta little job to do out there," Whitey pleaded.

He went overboard in a long, not too graceful curve and sent up a thin mushroom of water. Her voice split the air behind him.

"Oh no, you're not leaving me behind—how do I know what's going to happen to me?" There was a second splash and she bobbed up right beside him.

"Get back there, you little fool!" he spluttered. "What are you trying to do, drown yourself?"

IV

She kept abreast of him without any effort. "I can swim circles around you," she said.

There was a pull to the current that set their course for them automatically, just as it had the fugitive's. "All right?" Whitey kept asking. "Sure you're all right? I gotta get that guy out there."

"If you're going to get him, get him!" Dulcy said crossly at last. "I can last, but I can't make speed."

He went into the crawl and outdistanced her. His banged head throbbed; he'd been seasick, hit with a wrench, singed and scorched—but there was no place else to go but down if he quit.

By the time it felt as if he should have been all the way into Kansas, he was still only a quarter of the way to shore. But the quarry, he reasoned, must be having his troubles too. A fellow that stayed up all night shaking to jazz music wasn't cut out for a cross-river swim. They were sending up rockets behind Whitey, lighting the sky green. That ought to attract a police launch.

Weariness began to creep in, a shortening of stroke, a slowing-up. He went into a side stroke, to give slightly different muscles play. His legs began to drag after him like so much dead weight. He threatened to fold up and go down any minute, could almost feel something pulling at him from below. He had to quit altogether finally, and not a moment too soon, roll over on his back and float open-mouthed, like a stranded fish. He paddled backhand with one hand to keep from being carried too far out of his course.

A faint threshing, a slapping noise, came from somewhere nearby. The sound of someone agonizedly trying to stay up. At first he thought it was Dulcy, but the cry, when it came, was a man's. Whitey trod water, trying to locate the direction.

The cry came again, far over to the right but a little *behind* him, not in front. He'd almost passed the murderer in the head-down crawl, or else the other had lost all sense of direction and was heading back toward the boat again! By the time Whitey got to the man there he wasn't swimming any longer but was already in the earlier stages of drowning. The face that turned up despairingly to the sky was the same one that had been limned in white fire when the wrench glanced off Whitey's head.

Whitey came up behind him and caught him by the suspenders. Instantly he tried to turn and get a death-grip on his rescuer, coughing and retching with the water he was swallowing. Before Whitey could jerk away, one madly groping hand had caught inextricably in his shirt and they both went under together.

Whitey kicked like a horse, brought them up again. He pounded his fist like a sledge-hammer into the middle of the band-leader's contorted face. The impact was soggy but shattering. The clutching hand relaxed, the murderer floated unconscious on the water, harmless as a lily.

But the little strength Whitey had had left was gone now. He needed rescuing almost as badly as the bandmaster had a moment ago. Like the proverbial bulldog that won't let go, he kept his hold on the other's suspenders, keeping the two of them afloat somehow with one wearied, slowly circling arm that felt as though it were going to drop off his shoulder at every stroke.

Thin cries of encouragement were coming across the water; yellow pinpoints marked the portholes of the showboat. Two other boats were standing by it now, attracted by the rockets, and from one of them a second searchlight beam came into play and swept the water with sketchy strokes. The river was talcum-white where it hit.

For Whitey to reach shore was out of the question, even if he let go of the bandmaster and struck out alone. To get back to where the rescue ships were congregating was equally impossible. In about three strokes more he was going to go down.

Nearer than either shore or rescue ships, though, a peculiar round white object was showing in the glare of the interlocked beams. It looked like a large poker chip floating on the water. He moiled slowly toward it, with strokes that no longer bore any resemblance to the act of swimming. It tilted from side to side, but whatever it was it didn't go down. The three strokes were spent, but now the nearness of the objective, the feasibility of getting to it, lent him three more, and then another three—on borrowed time.

Dulcy's head showed up in back of the white thing, paddling it toward him. Water flushed the top of it but it stayed stubbornly afloat. As the space narrowed, she suddenly swung in between them, caught at his flailing wrist, and hooked it onto the circular rim of the white thing. He couldn't have made the gesture himself, the last inch would have defeated him. She quickly shifted over to the other side as the added weight made the object veer over toward him.

It was the bass drum from the showboat orchestra. Somebody had helpfully thrown it in after her.

"Let go of him," she panted, makeup running down her face. "He's gone anyway, and he's weighing you down." Whitey couldn't answer, but he held on. The reason may have been he could no longer extricate his numbed hand from the other's suspenders. The seeking searchlight-beams swept back and forth across them. A police cutter was rapidly drawing near, its green light dipping and rising in its hurry.

"He died on me in the water," apologized Whitey to his chief, sitting beside the hospital cot, "but at least I got him. A girl in the show threw him down and he went haywire, cut her throat, slugged an electrician to death, and then committed arson to cover up what—"

"Yeah, yeah," interrupted the chief. "Never mind about that now, he's dead and that closes the case. You stay under that blanket and don't be afraid of that whisky the boys sent you." He got up to go. "I'll probably have a little news for you after you've turned in your report. Somebody else waiting out here to see you."

Dulcy came in and shot the muffled figure in the bed a rather forbidding look.

"You all right?" he asked timidly. "I—I'm sorry if your evening was spoiled—"

"I give up," Dulcy said wearily. "I thought taking you out to that thing would get you away from crime for one evening. What's the use? Separating you from crime is like trying to part a pair of Siamese twins. It follows you around!"

(1935)

Hot Water

Hot water is two things. In slang it means getting into trouble, in geography it means a gambling joint just across the California state line in Mexico. Agua Caliente means hot water in Spanish. It means both kinds to yours truly, after what happened that time. I never want to hear the name again.

Ten o'clock Friday night, and all is quiet in Fay North's forty rooms and swimming pool, out in Beverly Hills. Fay has just finished a picture that afternoon and has said something about going to bed early and sleeping until next Tuesday. I have been all around, upstairs and down, seeing that the doors and windows are all locked and that the electric burglar-alarm is in working order, and I am in my own room just off the main entrance, peeling to pajamas and ready to pound the ear, when there is a knock at my door. It is the butler.

"Miss North has changed her mind," he announces. "She is spending the week-end at Agua Caliente. Please be ready in ten minutes."

I am not asked to go, you notice, I am told I *am* going. That is part of my job. Miss North parts with a generous helping of her salary each week, in my direction, and it is up to me to stick close and see that no bodily harm comes to her. It really isn't an unpleasant job for this reason: on the screen Miss North has become famous for playing tough, rowdy characters, but in real life she isn't like that at all. She doesn't drink, doesn't smoke, and never goes to parties or even night clubs; so all I really have to do is ride back and forth to work with her and shoo salesmen and newspaper writers away from the door.

But she has one great weakness, she is crazy for gambling. She never wins, but that doesn't seem to stop her. I feel sorry for her, but it is her money and none of my business what she does with it.

Anyway, she has stayed away from Agua for some time now, after dropping so much there the last time, so she is entitled to blow off steam, I guess, after working so hard. I shake my head about all the good sleep I'm going to miss, but I sling on my shoulder holster, pack a couple of clean shirts, and go out and wait for her in the car without saying a word. A plane would get us there in a couple of hours, but that is another thing about Fay, she won't get in one, so it means we have to drive all night to be there when the border opens at nine.

Well, she comes out of the house in about five or ten minutes and it seems just the three of us are going, her, me and the driver. For once she is giving Timothy the slip. He is her manager and a very good one, too, but he raised Cain about her losses the last time he was down there with her, and I guess she doesn't want him around to rub it in. He doesn't like the place anyway, doesn't think it's safe for her to go down there carrying so much money. She has brought several big bags with her, enough to stay for a month, but I guess that is because she is a woman and you have to dress up there. She gets in back and away we go.

"Well, Shad," she says, "I guess you could kill me for this."

"No, ma'm," I say, "you haven't had a day off in quite some stretch."

Shad isn't my name, but she calls it to me because when I was new on the job she got the habit of speaking about me as her Shadow.

"Timothy doesn't need to find out," she says. "We'll be back by Monday morning, and if he calls up tomorrow I told the butler to say I have a bad headache and can't come to the phone."

It doesn't sound to me like that is very wise; Timothy might come over twice as quick if he thinks anything is the matter with her, on account of she is such an important investment, but she doesn't ask for my opinion so I keep it to myself.

Then she says: "This time I can't lose! I'll show him, when I come back, whether I'm jinxed or not, like he always says. I'll make up all my losses, because I know now just what to do. I consulted an astrologer in my dressing room during lunch today, and she gave me a grand tip. I'm dying to see if it'll work or not."

First off I figure she means just another new system, every time we go down there she has a new system, none of which ever works, but later I'm to find out it isn't that at all. The funny part of it is that with me it's just the other way around. I don't give a rap about betting or games of chance, in fact I don't believe in it at all, but I never yet chucked down four bits or a dollar on any kind of a table at all without it collected everyone else's dough like flypaper and swept the board clean. So then I always picked the nearest sucker with a long face and made him a present of the whole wad—minus the original buck of course—and he went right back and lost it. The wages I get from Miss North are enough for me; I'm no hog.

Well, we drive all night, pass through Dago about seven in the morning, and roll up to the bridge across the Mexican border just as they're getting ready to open it for the day. Miss North only has to show her face and we clear it, only as usual one of the guardsmen can't resist hollering after us, "Drop around, don't be bashful!" which is the catch-word from one of her pictures. She's so used to hearing it she just smiles.

After that comes a sandy stretch with a lot of cactus, and then flowers, fountains, and a lot of chicken-wire architecture show up, and that's Agua. Miss North engages her usual layout and signs the book "Peggy Peabody" or something, to fool any reporters that may be hanging around. Everybody always stays up all night down there, but I suppose she has to have some place to powder her nose in and change clothes between losses. Anyway, I see to it that I have an adjoining room with a communicating door between. Then we separate to scrape off some of the desert, and in a little while she knocks on the side door.

"You're armed," she says, "so maybe you better take care of this for me until tonight," and she hands me a little two-by-four black toilet case with her initials on it in gold. "I'm so absent-minded I'm liable to mislay it just when I need it—"

Well, I'm just nosey enough to snap the latch and look in it—it isn't even locked, mind you!

"It's the stake for tonight," she smiles sweetly. "Fifteen thousand. I didn't bring much along this time because I'm so sure of doubling or tripling my ante."

"But, Miss North," I groan weakly, "carrying it around like this—"

"Yes, don't you think that's clever of me?" she agrees. "I just dumped out all the gold toilet articles. No one would think of looking in there." Then she says, "See you later," closes the door, and leaves me to do the worrying about it.

Well, the first thing I decide is, it don't stay in that beauty-kit, which hasn't even got a key to it. No matter where it goes, it gets out of there. So I empty it out—it's all ticketed just the way the bank gave it to her—stack it neatly inside a big, roomy envelope, seal it, write her name on the outside, and take it down to the manager's office. He's an American, of course, and perfectly reliable.

"Put this in your safe," I say, "and keep it there until Miss North or me calls for it when the session opens tonight."

"If her luck," he grins, "is like what it usually is, she might just as well not bother taking it out, because it will only come right straight back in again." Then he takes out a fat bundle of vouchers and tells me not to bother Miss North's head about it, but don't I think maybe she'd like to clear them up and start with a clean slate before she starts plunging again the next few nights?

"But Timothy wrote off everything she owed you people, right after she was down here the last time, and that's over two months ago," I object. "I heard him hollering, that's how I happen to know. Lemme see the dates on some of those."

Well, some are only from the weekend before, and all of them are later than the last time she was there.

"There's somebody been down here impersonating her," I warn him, "and getting credit from you. You better warn your bankers and notify the police."

His face drops and he tells me, "I never know when she is here and when she isn't. She always stops off under an alias anyway. Well, I can't afford to attract attention to a thing like this, it would stop the picture people from coming here, so we'll just have to forget about these, and I'll tip off my staff not to let it happen in future."

And he tears the whole lot of them up and dribbles them into the wastebasket. Most of them were only for medium-sized amounts anyway (which is another reason I know they're not Fay's), but it just goes to show there are some regular guys, even in his business.

Well, she comes downstairs after awhile, but I don't tell her about it, because she's down here to relax, in the first place; and in the second, it's Timothy's look-out, not hers, and everybody in her business has this impersonating stunt pulled on them at one time or another. It's nothing new.

She's wearing smoked glasses to keep from being recognized; but then, almost everybody else around is, too, so it don't mean much.

Well, we spend a quiet afternoon, me tagging after her while she strolls and buys picture postcards; and then at five she goes back to her room to get ready for the fireworks, telling me I can eat downstairs, but she's going to eat alone, up in her room.

Now, here's where the first mistake comes in. I have a right to stick with her, even if I have to eat outside her room door, but I figure everything's under control, that she's safer here than she would be in her own home, that I'm right down at the foot of the stairs if she needs me, and that she'll be down again as soon as she's through dressing.

So I sit me down in the big patio dining-room, and I tear a sirloin at four bucks a throw (not Mex, either). After awhile the dancing quits and the stars, I mean the ones in the sky, show and the big gambling rooms light up, one after the other, and things get right down to business. And still no sign of her. I know I haven't missed her, because I'm right on a line with the stairs and she'd have to pass me on her way in. So I dunk my cigarette and I go up to see what's keeping her.

Well, it seems I pick just the right time for it. A minute later and I wouldn't have seen what I did; a minute sooner and I wouldn't have either.

Just as I get to the top of the stairs and turn down the corridor leading to her room and mine, I catch a strange dame in the act of easing out of *my* door. She didn't get in by mistake either, one look at the way she's tiptoeing out tells me that. "Oho," I say to myself, "a hotel-rat—or rather a casino-rat, eh?"

Well, I want to see what she's up to and find out who she's working with, if possible, so instead of giving myself away I quickly step back onto the stair-landing and lean over the railing as though I am watching what was going on below. Her head was turned the other way, so I know she hasn't spotted me. She thinks the coast is clear. She closes the door carefully after her and comes hurrying along toward where I am. I turn around slowly and size her up. She is a tough-looking little customer, with jet-black hair and layers of paint all over her map that you could scrape off with a spoon. She is dressed like a dance hall girl, too—or like what people that never saw one think they are like—only personally I never met one that was such a dead giveaway. In fact, I wonder how she ever got into such a ritzy place with such a get-up. She's got a red shirtwaist on, and a yellow and black checked skirt, like Kiki, that hurts your eyes, only it misses her knees by a mile. But what interests me mostly is that in one hand she is hanging onto that toilet case that Fay turned over to me when we got in. I know it by the gold initials on it. She has lifted it from my room, without bothering to find out if it still has the money in it or not; maybe on account of Fay being right next door, she didn't have time. It is easy to see, though, that she must have overheard Fay tell me what was in it earlier in the day; that's how she knew what to go for. Probably eavesdropped outside our doors.

Well, she brushes by me close enough for me to touch her. She doesn't look at me at all, and I don't raise a finger to stop her.

It may sound funny, my not jumping on her when she is right at my fingertips like that; but the reason is I happen to know there is no money in that toilet case. And as I said before, I would like to see if she has a shill working with her, and where she is heading for with what she thinks she has. Besides, a slippery staircase is no place to tangle with the kind of a customer she looks to be like; the casino bouncers are down below, and she is going down there anyway.

So I let her get two steps ahead of me, and then I turn and start down myself, as if I just remembered something that required my presence below. And I have one hand loose, ready to collar her if she tries to break and run for it.

But she doesn't; instead, she slows up and takes her time, not hurrying any more, like when she first came out of the room. I can see that she is going to try to bluff it out.

She swaggers along real tough, and everyone is turning around to look at her. Then, when she gets down to the bottom, she happens to pass a guy with a cigarette stuck in his mouth—and doesn't she reach out and calmly take it away and start puffing it herself, without even a thank-you!

She passes by the main entrance without a look, and heads straight for the big gambling room, cool as a cucumber.

"Well," I say to myself, "if this don't beat everything for sheer, unadulterated nerve!" Instead of ducking, she is going to hang around the premises awhile and try her luck with money that she just lifted, which is so hot that smoke ought to be coming out of that case she is carrying this very minute—if it happened to have anything in it! All I ask is just one look at her face when she opens it and finds out what her haul is worth, maybe that will take some of the swagger out of her.

In I go after her, and I buttonhole the nearest bouncer, whom I know by sight.

"Send out for the cops," I say. "I'm going to present you with a pinch in just about thirty seconds. Camille, over there, squeezing her way in to the middle roulette table—keep your eye on her." And I tell him what she's done.

He sends out for the *policia* and he also sends for the manager, and then him and me and the other bouncer close in on her and get ready to pounce when I give the signal. But first I want to get a load of her disappointment.

Well, they're as thick as bees around that table—two or three deep—but that hasn't stopped her; she's used both elbows, both hips and her chin, and blasted her way through to the baize. We can't get in that far; all we can see is her back.

"Wait a minute," I motion them, "she'll be right out again—into our arms. She hasn't anything to play with."

You can hear the banker say, "Place your bets," and "Bank is closed." Then the clicking of the little ball as the wheel goes spinning around.

Not another sound for a minute. Then a big *"Ooh!"* goes up from everyone at once.

"Killing," says the bouncer, knowingly.

"Wonder what's delaying her?" I say. "She ought to have found out by now. Maybe she's picking people's pockets—"

The same thing happened a second time; a big long *"Ooh!"* sounds like a foghorn.

The manager shows up, and I tell him the story out of the corner of my mouth. "—caught her in the act, and followed her down here. But all she got was the empty kit," I snicker.

"That's what *you* think," he squelches. "I got my doubts! A voice on the wire, claiming to be Fay North, asked me to turn back that envelope, less than ten minutes ago. I took it up to the room myself—"

"Did you see her take it from you?" I ask excitedly.

"No, that's why I think something's punk. An arm reached out from the room, but she stayed behind the door. Claimed she was dressing."

"Good Gawd!" I moan. "And you turned over fifteen grand like that without—"

"You told me North or you would claim it. The call came from 210, that's her room, I checked it with the switchboard operator."

"That's *my* room!" I tell him. "North's is 211, she wouldn't be in my room; she's too much of a lady! This phony was in there; I saw her coming out. C'mon! We've wasted enough time. The hell with the payoff."

The Mex police had come in by now, two of them, both higher-ups, this being the casino. The manager and the bouncers shoo everyone aside, the crowd falls back, and we get a good look at what has been going on. The phony is left standing there all alone. But she is so taken up she never even notices. And she has the fifteen thou all right. Or at least she had it to start with; now she must have two or three times that. In fact, everything in sight is piled up in front of her, nearly chin-high. Her system, it seems, has been to blow the bills she bets with her breath, like handfuls of leaves, letting them land wherever they want to on the number mat. The banker is green in the face.

The manager taps her on the shoulder. "You're under arrest."

The Mex line up one on each side of her. She's hard-boiled all right, like I knew she would be.

"Run along and fly a kite for yourself. Can't you see I'm busy?"

I stoop down and pick up the toilet-kit, which she has kicked under the table. I shake it in her face.

"This belongs to Fay North. I saw you coming out of my room with it. The manager here turned over fifteen thou to somebody's bare arm in that room. Now, are you going to come clean or are you going to see the inside of a Mexican jail?"

Well, she keeps looking me in the eye and looking me in the eye like she wanted to say something, and then she looks at all the winnings piled up on the table like she was afraid of something, and she just shuts up like a clam. For a minute I almost have a crazy idea that maybe it is Fay herself, under a heavy character make-up, only just then I turn my head and I see the real Fay come sweeping in the doorway like a queen, heading for one of the smaller side-tables.

"Hold on," I say, "she'll tell me in a jiffy. If it was just the empty kit this one lifted, you can turn her loose for my part, but if she phoned down for that money she goes to jail, dame or no dame."

I run over and I stop Fay and say to her, "Miss North, did you call down awhile ago for that money the manager was holding for you?"

"I don't know what you're talking about," she says, and gives me an unpleasant look through her smoked glasses. "Don't put me in a bad mood now. Can't you see I'm on my way to the table? Please stay away from me, I gotta have quiet to concentrate—"

I go back to them and I say, "Okay, off she goes!"

"Why, you—!" she blazes at me, but she doesn't get any further. The two Mex lieutenants drag her out backwards by the shoulders, kicking like a steer, and there's quite a commotion for a minute, then the place settles down again and that's that. Since neither me nor the manager can talk spicko, one of the bouncers goes along with them to prefer the charges and see she's booked right.

Well, I'm afraid to go too near Fay, on account of she seems to be in a cranky humor and asked me not to distract her; so I sit down just inside the door where I can watch her and be the perfect bodyguard, without getting in her hair. She sure looks spiffy in her gold dress, but she keeps the smoked panes on even while she's playing. She has the usual luck, and runs out of the fifteen thou, which the house turned back to her, in no time flat. Then she starts unloading I.O.U.'s, and they come over to me to make sure there won't be any mistake like there was before, but I tell them to go ahead and honor them, it's the real McCoy this time.

About the time she's another four or five in the red, a houseboy comes in with a message for her and she quits and goes out after him. I get up to follow her, and she gives me a dirty look over her shoulder, so I change my mind and sit down again, saying to myself, "Gee, I never saw her as snappish as this before!"

But my equilibrium has hardly touched the chair once more, when there comes a whale of a scream from just outside the casino entrance. Then another, which chokes off in the middle like a hand was clapped over the screamer's mouth. Then there's a shot, and the sound of a big eight-cylinder job roaring away from in front of the place with its throttle wide open.

By that time the chair is rooms behind me and I'm tearing out the entrance with my own loudspeaker in my hand. There's nothing to shoot at but a little sinking red tail-light which is already clear of the casino grounds and just as I fire at it, it goes out, not because I hit it but because it's too far away to see any more. The porter is sitting on the front steps holding onto his shoulder for dear life, and one of her gold slippers which fell off when she was thrown in is lying there in the roadway.

There is also a scrap of paper a considerable distance away which they must have tossed behind them. I snatch it up as I dash for the garage where Fay's own car is bedded.

The driver is knee-deep in a crap-game, but luckily it is going on right inside the tonneau itself, so I just leap in at the wheel and bring the whole works out with me in reverse. He hangs on, but his three partners fall out, also one of the garage doors comes off its hinges, and almost all the paint gets shaved off that side the car.

Once out it would take too much time to turn it all the way around so I just make a dive through the casino flower-beds and the wheels send up a spray of rose-petals and whatnot. The casino steps are seething with people and I yell back, "Notify the border! They may try to double back and get across with her—" but I don't know whether they hear me or not.

As for notifying the Mex police, what could they do, chase the kidnap-car on donkeys?

"Snatched!" I tell the driver. "Right out of the doorway in front of everybody! I'll never be able to look anyone in the eye again if we don't head them off before this gets out. Reach over and grab the wheel."

He's been *tequila-ing*, but at least he knows what he's doing. He leans across my shoulders, I duck out of the way, and he hauls his freight over into the front seat. I give it the lights, and night turns into day ahead of us.

"Got gas?"

"Thank Gawd!" he says. "I filled her up when we checked in, to get it off my mind."

We finally get out of the grounds, and he tries to take the road to Tiajuana and the border.

"Left!" I tell him. "Left! They went the other way, I saw them turn."

"But there's not even a road that way—nothing, just desert—not a gas station from here to Mexicali! We'll get stalled as sure as—"

"Never mind the geography lesson," I tell him. "Don't forget, they're not running on maple syrup either."

The asphalt doesn't go an inch beyond the resort limits in that direction and as he says, there isn't even what you could call a road, just a few burro-cart tracks in the soft powdery dust. But one good thing about it: the tire-treads of their heavy machine are as easy to pick up as if they'd driven over snow.

As if I had to be told this late what the whole idea is, I take time off to look at the piece of paper I picked up outside the casino. "Fifty thousand," it says in pencil, "gets her back. Notify Timothy in L.A. that the joke is on him, he'll know what we mean. We'll cure her of gambling, also of breathing, if he don't come across." It is all printed out; evidently it was prepared before they drove up to the casino.

"Americans," I remark to the driver. "You can tell by the way it's worded. It's our fault if we lose 'em, they'll stand out like a sore thumb if they stay on this side of the line."

"Yeah," he agrees, "like a sore thumb with wings; they're making pretty good headway so far!"

That crack in the note about curing her of gambling makes the whole thing look twice as bad to me, because reading between the lines I get this out of it: Timothy must have engineered the snatch as a practical joke to begin with, to throw a scare into her and break her of the habit of running down to Agua and throwing away her money. But now his hired kidnapers have double-crossed him and turned it into the real thing, seeing a chance to get ten times the stage-money he paid them. And if there is anything worse than a snatch, it is a snatch with a double-cross in it. He knows who they are, and they know he knows; it's sink or swim with them and they won't stop at anything. Poor Fay is liable to come back to her public in little pieces, even after the ransom is paid.

We haven't once caught sight of them so far, even though they can't possibly make it any quicker than we can over a roadbed that consists entirely of bumps, ridges, hillocks, gullies, with scrub growing all over the place. And yet the treads of their tires are always there ahead of us in the glare of the heads, big as life, so I know we're not wrong. The visibility is swell too, everything stands out under the moon, the ground is white as cornstarch. It's not the seeing, it's the going, that is terrible. One minute the two left wheels are at a forty-five degree angle taking some mound, the next minute it's the two right wheels, and the springs keep going under us the whole time like concertinas.

"Go on," I keep telling him, "get some speed into it; if they can do it, we can! She paid ten grand for this boat."

"But it's supposed to be used for a c-c-car," he chatters, "not a Rocky Mountain goat. That *tequila* don't go good with all this see-sawing, either!" I take the wheel back from him for awhile and give him a chance to pull himself together.

A minute later as we ride a swell that's a little higher than most of the others, I see a red dot no bigger than a pin-point way off in the distance. In another instant it's gone again as we take a long down-grade, then it shows up just once more, then it goes for good.

"That's them!" I tell him. "They don't even know we're coming after 'em, or they wouldn't leave their lights on like that!"

"They wouldn't dare drive over this muck without any," he groans, holding his stomach with both hands.

"Watch me close in," I mutter, and I shove my foot halfway through the floor.

Immediately there's a bang like a firecracker, and a sharp jagged rock, or maybe a dead cactus-branch for all I know, has gotten a front tire. We skiver all over before I can get it under control again.

"That's been coming to us for the past forty minutes," he says, jumping out. He reaches for the spare and I pull his hand away.

"That would only go too. Let's strip them all off and ride the bare rims, the ground's getting harder all the time."

We get rid of them and we're under way again in something like five minutes' time. But that puts the others five minutes further ahead of us, and the going before was like floating on lilies compared to what we now experience. The expression having the daylights jolted out of you is putting it mild. We don't dare talk for fear of biting our tongues in two.

A peculiar little gleam like a puddle of water shows up a little while later and when I see what it is I stop for a minute to haul it in. It's that gold dress of hers lying there on the ground.

"Good night!" he says in a scared voice. "They haven't—"

"Naw, not this soon. Not until they make a stab at the fifty grand," I say grimly. "They probably made her change clothes, that's all, to keep her visibility down once it gets light—"

And away we go, him at the wheel once more.

The sky gets blue, morning checks in, and we can cut the lights now. There's still gas, but it's rapidly dwindling.

"All I ask," I jabber, keeping my tongue away from my teeth, "is that theirs goes first. It should, because our tank started from scratch at the casino, they must have used up some of theirs getting to it from across the line. They also got eight cylinders to feed."

A little after six we pass through a Mexican village, their treads showing down its main lane. Also, there is a dead rooster stretched out, with all the neighbors standing around offering sympathy to its owner. "They left their card here," I say. "Let's ask." We put on the brakes and I make signals to them, using the two Spanish words I know.

"How many were in the car that ran over that hen's husband?" I signal.

They all hold up four fingers, also swear a lot and tear their pajamas.

"Hombres or women?" I want to know.

All men, is the answer.

"M'gard!" groans the driver. "Maybe they give it to her and buried her back there where we found the dress!"

"She's still with them," I answer. "They got her into men's clothes, that's all. Or else there are four in the gang and they have her trussed up on the floor."

We have a little trouble starting, because they have all collected around us and seem to want to hold us responsible for the damage. A couple of 'em go home for their *machetes*, which are the axes they chop maguey plants with.

"We're cops," I high sign them, "chasing after the first car, which has *bandidos* in it." When they hear that, they send up a big cheer and clear out of the way. Unfortunately, we knock over a chicken ourselves, just as we're pulling out; a hen this time.

"It woulda been a shame to separate them two," says the driver, blowing a feather off his lip.

There are no firearms in the village, so we don't slow up to explain.

"Shoulda got water," says the driver. "We'da gotten a lot more than water if we waited," I tell him.

It's hot as the devil by nine, and every bone aches.

"We must be way to the east of Mexicali by now," I mention. "What are they going to do, keep going until they hit the Colorado River?"

"They must have some hide-out they're heading for between here and there," he thinks.

"They're looking for one, you mean. They didn't have time to get one ready. It was Timothy who cooked up the thing yesterday morning after he found out where she went to. She didn't even know

herself she was coming down to Agua until the last thing Friday
night—"

At nine twenty-two by the clock I say, "What're you stopping for?"

"I ain't stopping," he says, "the car is. Maybe you'd care to cast your
eye at the gas-lever?" I don't have to, to know what he means. We're
without gas; and in a perfect spot for it, too.

The wheels have hardly stopped turning before the leather seats
begin to get hot as stove-lids.

"All I need is a pinch of salt," he says, "to be a fried egg. Well, as
long as we're not going any place any more, here goes!" And he hauls
a long bottle of *tequila* out of one of the pockets of the car and pulls the
cork out with his teeth.

"Hold on!" I say, and I grab it away from him. "How about trying
this on the tank, instead of your insides? Maybe it'll run on this—"

I hop out and run around to the back and empty it in. He follows me
out with two more bottles.

"I laid in a supply," he says, "for that garage party of mine last
night—"

"Give it the ignition," I snap, "before it finds out what it's
using."

Well, sure enough, the engine turns over on it, and when I get in
next to him, it starts to carry us!

"You shoulda bought a kegful," I gloat, "it's lousy with alcohol!"

"Anyway," he mourns, "it'll take us to some different place to roast
in."

"I can't figure," I'm telling him, "why it hasn't happened to them;
they haven't had a chance to fill up since we've been on their tail—"

When suddenly he stops, this time of his own accord. "It has!" he
says. "There they are—or am I just seeing mileages or whatever they
call those things?"

They're so far ahead we can't even see the car; it's just the flash of
the sun on nickel we can make out from way off. But it holds steady in
one place, meaning they aren't moving any more, they've stopped.
There are three long, gradual, intervening hollows between us and
the flash, separated by two medium-sized rises, not high enough to
cut it off. But on a line with them, to the left, there is quite an abrupt

crag or cone-shaped mound, the highest thing for miles around. Its shadow falls the other way, they're right out in the blazing sun.

"They're stalled," I say, "or they would have gone around it into the shade. Cut way over to the left, if we can put that thing between us and them maybe we can sneak up and get the drop on them—"

It isn't the odds that matter, but I keep remembering they have Fay with them, and they are just the kind of rats if they see us coming would—I know the driver is armed without having to ask, she always insisted that he carry a gun on his person just in case. I replace the shot I fired at them from the casino.

"If they flash like that," he remarks, turning at right-angles to the left, "so do we—they've seen us by now."

"They're facing the sun, and it's behind us," I remind him, "won't be straight overhead until noon. They can't tell, unless they got energy enough to climb on foot all the way to the top of that crest. I don't think they even know we've lasted this far—"

We keep going in a big wide loop, and the hillock slowly shifts, first to dead center, then on around to the right. The winking flash their car gives off disappears as the crest gets in the way, and now we and they are on opposite sides of it.

"Now we'll close in," I say. "See if we can make the shade, anyway, before we get out of the car."

"You shoulda been a general at the Marne," he tells me admiringly.

"How do you know I wasn't?" I squelch.

The shade cast by the summit keeps backing away from us, distances being deceptive in that clear air, but finally when the ground has already started to go up, up, it sweeps over us like cool blue ink—and what a relief! I give him the signal to cut.

"We go the rest of the way on our own."

"Aren't you going to use the car for a shield," he says, "if they start firing at us?"

"There isn't going to be that kind of firing. Miss North is right in the middle of them."

We get out, and on foot we start up to the top on our side, instead of, as he wants, circling around the base. Looking down on them from above will give us a big advantage, I figure; they won't know whether we're a whole posse or just two fellows. It's a tough climb, too; the hill, which looked so smooth from way off, turns out to be full of big and little boulders, and with a tricky grade to it.

"Everything's under control," he heaves behind me, "except suppose it turns out they just stopped to rest instead of being stalled, and they've gone on while we been doing our mountain-climbing act?"

I don't bother answering, it would take too much breath away from my footwork. If they were just resting, they would rest in the shade, not out in the broiling sun.

We get to the top finally, and I motion his shoulders down, so they won't show against the skyline. Then we both stick our noses over and look. The car, being further out, comes in sight first—but there is nobody in it or near it.

"Don't tell me they've gone off on the hoof and left it—" he whispers.

"Sh!" I shut him up, and crane my neck higher. They're in closer to us, right under the brow of the hill, which is almost perpendicular on their side. Three of them are standing around talking it over, and there's a fourth one a few yards away sitting by himself on a boulder.

I nudge the driver and point with my gun. "What d'ye want to bet that's Fay North? He's the only one wearing smoked glasses, like she had on, and the poor guy's barefoot, d'ye notice?" Otherwise the figure has on dungarees, a shirt, and a cap pulled way down on its head.

Well, I have everything doped out beautiful. They haven't seen us yet, so we'll get the drop on them from above, make them reach without having to do any shooting at all, have her frisk them, and then march them ahead of us back to our own car. So I motion him to edge over further along the crest, away from me, so it'll look like there are more of us up here. He's been standing right behind me, gun in hand, looking over my shoulder. He turns to do like I say, and then something happens.

All of a sudden he's flat up against me backwards, pressing as close as he can get and quivering all over like jelly. There's a clatter, and he's dropped his gun. It sounds like a bee or hornet is buzzing around us. He's crowding me so that I can't get out of the way without going over the crest in full view of them, and he has no room to move, badly as he wants to. I twist and look past him, and aiming out of a cleft between two boulders alongside of us, at about chin-level to him, is a perfect honey of a rattler, coiled in striking position. It's so close to him the weaving of its head almost seems to fan his face—or it looks that way from where I am, anyway.

There's no time to think twice. I whip up my hand and plug three shots into it, close enough to singe the line of his jaw. There's no trouble hitting the thick bedspring coils, I could have almost reached out and touched them, if I'd cared for the pleasure. It strikes with a sort of a flop, but it's dead already, and hangs down like a ribbon. But there goes our chance of surprising them; in a split second we have to topple on our bellies and back away, the way bullets are pinging all over the rocks around us, and sending up squirts of dust. They are certainly quick on the draw, those guys.

The three who were together have shot apart like a busted tomato. One gets behind a bit of scrub; one gets in closer, where there's a little ledge to protect him. And one doesn't get any place at all, goes down on his knees as I get rid of my three remaining shots.

The driver has grabbed up his gun, and shoved over to the other side, to have elbow room. The figure sitting by itself further out has jumped to its feet and started to run toward the car. I can tell by the way she runs that it is Fay North, just as I thought. But she can't make time on the hot sand in her bare feet, stumbles and waddles. The one under the ledge suddenly darts out after her before I have finished reloading, and the second one breaks for it too, at the same time, which is what you call team-work.

The driver gets him the second step he takes, and he slides to a stop on his ear. But the first one has already caught up with her, whirled her around, and is holding her in front of him for a shield. To show us who she is, he knocks the cap off her and all her blond hair comes tumbling down.

"Hold it, don't shoot!" I warn the driver, but he has sense enough without being told.

The guy holding her starts backing toward the car with her, a step at a time. He's holding one arm twisted painfully behind her back, and you can see his gun gleaming between her elbow and her body sighted on us, but she's game at that. She screams out to us: "Stop him from getting to that car; he's got a tommy-gun in it!" Then she sort of jolts, as though he hit her from behind.

I burn at that, but there's nothing I can do. But the driver doesn't seem to have that much self-control. He's suddenly flying down the incline almost head-first, in a shower of little rocks and dust, arms and legs all waving at the same time. But at least not dropping his gun like before. When I see that, I break cover too, but not quite that recklessly, keeping bent double and zig-zagging down the slope.

Fay is almost hidden by smoke, the way the guy behind her is blasting away, but I see her suddenly come to life, clap her elbow tight against her ribs, imprisoning his gun and jarring his aim. He tries to free it, they struggle, and she gets a terrific clout on the jaw for her trouble. It seems impossible the driver didn't get any of that volley, but he keeps going under his own momentum, as though he can't stop himself.

Fay is out cold now, we are both almost over to her, but the thug with her is only a yard or two away from the car. He lets both her and the gun go and dives for it. He tears the door open and gets in. I jump over her where she is lying, without stopping, because once he gets his hands on that tommy-gun—

He has his hands on it already, as I light on the running-board, but that split second's delay while he is swerving it my way costs him the decision; I tomahawk him between the eyes with the butt of my gun. The tommy goes off spasmodically in the wrong direction and the windshield up front flies in pieces; then him and me and it all go down together in a mess in the back of the car.

The driver shows up in a minute more and sort of folds up over the side of the car like a limp rag, head down. There's blood trickling down from his shoulder.

"Gee, that was swell," I tell him when I get my breath back, "the way you rushed him from the top of that hill! If it wasn't for that he'd 'a' been sitting pretty behind this tommy-gun by now."

"Rushed him hell!" he grunts. "I lost my balance and fell down it, that's what happened!"

We truss up the guy in the car, who is all right except that my gun broke his nose, and then we go back to where Fay is sitting up in the sand, looking very bedraggled. Her shoulder is wrenched from the way he had held her, and there is a lump on her jaw, and her face is all grimy and dust-streaked. Even so, when we stand her on her feet and she takes off those smoked glasses, him and me both stare at her and blink and stare some more.

"I know—never mind rubbing it in," she groans. "After this, I'm through passing myself off as Fay North, rubber checks or no rubber checks. What an experience! I'm her stand-in," she explains, limping back to the car. "Same measurements, coloring and everything. I guess that's what gave me the idea. But all I ask you boys is to pick a nice cool jail for me where the sun never shines—if we ever get back to civilization."

When it finally dawns on me, which isn't right away, that the real Fay has been enjoying the hospitality of a crummy Mexican jail since the night before, due to me, I begin to wonder if it mightn't be better to stay out in the desert where I am than go back and face what I have coming to me.

About three o'clock a plane sent out from the casino to look for us sights us and comes down, and the girl and the driver go back in it, but we neither of us say anything about what she has done. I stay there with two cars, two dead snatch-artists and one live one, a pailful of water and a stack of sandwiches for company; and it's early Monday morning before I'm back in Agua with the rescue party sent out to get me.

She's been let out of course, but she's standing there waiting for me on the casino steps.

"Gee, Miss North," I mumble, "how was I to know that was you, in that black wig and all—?"

She shakes her finger at me and says, "Now don't try to act modest. You knew what you were doing, and I think it was simply wonderful of you! That was my new system, of course. Remember, I told you I consulted an astrologer the day we left Hollywood. She told me the trouble with my betting was I had the wrong aura! I was too blond and refined. She said if I'd send out tough brunette vibrations my luck would change. Of course I couldn't tell you, because that would have broken my winning streak."

"Then you're not sore?"

"Sore? Why, it was wonderful of you, Shad, the way you put me in jail to save me from being kidnaped. Such foresight—such cleverness! And I'm through with Timothy for trying such a thing on me. You're my business manager from now on—and I won't take no for an answer!"

As long as she won't, I don't try to say it.

(1935)